THE TARLETON MURDERS

By

Breck England

mango
PUBLISHING

Published by Mango Publishing Group, a division of Mango Media Inc.

Cover Design: Georgiana Goodwin

Layout & Design: Morgane Leoni

For permission requests, please contact the publisher at:

Mango Publishing Group
2850 Douglas Road, 3rd Floor
Coral Gables, FL 33134 USA

info@mango.bz

For special orders, quantity sales, course adoptions and corporate sales, please email the publisher at sales@mango.bz. For trade and wholesale sales, please contact Ingram Publisher Services at customer.service@ingramcontent.com or +1.800.509.4887.

THE TARLETON MURDERS

Library of Congress Control Number: 2017912934

ISBN: (paperback) 978-1-63353-649-4 , (ebook) 978-1-63353-650-0

BISAC - FIC022060 FICTION / Mystery & Detective / Historical

Printed in the United States of America

To my wife, Valerie.

ACKNOWLEDGMENTS

I owe thanks to Arthur Conan Doyle, whose "Adventure of the Speckled Band" I absorbed when I was about 8 years old. For me, the game has been afoot ever since.

I owe thanks also to Valerie, my wife, who graciously allows me the time to peck at my laptop at all hours writing stories like this one. I love her and respect her, and I want her and the world to know it.

I am also grateful to Annie Oswald, my colleague and friend, who helped me get this manuscript into the hands of the great people at Mango.

And finally, I thank Mango Publishing Group for kindly taking a chance on this book. May it prosper them and please you.

PREFACE

To Sherlock Holmes devotees, the discovery of Father Grosjean's manuscript ranks with the discoveries of the Rosetta Stone or the Dead Sea Scrolls, and the story of its finding is just as dramatic.

When the Boston College School of Theology and Ministry was founded a few years ago, a few musty boxes of memorabilia from the old Theology Department found their way to the school's new home. For months the college archivists put off looking at the boxes; only recently a couple of interns arrived to sort through them, catalogue anything of value, and discard the rest.

In a pile of old papers and lecture notes belonging to one Reverend Simon Peter Grosjean, who had taught theology at Boston College for 29 years, they found an ancient typescript.

Somewhat befuddled when he retired, Grosjean apparently forgot about his papers, including the manuscript. Although he had spoken in its pages of his intention to publish, it lay unnoticed in an old file box for more than a century until a bright young intern recognized it for what it was. The earliest written account of a Sherlock Holmes case.

"I felt like Nathaniel Hawthorne did when he found the Scarlet Letter," she said.

No one had suspected that Father Grosjean's work even existed, but with this astonishing discovery came answers to some bedeviling questions about Sherlock Holmes—especially about his connection to America.

That connection was clearly intimate, even nostalgic at times. "It is always a joy to meet an American," Holmes would say, sharing none of the British distaste for the "expressive" American language, and voicing a hope that someday America and Britain would re-unite under a common flag.

How did Holmes acquire such a rich acquaintance with America? In none of the canonical stories did he go there, yet the same stories make it clear that he knew a great deal about the USA.

For example, how did Holmes gain inside knowledge of the Ku Klux Klan, which supposedly didn't even exist in his day? Where did Holmes learn so much about American gangsterism? Was Moriarty actually an American? Indeed, who was the real Moriarty?

Two prominent students of Holmes's life deduced that he must have visited America at least once. The journalist Christopher Morley suggested that Holmes traveled to the U.S. between his college years and his meeting with Dr. Watson. No less an authority than W.S. Baring-Gould, Holmes's biographer, insisted that Holmes had to have been in America sometime in 1879.

Now the discovery of the Grosjean manuscript confirms these scholarly speculations. A former schoolmate of Holmes, Father Grosjean reveals the incredible story of the great detective's first major international case, a story unknown to Dr. Watson, although Holmes hinted at it to his friend. And at last we have it—the strange "record of the Tarleton Murders."

THE TARLETON MURDERS

By
Breck England

WATSON: *"These are the records of your early work, then? I have often wished that I had notes of those cases."*

HOLMES: *"Yes, my boy, these were all done prematurely before my biographer had come to glorify me. . . . They are not all successes, Watson, but there are some pretty little problems among them. Here's the record of the Tarleton murders. . . ."*

—A. Conan Doyle, "The Musgrave Ritual"

THE TARLETON MURDERS

Being a selection from the reminiscences of Rev. Simon Peter Grosjean, S.J., late of the department of theology of Boston College.

PREPARATORY

Chapter 1

In the year 1878 I was a teacher and chaplain to the Order of Our Lady of Mercy, an establishment of religious women who care for poor children at Charleston, South Carolina. It was a remarkable affair in relation to one of the nuns there that led me to seek out the assistance of a former acquaintance of mine, Mr. Sherlock Holmes.

The train of events was so dark and bizarre, even threatening to both the sister and myself, that I was utterly at a loss as to how to proceed. A knowledge of the political situation in the American South at the time should help the reader to understand why I felt I could not confide in the authorities at Charleston. I went about my duties well enough, but found myself helplessly pacing my room at night and then falling asleep at odd hours, suddenly waking from a daylight nightmare to the sight of my students staring in amusement at me.

In desperation—and feeling an unfamiliar sense of fear—I went into retreat for a week to pray and contemplate what to do. One night, as I completed my spiritual exercises before retiring, a slight flicker of hope came to me. I remembered how Holmes, my former schoolmate, was able to solve even the most intractable puzzles that were presented to him. It occurred to me that I might seek his advice.

Of course, since then the name of Sherlock Holmes has become world famous due to his extraordinary adventures chronicled by his friend John Watson. For years I have been tempted to bring my own singular adventure with Holmes to the attention of the world, but the demands of my vocation have forced decades of delay. Now that I am slipping into retirement and have more leisure for writing, I imagine the reading public might benefit from this tale of the great detective and his very first collaborator—*for I was Watson before Watson was Watson.*

As a schoolboy at Stonyhurst College, I knew Sherlock Holmes only a little, but all the boys were aware of his prodigious powers of observation. He astonished us more than once. I recall an instance when he exonerated one of my school fellows who was accused of pilfering. Personal things—cricket bats, leather schoolbags, watches—were disappearing overnight, and Holmes deduced that the college porter was the thief. His deduction rested on a mere trifle. The porter had an ireful watchdog that never slept and made us miserable with its barking—oddly, Holmes pointed out, the dog had made no sound during the time the thefts must have occurred. A boy out of bed would have sent the dog into a frenzy, but its own master would have occasioned no qualms in the dog. Impressed at Holmes's observations, the rector faced down the porter and the wrong was righted.

Still, my memories of the ingenious Holmes were somewhat troubled. He was in and out of school, for his family wandered about Europe a good deal. He was not popular. When the boy accused of theft tried to thank him for his help, Holmes turned his back and walked away. Most of us, myself included to my shame, used to make fun of the silent, shy, skinny Holmes, and we thought it a piquant thing to chevvy him about the schoolyard. Because he declined to play cricket with us, we considered him a bit of an auntie, which perhaps explains why he excelled at the more defensive arts of fencing and boxing. In these, no one challenged him: We sensed even then that he was all by himself in a battle with the world.

Blessed with the frame of a boxer myself, I sparred with him a few times. Although I had the shoulders, I lacked the agility of body or mind that Holmes enjoyed. He always out-fought me—and out-thought me!

Even so, Holmes was an indifferent student except in chemistry, where he showed uncommon zeal. In other courses, he paid little attention to the lectures and occasioned some mirth more than once when asked a question:

"Mr. Holmes, be so kind as to explain the concept of a free press?"

"Yes, sir, that would be when the porter irons my trousers for me."

I, on the other hand, was an exceptional student, particularly in theology, languages, and history. (That is why the brothers recruited me early on to join them.) However, I was hopeless at chemistry, so in our seventh year I was thrown into a room with Holmes, who was charged with tutoring me. I didn't relish the idea. Holmes strewed our room with clothes and yellow-backed penny-dreadfuls and on rainy afternoons when we were expected to study he would rasp idly at his violin or slip away heaven knew where to smoke a pipe. Except for our chemistry sessions, he was largely oblivious to me and I to him. In fact, we were nearly opposites. My love of good company and good food (I always joked that luncheon and tea were my favorite "courses" at school) made me the reverse of Sherlock Holmes, to whom a good dinner and good company meant nothing.

However, I was drawn to his perverse chemistry experiments. He would coldly kill small animals—mice and rats he had captured—with concoctions of monkshood and ground hemlock kept in phials and scattered at random about our room. From Holmes I came to respect the berries of a bizarre plant called the "cuckoo pint," with which he stunned and paralyzed a number of mice. He would lead me through the forest in search of these plants, and it disturbed me to find them breeding like shadows amongst the innocent spring flowers.

"Here," he would point with his gloved finger, "and here. There is death in these woods."

Of course, I knew of his mania for tobacco, and his furtive smoking didn't bother me—I rather liked the aroma of a good pipe myself—but then one night I found him in the laboratory vigorously *chewing* tobacco, which was of course strictly forbidden in school. He uncovered a cupful of maggots he had collected from a dead rat in the garden and expectorated into it. The worms thrashed about and were still. It was a revolting experiment that carried its own peculiar fascination.

Another time he put a brick in a pot, filled it with dried tobacco and water up to the brick, and set a teacup on top of the brick. He then covered the pot, heated it over the gas burner, and whispered, "Fetch some ice from the larder." I ran to the kitchen and brought back a bucket of ice, which he placed on top of the pot.

"Quick! Uncover the pot!" I seized the lid. Holmes carefully removed the cup and poured a steaming, light-brown liquid from it into a glass beaker. We repeated this maneuver several times until Holmes was satisfied; he knelt before the beaker and gazed at it for a long time before he spoke.

"A distillation of nicotine," he breathed. "An evil mystery. The essence of death, as lethal as cyanide, and yet I *cannot* live without it." Hungrily inhaling the remaining steam from the pot, he closed his eyes and went into a reverie from which I knew he would not emerge that night.

In the end, I did well at my chemistry levels.

Our acquaintance faded naturally as I went to seminary and Holmes to Oxford. Upon my ordination, I was posted across the water to the diocese of Charleston and lost track of him. I heard from some old boys that Holmes had left his studies to become a kind of "mender" of delicate problems for the aristocracy; and now, a mender was precisely what I needed. If anyone had a delicate problem, I did, and I could hardly wait until the morning to telegraph to England and inform him of the particulars.

Since I had no idea of Holmes's address, I wired the old rector at Stonyhurst for it, who obligingly inquired of Sherlock's brother (a heavy-boned, intimidating older boy we had known only as Big Mike), who in turn sent me the address of a convent *pensione* in Rome.

Rome! By a remarkable act of Providence, I was already booked to sail for Rome the following week. Sister Carolina, the nun who had created for me such a knotty problem, had decided to go into the cloister and wanted to make a pilgrimage to Rome before disappearing forever under the veil. My bishop asked me to accompany her, a request I accepted eagerly, for I had never been to Rome, and my heart was captivated at the thought of praying at the See of St. Peter, my patron!

Now I had an even more pressing reason for my pilgrimage: to find Holmes. If I had only known what a strange and dangerous journey lay ahead of me, I might have declined the bishop's request and stayed at home in Charleston to face my problem there. But as I reflect on it, I believe now that it was meant to be—and I wouldn't have missed it for anything.

ROME

Chapter 2

Enraptured by the late sun on a quiet piazza, we came at last to the address in Rome wired to me by the brother of Sherlock Holmes. Our little *carrello* stopped in front of a convent that looked as old as Christianity itself, the walls fissured like cobwebs and a Gothic window black with the smoke of centuries. I thought it was charming, and Sister Carolina tried to make agreeable noises, but I could tell it was just an old pile of plaster to her.

So this was our destination. After we had spent so many days tumbling on the ocean, in and out of one raucous Continental port after another, the fountain and flowers in this little square calmed and warmed my heart. Sun-browned children cooled themselves in the water, and a bony old priest in Roman hat and cassock hobbled round the corner in a sweat. Still, Sister shivered with autumn cold even though buried under heavy black robes and gloves. I hoped she would be able to rest here.

Abruptly, that hope was shattered, as was the Gothic window over our heads.

We both screamed as the glass exploded with a sharp retort. Green, blue, and red splinters blasted us like pellets from a shotgun. The children screeched, there were loud shouts from inside the building—but most startling of all, the lean old priest sprang into our carriage and seized the reins from the driver.

Shocked, I shouted at him to stop, but the priest whacked at the horse and we were off at full speed. All at once we were chasing a bizarre figure dressed in a peaked cap and a white silk gown, who vaulted from nowhere across our view and dashed into a side street.

As he ran, the muscular fellow tore at the silk and swept the cap from his head. Shreds of silk caught at us; the cap hit the horse full in the eyes. The animal leapt backward with a panicked scream. The priest struggled to control it, and the horse was off again in pursuit of the man who was now streaming tatters of white cloth as he ran.

We nearly overturned as we bowled into the busy Via Cavour. I was yelling "stop" at the priest and the priest was yelling "stop" at the man in tattered silk. Sister Carolina was a soundless, bouncing jumble of black habit, her face blanched and eyes tight shut. Baffled by the dusty traffic of omnibuses and *carrelli*, the priest urged the horse on mercilessly but in vain. The runner mixed with the crowd thronging the Termini, the grand new depot of Rome, and by the time our carriage reached it, the portals of the station had swallowed him up.

The old priest brought the wagon to a halt and stared bleakly at the crowd, oblivious to us. I saw to Sister Carolina, who waved me away faintly, and then slapped him on the shoulder. I was angry. I didn't care if he understood English or not.

"What is the meaning of this? What do you think you're doing, Padre? Are you mad?"

He continued searching the crowd.

"There is a respectable religious woman in this carriage who has just had the fright of her life! I demand you get out of it and leave the reins to the driver."

For his part, the driver was still hanging on, his old head down, sobbing and gripping the seat with both hands.

Then the priest slowly turned his glaring eyes on me.

"Tuck!" he whispered. He grabbed my hand hard, almost as a warning. "Calm yourself."

I couldn't understand what I was hearing. Tuck? No one had called me Tuck in years.

"It is I," he breathed in my ear. "Holmes."

"Hol-!" I almost shouted his name, but he held up a stern finger.

It *was* Holmes!

'Quiet!" he murmured. "You must not speak my name. Sit down and we will have this noble Roman charioteer return us whence we came." I stared in shock at him: The disguise was perfect—he had transformed himself into the very model of an Italian cleric, with cavernous cheeks and just the right touch of shrewd sanctimony in the eyes, a man of twenty-five who looked three times his age.

I settled back in the carriage and whispered to Sister Carolina, who was holding her gloved hands over her eyes and barely breathing. "It's all right. We're returning to the convent now." Holmes sat in silence next to the still skittish driver, who turned the carriage round reluctantly and never took his eyes off Holmes all of the way back to our destination.

Roman *police* were standing about the entry to the convent as a monumental nun swept shards of glass and stone away from the door, shrieking all the while in unintelligible Italian at no one in particular. We descended from the carriage, I paid the driver (a little extra, for he looked terribly queasy), and he brought down the baggage while the baffled police tried to decide whether to stop us or let us through. One constable with impressive mustaches stepped forward as if to question us, but the nun recognized Holmes.

"Signore, avanti, avanti." She ushered Holmes through the door. To the officer she shouted *"Via!"* and he stumbled backwards. Then noticing us, she gestured us toward the door and cried "Thees-a-way!" Then she slammed the door behind us.

It was cool and dim inside, for which we, in our hot, sweat-sullied clothes, were most grateful. Holmes introduced us to the giant nun.

"This is Sister Ugolin. She will see to you." Abruptly he turned and went back out into the piazza.

Sister Ugolin snorted. "It is always so with him," she said in forceful English, took hold of Sister Carolina's elbow, and guided us through the dark hall toward a reception room.

"Seester will stay in the 'ow-you-say cloister, and you, Padre, will be in a *cella* for the *uomini"*—she glanced up at my confused face—"thee room for thee men," she shouted at me as if I were deaf.

Taking stock of my bedraggled companion, she cooed "Oh *la povera* seester," embraced her, released her, and then hugged her even tighter against her vast bulk. I thought she was going to cry. For her part, Sister Carolina was in a daze. It had all been too much.

Clucking like a plump chicken, shouting promises about tea and *riposo* mixed with imprecations about *la finestra* (the broken window), Sister Ugolin herded us along to our rooms. Mine was a yellowish stone cell with a cot, but clean and quiet and supplied with a large white basin of fresh water, which, liberally rubbed on my dusty body, enlivened me considerably. Then I sat on the cot in my drawers and wondered what had just happened to us.

I had not known what to expect when encountering Holmes again, but this welcome was more striking than anything I had imagined. It's true that at school I was known as "Tuck." We often played at Robin Hood and his Merry Men, and because of my liking for food and drink I was "Friar Tuck" (I ran on the sturdy side, so the name fit). Everyone had nicknames, usually ironic—there was "Rhomboid" Fotheringale, so called because he was no good at maths, and "Ickle-Pretty" Gower, as homely a face as the Creator ever made. I believe even Holmes had a nickname for a time—"Soapy," of course, because of his lack of hygiene.

But why the elaborate fancy dress, and the exploding window, and the wild dash across the city after a man in a silken gown and a dunce hat? What was all that, then? And where on earth was that giantess with the tea?

A knock came at my door. It was Holmes, still in his disguise, although he was no longer hunched over with "age." He put his finger to his lips and motioned for me to follow him. I dressed and we slipped out across the square and behind a decrepit house across from the convent. We glanced up at a rope ladder that hung from the roof, but what really took our attention was a curious machine lying in pieces on the ground. Holmes picked up the pieces and expertly re-assembled them into what looked like a small cannon.

Holmes murmured, it seemed mostly to himself, "A Girardoni air rifle, created by a Tyrolean clockmaker a century ago and carried by the Americans Lewis and Clark on their famous expedition to the Pacific Ocean. The Germans call it the *Windbixel*—it is silent, potent, and deadly."

I whistled, as much at Holmes's display of knowledge as at the vile contraption itself. "So someone climbed up on the roof and fired this thing at the stained-glass window? But why?"

"Because the shooter knew it was my lodging." Holmes responded quietly.

"They were trying to kill you?"

"I don't believe so." He hesitated. "The motive is deeper than that."

"And that motive would be?"

Holmes said nothing—he was still examining the gun minutely.

I became impatient. "Holmes, I find myself *bouleversé* by all of this. I have my charge to consider, a devoted religious who has come to you for help—who is already frail, dealing with a fearful problem of her own, and now she has been knocked about like a sack of potatoes in a mad chase across Rome. I demand to know what's going on."

As if conscious of me for the first time, he looked up and smiled. "Forgive me, Tuck. I do know I haven't given you a proper welcome. Let's toddle back and see what Sister Ugolin has to offer us—if I recall, you'll be needing your tea about now."

The refectory, a small marble-clad room with a folding table, was laid with English tea (Twinings!) and biscuits powdered with sugar. Sister Carolina was already seated, working at her hobby. On our travels she occupied her time crafting rosaries, carrying with her a worn wooden box that contained the charms, beads, and black cord she needed, along with a small silver borer and awl. The effort calmed her nerves. Holmes shut the door behind us and the three of us huddled round the table, for despite the heat outside, the room was chilly.

"My dear Sister," Holmes was deferential. "Please forgive my discourtesy in not welcoming you properly. I have no excuse for putting you in danger, but if you understood the reason for my behavior you might think it not so remarkable after all. To my shame, I was not entirely prepared for the attack upon the convent, although I believed it likely, and my rashness in pursuit of the attacker I can explain by the fact that he is one of the most alarming characters in Europe today."

I was concerned about frightening Sister Carolina and thought to divert the conversation, but she leaned over the teacups and said, "Please tell us about him."

"His name is Stepnyak. He's a Russian radical, an assassin who has passed the last few years shooting mountain goats and aristocrats in the Balkans. Despite his revolutionary leanings, he has become rather a mercenary." Holmes waved the air. "Still, we're not here to talk of my cases. I received your wire, Tuck . . . er, Padre . . . but you said so little of your problem. I am truly pleased to see you, and now I am all attention. How may I be of help?"

Sister Carolina spoke, her soft Georgia cadence barely loud enough to be heard. "I've been troubled, Mr. Holmes. Troubled for many a year. And Reverend Grosjean says that you are the most discerning of men, so I am sure you will not find my difficulty too . . . difficult to solve."

"Actually, Holmes, I told her you were the most ignorant of men, except for everything to do with crime," I said, and turned to Sister. "He is a master at unveiling what people want to keep veiled. He knows every detail of the Gunpowder Plot, but nothing of who discovered America."

"Some might say that was a crime," muttered Holmes.

"Well, I'm not quite sure how to begin. . . ." Sister Carolina began, fumbling with the rosary at her belt.

"Before you tell Holmes your story, Sister, let him deduce it," I burst in. "Or as much of it as he can. He loves to show off. Rather like a pianist at a party who can't wait for someone to ask him to play."

Holmes gave a little snort of disapproval.

"Holmes, I've told Sister all about your unusual abilities. Such as the time you asked the rector if he had enjoyed sampling the chicken we were about to have for dinner. The rector demanded to know your meaning, and you pointed to the drippings from the spit on his shoes and the sooty bump on his head from hitting it on the hood of the fireplace."

"Don't forget the smear of chicken fat on his cheek," Holmes added, and we both laughed out loud. It was odd to hear laughter from Holmes—I don't believe I had ever heard it before.

"So what do you make of me?" Sister Carolina asked, looking sideways at Holmes.

Holmes regarded her with a neutral air. "Besides the obvious accoutrements that declare your calling, I would say that you are a woman who has suffered intensely. You've known deprivation and illness, regardless of the fact that you grew up in the American South in a well-to-do household with few cares. Though you have made vows of poverty, you have wealthy friends or relations."

Her face hardened just perceptibly.

"Of these things I am certain. As to your problem, I can only conjecture. Your present vocation is not the first choice of your heart, and from your age and provenance I surmise you lost much in the late American war—perhaps a soldier who was dear to you?"

He paused. Sister Carolina looked away.

"Now you have reached a crisis of some kind, and before you go into seclusion for the rest of your life, you must resolve it," he concluded gently. "Beyond this, I can see nothing."

"Reverend Grosjean did not exaggerate your powers, Mr. Holmes," she replied. "I was the daughter of a prosperous planter in Georgia. I came up with every privilege you could desire. I had frocks and chemisettes for every occasion, tea gowns underlaid with crinoline, lacy shawls, beautifully trimmed bonnets. Servants to answer every need. Balls and races and barbecues . . . it was at a barbecue that I saw him for the last time."

Her voice faded to a sigh.

"It was just at the commencement of the war. All the young men whooped and hollered and swore they were going to beat the Yankees, and my beau went off with them, but he never came back. None of them returned alive. He and his brothers all died the same day in the same place and they brought their bodies back to us . . . ." She tried, but could not hold back a sob that swallowed her frail frame.

I put my hand on her gloved hand, hesitated, then finished her story for her. "It appears that the three men, brothers named Tarleton, were killed within minutes of each other at Gettysburg. She would like to know why it was done, and who might be responsible."

"Tarleton. Tarleton, you say?" Holmes looked up, then shook his head. "At Gettysburg. The bloodiest battle of a bloody war—tens of thousands butchered in a matter of hours. What of three men in the midst of that carnage?"

Sister's eyes lit with anger and her voice halted. "They were the best men in the world. . . beautiful men . . . fighting for their homes and their people . . ."

"What's intriguing, though, Holmes, is that all three men were shot in the back," I said.

Holmes considered this. "It happens in the chaos of war—soldiers firing madly all about, through smoke and flame—bound to hit one of their own. I recall the Earl of Kingston who was torn in half by his own cannonball." He turned to Sister. "He was an unfortunate casualty of our own English civil war."

"But three brothers? All at once?" I tried to interest him in the problem.

"As I recall, the battle was hot and fierce and fought into the night. Imagine men with bloody sweat in their eyes shooting aimlessly at each other in the dark. And of course, there's the other possibility. . . ." Holmes gave me a glance full of surmise.

It took her a moment to catch his meaning, but again she was outraged and on her feet. "Mr. Holmes, no Confederate soldier would turn his back and run. Least of all the Tarleton brothers. Never. Never. It is unthinkable!"

Waxen with anger, she glided out of the room and shut the door behind her with a force I didn't think she possessed. We tried to rise, but she was gone in an instant.

I sighed and shook my head at Holmes. "Is this your way of treating your clients? Then I'm amazed you have clients at all."

"Well, Tuck. What did you expect of me? You must admit at least the possibility that the brothers were in, shall we say, retreat?"

I too was upset with him, but I put on my calmest voice. "It is most unlikely, Holmes. To Southern gentlemen, honor comes before all else, and the field of battle is foremost the field of honor. In the most hopeless battles, they would fight each other for the distinction of taking a bullet square in the breast."

Holmes was still gazing at the ceiling.

"Confound it, Holmes, we've come a very long way. How could you be so cruel to the lady? She came to you for help. You never did have any natural feelings."

"Forgive me," said Holmes airily. "I am a brain, Tuck. The rest of me is a mere appendix. You knew that. Her problem simply doesn't present any features of interest to me."

"Well, then, perhaps I can show you a feature of very great interest—a feature that explains why I have come nearly five thousand miles to find you."

Chapter 3

I took from my notecase a folded piece of paper and handed it to him.

"I received this letter—if that's what it is—in an unusual way. I found it, unenclosed, on the floor of my room after returning from my duties. It has been some weeks now, and nothing has come of it yet. But, in regard to your opinion of our problem, perhaps you might see things differently if you read this."

Holmes sniffed the paper, knelt, and spread it out on the table. "The paper precedes the Fenerty wood-pulp process, so it is rather old stuff. The writer smokes a fine Virginian tobacco. The ink is standard iron-gall, but stale, and the iron pen has been used for many a year—see how the nub has worn down."

"I'm sure that's all true, but what do you make of the *contents* of the letter?" I asked.

"Yes, let's have a read."

O.

LET T.HE TAR LET ON,

B.eware! Let the Feathers reveal,

Raging bloody w.ax Fire be set,

On thy Bans! Awe thy Confessi.onal Seal!

Thou shalt drink Fate. in Wine, be it distilled Gall!

Hell's bread shalt. avenged in Tartarus eat!

Even Thy Goddess in the d.epths of Acheron shall fall!

Revenge! T.hou shalt drink the shame of it Sweet!

Shad.owed Brotherhood! If we Heaven's will cannot avert, Hell

Let us move. Charon bring thee o'er his Flood to meet,

In Ro.bes and burning Cross and Blood Drops to lie,

Even there. where the Prince of Air forever flames up howling,

PETIT AND PERDITION! BAP.ST AND BLAZES! STRICKEN AND SEALED!

CHAOS AND CURSES!

DO NOT OPEN PANDORAS BOX OR YOU WILL FEEL THE WRATH
OF THE KU, KLUX, KLAN!

"A sort of misshapen sonnet? Fourteen lines, but badly executed. It doesn't scan well at all," said Holmes.

"Your opinion of the verse," I said, "is not pertinent. You're acquainted with the Ku Klux Klan?"

"Yes, indeed," Holmes replied, still contemplating the mysterious text. "One of the most dangerous criminal organizations in the world, all the more so because it doesn't exist." He barked a laugh.

"Doesn't exist?"

"The Klan was supposedly 'disbanded' years ago, in a ploy that enables some of the most influential men in the South to work their treachery in the dark—at the same time denying that there is any such thing as the Klan."

"I know there's a good deal of anti-Catholic feeling in the country, and the Klan is known for it. Clearly, this letter is a threat against the Church. The allusions to the sacrament of the Eucharist, to the confessional . . . ."

Holmes looked up at me from his study. "Oh, surely, it's more than that."

I paused. "Yes. It's evidently a threat against myself as well. The mentions of Petit and Bapst . . . ."

"Who are . . . ?"

"Jesuits, like myself. They were Swiss, I believe, posted to America by the order. Father Benjamin Petit was driven west with the Indians and died on the trail. Bapst was the object of a hideous attack—tarred and feathered by a mob—and now lives with nightmares of it."

"So the Klan has nominated you as a candidate for martyrdom. As a Jesuit, that should please you." Holmes took the paper by the corners and held it to the window. "No watermark. And of course, it's more than a shocking piece of doggerel. I don't know if you're aware, Tuck, that my first case involved a disquieting letter."

"Indeed."

"Yes. An acquaintance from university invited me down to his father's estate. The father was an affable, wealthy old man of somewhat mysterious origins. One day he received a letter that sent him into a fit of apoplexy, yet upon our reading it, it seemed innocuous enough. After a bit of study, however, I determined that it was in code. The true message was conveyed by every third word of the text—a message that indicated that the illegitimate source of the old man's wealth was discovered and that he should fly the country immediately. He died of the shock instead."

"What was the source of his wealth?"

"It is of no matter. Let's just say the law would not have smiled on him. I rather regret the old man. He was the first to suggest to me that I might make a career of crime—I mean, the detection of it. His suggestion rescued me from a life of unrelieved tedium, and I am grateful to him for that."

"I gather then that you see some hidden message in this document?"

"Yes," Holmes replied, "and it is so easily deciphered that I gather you see it as well."

"I believe I do, but I would like you to confirm it for me"

"Very well. Take the first two lines: O LET THE TAR LET ON. You've told me that the dead brothers lamented by Sister Carolina were named Tarleton. That is easy enough. Then there is a simple acrostic, formed by the first letter of each line thereafter:

B

R

O

T

H

E

R

S

L

I

E

"'O, let the Tarleton brothers lie.' It is a childish code, but it does make the Sister's little problem much more enticing. Do you have any idea why such a message would come to you?"

I sighed with relief and nearly embraced Holmes. I too had worked out the message, but it had taken me a good deal longer than it took him (I hesitate to say days, but it was true). At last I could share this strange burden with another.

"I don't know why it was sent to me. I have no particular connection to the Sister—any more than to the other religious—so I can't think how her predicament involves me."

"Did Sister also receive a letter?"

"Not that she has mentioned. I thought it best to keep the letter to myself rather than to alarm her with it."

Holmes was up and pacing. "When did you learn of the questionable death of these Tarletons?"

"From my first day at the convent. Sister Carolina asked for a word with me, as I was the new chaplain, and she confided the whole story immediately. Apparently the former chaplain had no sympathy for her, but I feel a certain duty to listen and try to succor my charges in their woes if I can.

"I told her I would look into it, but frankly didn't know what I could do. My thoughts were the same as yours—three men shot at Gettysburg among thousands, in the confusion of the battlefield—and possibly by their own officers, if they were deserting. But she was importunate, constantly at me about it, and I decided to make some inquiries if only to calm her mind a bit."

"To whom did you make these inquiries?"

"Along with other clergy, I attended the Mayor's celebration of the first year since the Yankee soldiers left Charleston. It was a grand party in the grandest room in Charleston—the gallery of the city hall—and stuffed with grandees."

"It does sound very grand," Holmes mocked me.

"After dinner, I found myself conversing with a number of prominent men. They were reminiscing about the late war when I took advantage of the moment and told them Sister Carolina's story. I asked if any one of them could help me resolve the issue for her.

"One of them suggested I write to the War Department. Another thought I might try interviewing members of the Tarletons' regiment, if any survived. The others scoffed at the idea of discovering the truth as a hopeless quest at this late date."

"Have you discussed the matter with anyone else, before or since?"

"I have not."

"And the letter appeared after the party?"

"Directly afterward. I think it appeared the next day."

"Then the letter is unmistakably the fruit of your conversation that night," Holmes said. "Can you recall the names of the men in your circle, at least one of whom must be connected with the Klan?"

"I've had the same thought and tried to re-construct the group in my memory."

"This is becoming too workmanlike." Holmes stood, grumbling. "Perhaps the murders were due to a simple personal vendetta. We'll take this up later. The inhabitants of the *pensione* dine early, and it is nearly their time. The nuns will be bringing their pail of slop and hard bread into the refectory any minute, and through fear of Sister Ugolin, I deign not to be late."

My heart sank at the thought of slop and hard bread, and that Holmes might be losing interest in my predicament. At any rate, I felt that I had neglected Sister long enough. I folded the letter and was about to return it to my notecase.

"May I take the letter and study it a bit further, Tuck? It may reveal more secrets."

"Certainly. I hope you can make more of it than I have done."

A half hour later, we were seated at dinner with a dozen or so other guests—all of them English pilgrims to Rome. As befits the English, we exchanged barely a nod with each other and no words beyond a rigid "good evening." Sister Ugolin and her staff of two squabbling nuns sailed through the room ladling out soup she called *minestrone*—a concoction of boiled chickpeas and vegetables.

I tasted the soup and found it delightful, as was the crusty bread that came with it. Even Sister Carolina, with her delicate appetite, was lapping it up.

Holmes sat across from us, slumped over once again in his immaculate imitation of an Italian priest. He tried pushing the soup away, but Sister Ugolin descended upon him brandishing her giant ladle.

"*Mangia!*" she threatened. "Eat!"

"Tyrant," he muttered, and picked up his spoon.

We ate in silence for a moment, then Holmes turned to Sister. He spoke low. "I feel I must apologize to you. I'm afraid I may have seemed dismissive of your problem. I confess that at first, I believed it to be outside my sphere of interest, but on consideration, I would like to help you if I can."

Sister Carolina looked up from her soup but did not meet his eyes.

"I do not welcome your help, sir. A man so impulsive, so prejudiced as you, against a people and a cause you know nothing about, inspires no confidence, I must say."

"Forgive me, Sister, I am only too conscious of my shortcomings. Tuck . . . Father Grosjean probably described me to you as an unfeeling, unpleasant sort of person, and quite right if he did so. But, I assure you, what poor faculties I have in detection are entirely at your service."

I myself was taken aback by Holmes's sudden eagerness. "You are full of surprises, old man," I said.

At that moment the refectory door blew open as if with a violent wind, and a man stood there in a long, fluttering white silk robe, a mask, and a peaked white cap perched on his head.

Chapter 4

With most people, there would be pandemonium at the appearance of such a figure. But we were English, and instead of hysteria there was frozen silence.

Except for Sister Ugolin, who went at this apparition with her ladle and a deluge of angry Italian, her two sisters adding to the din. The man held them off and answered with a stream of *basso* German.

He pulled off his cap, revealing a burnished mustache over a big grin, and found Holmes. *"Mein Kamerad!"* he rumbled, descending on Holmes in a full embrace.

Holmes stood and propelled the man out of the room. I followed, swinging the door shut behind me, anxious to find out what this was all about. In the corridor they were already whispering at each other.

"Tuck, this is my friend Sergeant-Major Sprüngli. He is from the Pope's personal guard."

Looking at his cherubic face and white gown, I felt I was standing in front of Michael the Archangel. He lacked only a pair of wings.

"You astound me, Holmes. For a moment I thought this was the man you were pursuing today."

"No, the Sergeant-Major has been my right hand here in Rome. We did a good morning's work today, didn't we, Sprüngli?"

"Ja ja! A very gut morning!" The man laughed from his belly and once more crushed Holmes to himself with his sinewy arms. "I think Stepnyak will not return, no?" He stepped out of the robe and handed it and his bizarre cap to Holmes. "I these to you give. No need now."

"Thank you," said Holmes, who rolled them up under his arm. "And now let's examine the latest outrage." We followed him out of the convent and into the piazza. Holmes showed Sprüngli the exploded window, which workers were already boarding up, and the rope ladder we had found earlier in the day.

Then Holmes took us to his room in the convent.

Although he had been a guest in this room only a few weeks, Holmes had already created a mess worthy of a violent earthquake. Clothes, journals, phials of chemicals, newspapers, orange peelings, sheets of music, a pocket version of Petrarch, and the remains of his correspondence lay in loose piles everywhere, covered with a fine powdering of tobacco dust. He flung Sprüngli's fancy dress into a corner, swept the litter from a couple of chairs, and motioned us to sit.

"He left this weapon behind," he said, handing the air gun to Sprüngli and filling his pipe with tobacco he pulled from an old stocking.

"*Ach, der Windbixel!* This have I never seen. It is wonderful, no?" He cranked it and took aim through the wooden sight. "It is so *schweigend*. How do you say . . . ?"

"Silent," Holmes responded. "I think it belongs in the Papal armory with the other infernal machines on display there. Please take it, as a memento of the day we saved your master from a dreadful death. "

At last I spoke up. "Would you please give me some idea of what's been going on here?"

The two men stared at me and laughed. "Of course," Holmes said. "And we must include Sister Carolina, for the story we have to tell concerns her as well."

A half hour later we were back in the refectory, now swept and empty, and Holmes was filling the room with pipe smoke. Sister Carolina had remained behind and introductions had been made.

Sister was cold but cordial. "Please be brief, Mr. Holmes. I should like to retire soon," she said, concentrating on her rosary kit. She had started another string from the bag of small dried berries she carried.

"Certainly, Sister. You have had a trying day, although I believe our story will interest you—and most particularly its sequel." He threw a sly smile at Sprüngli and settled back in the blue mist from his pipe.

"Our adventure began some weeks ago with a message from my brother Mycroft. You may remember him, Tuck?"

"Oh, yes. Big Mike."

Holmes gave me a wry look and went on. "Mycroft is a big noise in the Foreign Office, or the Home Office, or some dashed office, and he asked me as a favor to pay a call on one of the most eminent Roman Catholic churchmen in England.

"I did so. This august person told me that the new pope was too free-thinking for the tastes of certain high-placed dignitaries of church and state across Europe, some of whom were in fact contemplating assassination. He told me he had no taste for the new pontiff either, but didn't want him to be the first sitting pope to be murdered in nine-hundred years."

Sister Carolina crossed herself.

"Just how eminent was this churchman?" I asked.

"I hesitate to say, but it might interest you to know that a red hat was on the table."

I whistled, surprising both Sister and myself.

"*Unmenschen!*" the sergeant grumbled.

"I was told that the services of a master criminal had just been obtained, so I was urgently offered the task of preventing the assassination," Holmes went on. "I had little doubt who the master criminal was. I immediately went to the Thames at low tide, dug up some foul mud, and employed a boy of my acquaintance to scatter it round the threshold of the criminal's house at 198 Piccadilly. Then I took the next boat train for Rome, hoping I was a step ahead of them and not too late."

"A master criminal in Piccadilly? Mud from the Thames?" I was trying to keep up.

"Pay attention, Tuck. How on earth do you get through the confessional? I took with me only my make-up box and my scrapbook of murderers. For years I have collected in my book items from the London newspapers regarding every assassin, cutthroat, and hired dispatcher I could learn of. After long study on the train, I deduced that the most likely candidate for a papal assassin was one Sergey Stepnyak, a brutal Russian who has done political murders all over the Balkans and has been connected with Italian anarchists. He is known in London as well, as a revolutionary agitator who hates any form of authority. His most recent feat was the daylight stabbing of the head of the Russian secret police.

"So, once in Rome, how to find Stepnyak? I enlisted the aid of Sergeant Sprüngli here." At the sound of his name, Sprüngli brightened. "He possesses a most admirable bloodhound . . ."

"*Schniffler!*" Sprüngli laughed and woofed like a dog.

"Yes, Schniffler," Holmes continued. "I borrowed the dog, acquainted him with the smell of the mud, and sat with him in the arrivals area at Termini. Luckily, the Romans have been astute enough to build one central railroad station, so anyone arriving from London must come through there."

"I begin to understand the mud," I said. "The hound would recognize any arrival who had been in contact with your 'master criminal' in London."

"It is elementary. Day after day I sat in the waiting area near the arrivals platform with an utterly bored animal, until I began to doubt my plan. But then two weeks ago, as the Calais-to-Rome express arrived, the hound came alive. A most peculiar set of pilgrims descended from the train—*penitentes* masked and dressed in long gowns and bizarre cone-shaped caps."

Sister Carolina had been trying to follow the story. "Excuse me . . . *penitentes?*"

"Penitent ones," I explained. "They are penitent sinners who wear this costume to maintain their anonymity. The cone-shaped cap symbolizes rising up to heaven."

"Yes," said Holmes. "It is an excellent way to maintain anonymity, as you say. And in Rome, it is also a convenient way to get close to the Pope, as groups of *penitentes* are often honored with an invitation to hear him speak or even to meet him inside the papal palace. So when the hound sniffed the mud, he went straight for the source of it."

"*Schniffler!*" Sprüngli laughed and woofed again.

"Indeed, good old Schniffler," Holmes echoed. "He steered me toward one of the pilgrims, and then I called him off. I followed the pilgrims out of the station, where they piled into carriages and went off to lodgings at the Casa Rosario.

"The next day I joined them. Sprüngli found me the regalia, and I managed to play the *penitente* without causing a stir among them. For ten days or so we made a tedious circuit of the shrines of Rome—Saint Mary Major, St. Paul's Outside the Walls—we even climbed the Holy Stairs on our knees, while I kept the suspected assassin constantly under my eye. At last I learned we would be accorded an audience with the Holy Father on our visit to the Vatican; this would be the killer's opportunity to strike.

"Then the picture changed. Sprüngli informed me that the Shamrock had arrived."

"The Shamrock?"

"The steam yacht that belongs to our master criminal from London, a splendid vessel with a twenty-man crew lying as we speak in the port of Ostia, only a few miles from here. I was surprised. Having recruited his Russian pilgrim, he should have been as far from the scene as possible: it is not his pattern to be found anywhere near the crimes he puts in motion. I thought something else was afoot, but could not tell what.

"Within a day I knew I had been discovered. Twice I caught Stepnyak staring at me, those Slavic eyes menacing me through the slits in his mask. I tell you, Tuck, in those moments I felt a chill of fear that I am usually a stranger to. Of course I took measures never to be alone with him as we continued our *hajj* round Rome.

"Then this morning came the papal audience. On this last day of the pilgrimage, excitement ran high among the *penitentes*. I knew Stepnyak or perhaps some minions from the Shamrock would move against me before they made any attempt on the pope, so I altered my arrangements. The pope himself was apprised of this, and a man with more iron nerve I have never met. He readily agreed to my plan.

"Early this morning, the *penitentes* trooped together through the square of St. Peter's and into the great basilica, where along with many other pilgrims they were to be met by the pope and his entourage. Kept waiting for an hour or so, they were finally informed that the Holy Father was in his garden conferring on a matter of great importance, but that he would be with them shortly.

"A few moments later, one of the *penitentes* slipped away from the crowd and crept carefully through the sacristy and out to the garden of St. Martha's square. There the assassin found the pope himself talking to an elderly priest. At once he took aim at the pope with his remarkable weapon. The priest, however, flung himself at Stepnyak and struck at the gun with a heavy cane, fouling his aim. Unable to hold him, the priest shouted for the guards, who came swarming from the surrounding buildings to capture him, but with his great strength he fought himself free and scrambled up the vines on the city wall. The guards fired at him with their new Vetterli rifles, but he was over the wall too fast for them."

I couldn't suppress a laugh. "I gather that the old priest was you."

Holmes smiled. "He did seem youthfully agile for a man of such great age."

"Then obviously you were not with the *penitentes*: Stepnyak would have noticed that you were missing. Why didn't he?"

Then Sprüngli laughed. "We change clothes! I pretend to be Sherlock Holmes with pilgrims, and Holmes guards Holy Father! Just before assassin step away, a man—American man, very short—tap me on shoulder and ask me many questions—'who am I? what means hat and gown?' He keep me talking so I would not notice assassin, and I play his game."

"I see. That's why you were wearing the fancy dress, Sergeant. The gang thought you were Holmes, while Holmes, dressed as he is now, was in the garden with the pope," I was half explaining to Sister Carolina, who glanced back to tell me she understood perfectly—I didn't need to clarify for her.

"It seems unnecessarily dangerous," she said. "You put the Holy Father in great peril."

Holmes turned earnest. "It was necessary to draw out the assassin and foil his purpose. However, I do recognize that our plan was a hazardous one, and that is why I pay such tribute to the nerve of the pope. He is a canny one, as you will soon know for yourself."

"What do you mean?" she asked.

Holmes attempted a gentlemanly smile, and nearly succeeded. "I have been summoned to the Vatican to receive—in private—the personal thanks of His Holiness, and I am invited to bring with me whomever I wish."

"We are to accompany you?" I asked, awestruck. "To a papal audience?"

"If you are so inclined, I would be pleased if you, Tuck, Sister Carolina, and Sergeant Sprüngli would do so. Tomorrow."

Chapter 5

The next morning after a breakfast of Sister Ugolin's volcanic coffee and hard rolls, we climbed into a brougham sent by the Vatican and made our way through the streets of Rome toward the titanic enclosure of St. Peter's. Holmes, at last devoid of make-up, wore a respectable cutaway, waistcoat, and top hat. I had invested in a new starched collar, while Sister Carolina required us to stop at a leather shop in the Piazza Barberini so she could choose some new gloves. She returned with several pair.

"You have dropped your disguise," I observed to Holmes as we crossed the Sant' Angelo Bridge.

"I shall not again enter the presence of the Supreme Pontiff in fancy dress. Besides, there is no reason for it now," he replied. "The pope is safe and his guards are highly vigilant. Stepnyak is surely on his way back to Russia and out of reach—that is, if he values his life. Our master criminal does not tolerate failure."

"Who is this 'master criminal,' Holmes?" I asked.

"We'll talk of him later," Holmes cut me off, looking askance at Sister Carolina. "We've nearly arrived."

Gazing up through the window, I saw the colonnade of St. Peter's square coming into view and was stunned at the grandeur of it all. The façade of the basilica was far larger than I had imagined, a grand golden frieze shadowed with dust in the morning sunlight. We were met at the entry by Sergeant Sprüngli, whose face was no longer so jolly. His mustaches were drooping.

"Herr Holmes, please come with me. I have news."

We descended, waited several minutes while Sprüngli whispered to Holmes in German, then I approached them. "What news?" I asked.

"There has been in the Vatican museum a robbery, and the Shamrock has steamed away. But we are due in the audience rooms, so let us go."

Sprüngli, looking trim in his modern blue uniform, led the way for us. The next hour was a towering experience—to meet and be embraced by the Holy Father himself, although I had done nothing to qualify for such a moment—well, it felt as if I were entering heaven.

My feelings did not compare to those of Sister Carolina, however, who disintegrated in tears as the Holy Father took her hand and lifted her from her knees.

Holmes, on the other hand, was formal, bowing firmly as he was presented. He murmured a low apology for allowing the would-be assassin to escape and failing to anticipate the rifling of the museum. The pope dismissed all of this with a shake of his head. Congratulating Holmes on foiling the assassination attempt, he raised his hand to bless my friend and placed a small box in his hand. Holmes trembled slightly, but was his unyielding self again in an instant as he backed correctly away from this august personage.

Afterwards, Sprüngli kindly led us on a visit to the Vatican museum. Resplendent in their Renaissance dress of gold and purple, the Swiss Guards were everywhere, saluting Sprüngli as he passed.

"We take more care now. Guards must watch, watch. *Was eine Schande,*" he muttered.

"'What a shame,'" Holmes whispered in my ear, and it was not just a translation.

I prevailed on him to open the box the pope had given him, in which lay a medal, an eight-pointed ivory cross with golden sunbursts between the arms. At the apex of the cross was carved a cavalier's tiny spur, its rowel etched with dozens of delicate barbs.

A gasp came from Sister Carolina. "Why, it's lovely. What is it?"

I explained, "It's the Order of the Golden Spur, an award for meritorious service to the Church." I did not go on to say that it was one of the most common of Catholic medals, handed out by the bushel to just about anyone who had money or influential friends. Holmes apparently knew this as well, for he sniffed and pocketed it without comment.

At length we came upon the scene of the robbery. Guards stood at attention round a massive glass case with its lid lying open. Among a lovely set of cameos, there were empty spaces with handwritten labels now attached to nothing but torn threads. A tonsured librarian was bending over the case and taking notes.

"A tremendous failure," Holmes said, mostly to himself. I could tell he was in acute distress.

The librarian looked up and, to our surprise, replied in English with a Yorkshire tinge. "Indeed. It all happened yesterday. The guards in this room were distracted by a noise of gunfire and ran to the garden. When they returned, this case had been rifled. The guards have been severely disciplined."

"You're English?" I asked.

"Oh, yes, excuse me. I am Dom Beazley. I came here a number of years ago from Ampleforth Abbey to assist the Vatican librarian."

We introduced ourselves. "What has happened here?" Holmes spoke up. The Dom looked at Sprüngli, who nodded his assent.

"This case contained a number of priceless antique cameos, including a magnificent onyx depicting Bacchus and Ariadne, as well as the famous Gonzaga Cameo portraying the Pharaoh Ptolemy from the fourth century before Christ. It is a profound loss," the Dom shook his head sorrowfully and went back to his notes.

"I've been blind," Holmes said as we walked away. "In my anxiety to oblige the pope, I completely overlooked the likelihood that our friend from Piccadilly would have more than one aim in mind."

"How could he have anticipated that the guards would leave their posts in that way?" I asked. "Surely it was some opportunist taking advantage of their absence."

"No, no. Only the most valuable cameos were taken, which indicates premeditation by an art expert. And our diminutive London friend is nothing if not an expert."

"You mean the short man who spoke to Sprüngli . . .?" Now I understood.

Holmes was vehement. "He counted on me to produce the distraction. He foresaw my every move, calculated that the assassination attempt would draw the guards away, and that under cover of the chaos he could lever that case open and come away unnoticed with some of the incomparable treasures of the Vatican." Holmes was actually grating his teeth. "I am a pastime for him, a diversion—a sport!" He smacked his cane against the marble floor and strode away smarting.

We lunched at a small outdoor trattoria near the Tiber. Mounds of pasta with cheese and huge bowls of ripe apricots and peaches lifted my spirits, although Holmes remained in a funk. Sister Carolina still radiated from her encounter with the pope and had little appetite. I made up for both of them. Smoking like a locomotive, Holmes touched only his cup of the foaming Vesuvian coffee I had learned to love in Rome. It was so much more substantial than the warmish bilge I had become used to in America.

"Man shall not live on tobacco and coffee alone," I admonished him, picking up a copy of the Vatican newspaper. I had enough Latin to read it quite easily and ran across an item that made me laugh out loud.

"Listen to this, Holmes. *Ab heri et a voce magna in hortis Vaticanis* . . . Oh, I'm sorry." My two companions were staring at me uncomprehendingly. Sister knew only the Latin of prayer. Holmes had picked up some of six living languages in his youthful travels round Europe with his parents, but, like Shakespeare, "small Latin and less Greek." Latin had been obligatory at our school, which is why Holmes never learned it.

"Allow me to translate." I read: "'Yesterday a loud noise of gunfire was heard from the Vatican gardens at about 10 o'clock in the morning. It caused considerable alarm throughout the City, until it was explained that a groundskeeper had used a shotgun to frighten away birds that were eating the grapes in the vineyard.' What a splendid joke. I shall never believe a newspaper again."

"They are rarely to be trusted," Holmes said absently, as if talking to himself. "The Shamrock is surely in international waters by now. The assassin Stepnyak has disappeared behind the great forest wall of Russia, a world of its own. We shall not see him again. Everyone has escaped my grasp." Then he shook his head as if to clear it and looked intently at Sister Carolina: "But now we turn to the problem of your three honorable men whose murder we must solve."

Sister Carolina came out of her reverie. "Murder? Then you believe the Tarleton brothers were murdered after all? Not just casualties of war?"

"I do indeed, Sister. It was cold, deliberate murder. That is beyond question. I am even fairly sure I know who did it. The next question for us now is, how and why was it done? Sister Carolina, my interest in your problem is more than eager—I must pursue it if I have to go to the ends of the earth."

"But you were so dismissive before . . ."

"Yes, before. But *now* . . . *now* a light has begun to shine in the darkness. Perhaps it is the holy influence of our morning's encounter with the Vicar of Christ, but I begin to see the remotest chance that we might solve more than one problem by pursuing this case. I hope that you will permit me to do so, both of you—and that you will accompany me."

"Gladly," I said, and the Sister echoed me. Her feelings toward Holmes had relaxed somewhat as she watched the Supreme Pontiff paying honor to him.

"I must warn you," Holmes said after a moment's hesitation. "This is a dark business. The point of light I see in the distance may turn out to be a furious fire that could consume us all. You must know that we are entering a zone of danger, and I cannot guarantee the result will be a favorable one."

"Mr. Holmes," Sister replied soberly, "I am about to leave this world behind. Before I do, I will see justice done. If I leave the world one way or another, it makes little difference to me."

"In this case, and after so long a time, justice is lame, and she must lean on me." Holmes stood after downing his coffee. "Now we must be off. I hope you will not mind cutting your Roman pilgrimage short . . . ."

"Back to America," I sighed, dreading just a bit crossing the ocean once again.

"No. At least not yet. For now, we re-direct our pilgrimage to London."

Chapter 6

It was no easy task to get passage, as the trains were crowded with tourists on their way to the world's fair in Paris, but Sergeant Sprüngli used his most officious manner to obtain places in a compartment for us. He was nearly in tears when it came time for us to say goodbye, and he waved at us from the platform until we lost sight of him.

The other passengers in the compartment were also English—Colonel Wurmston, an intolerably loud old gentleman in an old frock coat, old medals, and thick old whiskers, and his wife, brave in baubles, whose scorn for Catholics was demonstrated by her cold silence toward us. She made a show of sweeping her monumental dress out of the way to accommodate Sister Carolina and then turned her face from her for the rest of the day.

Her husband complained endlessly about Rome. "Never beheld such folly in me life . . . The Corso is impossible for quiet respectable people . . . silly Italians so given up to pleasures . . . a great annoyance, a very great annoyance . . . I ask you, where are the authorities?"

Desperate to change the subject, I said, "So you must be looking forward to Paris."

Then came a volley of attacks on the French.

At that point, a smart blonde woman in an amazingly tight-waisted dress looked through the window and swept the door open. "Is this place free?" she asked, her hand out to the seat next to mine.

"It is," I replied, and she fluidly made herself at home. A golden slide chain and locket gleamed on her breast. Her striking frock, sans bustle and crinoline, was light against her body and cut a bit too low for the time of day. It contrasted pleasantly with the bed furnishings that enveloped the Colonel's lady, who grunted her disapproval.

"I'm sorry to intrude on your party," the newcomer said. "I am Mrs. Katherine Wells, on my way to London to rejoin my husband." Holmes, who had been napping in the corner with his pipe, gave her a brief diagnostic look with one eye.

I was about to introduce ourselves and explain that we too were on our way to London when Holmes started from sleep and threw hot ash from his pipe over my knees. "I'm so sorry, my dear Padre," he cried, flicking the ash off of my trousers with his handkerchief. "How clumsy of me!" I glared at him in surprise.

"Excuse me, dear lady," he now said to Mrs. Wells. "I am Captain Basil, accompanying my cousin and his sister to the Paris Exposition. I wonder if you have seen it. It is said to be a spectacle unequaled."

"I have seen it, and you are right. It is unequaled. You shall enjoy it, I'm sure."

"Your husband must be in shipping, as you are from Liverpool, I take it?"

Mrs. Wells smiled. "My speech gives me away, doesn't it? The lilt of Merseyside? I am originally from Liverpool, although I have lived for some years in Paris and London. But no, Mr. Wells is an independent gentleman."

"An American, I presume."

This time, the lady looked just a bit startled. "Why yes, from New York. How did you know?"

"Your necklace. It is Tiffany and Company, isn't it? The famous New York jeweler?"

"You have a keen eye, Captain Basil."

Colonel Wurmston then fired a broadside against America until his wife silenced him with a sharp command.

"Are you interested in jewels, Captain?" Mrs. Wells asked.

He looked out the window as the train chugged along the seashore. "An obsession of mine, Mrs. Wells. I have a particular interest in antique cameos," he said, turning back to face her.

"And what brought you to Rome?" Her question was almost bland.

"Every Catholic longs to see Rome before he dies, isn't that so, Padre?" Holmes addressed me.

"Yes, of course," I nodded, bewildered at Holmes's stream of lies.

Mrs. Wells gave me a terse smile, then looked past me at Holmes. "I thought that old saying referred to Naples."

"'See Naples and die.' They do say that. In our case, we were able to see Rome without dying. Perhaps we shall see Naples someday. But not on this journey."

Gesturing at my pocket watch, Mrs. Wells consulted me for the time and then announced she was going for tea. As quickly as she came, she was gone.

"Saucy parvenue," sniffed Mrs. Colonel Wurmston. "Flitting from one compartment to another, showing herself to men and talking of jewelry." She held her hand over her voluminous necklaces. "She's probably a jewel thief herself."

Holmes said, "If she is, you'll attract none of her interest. Your ornaments are all paste, Madam."

"Paste! You dare . . . you . . . he's insulted me!" she babbled at her husband.

"Scoundrel!" the Colonel shouted. "You impertinent . . . I'll meet you outside!"

"You won't. You know as well as I that your wife is not worth a box. She has nearly bankrupted you. Look at your boots. And your tweeds are disintegrating while she luxuriates in yards of silk. You will not fight for this elderly social-climbing bigot who deigns to cut my cousins dead—fine religious folk who have dedicated their lives to the service of God."

"I will not stand for this. I am a gentleman. I hold the Queen's commission!" Wurmston growled.

"Which you purchased, and then sat drinking port behind the Crimean lines while thousands of infantrymen shed their blood and lost life and limb. You flaunt your Crimea medal on your lapel as a symbol of your armchair courage, but like so many amateur officers in that disastrous war you are a contemptible old coward." Holmes's voice was cold and calm.

"You will not fight? You are the coward!"

Holmes chuckled. "No, I will not fight you. But the Padre here . . . well, you have no doubt heard that Catholic priests are often superb boxers."

I choked with surprise, then smiled apologetically.

The Colonel winced. "Your betters shall hear of this!"

"Sir, my betters do not jockey for spaces in a second-class railroad car."

The wife glared at Holmes as if she would spit at him. At last she hissed, "Papists!"

Holmes threw his head back and laughed.

The Wurmstons rose and blustered out of the compartment. "We will hear no more! Swine!"

Ruefully, I said, "Holmes, you've wounded them."

"'The wound is the place light enters you,' says the great poet of Persia. Perhaps they will begin to see themselves more clearly for what they are, and be the better for it."

The rest of the journey passed uneventfully. Holmes and I dozed while Sister, as patient and untiring as the spinner of destiny, wove another rosary in the darkness.

Many hours later we descended at Paris. Holmes hurried us across the capital to catch the Paris-Calais express. I couldn't help but notice the many Parisian woman in the station wearing natural frocks like the one Mrs. Wells wore. Whatever else she was, her sense of fashion was *très au courant*.

Arriving at the train early, we came across a compartment with only one passenger, a woman in rusty brocade with a scarf flaring like a sunset round her neck. She nodded smartly at us as we entered and continued reading her newspaper, *Le Figaro*.

"A compatriot of yours, I'd say, Sister Carolina," Holmes smiled at the lady as he sat down.

The passenger glanced up at Holmes. "Do you refer to me, sir?" she said, with an unmistakable American accent.

"Pardon me, ma'am, but it is a little hobby of mine to guess at the provenance of strangers."

"Oh?" she replied, intrigued, "What do you make of my 'provenance,' as you put it?"

"You are an American lady who has lived in France for some time, unmarried, a professional painter in pastels and oils. Your work has recently been rejected because it is deemed to be unconventional, but you have not lost confidence in your artistic philosophy. Although you belong to a family of some means, you are determined to live from the proceeds of your paintings."

The woman gaped at us in astonishment. "You have been following me." She put down her newspaper and seized a good-sized wooden box lying next to her as if to defend herself with it.

"Not at all," Holmes said. "I have never laid eyes on you until this moment."

"It is so," I piped in. "Quite remarkable, isn't he?" Sister Carolina was chuckling disdainfully.

"What you say is quite true, but I'm at a loss as to how you could possibly know these things. Perhaps you've been following my career?"

"I fear not, although I'm sure it will be a brilliant one. You are clutching to yourself an oaken box labeled *Pastels Tendres,* containing the prized pastels of an artist. Your general demeanor of independence and briskness of welcome indicate America, not to mention a certain national look which Americans are acquiring—what the French would call *enfantin*. But you have settled in France: you wear a well-used French gown and bonnet, which means you are no tourist, and you read *Le Figaro* easily. Your clothing indicates that you are in straitened circumstances—as are most artists trying to live from their art—but your pince-nez are solid gold, clearly a gift from well-to-do family connections. No gentleman would buy such a gift for a lady. It is too useful."

The lady was impressed. "Extraordinary! My father is indeed prosperous, but I will not have him supporting me—although I do not begrudge a gift now and then. And I lack a wedding ring, obviously. All true, but how do you know of my unconventional style of painting, and my recent disappointment?"

"Your fingers are stained with unmixed oil paint, which no orthodox painter would use. Your approach must therefore be irregular. From this I surmise a recent rejection, as you are leaving Paris, the artist's holy of holies, possibly forever. The volume of your luggage in the overhead bin reveals as much. Other than these small indications, you are a complete stranger to me."

"Well, then, we are strangers no longer," the woman replied. Smiling, she extended a hand to Holmes and me and shook ours vigorously. "Mary Cassatt, originally of Pittsburgh, Pennsylvania, most recently of Paris. And you are right, I have not lost confidence in my art."

"Of course not, Miss Cassatt, your deportment, the set of your jaw, the way you grip your paint box—you are justifiably sure of yourself. My name is Captain Basil, and these are my cousins, Reverend Basil and his sister Mary."

"Are you on a pilgrimage together?"

"A pilgrimage of sorts," Holmes replied. "And now you will be getting off the train."

Her eyes widened. "Do you think I should? I had thought to get away from Paris, to escape . . ."

"Miss Cassatt," Holmes replied, "a century from now your work will be praised and studied and fawned over by the whole world. You have no time to lose. You must stay."

"Captain Basil, with your powers of observation, you have confirmed for me that my approach is the right one. The power of the picture is in the small things, the things others don't see, the light-catching things that go unobserved by our dull eyes." She paused, gazed out the window for a moment, then arose. "I will be turning back my ticket now." And she left the compartment in search of the agent.

"Holmes, you are a healer," I remarked.

"Like you. Our professions are similar, Tuck—we are both engaged in the cure of souls."

The train was just leaving the station when Miss Cassatt was replaced by a young man who popped through the door in a sweat. He nodded at us and sat down by the window, shedding his coat. "Almost missed the train," he said. "You speak English?"

"Yes, we are English. I am Reverend Basil, my sister Mary, and my cousin Captain Basil." I was playing the game quite smoothly now.

"Clement Yeobright," he said. "On my way home at last. Do you mind?" he took out a cigarette.

"Not at all," said Holmes, who lit it for him from his black clay pipe. "Where is your home?"

"Egdon Heath in Wessex."

"Sounds desolate," Holmes observed, blowing smoke in his direction.

"Oh, not at all," the young man said, learning forward with some energy. "It is most exhilarating and strengthening and soothing. I would rather live on those hills than anywhere else in the world."

"You, a young man, are leaving Paris, the most brilliant of cities, to bury yourself in the heath of the West Country?"

"I hate Paris," Yeobright snapped. "It is false and flashy and . . . effeminate."

"And yet those things hold a certain attraction for you," Holmes replied.

"What do you mean, sir?" Yeobright sat back warily.

"I mean you have been working for some time as a jeweler in Paris. Diamonds are your business, and you have been quite successful at it. They are gaudy things, are they not?"

"I'm leaving all of that behind." Then he stared at Holmes with that stunned expression I had become used to. "How in blazes did you know all of that?"

"Your sleeves are whiter to the elbows than the rest of your shirt. This comes from wearing sleeve stockings, which is typical of a jeweler. You have a faint white stripe on your forehead from a visor with a loupe attached, also typical of a jeweler. You wear a diamond stickpin of unusual purity. That and your natty clothes suggest that you are—or recently have been—a diamond dealer of substance."

"You are a close observer. Yes, I have been doing well."

"Pray, what is 'doing well'?"

Yeobright made no answer at first. He looked out the window at the flat French countryside, then abruptly said, "That is precisely the question, sir. What is 'doing well'? How does any man worthy of the name pass his time?"

"For my part, I collect vintage cameos," Holmes said coolly.

"Indeed." The young man showed no interest.

"Of course, I don't carry them with me. Thieves infest these trains. In fact, just weeks ago a gang stole 700 thousand francs in Egyptian and Spanish bonds from this very train, the Paris-Calais Express."

Yeobright continued staring at the landscape. "I had heard something of that," he murmured, but he was no longer with us. His mind had drifted into some charmed atmosphere of his own making, and soon he was snoozing against the window.

Some hours later, Holmes and I sat outdoors on a bench astern the cross-channel ferry. We both preferred it to the main cabin, which was stale with the odor of seasickness—although Holmes fouled the fresh air with his old pipe.

"Young Yeobright is the man of the future," shouted Holmes over the wind. "Immense potential, utterly aimless."

"He seemed quite nice to me," I shouted back.

"Nice men like Yeobright impose their will on others to no real purpose. He will create a wake of unhappiness as he searches for something to live for. All in vain."

"That is the future you see for mankind?"

"It is."

The wind weakened for a few moments.

"Is it the future you see for yourself?" I asked.

"Ah, there," Holmes stood and set his face toward the channel spray, raising his black walking stick against it. "I have something to live for. To delve into the mystery of all things. It is the mystery that matters."

"Then we are indeed in the same occupation. Mystery is my business as well."

"So it is, as I said. We do the same job, you and I," Holmes gave a wry laugh. "And I venture a guess that it is permanent employment."

As we approached the port of Dover, we entered the main cabin where Sister Carolina sat working on her rosary kit. "Another," she said, and held it up hesitantly, a small silver cross drooping from a circlet of parched red and black berries. "It is a gift for you, Mr. Holmes," she sniffed. "I do not know how else to thank you for . . . the Holy Father . . . such a moment."

"I accept it with pleasure," said Holmes, taking it reverently from her hand. His cool voice warmed slightly. "Although my failures thus far outnumber my successes," he muttered in my ear.

We soon debarked into the autumnal damp of Dover. During my years in the Carolinas, I had forgotten how the cold English air could stab like a knife in the spine. While we were collecting our belongings, I caught sight of the comely Mrs. Katherine Wells coming down the gangplank, now snug in a coat and hat of black woolen brocade and followed by men carrying trunks. She glanced at me and waved as she entered a waiting brougham, then was off.

"Holmes! Katherine Wells was on the Dover boat with us!"

"Yes."

"Now she knows we were lying about Paris being our destination."

"She never believed that it was," he muttered. "And lower your voice. Have you any money for the porter?" I dug into my pockets for some coins.

From the Dover station we took the London train and at last arrived in the metropolis. Holmes's demeanor changed as we approached the city. He pulled his collars up and his hat down, stayed furtively behind the porters when we left the train, and made quiet arrangements with two separate cabmen on Cannon Street.

"We part here, Tuck. In this cab I will take Sister Carolina to a religious house I know of. She will be safe there. You have a sister in the city, don't you? Take the other cab, please, and stay with her until I call on you."

He and Sister Carolina disappeared into their cab.

I didn't expect them to disappear from the face of the earth. Yet that is what happened.

LONDON

Chapter 7

Four days later I was walking through Hyde Park with my four-year-old nephew. My adventure in Rome now felt like a dream. Had it really happened? I had heard nothing at all from Holmes or Sister Carolina since leaving them at the station. As I felt responsible for her safety, I was growing anxious.

What if something had happened to them? I would be totally ignorant of it, possibly forever. After all, I had no inkling of Holmes's address, nor of the place he would have taken the Sister. I recalled how Holmes had been on his guard as we last parted and wondered if perhaps he had fallen foul of the 'master criminal' he spoke of so cryptically.

I had none of Holmes's instincts, so couldn't tell if I myself were in danger or not. It didn't appear so. I had arrived to a squealing welcome at the house of my sister and her husband in Campden Hill and made the acquaintance of her son, a noteworthy boy of four ("four-and-a-half," he reminded me soberly), big for his age, who engaged us in conversation with full, florid sentences. I had never known a child to speak so. His mother told me that the gift of language had fallen on Gibby like a tongue of flame. As soon as I met him, he tested me with a provocative and quite unanswerable question: "Uncle Simon, when I jump from a chair, do I fall to the earth, or does the earth fall towards me?"

While awaiting a message from Holmes, I paced my sister's house like a bored cat, with Gibby continuously flinging questions at me, and she finally asked me to take Gibby on an outing to the park if only to be rid of us.

I had some qualms about leaving the house, especially with a child in tow, but I was overwhelmingly curious to see something in town. So I agreed to go. It was a brilliant, fresh fall day, and I couldn't conceive that anything could happen to us in daylight in the heart of the world's greatest city.

We bundled up Gibby against the cold and he and I set out. He became something of an attraction on the pavement. A young idler propped against a street lamp grinned at the little boy as we passed. Ladies stopped to admire him and the eager chaos of his red hair.

The child nattered on as we strode along just inside the gardens by the Kensington High Street. "Uncle Simon, why are you so burly?"

"Burly?" I laughed. An odd word for a four-year-old. "We come from a large family."

"It is a large family in numbers . . . and it is also large in size," the child giggled. He floored me with this one. It's true, I was one of twenty-three children, and my brothers and I were all broad and muscular. At age four, Gibby was already distinguishing the significations of words as if he had the dictionary in his head.

"Uncle Simon, why are you a priest?"

I gave him a sort of childish answer. "Because the Lord loves little children, and he needs me to baptize them."

"Yes, I know. I was baptized in the church by the water tower. Do you know why? Father says it took a great deal of water to make me a Christian."

He laughed at his little joke, while I stared down incredulously at the wild mass of red hair that roofed over such a precocious brain.

"Someday I should like to be a priest," he chirped.

"Why, Gibby?"

"To get rid of my sins. And help other people get rid of theirs."

It was a stunning summary from the mouth of a babe—a little formula I have cherished ever since. "That is an excellent reason to be a priest, Gibby. Thank you for your wise words."

He grinned up at me.

We soon found ourselves at the end of the park, toddling alongside the anarchy of Piccadilly among a crowd of rude boys. I could tell Gibby was beginning to tire—it had been a long walk already—but I had to go just a little further.

There it was—number 198 Piccadilly—according to Holmes, the address of the master criminal of London. Set in the stately façade was an immense barred gate, next to which a London policeman stood watching the passersby. I had anticipated something else—a moldering Gothic tower, or perhaps an archway leading to sinister caverns—but it was just a townhouse typical of Mayfair.

What had I expected? To glimpse an imprisoned Holmes gesturing to me from an upper-story window? To catch sight of Sister Carolina being carted off into the white-slave trade?

I couldn't resist speaking to the policeman. "Is anything wrong, constable?"

"Nothing sir, er, Padre."

"What brings you here to this particular gate?"

"Just standing my post, sir."

I examined the pavement round the gate looking for traces of river mud, but found nothing but the usual London dust. I got down on all fours and sniffed about in vain for the odor of the Thames before I realized what I was doing.

"Are we playing a game?" Gibby asked.

I looked up to find that the constable and three or four pedestrians, a lady and gentleman and a couple of stray beggar boys, had stopped to stare at me. The constable was tapping himself with his stick, so I stood and brushed off my knees. "Er, thought I could smell gas. You know, these old underground gas pipes aren't to be trusted."

After I had loitered a while, hoping to catch someone, anyone, going in or out of the house, the constable suggested I move along. "The little fellow looks tired, Padre. Per'aps you should cab it home. "

I agreed, and he signaled for a hansom cab that had been waiting across the street. "Where to, sir?"

"Campden Hill."

The constable shut us into the cab, had a word with the driver, and we were off. Nothing out of the ordinary—until we moved beyond the park in Knightsbridge and missed the turning for Campden Hill. Then I knew something was going wrong.

All at once the carriage reeled forward at high speed, listing from one side to the other and going faster and faster, winding madly through the traffic for no reason I could see. I reached out for Gibby and held him tight as we spun off the street toward Hammersmith.

"Slow down! Stop!" I shouted, beating on the trap door in the roof of the cab, but it was locked. "Stop, I say. There is a child!" The driver gave no answer but lashed the great black horse even faster. We sped on, turning wildly almost backward into a lane spiky with barren trees. The child and I banged hard against the windows. Branches slapped at us as we hurtled over ragged roads through the outlands of Shepherds Bush. The driver's whip slapped again and again across the flanks of the laboring horse.

My hammering and shouting did no good. I managed to roll Gibby into a lap blanket and clasped him tight against myself to protect him, but he made no sound except an occasional "whee!" Flinging gravel from the wheels against the windows and even over the fender, the cab lurched and bounced so violently that several times I thought we would overturn. We could do nothing but endure it.

Then as quickly as it had begun, the mad ride was over. We had come nearly full circle and stopped at Campden Hill. The latch abruptly opened. Without pause I pulled Gibby, blanket and all, out of the doors and turned in anger to the cab driver. Buried in a scarf and low hat, he laid his whip over my face, just missing my eye, shouting "Get out of it and stay out!" Then he was off again at speed.

Gibby and I limped to my sister's house. The idler still slumped against the street lamp looked sinister to me now, and I glared at him. My cheek stinging, my head reeling, I was outraged and my sister horrified when I told her the story. She breathed out threatenings and slaughter, but my brother-in-law, Ed, was more philosophical, eventually succeeding in calming her down. As for Gibby, he merely looked up at me and asked, "Can we do it again?"

"Why?" my sister asked. "What would cause a London cabbie to take leave of his senses like that?"

I had told my family nothing about my adventure with Holmes. They knew I had been to Rome, but they thought I had stopped at London on my way back to the States just to see them. Of course I suspected that the driver had been suborned by Holmes's enemies and that this show of violence was intended to warn me off. Now it had touched my family, and I resolved to wait no longer to hear from Holmes.

After a short rest and a little refreshment, I started out again, this time taking the Metropolitan from Kensington Station to Westminster Bridge. As the train rattled along, I kept looking round at my fellow passengers. Which of them might be stalking me? Watching me? Hanging from a strap was a beefy fellow in a bowler hat, next to a short man who glanced at me occasionally through gemlike spectacles. Was he looking at me, or I at him? He shifted his weight. Which of us was the more nervous?

At Westminster I leapt from the train and ran out into the knife-like wind off the river. Walking quickly, I made my way to the entrance of Whitehall, first looking round for any sign of pursuers. No one in the busy plaza was taking the slightest notice of me, so I addressed myself to the guard at the grand archway and asked to see Mr. Mycroft Holmes.

Sometime later I faced a puzzled junior clerk who informed me that no such person was employed in the government.

But I had received a wire from Mycroft Holmes at Whitehall only a few weeks before, I explained. No, unfortunately, I didn't have the wire with me. The clerk shook his head, looked officially sympathetic, and disappeared back inside the halls of empire.

Now I was well and truly baffled. Sister Carolina had utterly disappeared, so had Sherlock Holmes, and now his brother didn't exist. No trace of any of them remained. Standing there on the street immobilized, for a moment I had the crazed thought that it had all been a fantasy of mine, that I was dreaming or gone mad.

But what of the cabbie's brutal treatment of the morning? Surely that was a message from someone. No, it was no fantasy. I was in grave trouble and now quite alone. I sent up a few Hail Marys and tried to think of what to do next.

It occurred to me, or I had read somewhere, that to find a lost person one should go back to the last place the person was known to be. That would be the Cannon Street station, where Holmes took one cab and I another. Perhaps if I went back to that spot, looked for the cabbie who had taken up Holmes and the sister . . . but would I even know him if I saw him? Also, I was now rather shy of London cabbies.

Nevertheless, I took the Metropolitan line again toward Cannon Street and found the kerb at the station where Holmes had left me. It was hopeless. There were dozens of hansom cabs in the queue, the drivers submerged in woolen scarves against the cold, none of them in the least distinguishable from the others.

As I stood there forlorn, a boy approached me with a note, which said I was to follow him into the post office next the station.

"Are you sure you have the right person?"

"Yes, sir. You are Father Grosjean, sir?"

"Yes, I am."

Startled, and lacking the caution I should have shown, I went with him to the post office. What else was I going to do?

The boy led me to a clerk with a wisp of a red beard who introduced himself briskly as "Bernard Shaw, an Edison man." He took me into a private room hung with electrical wires and set me before a device the like of which I had never seen before. A horn protruded from it, and the clerk affixed a heavy instrument to my head so it covered my right ear.

"What is this?'

"It's a telegraphic telephone, your reverence."

"A what?"

"An electrical apparatus for speaking over long distances. Its purpose is to advance the illusion that communication can actually take place."

I had heard vaguely of such a thing but discounted it as fantasy, until I heard a roaring noise in my head and a voice spoke to me.

"Father Grosjean?"

I didn't know what to do. The metallic voice repeated my name.

"Speak into the horn," Shaw whispered with an impatient smile.

"This is Father Simon Grosjean," I intoned slowly into the device, wondering if I were about to be electrocuted.

"Is there anyone in the room with you?"

I looked round expecting to see Shaw, but he had withdrawn and closed the door.

"No, I am alone."

"This is Mycroft Holmes speaking. I am sorry I couldn't acknowledge you earlier today, but the world situation is such that no one must have any connection with me for the present. I felt bad watching you from the window as you left, so I determined to make contact with you in the most private way possible."

"But how did you know to find me in Cannon Street?"

"Please, Father Grosjean. I prefer not to discuss our methods."

"But I didn't notice anyone tracing me."

"When I trace you that is what you may expect to notice."

I still couldn't believe a machine was speaking to me and wondered if this were some elaborate ruse. Was I hearing someone in the next room talking through a pipe?

"How am I to know certainly that this is Mycroft Holmes speaking?" I asked.

The machine gave a rumbling gurgle, which I soon recognized as a laugh. "Very wise of you, Father. I would want to make certain myself. Ask me a question to which only you and I would know the answer."

I thought for a moment, then asked, "By what nickname were you known at Stonyhurst?"

A space of silence, then "Big Mike." A little wry resentment in the voice?

"Thank you, thank you, Mr. Holmes. I do apologize. I was afraid I was losing my mind when they told me you didn't exist."

"Well, I exist. What can I do for you, Father?"

I explained my predicament and the fearful ride I had taken in the morning. "I just want to know what's going on—where to find your brother, to know nothing untoward has befallen him."

"One never knows, Father. Something untoward is likely to befall Sherlock one day, given his taste for hazardous adventures." I was surprised at his coolness. "But you might possibly find him at this address. Commit it to memory, but pray do not write it down."

I did so. "I am most grateful to you, Mr. Holmes."

"My pleasure, sir." The roaring noise resumed after a loud click. I removed the apparatus and poked my head out the door where Shaw was waiting.

"I'm finished with the machine," I said. "It's a remarkable contrivance, this telegraphic what-d'ye-call-it."

"Isn't it? We've had it less than a month. We held our first communication with Norwich just a few days ago."

"Norwich! That's more than a hundred miles from here! Who on earth could come up with a contraption like that? It's utterly unreasonable."

"Perhaps all progress depends on unreasonable men," said the perky Shaw. He shook my hand and I was in Cannon Street again.

The address tucked in my memory was somewhere in the east of London. I knew the city feebly, but had no doubts about this location. It was in one of the city's worst pockets of crime and filth, near the docks on the river where the scum of the whole world drifted in on the wake of the vast merchant fleet of Great Britain.

Chapter 8

Far beyond the east end of the Metropolitan line, I found myself in a worn cab slogging along behind a horse whose demise appeared imminent. I had been wary of taking a cab, but the bony driver looked so tired that I couldn't muster up fear of him. When I told him where I was going, he sniffed hard, looked up to heaven, and said, "That's no place I'd be caught *without* a clergyman."

My collar and cassock as our assurance, we entered the closest lanes I'd ever seen, squeezed between haggard, water-scoured warehouses of gray wood, peopled only by an occasional wretch lying drunken in a doorway. Although it was still afternoon, fog and the smoke from burning detritus darkened our path through the back burrows of the dockyards. Evil-looking boys darted in and out of the alleys, no doubt looking to waylay people like me.

"Here it is, sir," the man announced hoarsely. We had stopped under an ancient eave with slats swollen and eroded like a mouth full of rotting teeth. I stepped out and asked the cabbie to wait for me, but he said he would rather live long enough to have his dinner, turned round, and lurched away with surprising speed.

Under the eaves was a slowly collapsing frame building that looked as if it had barely survived the Middle Ages. I knocked on the moldy boards that had once been a door and waited. No answer.

I knocked again, louder, but again there was no answer. What if Holmes weren't there? Worse yet, what if someone else were there, someone I would prefer not to deal with? How would I ever get out of this labyrinth of ruins and back to Campden Hill?

By this time I was perishing with cold, and a misery of a rainstorm had decided to squat over the city, so I decided to enter the warehouse of my own accord. No lock would have served the disintegrating door, so I pushed my way in and waved aside a dust-covered hanging that revealed steps leading underground. I descended, and as my eyes grew used to the dark, I detected what appeared to be a mass of squirming bodies.

"Dowse . . . that . . . light!" came an agonized groan. I looked round. What light? Were they referring to the almost imperceptible grayish light from the open door above? I quickly replaced the hanging.

"Excuse me," I called in a weak voice. "I'm sorry to intrude, but I'm looking for a friend." I was answered by a cascade of coughing and a giggle that sounded like a raven's screech.

"You have no friends here," a tuberculous voice answered.

A candle was abruptly lit and a man appeared, a well-kept, middle-aged figure with pale lips and eyes under his twisted black hair. Carrying the candle, he stumbled toward me as if sightless, then felt his way up the stairs to the door.

"Ye'll remember the market price, now, and pay according," came the screeching voice from below. "Ye'll remember like a good soul, won't ye?"

The man shouted something unintelligible. I pursued him out the door.

"Excuse me, sir. Sir!" I touched his arm and he shook me away. Holding his hand over his eyes, he looked like a respectable churchwarden who had just come from Mass into the daylight. I didn't dare speak Holmes's name, so I merely said, "I'm looking for a friend who is missing. He is tall and thin, about twenty-five years old. Prominent nose . . ."

The man cut me off. "What is it o'clock?" he stammered.

"About four of the afternoon."

"It can't be. It just can't . . ." he moaned and drifted unsteadily away. Then he turned and said helplessly, "Um, no one like that. No one in there." He pointed at the grim house and continued down the lane.

I had reached another impasse and was soaking from the drizzle. I decided to wait for it to stop just inside the door of the house. I was under no illusions about the place, and my fear of it had diminished. Once or twice I had accompanied the sisters to minister in such places near the wharves of Charleston, where the hopeless smoke away their lives on the dismal harvest of opium from the East. Such people are to be pitied, not feared.

The place was warm and the rain hypnotic. I have no idea how long I stood there watching, but as it got dark outside I became conscious of a low conversation going on down the stairs. Curious, I pulled the curtain aside and peered in. By the red glow of the pipes I could see three figures—a lascar, a blowzy Chinese, and a filthy rag of an old woman—the latter two lying in a stupor and mumbling quietly to each other on a collapsed bed that nearly filled the tiny cell. Their faces, drawn and drained by the poison, resembled each other so much that the woman looked

Chinese and the Chinese man looked like an old fishwife. The lascar slept the sleep of a corpse—and perhaps he was one by now.

I was about to turn away from this miserable sight and leave the place when I heard a faint "Tuck."

It's not possible, I said to myself before realizing it was bally well possible. Anything was possible with Holmes.

"Holmes?" I whispered. He must be hiding in the house somewhere.

But the voice had come from the bed. Slowly the Chinese man slid upwards to his full height and shed about a hundred pounds in the process. I would never have believed it.

"Holmes. You . . . you . . ."

His voice was hushed and grave. "I instructed you to wait until you heard from me. Why have you disregarded my instruction? It was for your own safety, and that of another."

"I was afraid something had happened to you. An accident or . . . . It's been four days! I've heard nothing!"

"You were supposed to hear nothing. I wanted you out of this for the time being. Now you may well have brought them down upon us."

"Them? Who?"

At that instant we heard a whistle from the courtyard and then muted voices at the door above our heads. Holmes put his finger to his lips and resumed his Chinese disguise, losing two feet of height and shrinking into an oily ball of fat in the light of a candle.

He went to the door. I heard the voices, then a quick muffled shout. "Tuck!"

I ran upstairs squarely into the stomach of a big hooded fellow who stank of sour gin. The man staggered back. Balancing on his rear foot, Holmes was circling another man, short but thick, who struck out at him with a roar and a fist like a tree trunk. My man turned on me with a brutal blow to my chin. I hadn't remembered how shocking it was being punched in the face; but it raised my blood and my old school training, and I clouted the man with an upper thrust of my right and a thump to his temple with my left.

I have always had powerful shoulders. I hit him so hard that he flew sideways off his feet against an outer wall. I could see a window in that wall, so I threw myself at him, wrestled him up, and heaved him like a beam of wood out the window. I hadn't realized the house backed onto an inlet of the river: a dull splash was followed by a good deal of drunken roaring.

I turned to find that Holmes had bloodied the other invader into unconsciousness.

"Quickly," Holmes said. "We must be off."

From below stairs came a cry. "The market price is dreffle high just now, and business is slack . . . so slack. . . ."

"Have you any money?" Holmes whispered urgently.

"I have a sovereign."

"Give it to her." I tossed the coin down the stairwell and the old lady snatched it, shrieking at her good fortune. I was surprised at her sudden nimbleness.

Moving like lightning, Holmes ripped the clothing off the man on the floor and swathed me in his foul scarf and filthy coat and hat. "Now!"

We dashed out like rats caught in the light and ran through a warren of warehouses smelling of fish and tar until we arrived at the wobbly end of a pier. I thought I could hear voices behind us, but couldn't be sure. We climbed down a ladder into a small boat tied to a piling, cast off, and began to row away from the dock.

The sky was murky by now, the opaque gray of the afternoon gone, and we pulled our way quietly upriver staying in the longshore current. In the daylight we would have made a bizarre sight—a fat Chinese and a tramp in rags taking a little exercise on the Thames. But we were well concealed by the fog.

I was more than baffled by what had just happened. "Holmes, what on earth—?" I began, but he shushed me with a low hiss. Of course, I thought, we might be invisible, but we could be heard easily across the water; so we rowed on in silence for what felt like hours, floating past curling lights on the water from a bridge or gas lanterns on the embankment. My hands froze, my shoulders cramped, my jaw ached from the fight, and I sent up a good number of Hail Marys that were earnestly meant. Happily, I was answered by an end to the miserable rain. I could even see a star or two through the clouds.

At last we arrived at the abutments just below the entrance to St Katharine Docks, where we found a stone stairway.

"I will leave you here," Holmes said. "Go up the stairs, back to Cannon Street, and ask for a cabbie named Bratfish. He will return you safely to your family."

"You're not tying up?"

"No, I have more to do this night. But pack your belongings and be at Paddington Station at dawn. Wear mufti, particularly a heavy scarf round your face. Book yourself onto the 6:59 for Liverpool. We will meet you there."

"We? Sister Carolina also?"

"Yes. Now this time, do as I ask."

"I won't fail."

I watched Holmes disappear again into the fog.

Chapter 9

There was something French in the makeup of my family. It came from our paternal line—tough, extraordinarily tenacious people who came to England in the time of the Huguenots. Our family name, Grosjean, is French for "Big John," undoubtedly a relic of a formidable ancestor of that type. My sister is a concentrated version of those traits, while my character is of my mother's more phlegmatic Anglo-Saxon vein.

Consequently, my sister met me in a tearing rage at the door that night. "Where have you been? We've been so frightened, afraid of every sound outside the door, afraid even of calling the police!"

"Don't exaggerate, my dear," my brother-in-law said.

"Look at him!" she shot back. "He looks like the Tsar's armies marched over him in the mud. A fine figure of a priest! What has happened to you?"

I didn't know how much of my story to reveal, but my sister was not one to be lied to and in a way had a right to know why the shadow of danger had fallen over her household. So I told her a version of the truth, that I was assisting my old schoolmate Holmes on an inquiry concerning the Church. It was a question more political than religious, I assured her, but certain unsavory parties had an interest in it. I also promised to leave in the morning and all would be resolved.

She hesitated, staring at me. "Your friend is a detective?"

"I want to be a detective," came a small, clear voice from behind us. It was Gibby, who had slipped out of bed.

I smiled at him. "I thought you wanted to be a priest?"

"I can be a detective *and* a priest," he insisted.

"Why would you want to do that?"

"I could detect sins and then get rid of them for people."

His parents and I could not suppress a laugh. "Gibby, that's a very good reason to be a detective priest." I went on, "I must leave in the morning, but may I tell you a bedtime story now?"

"Oh, yes, Uncle Simon. The story of St. George and the Dragon."

I looked at my sister. "Go ahead," she sighed. "Up to bed with you. Both of you."

So I lay next to the little boy in the darkness, barely able to stay awake as I mumbled my way through the old tale of a knight who saved a princess from a horrible dragon. In my half-dream the knight took on the form of Holmes and the princess the form of Sister Carolina. The dragon remained a dragon, choking out smoke from a red pipe in a black underground cell of London.

Then Gibby murmured, "St. George no longer fears the dragon. Now he must fear the princess."

The next morning I put on an old suit of my brother-in-law's, a derby too small for me, and wound a thick wool scarf round my mouth. A discarded greatcoat completed my attire, and I looked like a man who was trying to wear the clothes of his adolescence—in short, I was straining at the seams. I traveled in the darkness in a nearly empty Metropolitan to a nearly empty station, where I was startled from behind by a boy in a ragged porter's waistcoat.

"Tuck?" he asked quietly. "I'm Deputy. I'm taking you to Mr. Aitch."

"How did you know me?" I asked the boy, and then felt foolish, as I was the only passenger in the vast hall who had just booked the 6:59 to Liverpool.

Deputy led me to a locked compartment on the waiting train. He knocked and the door opened on Sister Carolina, now dressed in a plain brown nun's habit and wearing spectacles. Of course Holmes bore no resemblance to himself. His costume was an odd combination of drudge and dandy—a top hat, a rude tie, an old frock coat, and a large pair of dirty Wellington boots. But most remarkable was the pinkish goatee, expertly applied and utterly transformative.

Deputy introduced me as if we were at a high-toned London club. "Mr. Tuck, may I present your travelin' companions, Sister Alphonsa and Mr. Escott, a well-to-do plumber from Brixton."

"Sister," I said, touching my hat. "Mr. Escott. May I join you?"

"Certainly sir," Holmes replied affably, applying a match to his clay pipe. "Plenty of room, plenty of room. I say, sir, have you any money?"

I sighed and produced a coin for Deputy, who smirked and left the train. Holmes locked the door behind him and drew the window curtain.

Immediately I examined Sister. Her face was tired and white. "Are you all right? I was deathly afraid for you. I had no idea where you were . . . "

"I'm well enough," Sister replied coolly. "Mr. Holmes kindly arranged for me to stay at a place called the Nuns' House, quite à propos, and has explained the need for my temporary change of identity." She sniffed disapprovingly, pulled out her étui, and began work on yet another rosary. "I suppose it's all for my protection."

"It is indeed, dear Sister," Holmes replied. "And it's all part of the excitement." He rubbed his hands with enthusiasm. "This is truly the most intriguing case I have yet encountered. We are going to have a splendid time together."

Sister and I looked at him in disbelief.

"You may find it intriguing, sir," she said, "but for me it has been an ordeal. Being hurried here and there across continents . . . I could wish for less intrigue."

"Holmes, I am on pins and needles waiting for you to tell us what you have been doing."

His eyes gleamed. "I have passed three days between Somerset House and the British Library, and I believe I have come close to tying one loose end of this case to the other."

"Somerset House? The national archive?"

"On Thursday morning a self-made upstart, a plumber named Escott, visited the Registrar General to make inquiries about his ancestry. He believed he might be the rightful heir to the Earl of Shrewsbury, as his mother was named Talbot—as you know, the earldom belongs to the noble Talbot family. The registrars thought they would make a good joke of young Escott, so they actually let him examine the archives of Talbot births and deaths and marriages.

"Obviously, the names Talbot and Tarleton are close together in the alphabet, and Escott found himself by chance rummaging among the records of the Tarleton family—a most fruitful chance, I might add. To his not very great surprise, Escott learned that the Tarletons of Britain are somewhat involved with the history of the American South—one Tarleton in particular.

"His name was Colonel Banastre Tarleton, a commander of dragoons who made a mixed reputation fighting the Americans in the Revolution. In the late spring of 1780, Tarleton's men attacked a force of Continentals at Waxhaws Creek in the Carolinas, who, outnumbered, raised a white flag. The account is confused, but it appears that the British attacked the surrendering army and butchered them where they stood. Thus the incident became known as the Waxhaws Massacre and Tarleton as 'Bloody Ban.' It was a pivot point in the war, as many American loyalists, revolted by Bloody Ban's massacre, turned against the British, and militias sprouted up everywhere. Within a year, it was all over, and the Colonies were lost."

Sister interrupted. "What does this battle—almost a century ago—have to do with my Tarleton boys?"

"That, dear sister, is the loose end I must tie up. But there is an undoubted connection, as you will see." Again checking the window and the door, Holmes unrolled the bizarre message I had received in Charleston. It now looked much worn from Holmes's repeated handling.

"What is this?" Sister asked, her face graying even more.

I explained the letter and the coded message we had found. Stiffening with fear and distrust, she drew back from me into the corner of the bench. "You have said nothing to me about this. You, my friend, my pastor, have kept it all from me for these many weeks?"

"I thought to protect you—I didn't want you to be alarmed."

She took a harsh breath and glared at me. I thought this unfair. I really had wanted to shield her from those morbid threats and expected that she would be grateful at our progress in unraveling the mystery of the Tarletons' death. However, even after many decades of listening to women in the confessional, I can still state unequivocally that I do not understand them at all.

Holmes was holding the letter up to the window light. "You see, I have deciphered more of it.

O.

LET T.HE TAR LET ON,
B.eware! *Let the Feathers reveal,*
*Raging **bloody** w.ax Fire be set,*
*On thy **Bans!** Awe thy Confessi.onal Seal!*
*Thou shalt drink **Fate**. in Wine, be it distilled Gall!*
*Hell's bread shalt. avenged **in** Tartarus eat!*
*Even Thy Goddess in the **d.epths** of Acheron shall fall!*
*Revenge! T.hou shalt drink the shame **of** it Sweet!*
*Shad.owed Brotherhood! If we Heaven's will cannot avert, **Hell***
*Let us move. Charon bring thee o'er his Flood **to** meet,*
*In Ro.bes and burning Cross and Blood Drops to **lie**,*
*Even there. where the Prince of Air forever flames up **howling**,*
PETIT AND PERDITION! BAP.ST AND BLAZES! STRICKEN AND SEALED!

CHAOS AND **CURSES!**
DO NOT OPEN PANDORAS BOX OR YOU WILL FEEL
THE WRATH OF THE KU, KLUX, KLAN!

Holmes had circled with a pencil a word in each line. "You see," he said eagerly, "start with the first word of the first line, then the second of the second line, the third of the third, and so on. Read diagonally from the upper left-hand corner to the bottom right-hand corner."

I read it slowly, with a darkening chill: "'Beware bloody Bans! fate in depths of Hell to lie howling curses!'"

Holmes was grinning at me.

"Bloody Ban's fate?" I asked.

"What do you think? Chance or design?"

It was evidently not chance.

Holmes sat back in his seat, all at once contemplative. "Put the two messages together and you have 'Let the Tarleton brothers lie, or beware Bloody Ban's fate in depths of hell to lie howling curses.' Evidently, Tuck, if you don't let the whole question of the Tarleton murders alone, whoever wrote this letter intends to send you to hell." Then he peered down at me. "Well, to your death in any case."

"It's horrible," Sister Carolina intoned from her corner.

Holmes continued in his neutral voice. "The reference to Bloody Ban Tarleton of Revolutionary War fame connects him to your Tarleton brothers who died at Gettysburg. The question is, what is the nature of that connection?"

"Perhaps there is no connection at all," she said. "Perhaps it is all in your imagination and merely a coincidence in the arrangement of the words."

"Of course, I considered that possibility until I discovered yet another hidden message in the letter." Holmes held it up again to the light and invited me to read the fourth word in from the end of each line:

"*Let . . . wax . . . awe . . . be . . . avenged . . . of . . . shame . . . upon . . . his . . . blood . . . forever . . . sealed.*"

Holmes read it this way: "'Let Waxhaw be avenged of shame upon his blood forever sealed.' It strongly suggests that the death of the Tarleton brothers had something to do with revenge for the Waxhaws Massacre upon Bloody Ban's descendancy."

"So your theory is that someone killed Col. Tarleton's descendants in order to settle a score over a century-old massacre? It seems very far-fetched," I said.

"Doesn't it? But you yourself, Tuck, have spoken of the Southern gentleman's obsession with honor. Memories are long in the Old South, aren't they?"

"Indeed they are. But why would the Ku Klux Klan become involved in such a petty old disgrace? And why threaten me over it?"

"Because you threatened them. You talked at the fête at the city hall about delving into the deaths of the Tarletons, which, as it appears, makes certain people—perhaps very prominent people—uneasy in the society of Charleston."

"Then the answer to the mystery lies in that circle of men I spoke to that night," said I. "If I can remember who they were, we should be able to investigate each one and identify the culpable party. Someone who bore a long grudge against the descendants of Colonel Banastre Tarleton."

"Perhaps," Holmes responded, casually enveloping himself in pipe smoke. "There is, however, a problem with my theory. It doesn't account for one glaring fact."

"Which fact?"

"That Colonel Banastre Tarleton had no descendants."

Chapter 10

We passed an hour or so clacking up the Midlands railway beneath a cheerless autumn sky. Sister worked anxiously on a rosary, her gloved hands busy boring holes in dried berries with a silver bodkin and then lacing each berry onto a cord. On the other bench, veiled like a mountain under a cloud, Holmes disappeared into his thoughts.

For my part, I didn't know what to think. If Tarleton had no descendants, then the killer of the boys at Gettysburg had made a grotesque error—or was simply striking out madly at anyone with the Tarleton name.

Another possibility occurred to me. Although Colonel Tarleton lacked legitimate descendants, could he have had the other kind? "Let Waxhaw be avenged of shame upon *his blood*." Tarleton's blood didn't have to be lawful blood.

Wouldn't it be intriguing to know the origin of the Tarletons of Georgia?

Still, who would care at this late date? The only individuals I spoke to about the Tarletons were some of the most eminent men in the South.

Which led me to the other bedeviling question: Just who *were* those men in that circle at the Charleston fête? I remembered the amber paneling of the room, the Trumbull portrait of George Washington, the powdered skin of the ladies warmly wrinkled in the light from the sconces; but I met the men only briefly and they were indistinguishable to me—mostly fat old soldiers in black suits or Confederate regalia.

As I tried to conjure up names and to picture their faces, gradually they came back to me.

There were two governors in the circle: General Hampton of South Carolina, and the other from Georgia; Mayor Sale of Charleston; the mayor of Atlanta—Calhoun, I think; and three or four more. I just couldn't remember. . . . A Mr. Gary, or Kerry? A Mr. Buford? A distasteful younger man named Tillman, it seems. . . .

I stood to fetch my notecase when Holmes handed me his, along with a pencil. "Here," he said, "Write them down."

"Write what down?"

"The names of the men you spoke to in Charleston."

I was startled. "How on earth did you know that I was thinking about them at this very moment?"

"You were contemplating the lack of a Tarleton descendancy and it occurred to you that there might be an illegitimate strain. Then you asked yourself who would care; the answer, obviously, would be those who knew about your interest in the Tarleton murders. At that point, you began to rack your brain for their names."

"But you would have to read my mind to know all of that."

"I am not a mind reader," Holmes said. "From the logical starting point, I followed your thoughts by reading your face and the motion of your lips. I watched you struggling with names and when you stood up to rummage for your notecase, I knew you had succeeded in remembering them. It is an old trick, made famous by the American genius Poe in his detective tales."

I chuckled and shook my head as I wrote. Then Sister spoke from her corner.

"Your powers seem beyond the human, Mr. Holmes. I have been bothered by your characterization of me in Rome . . . that I had suffered . . . known deprivation and illness, although I have been well-to-do and enjoy wealthy relations. It is all true, but how could you have known these things?"

"Dear Sister, look at your hands. The profound callouses on the palms, although years old now, indicate a period of rough labor to which your hands were unaccustomed. A lady like yourself would scarcely have done such labor unless it were necessary for survival. Your overall drawn demeanor points to a draining illness in the past, from which you have fortunately recovered.

"I deduce wealthy relations from your gloves. You have many fine leather pairs, which you change frequently, and you purchased more of them from an expensive shop in Rome. Fine kid gloves are a luxury not generally associated with a religious woman under a vow of poverty, thus indicating a source of income that is not yours."

Sister folded her hands as if to hide the gloves. "That is admirable, Mr. Holmes. I have indeed suffered as you say during the late war, and I have fought the typhoid, and I do depend on the kindness of my family for a few small indulgences."

"All of this is elementary," said Holmes. "But I sense that I have not truly fathomed your mystery, Sister Carolina."

"My mystery, as you call it, is why my friends had to die. My purpose is justice. That is the only mystery with which you need concern yourself," she responded, bending her head again over her handiwork. "It appears to me you have made little enough progress in that direction, for all your powers."

Holmes laughed and pulled from his coat a flat piece of card paper. "In my hand I hold a considerable milestone in our progress, due to my hours in the British Library." He held it up for us to see. "It is a postal card which I purchased in London only two days ago."

The copy of a painting of a woman from a century before, the card read "Mrs. Robinson entitled Perdita by Gainsborough."

As we peered at the picture, Holmes explained. "Mrs. Robinson was a young actress who took command of the English stage in the 1770s. Her performance as Perdita in Shakespeare's Winter's Tale captivated the Prince of Wales himself, and she became his mistress. When he tired of her, another suitor became enthralled with the abandoned lady—his name was Colonel Banastre Tarleton, recently returned from the Revolutionary War in America.

"For him, she gave up the stage and moved to his family seat at Finch House in Liverpool where she languished for many years. Despite her hopes, the haughty colonel never married her—she was, after all, not his equal in society—but there was a confinement in 1783 which left Perdita inexplicably crippled for the rest of her life. It was given out that the lady miscarried."

"Holmes. You believe there *was* a child," said I.

"It is a capital error to theorize without facts, but that is a possibility I mean to run to ground."

"Thus our journey to Liverpool."

"That is one reason for it."

We gazed for a while at the melancholy portrait of a woman in ruffled silks with blue ties at her bodice and a small dog at her side. Even the grey landscape breathed abandonment.

"Perdita," I whispered. "'The Lost One.'"

"Lost indeed," said Holmes. "Eventually, Bloody Ban tossed her aside and wed an acceptable lady, but there was no issue of that marriage. So, if the unlamented Tarleton does have descendants, it is likely to Perdita that we must look."

A tiny detail of the painting caught my eye. "She holds something in her hand."

"You noticed that," said Holmes, smiling.

"A miniature? A little picture within a picture? A cameo?"

"A depiction of someone, perhaps the Prince of Wales, perhaps Tarleton, perhaps . . . ."

"A child?"

"I have examined the original Gainsborough at Hertford House—the Marquess owed me a favor—but the image is too small and dark to make out," Holmes replied.

"So your powers of perception have met their limit," the sister said, piercing another bead with a blunt needle.

Just then came the sound of the tea trolley from the corridor. Holmes leapt up and offered to get tea for everyone, which surprised me—he usually had no time for food and drink. "Have you a few coins?" he asked me.

Moments later he returned with two cups of tea and biscuits on a tray. "Only two?" I asked.

"None for me," said Holmes as he passed us the cups. Opening the curtain a bit, we sipped tea and watched as gales of leaves blew past our coach in the Shropshire landscape, now growing dark. The fuming mills of Birmingham and Wolverhampton were behind us, the colder country ahead of us, and as we clipped along I felt the pull of the north where I had spent my childhood school days. I thought of late autumn teas at Stonyhurst after the day's studies, nighttime in the afternoon, and chatter and singing by the fire.

I began to drift off to sleep but was awakened by an abrupt snore from Sister Carolina, followed by a chuckle from Holmes. He held up a small vial of clear liquid in his hand.

"She will sleep for a time. I wanted to have a word with you alone."

"And I want to have a few words with you," I snapped. "You've medicated Sister without her knowledge?"

"Just a drop or two of chloral hydrate. It will hardly do any harm. . . ."

Anger welled up in me. At last I could speak freely. "That is just one instance of your callous behavior. You've been outrageously irresponsible. . . Abandoning us to some obscure gang of brutes . . . They attacked me and my nephew, my *four-year-old nephew*! Dragging us across London in a reckless chase . . . ."

"Your nephew loved it," said Holmes calmly.

"How did you know that?"

He leaned forward and spoke intently. "Not for one moment have you been out of my sight. If you hadn't disregarded my instructions, you would have been safe."

"You were watching all the time?"

"My irregulars were watching and reporting to me. They are boys of the London streets—invisible to the fine Christians of the City—whom I recruit to do *my* work instead of the work that would put them in prison. They roam the streets on missions for me by day and sleep warm at the gasworks by night. The boy who brought you here, Deputy, is their leader. Not his real name of course—all the boys in the gasworks are called 'Deputy.'"

I was taken aback, but still hurt. "That's all very well, but then I find you sprawling in an opium den in the slums, polluting yourself with a crowd of maniacs. I begin to suspect that your craving for tobacco is only the slightest of your obsessions. . . . That filthy woman . . . ."

"That filthy woman," Holmes bent close enough to breathe in my face, "is the richest source of information about the underworld in the entire city of London. Before you throw stones at her, you would do well to learn something of what goes on in the lives of the miserable people who live beneath your respectable feet, Father Tuck."

Somewhat chastened, I asked, "Well, then, who is she? What information . . . ?"

"No one knows her real name. She is called Princess Puffer, and she knows enough about the criminals that haunt this city to put them all in jail for good, and they know she does. That makes her safe from them. Frankly, her knowledge is also her source of income, for many fear her speaking.

"Not all the ravings that fill her den are meaningless rubbish. She has a keen ear for the shameful secrets that leach up from the depths of those tormented souls, and she knows how to profit by them."

"A skillful blackmailer."

"Oh, yes, but not a vicious one," said Holmes. "She holds a knife at the underbelly of London, it's true, but she holds it steady."

"Then how is it she shares her information with you?"

"Because I hold a knife at her throat. I know enough to end her career quite abruptly, and that makes us the best of friends."

I was curious about something. "A respectable-looking man came out of that den just as I arrived. He appeared every bit the tormented soul you speak of—I wonder who he is."

"His name is John Jasper," Holmes replied, offhand. "According to the Princess, he is of all things a cathedral choirmaster who mutters in his stupor about killing someone named 'Ned.' She seems uncommonly interested in this Jasper, which in turn piques my interest as well, so perhaps one day I shall look into it. But for now we have much bigger fish to land."

"What information did you get from her?"

"Enough to confirm my darkest suspicions. You and the Sister, and now I, have become targets of the most dangerous society in England, and perhaps in America as well." His voice dropped even lower and he looked about the compartment as he said it. Sister still breathed quietly in her corner.

I was incredulous. "That can't be true," I said. "Whoever they are, what would they want with Sister and me? We are the most inconsequential of people."

"We are all inconsequential until we enter into the calculations of evil. The head of that society—well, suffice it to say I could not rest, Tuck, I could not sit quiet in my chair, if I thought that such a man as that were walking the streets of London unchallenged."

"What man? Is he the master criminal you've spoken of?"

"He is the Napoleon of crime, Tuck. He is a capital brain—a planner, a strategist, a director, a controller, at the center of the inner circle of much of the ill-gotten wealth in this world. He is within three or four steps of every criminal enterprise on both shores of the Atlantic. Like most rich men, he does little himself, but he moves invisibly, like a toxic fluid, from one grand crime to another, enriching himself unimaginably each time."

"He sounds like one of these barons of Wall Street," I observed.

"It is a distinction without a difference, my dear Tuck. His Piccadilly address— where you went sniffing about like a bull terrier—is the clearing house for most of the big robberies in Europe and America. His fine 'Italian hand' can be traced to almost every one of them, but never proven. Against him, I have found it impossible to get evidence which would convict in a court of law, and am forced to confess that I have at last met my intellectual equal."

I disregarded his smirking reference to my adventure at 198 Piccadilly. "Does this fiend have a name?"

"His names are legion, and additionally I have my own private name for him. You will perhaps recall twin boys at school some years behind us who took great pleasure in mocking me. They were brilliant, both of them, one a mathematical genius and the other as devious and malicious a schemer as I have ever encountered. He has just been named attorney general for Ireland."

"You refer to the Moriarty brothers."

"Precisely. This master criminal combines in one person the calculating brain of the one and the artful malevolence of the other, so I call him 'Moriarty.'"

"But how do we concern this Moriarty?"

"It was he who organized the attack on the Pope, and by my interference I have drawn his attention to myself. I confess it is a fearful thing to enter into the labyrinth of this monster."

"Thus your painstaking disguises and cunning in moving about. Is it by our association with you that Sister and I have become his targets?"

"In part, but the issue is much deeper than that. There is something afoot, a scheme of large proportions that is linked to the Tarleton murders."

"What scheme?"

"It is taking shape only vaguely in my mind, but I believe it to be a monstrous shape. If Moriarty remains true to form, I have little hope of ensnaring him, but every hope of foiling him."

"I begin to understand your sudden eagerness to take on Sister Carolina's case. But can you not explain to me her connection to Moriarty?"

"For her own good—and for yours, I might add—I prefer to keep it to myself for now," replied Holmes. "There are things it were better for you not to know. But our journey to Liverpool, I hope, will establish the connection firmly in my own mind, and if I am not mistaken, we have nearly arrived at the ferry to that great city. Let's summon the Sister from sleep and cross the Mersey."

Chapter 11

Travel is wearing, and I slept the sleep of a worn-out man that night. Holmes and I had installed Sister Carolina in a friendly convent guesthouse and gone on to a cheap hotel near the waterfront, where I dropped like death into bed. So I was shocked awake in the darkness when Holmes pulled on my foot.

"Up, Tuck. It's time to be off." I lit a candle and consulted my watch. It was five o'clock in the morning, a fact I pointed out to him with some annoyance. He responded by pulling my foot hard enough to wrench me out of bed.

"What about breakfast?" I asked.

Holmes groaned. I dressed in my brother-in-law's old suit and we were out in the frozen street, where I managed to find some hot tea from an ice-covered tea shop and Holmes found a sleepy cab driver.

"Where are we going?" I asked, burying myself deep in my too-small coat and drinking tea that tasted like boiling seawater.

"To the plumber's."

Of course. To the plumber's. I was too cold and tired to inquire further, and fell into a daze that lasted until we stopped at a mechanic's shop, from whence I heard the squeal of hungry hogs, along with the rattle of machinery.

Holmes leaped out and rapped at the door, which was opened by a loose-jointed young man pulling his braces over his shoulders and shaking out a prodigious head of black hair.

"Mr. James McCartney, plumber?" Holmes boomed at him.

"It's Jimmy," the young man grinned. "You Mr. Escott? Got your wire and I am at your service."

"Then let's get on with it." Holmes vaulted back into the cab, while McCartney collected his coat and toolbox.

He squeezed in next to me and gave me an ironic smile. "I'm Jimmy. Close friends already, eh?" He spoke in the voice of a man with a severe cold in his head, but then so did everyone else I had met in Liverpool.

I gave Holmes a curious look, and he whispered to me that we needed a real plumber for the job we were about to do. Again I was too preoccupied with keeping myself warm to worry any more about it. "Jimmy" mused at me as we clipped along. "Soily business, plumbering. Most as soily as raising hogs. But that there's Christmas bacon, idn't it? Party's on. Only comes this time o' year, you know."

After about an hour of the young plumber's random singsong, we alighted at the gate of a house that looked to be moldering away in a tide of sleet. "Wind blows hard and cold this time of year," Jimmy said with delight, strangely invigorated by the nightmare weather. I growled and followed him and Holmes round the house to the servants' entrance.

"Remember, McCartney," Holmes said. "We are here to make an inspection: that is all. You will be paid well to inspect. There is no need to do any actual plumbing."

"No worries, sir."

Holmes pulled the bell rope, and we waited a freezing eternity for an elderly housekeeper to open up.

"Finch House?" Holmes asked. "I am Mr. Escott of Escott and Tuck, consulting plumbers. This is Mr. Tuck, and this is Mr. McCartney. We wired you?"

"Here so urly?" the old woman gurgled in the clogged local accent as she motioned us into a kitchen that smelled of warm decay. "My, such ambitious young men. And so sturrdy, too. Come in, come in. I am Mrs. Throstle. Tea?"

I accepted gratefully, Holmes declined, and Jimmy pattered, "A cup o' English tea, very twee, very twee. . . ."

"To work, McCartney." Holmes was blunt. The young man rustled through his tools and began examining the kitchen pipes while Holmes gestured at me to sit next to him at the servants' table. The old woman plumped down exhausted by the effort of pouring tea for us.

"As we advised, Mrs. Throstle, we are here on behalf of a party interested in purchasing the property, merely to inspect the drains and report back to him," Holmes lied smoothly.

"And very wise, too," the housekeeper beamed. "The family have been trying to sell for so long, but no one wants it. I fear the old place is like me—the foundation all eaten up and rising damp in the cellar. No doubt the old pipes are as bunged up as me own pipes."

I smiled for the first time that day.

"Damp in the basement, damp in the wall," Jimmy purred, clanking at the pipes with his spanner. "Water's drippin' from the standpipe," he announced.

Holmes looked at him with annoyance, then turned back to the housekeeper. "How long have you been with the Tarleton family, Mrs. Throstle?"

She laughed softly. "I was born in survice. Mum and Dad were both born in survice to the Tarletons. So you could say I've always been with the family."

I began to understand what we were doing in this blighted old house so "urly" in the morning.

"It's a storied family," Holmes gave her an oily smile to encourage her.

"Oh, and such stories, too. Before they was bankrupted, they was slavers, all of 'em. That's where the money come from." She took a mouthful of tea. "Me dad would be right chapped at me for talking of it. But that's what they was. Slavers."

"Yes, that was a terrible business," sighed Holmes.

"A soily business!" added Jimmy, who shrank at Holmes's threatening glance. "Er, drains all mucked up."

"But wasn't there a family hero? Colonel Tarleton?" Holmes asked.

"Family hero," she clucked. "I wouldn't put it like that. You mean our Bloody Ban, don't you."

"You wouldn't put it like that? If I remember right, he distinguished himself in the Colonies."

"That I wouldn't know. They was slavers, all of 'em."

Holmes leaned in. "The family who are selling the house, are they the Colonel's descendants?"

"Oh, no. Not at all. It's the cousins. Sir Ban and Lady had no children, you know. La, they didn't care for each other, you might say. Me old grandmum told us. Toast?" The old lady shifted to warm some bread on a long fork over the fire.

"None for us, thank you," said Holmes. I longed for toast and grimaced at him, but he took no notice. "No children at all? And what of Perdita?"

At the mention of this name, the old woman's eyes tightened and she pulled at the strings of her bonnet as if to close it round her face. "What of Purdita?" she echoed. "What of her?" I feared that Holmes had probed a bit too deeply.

Her eyes now shut, she sniffed gently at the toasting bread, and for a moment I thought she had forgotten about us. Then she laughed, "Me old brain. Memories blocked up."

"Sweeeet memories," Jimmy crooned from the hole he was digging under the sink. "Valves all corroded."

"Save it for your report," Holmes shot back at him, then turned to the pensive Mrs. Throstle. "Didn't Perdita have a child?" he asked straight out.

The old lady bent her head, embarrassed. "It's not something that was talked about. Grandmum was so very close about it, she was a midwife, don't you know. But it's so long ago now, nigh on a hundred year I'd say. No doubt they're all dead now that knowed aught about it."

"About what?" Holmes coaxed her, gently. "About the child?"

"Little Rafe, they called him. They packed him up and sent him to the Indies with old Tiggonah. She died horrible, they say. A allergator got her, they say." Mrs. Throstle began to nod over her fire. "How would that be? To be et by a allergator."

"I'd save you from the allergator, Missus," Jimmy sang out from his hole.

"Sweet boy. And look at all the beautiful hair he's got on top—we could mop the floor with that," she chuckled, watching Jimmy's head poking out from beneath the sink. Then a pause, and she slipped back into her reverie. "She never was the same after that. Just brooded away in a despond from losing her child to the Indies, raving in a frenzy, writing poems and such—that was our Purdita."

"I thought she miscarried," Holmes said.

"You're fearful well informed, aren't you sir? Well, it was given out as such, but the master had lots of ships running in those days and he put the baby and the slave woman on a ship. They was never seen again. She was et by an allergator, they say."

"Why was the baby sent away?"

"Why? 'T wouldn't do now, would it, for the master to be raising up a child from the wrong side of the blanket, as folks say? So off they goes to the Indies." In the earthy warmth from the fire, Mrs. Throstle was becoming somnolent, and I could see that Holmes was becoming impatient.

"We have all of the information we came for," he muttered to me.

"All?" I asked, but he was up and keen to go.

"McCartney! We've finished. It's time to be on our way."

Jimmy's face appeared from the depths, bewildered and streaked with grime. "I've not finished. I'm almost at the bottom of the pipe, and when I gets to the bottom, I goes back to the top."

"You've reached bottom and we're leaving. Come along."

"Right-o. As you say." Jimmy grinned and wiped his face with a rag that rendered it blacker. We made our goodbyes to the housekeeper and sallied out into the sleet once again.

"Never did find that leak," Jimmy lamented as we crowded back into a cab. "But then that's the joy of plumbering. There's always refreshers. 'When you ask a working man, does he ever stop? No, he work until he drop.'"

Jimmy was nothing if not lyrical. We let him off at home and Holmes ordered me to give him a half-sovereign.

"A half-sovereign?" I protested, diving into my pockets for a coin. It was a lot of money for a morning's useless work. "He's a poor man," Holmes whispered.

"So am I," I whispered back.

"You have vowed to be poor," he rejoined.

"What about my report? Don't you want to hear it?" Jimmy called after us, but goaded by Holmes, we were galloping back toward the waterfront.

"Things are coming nicely," Holmes said, breathing in the salty air before lighting his pipe. "Mrs. Throstle has woven a good many threads together for us, and the tapestry is beginning to take shape."

"So Tarleton did have a child, which opens the possibility of descendants. But she said the child was taken to the Indies . . . ."

"The West Indies, Tuck. The New World, not the Old. What she told us fits well into what I already knew about the Tarleton family. They were indeed in the slave trade, and in a very significant way. Colonel Tarleton's father and brothers controlled a good tenth of the trade triangle between Africa, Britain, and America, and the brutal way in which they conducted the trade brought much unwanted attention from Parliament.

"Thousands, perhaps tens of thousands of African slaves died in the horror of Tarleton ships, and although the brothers fought for it, the vicious traffic was at last abolished in part because the Tarletons were determined to keep it going. The anti-slavery movement began in Parliament about the time the child of Perdita and Colonel Tarleton was due. I surmise that the family could not afford a scandal at that delicate moment, so the child was packed off to the Tarletons' plantation in the West Indies, where he could grow up well away from it all."

"That is a lot of surmising," I observed.

"But it is all based on fact. We even know the child's name—Rafe, or Ralph— probably in honor of an old Tarleton patriarch, Ralph William."

"You have become an authority on the Tarleton family."

"The fruit of my hours in the British library these past days. If the imbecilic British police could find their way to the library, or were even aware of its existence, much of their endless footwork would be unnecessary."

"So you have now linked the Old World Tarletons to the New World," I said. "Where do we go from here?"

"To the New World! Or rather, you go. I am staying behind."

"What do you mean?"

"You and Sister are booked for passage to Philadelphia tomorrow morning."

"What? You have already arranged it?" I was stunned.

"Yes. You will board the steamer Nebraska at ten o'clock under your own names, in keeping with your passports. You have finished your pilgrimage to Rome and visited your family in Britain, and now you are as a matter of course returning to your duties."

"But . . . what about the case? What are we to do without you?"

"You are to do exactly as I tell you."

I couldn't accept this. "I am not one of your London irregulars to be ordered about. I insist on being consulted, not commanded. . . ."

"Believe me, your life depends on doing what I ask."

"Consulted, not commanded!" I said again. "And I will not be put off by talk of some obscure threat I don't understand. I must know precisely what our position is before you ship us off to who knows what fate."

As we were approaching our hotel, Holmes was silent for a time. "Very well," he muttered, somewhat disdainfully. "Let's find a little privacy and I shall 'consult' with you."

Back in our chilly room, Holmes locked the door behind us, sat on the bed, and breathed out smoke. I could tell that he was calculating in his mind just how much to share with me. For my part, I realized that crossing the ocean meant that I might never lay eyes on Holmes again, and I felt an abrupt pain at the thought. A few days with him had awakened in me a strange comradeship I had never experienced before. Now he was sending me away.

As if he sensed my feelings, Holmes spoke almost gently. "Tuck, I have been guarded with you because, in this affair, the shadow of danger to our lives is real, and it is death to know too much about certain people. That is the case with Moriarty.

"As I have said, by disregarding my instructions in London you have already put us and your family in jeopardy. Your adventure with the cabbie was intended to warn you off. Our encounter at Princess Puffer's was another warning.

"Moriarty does not commit murder casually—there must be a significant reward—but he will act to remove a threat if he deems it to be serious."

"Holmes," I said, "I am willing to do as you think proper, but you cannot expect me to merely return to Charleston and forget all about it."

"If only you could," Holmes replied with a pained smile. "If only you could go back to America and forget all about it. In fact, I took some pains to keep you out of the web of this monster, but you are entangled in it now so we must see it through."

"What do you mean?"

"I mean that Moriarty's web stretches to Charleston—and well beyond. To escape that web, I will ask you to do a certain task in Charleston that will likely put you in further danger. But sometimes it is necessary to push forward in order to go back."

"You have spoken of a connection between Moriarty and the killing of the Tarletons at Gettysburg," I said. "Does the task you speak of bear on this connection?"

"It has a direct bearing."

"Holmes, what is the connection? What could possibly link an American battlefield killing to a master English criminal?"

"Moriarty is not English. Nor is he American. I am not entirely sure of his provenance, although I suspect it lies somewhere in central Europe. As for his connection to the Tarletons, let me show you."

Once again he pulled out of his waistcoat pocket the document he always kept to himself and spread it out on the bed. "Here," he said, "surely you've noticed the seemingly random sprinkling of dots that look like full stops. There is one dot per line, except for the last line."

O.

LET T.HE TAR LET ON,

B.eware! *Let the Feathers reveal,*

*Raging **bloody** w.ax Fire be set,*

*On thy **Bans!** Awe thy Confessi.onal Seal!*

*Thou shalt drink **Fate.** in Wine, be it distilled Gall!*

Hell's bread shalt. avenged in Tartarus eat!

*Even Thy Goddess in the **d.epths** of Acheron shall fall!*

Revenge! T.hou shalt drink the shame of it Sweet!

*Shad.owed Brotherhood! If we Heaven's will cannot avert, **Hell***

*Let us move. Charon bring thee o'er his Flood **to** meet,*

*In Ro.bes and burning Cross and Blood Drops **to lie**,*

*Even there. where the Prince of Air forever flames up **howling**,*
PETIT AND PERDITION! BAP.ST AND BLAZES! STRICKEN AND SEALED!
*CHAOS AND **CURSES!***
DO NOT OPEN PANDORAS BOX OR YOU WILL FEEL
THE WRATH OF THE KU, KLUX, KLAN!

"Yes, I bludgeoned my brains over those dots but could make nothing of them," I replied.

"Nor could I, until I recognized them as a simple alphabetic code. There are twenty-six letters in the alphabet, and each letter has a number—A is one, B is two, C is three, and so forth. When you count the letter spaces over to each dot, you arrive at a letter. Try it."

We created this table to make our work easier.

A	B	C	D	E	F	G	H	I	J
1	2	3	4	5	6	7	8	9	10
K	L	M	N	O	P	Q	R	S	T
11	12	13	14	15	16	17	18	19	20
U	V	W	X	Y	Z				
21	22	23	24	25	26				

Then I began counting the letter spaces in each line until arriving at the dot. There was only one letter space in the first line, so the letter must be "A." The second line had four letter spaces before the dot, so the next letter must be "D." We continued in this way until we deciphered all fourteen letters.

ADAMWROTHDIDIT

It meant nothing to me. "Adam Wroth did it? Who is Adam Wroth?"

Holmes stood and listened for a moment at the door, then verified that it was locked.

"It is an intriguing name. I believed it is misspelled, perhaps deliberately, for the man in question is certainly 'wroth,' that is, filled with cruelty. I told you that Moriarty's real name is unknown, but there is some evidence that he was born 'Adam Worth' somewhere in Germany. If Moriarty is indeed Adam Worth, he has not been known by that name for many years."

"This evidence you speak of . . ."

"In response to an inquiry I made to Pinkertons, the famous American detective agency. Adam Worth was well known to them. When he made America too hot to hold him, he escaped to Paris where he opened an American bar and made a fortune in illegal gaming.

"A mathematical prodigy, Worth subtly cheated his guests of many thousands of francs in ways they were never even aware of. Then some five years past, a Pinkerton man—Allan Pinkerton himself—happened to enter the bar and recognized him, so Worth moved his operation immediately to London. Each year, as I told you, he has become more and more powerful.

"A remarkable genius of crime, he has been untouchable—until now. When I first deciphered Moriarty's real name in your poison-pen letter, I realized at once that I might—at long last—have in my hand the only tangible evidence I have ever found of Adam Worth's involvement in an actual crime."

"Which made you all the keener to take my case." I was still staring at the now worn-out document in Holmes's hands. "But what could this man Worth, or Wroth, have to do with the Tarletons?"

"That is precisely what you must discover, Tuck, on the other side of the sea."

TRANSATLANTIC

Chapter 12

As we steamed away from Queenstown, I was bored and anxious at the same time. I stood on the stern leaning at the taffrail, watching the ocean eat up the land and the dark sky and water converging on the horizon.

We were eight tedious days from Philadelphia. My third crossing of the Atlantic had none of the fretful charm of the first or even the second. This time I was facing a task that disturbed me deeply but that I could not avoid. As a priest, I recognized that fear should not dominate my life, and it did not; but I confess that I dreaded what was to come and wished it were over and done with. I would not be sleeping well on the steamship Nebraska.

The ship began laboring into heavier water, so I went below to the library in search of a book to while away the time. Almost at once I found a slim volume of poems by Mary Robinson—our Perdita. I opened it idly and read.

> AH LOVE! thou barb'rous fickle boy,
> Thou semblance of delusive joy,
> Too long my heart has been thy slave:
> For thou hast seen me wildly rave,
> And with impetuous frenzy haste,
> Heedless across the thorny waste,
> And drink the cold dews, ere they fell
> On my bare bosom's burning swell.

The couplets kept rhythm with the sway of the ship, and I felt what Perdita must have felt, passing day after day in hopeless, frenzied pleas for her delusive lover to keep his pledges to her. I felt what it must feel to be abandoned, coldly pushed aside, and robbed of her only child.

Perhaps I might be instrumental in bringing her the only earthly justice she would ever get.

I sat in the library reading until it was too dark, then went to my stateroom to wash up before dinner. Sister Carolina and I had been invited to the captain's table for our first night on the main, and when we arrived in the dining room it was quite inviting with lamps on the walls and white cloths on the tables. A small orchestra played for us thirty or so first-cabin guests, all kitted up in formal wear except for Sister and myself. It was paradoxical to think that this decorous scene was playing out in a box suspended on black ocean water five hundred feet deep.

As we were a bit early, we found our places at the captain's empty table and munched celery as we listened to the music. The orchestra played mediocre music-hall tunes, although I thought the violinist exceptional. Soon a couple joined us, pleasantly white-haired Americans on their way home from "the trip abroad." Then another couple arrived, and I found I was not the only clergy aboard: a shiny-faced Dr. Shlessinger, an Anglican missionary from Australia, and Mrs. Shlessinger. They were followed by a man and woman who couldn't be husband and wife from the furtive looks they gave everyone else—the man had the snaky mustache and flattened hair of a circus performer; the "woman" with him was clearly a female impersonator.

I exchanged greetings with everyone; sister was her reserved self and settled for a drawn smile. We all shared banalities about the weather, worries about the lateness of the season, and apprehensions about icebergs.

Then I looked up and nearly dropped my celery.

Three people were approaching our table. I didn't recognize the men, one of whom was short with an easy manner and well-combed side whiskers and the Order of the Golden Spur on a ribbon round his neck, the other tall with the goatee of Napoleon III and the same badge affixed to his coat; but the woman was our acquaintance from the Rome-to-Paris train—the seductive Mrs. Katherine Wells.

"Padre!" she sang out as she caught sight of me. "What a delight to meet you again."

I stood. "How wonderful to see you, Mrs. Wells. You'll remember my traveling companion, Sister Carolina." Sister gave her a sour smile, and I turned to the gentlemen with her. "Do I have the pleasure of meeting Mr. Wells in one of you?"

"No, my husband is in America waiting for me," she said. The tall man was a Count Schindler of Brussels. As for the other, "This is my old friend Mr. Henry J. Raymond of New York."

Raymond bowed and introductions round the table followed. His name caused a stir with the white-haired couple, who whispered to each other and then both gazed intently at the man as if they knew him.

The steward seated Mrs. Wells next to me. Once again I was taken with her mound of soft blonde hair glowing in the lamplight and the warm fragrance that I had first noticed that night in the train crossing Italy. Again, I am a priest, but also a man perfectly able to appreciate the aesthetic appeal of such a woman.

At last we were joined by the ship's captain, a diffident man buried in a beard, who had little to say after bowing to the company and taking his seat.

We were confronted with an enormous dinner, starting with julienne soup and baked halibut in wine sauce and calves' feet jelly, followed by our choice of corned pork and cabbage, fillets of chicken with mushrooms and spinach, or mutton with caper sauce—or all of them! Although I was feeling a bit queasy from the movement of the ship, I have always had difficulty turning down a fine dinner and ate more than I intended.

As they brought the after-dinner brandy, Mrs. Wells turned playfully to me. "My dear Padre, would you serve me as a father-confessor tonight?"

"I'm sure you have nothing of any moment to confess, Mrs. Wells," I replied.

"Really, Padre, I have never been so belittled," she laughed. "We have just been in Italy, so we both know how the Latin heat can melt away even our coldest English scruples. It's just that I found your companion on the Paris train—Captain Basil, was it? your cousin?—a very attractive man, and I wondered what has become of him."

Bemused, I told her that he had returned to England. She smiled thoughtfully.

"I confess that he made my heart flutter," she said. "Where does he live? What does he do?"

"He lives in London, I think in the neighborhood of Bloomsbury. He is a very . . . um, prosperous plumber."

"Oh, no, I don't believe that for a moment. His hands were so beautiful, so soft and expressive, such long, lovely fingers."

"He is a *consulting* plumber," I added.

"Ah, so he never dirties his hands himself. A military man turned prosperous tradesman. How rare. Is he very rich? He must be to have cultivated such an interest in vintage jewelry."

"I don't think he is so very rich, but he is selective in his obsessions."

"And what, besides antique cameos, obsesses him?"

"Tobacco, mostly. And penny dreadfuls. He is always reading them."

She sniffed a little. "You disillusion me. I had quite a different picture of the man. He seemed to be so intelligent, analytical . . . probing."

"There you are not wrong. Intelligent undoubtedly, and he is very analytical when it comes to muck and corruption—in water pipes, I mean. As for probing, he generally leaves that to others."

"I confess some disappointment. When I saw you, Padre, I was hoping your cousin might be nearby."

"His business in London presses him a good deal."

"But you'll do," she said, her voice almost a caress. "Pity about that collar. It's not often one meets a handsome young clergyman—they always seem so old—but I've always thought the white collar and black cassock something of a challenge. . . ."

Mr. Henry Raymond, who had been listening, came to my rescue. "Padre, I warn you," he said between good-humored puffs of his cigar, "Mrs. Wells finds all men a challenge, particularly those who appear to be beyond reach. Isn't that right, Count?"

That rigid gentleman stiffened even more, but said nothing. He had been busy with the port and brandy, which oddly enough loosened him not at all. Inadvertently I turned to Sister Carolina and found her glaring at me from beneath her hood like the grim reaper. All she lacked was a scythe.

The captain had risen and was speaking.

"Ladies and gentlemen," he began. "Please attend me. I am Captain Radley, and on behalf of the American Steamship Line I welcome you all as we begin our crossing of the main. We must anticipate a stormy voyage, as we are the last to cross this season, but I assure you we shall make landfall in good order on Monday week.

"For your interest, we are carrying thirty passengers in the first cabin and forty-two in the third cabin, along with our ship's complement of twenty-four. Our cargo includes fifteen hundred tons of machinery." This was all delivered in a loud but invariable tone.

"Now, let us enjoy a brief concert by our ship's orchestra, with solos by our guest, the renowned Norwegian violinist, Herr Sigerson."

A rattle of applause, and the small band took up a nautical ditty I'd never heard but sounded appropriate for seagoing. It was charming, although it seemed to discomfit our young couple of indeterminate gender. They frowned and whispered at each other all the way through the piece.

"The latest thing from the London stage," Mr. Raymond smiled, leaning over to us during the applause. "The overture of a play called *H.M.S. Pinafore*. It's enchanted the entire capital. You should see it."

This was followed by Sigerson, the violinist, a spindly man with a sheaf of white hair that looked like a tree formed by the prevailing winds. He stood quiet for a moment, then slowly embraced the violin and stroked it lovingly through the most tranquil theme I've ever heard—a song without words by Mendelssohn. It calmed the company into a trance, and even Sister Carolina had a sad smile on her face, while outside the cabin the wind relaxed its constant roar as if in sympathy with the music.

As we applauded, Mrs. Wells murmured her admiration. "What a musician! Such hands, such long, lovely fingers."

The violinist then plunged into a Paganini caprice that flew past like lightning, but stripped of its Italian humor and infused with a strange Nordic foreboding.

"Rattling!" said Mr. Raymond, pounding the table. "Remarkably good. What a performance! The man ought to be playing at Boston Museum."

After the concert we all excused ourselves for the night and made our way back to our staterooms. I tried to mollify Sister Carolina over my comportment with Mrs. Wells, but she muttered a few things at me about the instability of the human heart and shut her door decisively. "Good night, *Father*," she said.

There was something different about my own room. Surprisingly, I didn't notice it right away. After all the room was so small I could barely lie down with any security, but there on my bed was an envelope. A small piece of note paper inside contained one line of plain writing in some kind of code:

Numeri 8, 6, 1 – 8, 26, 25 – 16, 46, 32 – 2, 32, 2 – Actus 21, 2, 14

Of course I recognized the words from the Latin Bible: Numeri is the book of Numbers and Actus the book of Acts. But I had no idea what the numbers meant. I understood two numbers—chapter-and-verse—but I had never seen *three* numbers before in a scriptural citation. Puzzling over it, I thought perhaps it might refer to page numbers, but that made no sense at all. Perhaps it was some arcane numerological code based on the Bible. I had heard of such things, but who would present me with a message I could not possibly read?

Unfortunately, I had no Latin Bible at hand, so I could not break any code that depended on it, but I did have in my trunk the little old Douai Bible in English that goes everywhere with me. Baffled, I opened it to the book of Numbers and positioned the message next to it on my bed, hoping to connect the two somehow.

Each trio of numbers was set off with a dash. "8, 6, 1 – 8, 26, 25 – 16, 46, 32 . . . . Three numbers and a dash," I muttered to myself. "Three numbers and a dash."

Then it came to me. I remembered the alphanumerical code in the Klan document that Holmes had deciphered. Perhaps the first two numbers represented the chapter and verse, and the third number a word within the verse.

"Numbers 8:6, first word: TAKE. Numbers 8:26, twenty-fifth word: CARE." I knew I was on to it. "Take care" of something.

"Numbers 16:42, thirty-second word: WROTH. Numbers 2:32, second word: IS. Then the book of Acts 21:2, fourteenth word: ABOARD.

Take care wroth is aboard.

Chapter 13

I didn't sleep. The ship vibrated like an old tree as the wind scraped at it without ceasing, whining through the rigging all that night. I was haunted by the message left so starkly on my bed: if I had deciphered it correctly, Holmes's "Moriarty"—the arch-criminal Adam Worth, or Wroth—was on the ship with us!

Just as alarming was the realization that someone else on board knew of our entanglement with Moriarty. Who could it be? Certainly not Sister—she was as oblivious as I and could not have left the note in my room. Mrs. Wells? She was the only other person on the ship with whom I had any acquaintance at all, as slim as it was. But what could she know of us?

Not for the first time, I wished that Holmes had made the journey with us. He had insisted on remaining "in the lair of the beast himself." "If you do as I instruct," he had said the night before our departure, "you will soon find the Tarleton murders solved and the entire affair safely concluded."

"But what of Moriarty?" I had asked.

"You will be pursuing the foxes. I must pursue the wolf."

I pointed out that getting embroiled with the Klan was hardly as innocuous as fox hunting, but Holmes would say no more. His instructions were simple enough, and his assurances straightforward; yet here I was alone with my charge in the middle of the Atlantic apparently caged up with the wolf himself.

Once it was light I invited Sister Carolina to our morning mass in the passenger lounge, which, as it was Sunday, the purser had kindly permitted us to use. Wearily I went through the rites, but was gratified that a couple of Portuguese sailors joined us. Their plain faith encouraged me: Perhaps I was not so very alone after all.

I now had two tasks on my hands: to discover which of our passengers was the arch-criminal, and which one had warned me about him. My experience with the cabbie in London had taught me that Holmes had eyes everywhere—someone on board must be part of his small but effective organization—perhaps an officer of the ship, a steerage passenger, one of my fellow travelers, or even the Portuguese sailors. At the end of the service I shook hands warmly with them, fancying them already my allies.

I went to breakfast hesitantly, as my stomach was a little off from nerves, but then the piles of sausages, puddings of all kinds, and even fresh eggs and excellent tea overpowered my anxiety. The Americans do a far better job of an English breakfast than the English do.

Still, each face in the breakfast room could belong to our antagonist, so I searched each one I encountered for any sign of recognition. I found none. They were all equally strange to me. I decided I would try to employ Holmes's methods to see if I could ferret out Moriarty from the crowd. Surely such an evil genius could not completely suppress his nature—the mark of the beast must reveal itself in some detectible way.

Sister Carolina and I were seated at table with two others, both Americans—a wealthy, sad-looking lady, a Mrs. Miller, and her son, a ravenous and disrespectful little mope who sneered at me through the entire meal. She told us she was returning home after her year in Italy where she had lost a daughter to "Roman fever." Whether this was an actual or a figurative fever she did not say, and I did not probe. It was not unusual for young Anglo-Saxon females to be agitated to death by Italy, or more precisely, by the men of Italy.

"May we join you?" I looked up to see the Rev. Dr. Shlessinger and his wife shining down upon us with benevolence. His bald head and big red cheeks, freshly shaven, glowed in the early light, and he took a seat next to the mournful Mrs. Miller. I thought this a blessing, as perhaps he might be able to comfort her, or at least take some of her son's spiteful gaze off me. Then it occurred to me—could this hale clergyman be Moriarty?

There was something unsettling about him—a pitilessness in the mouth. And when he turned, I noticed his left ear was frightfully mangled, as if a cruel dog had chewed on it. Holmes would see much more, but even I could detect a scent of criminality in him. What was attracting this man to our presence? Twice he had taken a place at our table. It could not have been a desire to consort with other religious—after all, the Protestant clergy I had known could hardly bear the odor of "popish priests."

I tried to think of some innocuous way to draw him out, and then I remembered Holmes's saying that Moriarty was obsessed with mathematics. I waited for an opportunity in the conversation. When Mrs. Miller commented that the morning seemed unusually fine for late autumn, I spoke up. "It *is* unusual. The law of averages is surely against it. And talking of mathematical laws, I happened to read some interesting news the other day about the binomial theorem."

Everyone, including the Rev Dr. Shlessinger, stared at me uncomprehendingly. The Miller boy's mouth hung open full of pudding.

Annoyed, Sister Carolina shushed me and we finished our breakfast. My effort had failed. Perhaps it was too obvious. On the other hand, perhaps it had worked and Shlessinger was innocent—after all, he was doing a fine job of cheering up Mrs. Miller with his resonant talk of the gospel. She was clearly taken by him.

The squally night had indeed given way to a placid morning, so we walked on the deck after breakfast and watched the icy green sea streaming past. I took the opportunity to study carefully our fellow passengers, who were coming at last into the sunshine like small animals peeking out after a storm. A flock of children from steerage played out their pent-up energy, running and squealing, annoying the first-cabin passengers while their pale and peasant-like mothers tried to gather them up again. It was whispered that they were all Mormons, members of an impoverished sect from Scandinavia making their way to their promised land in Utah. I doubted I would find Moriarty among them.

At length we lounged on chaises brought out by the crew. Sister Carolina went to work as silently as always, weaving away at her rosaries like one of the Fates. The ocean light, though hazy, was bright and permitted me a good look at others as they strolled past. Stuffed with sausages and contented at the weather, the gentlemen in their gray morning coats bowed to me, or rather to my collar, while their more devotedly Protestant wives gave me the slightest possible dip of the chin. To my disappointment, or relief, none of them looked very evil.

I had hopes of seeing Mrs. Wells again, but she did not put in an appearance.

We heard singing, and out of curiosity I walked to the common area below the smokestack where the Mormons were holding a service. The men were sturdy, the women stark and unadorned, and the children on the verge of squirming out of control. A plain man who looked like a dairy farmer led the singing, which was in some Nordic tongue, and then began a sermon from his holy book. Although I understood none of it, I sensed a stern candor in this preacher with the beard and smock of a stolid workman. His directness commanded respect, and even the wriggling children calmed down and listened to the story he told, whatever it was. I thought perhaps the earliest Christians might have met like this.

Returning to my lounge chair, I found that an American couple had taken up places next to us. The gentleman, who looked considerably older than his beautiful companion, introduced himself as Mr. Adam Verver. The youthful lady was his wife Charlotte.

Adam! The name chilled me. Verver? Could this man be "Adam Worth"? Had Holmes's arch-villain sought me out to toss me overboard? To take me by surprise and rid himself of a troublesome priest?

If so, he was awfully slow about it. We exchanged a few pleasantries about our European tours and the man buried himself in newspapers while his wife, the very picture of doom, stared out to sea. One of those melancholy ladies, I thought, grand in a suit of gray as soft as a bird's breast, and unhappy in her uneven marriage to money—for the couple had the air of money all about them. It didn't take a Holmes to discern that.

By contrast, her husband had all the appearance of a self-satisfied baron of industry. I studied him carefully, trying to be subtle about it. A small diamond pin fixed his cravat, diamonds linked his cuffs, and a diamond stud held his collar in place. Gloves, soft fedora, cane—everything about the man was immaculate, although I guessed at a severe sort of dissipation in him. "Steel" was the word I would use to describe his complexion.

"You observe me closely, sir," Verver spoke from behind his newspaper. I flinched. I hadn't thought I was being so obtrusive.

"I, um, I thought perhaps I'd seen you before, Mr. Verver," I lied.

"It is possible," he said. "We have both been recently in Italy, and may have moved in similar expatriate circles."

I agreed, stammering. "What were you . . . why were you visiting Italy?"

"I have acquired an Italian prince as husband to my daughter, so we have been stopping with them. And you?"

"On a pilgrimage to Rome with my cousin here, Sister Carolina."

"I'm a bit of a pilgrim myself," Verver put down his newspaper and lit a cigar. "In search of valuables. I'm a collector, you see, and I've been scouring Europe for beautiful paintings, old Persian carpets, an extraordinary set of Oriental tiles . . ."

"A prince for your daughter?"

Verver smiled. "I suppose that is a prime sort of acquisition."

"What about antique cameos?" I dared to ask.

"Do you have any?" Verver looked interested. I couldn't tell if he was being genuine or not.

"No, I just enjoy looking at them. I admired many beautiful examples in the Vatican Museum in Rome."

If he was guilty of stealing the Vatican cameos, he showed no sign. "Ah, a museum. In fact, that is the aim of my collecting," he said. "I am planning a museum in America, to bring the treasures of the Old World to the New. The great American working classes need a little refining." He winked and added, "And it won't hurt if I can make a dollar off the mugginses who come to gawp at my cache, will it?"

"Not at all. Everyone benefits. You must be blessed with great resources to do such a great work."

"Father Simon, I'm an unapologetic worshiper of Wall Street. An acolyte of the mighty dollar."

"You are on the side of the robber barons?"

"I would rather put it this way," he leaned towards me. "They are on my side."

"God has been good to you, then."

"I don't know about God. My life is about machinery, the antidote to superstition."

Ignoring this dig, I ginned up some courage and threw out more bait. "I too am interested in science . . . mathematics, actually. I was just reading something interesting about the binomial theorem."

"The what?" Verver examined his cigar. "My own interest in mathematics is purely practical. 'If I bid on two Gainsboroughs instead of one, will I get a discount?' or 'How much does that iron shutter weigh?' That's my business, you know—iron."

Iron shutters. Was this a reference to a prison history? Or a threat? Was he going to kidnap us? Imprison us behind iron shutters? Was he being enigmatical or literal? I couldn't tell.

A warm haze had set in, and Mrs. Verver in her pigeon-gray suit nearly disappeared into an outline on the far side of her husband. A lovely acquisition indeed. The scene reminded me of one of Mr. Whistler's gauzy studies. One felt stark futility emanating from her, a woman buried alive within iron shutters; as for Mr. Verver, I got the impression that the cloud was his native element, although a metallic spark of lightning could strike at any moment.

Despite the haze and her enormous bonnet, too much sunlight was penetrating Mrs. Verver's skin. She moaned, "I need my calamine lotion." Verver stood with the help of his cane and bowed to us. "Siesta time!" he announced and took his wife's arm. As I watched them withdraw, I was quite sure I had found my man.

The unsettling thing: He had also found me.

Chapter 14

Oh joy, oh rapture unforeseen,
The clouded sky is now serene,
The god of day—the orb of love,
Has hung his ensign high above,
The sky is all ablaze.
With wooing words and loving song
We'll chase the lagging hours along,
And if we find the maiden coy,
We'll murmur forth decorous joy
In dree-ee-ee-eamy roun-dee-lays.

The duet was enchanting, and the diners managed to get their feet to applaud despite the rolling of the ship. Our sixth night out, we were used to it by now. Sister and I had become pretty well acquainted with our table party, now raucously clapping for the two artistes who had delighted us with several after-dinner songs. Sigerson piloted the orchestra with a firm hand on the helm of his violin.

Henry Raymond, Mrs. Wells's friend with the big black whiskers, asked the waiter to invite the singers to our table, and "Charlie and Bessie" came right over. They were the couple who had shown such irritation at the orchestra on our first night. Intriguingly, Charlie had sung the soprano part and Bessie the tenor.

"Charlie and Bessie, that was capital, just capital!" Raymond shouted over his cigar. "You must meet my friends. This is Father Simon, Sister Carolina, Count Schindler, the Shlessingers, and the good Mrs. Wells."

The young couple bowed. Raymond went on a little loudly, "Capital tunesters, those Gilbert and Sullivan fellows. Now wasn't that song from their new play the Pinafore?"

"Yes, sir. It's the closing number."

"Are you going to perform the play in America? New York, perhaps?"

"We hope to stage it, yes."

I broke in. "You seemed displeased the other night when the orchestra played the overture to Pinafore."

Charlie's face darkened, but Bessie went on in her incongruously deep Cockney voice, "Well, it's like this, we feel like that's ours, you see, our music. And we don't like others playing it."

Raymond sat back and regarded them for a moment. "Surely it's Gilbert and Sullivan's music, isn't it? You're pirating it, aren't you?"

The two artistes looked uncomfortably at each other.

Then Raymond laughed. "Here's my card. You two are going to need some help in the land of liberty, and I'd be interested in backing you. Come and see me when you get to New York."

"Oh, we will, sir! Thank you, sir!" Relieved and excited, they danced away.

"You're not serious, Harry," said Katherine Wells with a giggle. She wore a dress which she had informed me was of "rose silk *faille*," a white feather boa, her tiny golden locket, and, intriguingly, a cameo on a black ribbon round her neck. In the lamplight, she came near to causing me to forget my vocation. Night after night, she came out like a star—never appearing during the day, but a dream of beauty at dinner and afterwards as we lounged and talked. Sister would retire to her weaving, while Mrs. Wells found something appealing about my listening ear.

She had asked my opinion of nearly everyone in the dining room. She apparently had nothing else to do and nothing to occupy her thoughts but to inquire about, and talk about, our neighbors; so we speculated and surmised together as the others played cards or smoked and drank brandy while the ship swayed beneath us.

One evening I had asked *her* about someone—Adam Verver.

"Rich as Croesus. Wife married him for the cash, but she didn't take stock of him coming with it." This was so starkly put that I glanced at her in surprise. There was a breath of the Liverpool docks in her voice.

Verver was engaged across the room in a genteel card game, with his bored wife seated next to him. I'd had no further encounters with him other than the occasional tip of the hat, a fact that mildly surprised me.

"You don't find something . . . menacing about him?" I asked Mrs. Wells.

"Oh, he's a menace, all right. Just look at *her*."

"Something . . . corrupted?" I tried again.

At this Mrs. Wells had turned quiet and then sighed—severely, I thought, if that were possible.

"Most blokes are," she said with an empty smile. "That's why I was interested in your Captain Basil. He struck me as an unspoiled sort."

Unspoiled? I suppose so, I thought. And infuriating.

After that, she had fallen into a sad silence, and I eventually excused myself for the night.

But now Mrs. Wells was all frills and giggles. "What will you do with this 'Charlie and Bessie' if they do turn up on your doorstep, Harry?"

"They're pirates, aren't they?" the little man cackled. He had drunk one brandy too many. "Right down my line, Kitty."

"Yes, I suppose you'll know exactly what to do with them," she said with a twinkle of contempt in her voice. At this, Count Schindler, who never spoke, leaned over to Mr. Raymond and whispered something in his ear. I couldn't tell what, for the purser had taken the floor as a kind of master of ceremonies.

"Ladies and gentlemen, tonight we have the pleasure of a magic lantern show by the Reverend Doctor Shlessinger, who will lecture on his mission among the poor benighted savages of the Amazon coast."

Chairs scraped, ladies clapped, and the men in the room took on the look of animals in captivity, but no one left. The staterooms were the only refuge of escape, and most of the couples aboard were by this time avoiding each other. Even the men of the orchestra, including the rigid Sigerson, lounged against the bar to see the show. Shlessinger began to set up his apparatus as everyone re-arranged themselves.

A timid gray couple I had met the first night happened to sit nearby. We exchanged pleasantries, and the husband leaned vaguely in the direction of Mr. Raymond. "Excuse me, sir, but would you be *the* Henry Raymond, the editor of the New York *Times*?"

Emitting a glow, Raymond asked, "I'm afraid you have the advantage of me, sir. And who would you be?" The fellow was a prosperous farmer from Wisconsin, bringing the little wife home from a long-promised European tour, and such a tour it had been, Paris, Venice, Florence, Rome, London, and he so admired you, Mr. Raymond, and the New York *Times* and abolitionism and he had been a volunteer in the 5th Wisconsin and . . . . Like many nervous men he couldn't stop talking.

Eventually he subsided, and the stewards finished making a theater of the dining room. The Ververs took seats in front of us. Verver turned and nodded slightly to us, then bowed extravagantly to Mrs. Wells and her companion.

"Raymond," Verver acknowledged him.

"Verver," Raymond replied, and they struck up cigars simultaneously. When the lamps were dimmed, all the gentlemen's shirts glowed in the reflection from Shlessinger's miraculous lantern. The grand missionary stood to introduce his topic, "mission work among the Maroons of Brazil."

"At last something other than drinking and playing cards," Sister whispered to herself. "But I wonder, what is a Maroon? Is it like a mulatto?"

I chose not to answer, partly because I didn't know the answer, but shushed her instead.

"In keeping with our Lord's great commission in the Gospel of John," Shlessinger boomed, "my beloved wife and I have worn ourselves out in service to the Maroons of Brazil—to make disciples of these wretched creatures."

He showed us pictures of the miserable Maroons who were supposed to be the descendants of runaway slaves. Shockingly, they all lived together in promiscuity and seaside huts called *mocambos* and harvested manioc to survive. The ladies gasped at the scandal and squalor. However, as Shlessinger dropped one slide after another into his magic lantern, I began to suspect he was spreading something other than the gospel.

For one thing, the great commission to go and make disciples of all nations is in the book of Matthew, not John. And for another, the scenes in the slides looked suspiciously familiar to me. The more I saw, the surer I was.

When he finished, Shlessinger embraced the light applause from the audience and beamed ruddily at the ladies like a boiling lobster. He announced he would now take questions, as well as a collection "for the poor Maroons."

"Is a Maroon the same as a *mocambo*?" one quavering lady asked.

"You say they eat . . . 'manioc.' Is that what they call . . . human flesh?" asked another, cringing.

Then I ventured. "I find it interesting, Doctor Shlessinger, that in your pictures the Maroons wear the same jean cloth and homespun dresses as the field hands round Charleston, where I live. And their little huts look extraordinarily like the clapboard houses I've seen on Hilton Head and Port Royal Island. What do you make of that?"

Shlessinger muttered something about their "common West African origin" and then hastily moved on to the next question.

Mrs. Wells leaned in to me. "What could you be suggesting, Padre? That the reverend doctor has confused North America with South?" Next to her, Raymond stifled a chuckle.

"I'm suggesting that he picked up these magic-lantern pictures in the States," I kept my voice low. "They have nothing to do with Brazil."

"When will you be returning to Brazil, Dr. Shlessinger?" asked a pious lady on the front row.

"I'm sorry to say that I may not be able to return." Shlessinger bowed his head and shook it slowly and sadly. "I had hoped to establish a school among these base and vile people, if only to give succor to their children . . . ."

"But do you think it wise to send colored children to school?" Sister Carolina spoke up.

"My dear Sister," Shlessinger intoned, raising his bald face to the heavens, "The Lord has sent me in search of the black sheep of the flock so they may know the simple gospel, not the worldly learning of men, which would simply confuse and annoy them. And now, my return depends utterly on the gracious bounty of my hearers. Anything you can contribute, my friends, anything at all—the smallest coin is as valued as the most precious jewel, I assure you—will be greatly appreciated, and will redound to your account in heaven, I have no doubt. Blessings on you all."

Taking the hat from his wife, he roved round cadging the audience for donations. The bar was now open so the party could cap the night. Sister refused, so I took a small glass of port with Mrs. Wells and her friends.

"A confidence man, then?" she asked me.

"If Shlessinger truly is a missionary, I will eat the feathers in your lovely wrap," I said.

Raymond, irrigating himself once again, couldn't stop laughing. "The fellow is as bare-faced as any I've seen."

"And that's more than a few," Mrs. Wells murmured into her drink.

Raymond went on, "Just the sort of fellow I like to have in my employ."

"A swindler?" I asked.

"A showman," Raymond replied. "Men like Shlessinger attract an audience." He nodded at the man, who was ingratiating himself with a flock of grand dames adorned with piety and pricey jewels. His hat was filling up.

"At heart Henry is an impresario," Mrs. Wells explained, coldly. "He loves a good spectacle, so he collects showy people like Charlie and Bessie and this reverend gentleman with the bogus pictures—and many, many others."

"I thought you were a journalist, Mr. Raymond."

Raymond chuckled again. "Journalism, Padre, is the greatest show on earth, to borrow a phrase from the good Mr. Barnum . . . and, speaking of spectacular frauds, Mr. Shlessinger approaches."

"As you clink the social glass, my friends," Shlessinger said, his hat in hand, "I'm sure your magnanimity extends to the poor Maroons of Brazil."

"I haven't my notecase with me, sir, but if you will accept my card and come to see me when we debark, you will not be displeased at what I can do for you," Raymond said. His eyes on Shlessinger made the latter shiver either with pleasure or some presentiment of danger—it was hard to tell which.

"And yourself, Padre?" the fraud asked, turning to me. "A mite from the man of God for the widows and orphans among the Maroons?"

"I fear I have nothing for you," I said. I was clean out of coins (due to Holmes), but I would not have given if I had.

"All gone for Peter's Pence, is it?" he smirked, then walked away muttering "Papists and Mormons. What a ship of fools."

I finished the port and excused myself from the party, as it was getting late. Mrs. Wells thanked me for being so attentive to her.

"I'm afraid I have bored you these many evenings, but you are such sympathetic company, Padre. I wish I could tell you what it has meant to me."

"Bored? Not in the least," I replied, and meant it. "It's been delightful. By the way, I didn't realize your friend Mr. Raymond was such a prominent gentleman. Editor of the New York *Times*?"

"Prominent, he is," she shrugged and led me toward the door. "Now, I do have something to give you." Almost motionlessly, she shifted a small envelope from her hand to mine.

I put the envelope in my breast pocket without looking at it. "Then I'll bid you good night, Mrs. Wells." I bowed and called for Sister, who sat abstractedly staring at the crowd, and we made our way back to our rooms. Once my door was shut behind me, I ripped open the envelope, which was blank, and inside found another envelope sealed shut but with this writing:

Please deliver to Captain Basil.

Chapter 15

To Captain Basil?

I ate a little piece of my heart out, but remembered my dog collar. Of course the note wouldn't be for me. But should I open it? Even if I posted it on the ship, it wouldn't get to Holmes for weeks, and what would he care? He would have no interest in a love note from a near stranger: it was not in his character.

But if it was not a love note? What could it be?

The ability to wander the forest of ethics and find one's own way is famously imputed to the Jesuits, and at least in my case the imputation fits well. It took me only a few minutes to convince myself that I should open the letter to "Captain Basil."

There was nothing in the letter but a crudely penciled diagram, on the back of it some numbers. I had never seen such a figure, like a watch gear imposed over a snail shell imposed over a pyramid.

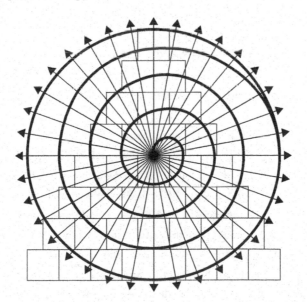

The numbers on the back of the paper were arranged in four vertical columns:

33-3	4-3	0-1	36-1
10-1	1-1	3-1	3-1
26-1	20-21	20-15	3-1
18-20	23-1	4-3	22-5
22-5	20-15	22-5	20-15
18-20	16-10	34-1	25-4
4-3	3-1	4-3	4-3
20-10	18-20	1-1	1-1
18-6	36-1	22-5	20-21
3-1	4-3	4-3	22-7
11-4	1-1	18-6	11-4
20-10	4-3	10-1	18-20
1-1	18-20	4-3	7-1
20-15	18-20	18-20	1-2
25-4	20-10	1-2	14-1

"Another cipher," I sighed.

Staring at it for an hour, utterly baffled, I did not even attempt to break the code. There was something naggingly familiar about the diagram, but that late at night and under the spell of the warm port, my thinking was woolly to say the least. I roused myself long enough to make a copy of the drawing and the table of figures, then returned the original to its envelope just in time for my lamp to burn itself out.

The weather was rising outside when a light ruffle of sail and a flourish of wind sent me off to sleep.

In the deepest part of the night a storm erupted. I awoke to the sound of cracking wood and a roar like the groaning of a giant animal. Doors crashed and shutters dithered in the wind. Something metallic bounced violently along the deck, the ship's bell banged frantically, and underneath it all was the whine of the wrathful ocean.

I gripped my bed, praying with each blast of wind that it would weaken, but it grew only stronger. I could taste the salty mist of it and feel the force of it even as I crouched under my blanket. I was sure the ship would break up any second.

Worried about Sister Carolina, I got up and clambered about getting my boots and coat on as the deck reared from side to side. I forced my door open against the wind. The ship was hurling itself into the air and then plunging into the water in a thunder of spray. Whiskers of cold, black rain raked at my face. Groping my way, I found Sister's door and pounded on it.

"Are you all right, Sister?"

She responded weakly, and I told her to cover her head, hold tight, and pray. What else could I do? Thoughts of the storm on Galilee went through my brain, and I felt my faith draining away.

Just then I heard shouts from up the deck and could barely make out a group of men congregating there. "Father, we need you," someone called, so I pulled myself forward clinging fast to the bulkhead

It was the captain, who wore a bandage round his head. He had been hit with force and seemed confused. It was too dark to recognize the others crowding round him. "The hatches!" he croaked.

I looked round and saw the great wooden hatches in the foredeck coming loose from their iron clasps. With every lunge of the ship, water surged through them into the hold. I could hear the cries of women and children below.

"Bring up the hatches from the lower deck," the captain called, almost in a faint.

I didn't understand at first, but then I heard a stronger voice behind me. *"Prest! Come vit me!"* It was Sigerson, the violinist. He motioned to the other men, and we followed him aft, grasping at the railings hand over hand to keep from being blown overboard. We found four hatch doors snugly attached to the lower deck, which was taking much less of a beating. The big Mormon farmers wrenched one off with grappling hooks and we carried it forward against the wind, where Sigerson directed us to remove the most damaged forehatch. Hammers were found, and the Mormons soon had it battened in place. We did the same with two more of the lower hatch doors.

Then all at once the ship dived into a deep trough and a massive wave raced toward us. The foreboom snapped, coming within inches of smashing my head and sweeping the two men behind me into the flood. Fixing a rope fast to a spar, Sigerson passed it to me. I tied it round my waist and passed it to the next man. It was Henry Raymond. Thus linked together, the three of us hoisted the last of the lower hatches on our shoulders and struggled forward with it. The two remaining sturdy Mormons hammered it down, and at last the hold was safe from the surge of the storm.

On the deck we huddled together with our injured captain, who was becoming delirious. I wanted to get him inside, but none of us dared walk on the pitching surface. It was as slippery as cream. Then the wind turned fanatical, screaming and blasting away at the ship, pushing it alarmingly to port. The captain pulled my head down and panted into my ear. "She's sitting athwart the wind. The helm . . . into the wind. . . ." It was all I could make out, but Sigerson understood. He loosed himself from us and disappeared into the black spray, his lean hands clutching at the wild lacework of ropes flailing over his head.

The deck tilted further and further downward, and still further. I found myself staring literally into an abyss, holding fast to the captain with one arm and to the rope with the other, praying and willing the ship to come level. Just as I feared I would lose my grip, the vessel made a great groaning noise, curved slowly into the wind, and righted itself.

But the ship still lurched like a mad horse. At length Sigerson reemerged from the blackness holding a cable and motioning us to pull ourselves to safety.

Just as Sigerson approached, I thought he stumbled and collapsed on Henry Raymond. For a few minutes I imagined them wrestling each other in the darkness, struggling for something to cling to as a river from the foredeck streamed over the two men and launched itself like a waterfall into the sea. I grabbed at a waving hand and pulled its owner out of the torrent with all my strength. It was Raymond's hand.

He lay retching salt water, clutching my arm and tugging himself in convulsions toward me. I had no idea what had happened to Sigerson, but I reached out, found the cable, and dragged Raymond and the injured captain across the weather deck. It felt like forever before I could discern the pale lamplight coming from the lounge.

Inside, a dozen or so passengers, groaning and sick, lay lashed to the deck as the ship's doctor hovered over them. Drenched and trembling myself, I volunteered to help as I could. At last fainting away, the captain waved us off to tend to the others. When we came to examine Raymond, we found him still in evening dress, exhausted but uninjured—he opened one eye and looked me over, then closed it again in sleep.

At length the rocking of the ship, the dull warmth of the room, and the mutterings of the sick put me to sleep as well.

When I awoke hours later, the storm still thrashed away at us, although it was light. The ship continued to soar and then dive into the wind with a rhythm that became strangely comforting as it was now quite predictable, and everyone began to breathe more easily. In the lounge the smell of sick turned my stomach, so I decided to venture out into the reviving wind. I braced myself behind a mast and, with the sensation that I was astride a great, slow horse, let the spray bathe my face.

Gradually, almost indiscernibly, the wind diminished. By eight bells, the indignant ocean had reconciled itself to our presence almost to the point of allowing us to stand and walk upon the deck, and a few passengers emerged once again, their faces green as the sea, shambling like drunks into the open just to get a gulp of air.

For the next two days we endured the unceasing misty wind as we proceeded at dead slow toward land, at last sighted on our seventh day out. There were no more gay evenings in the lounge, and meals were taken in silence. The third mate and two of the Mormon pilgrims had been swept overboard, so a general sense of gloom pervaded the ship. It was heart-rending to watch the Mormons gather on deck and pray mournfully over their loss—two wives were left alone with small children—but they appeared to rally round each other and quietly dispersed below once again.

Then I realized that Adam Verver was standing next to me watching the sad scene.

"What a catastrophe," I breathed.

"Hadn't we better wait a while before we call it a catastrophe? After all, we don't yet know what the losses amount to." And he walked away swinging his cane, his boots shined and his ascot correct.

I busied myself comforting Sister Carolina, who had dropped into a kind of terrified trance, and making inquiries about the welfare of the passengers, in particular Katherine Wells. I was met at her stateroom door by the taciturn Count Schindler, who gave me to understand that she was resting and would continue to rest until we reached port. It was made equally clear that I would not be disturbing that rest.

I also looked up and down for Sigerson. I wondered if he had come through alive, and I wanted to congratulate him for his resolute handling of the crisis. I learned that the helmsman had been rendered unconscious by the same lurch of the ship that had injured the captain, and that Sigerson had revived him so he could steer properly. We all owed our lives to the violinist. The porter told me not to worry: Sigerson and the other musicians were all "O.K.," in that peculiarly American way of signifying no need for concern.

At length we made our way up the smooth Delaware River to Philadelphia, and the ship was one commotion of activity from bow to stern. Once on land, my legs felt like tree stumps. While awaiting our baggage, I hovered round the passengers' gangplank hoping for a last moment with Katherine Wells.

I bade a pleasant farewell to Mrs. Miller and her intolerable son and a less pleasant farewell to the Shlessingers, who cut me dead. Adam Verver descended as if from Olympus, trailing bags and trunks and, on his arm, enwrapped in a luxurious cream-colored boa, his stupendously beautiful goddess-wife.

"An eventful crossing, Padre," Verver paused to acknowledge me.

"Indeed." I glanced at Mrs. Verver, who looked as if she were about to be buried alive, and felt an urgent blessing was called for. *"Pax vobiscum,* Mrs. Verver."

"And with you, Padre," her husband said with no attitude at all, bowed, and continued his progress.

When nearly everyone else had left the boat, Mrs. Wells came down—subdued but still grand—closely supported by her two retainers, Raymond and Schindler.

I had not encountered Raymond since the night of the storm. He was inconspicuously elegant once again, his dress tactful and his black whiskers carefully managed. "Padre!" he greeted me. "We weathered the tempest together, didn't we? For a few moments, I was afraid we were going to end up a couple of Jonahs."

"Indeed," I smiled. "But, like Jonah, 'I cried out of my affliction to the Lord, and he heard me.'"

"I'm glad you could depend on the Lord, Padre. I was depending on those big shoulders of yours. I'm in your debt, sir."

I shook my head, but Raymond was already walking away. Mrs. Wells stopped him and came back to speak to me.

"I'm so happy to have made your acquaintance, Father. If you ever come to New York, please call on me." She put her hand on mine.

"It would be my pleasure. Bless you."

She hesitated, then quietly asked, "Did my message get through?"

"Your message? Yes, I posted it with the porter."

"Ah," she halted. "Posted. Of course. Well then. Goodbye, Father, and happy journey."

"Kitty!" Raymond was calling, and she was swept into the crowd with her retinue. I didn't tell her about the copy I had made and could still feel rustling in my breast pocket.

CHARLESTON

Chapter 16

In after years it was known as the Great Gale of '78. The storm we stumbled into had marshaled its forces as a hurricane in the West Indies and then marched across the States as far north as Philadelphia, ravaging towns, crashing church steeples, even twisting iron rails from the ground before it swerved out to sea to meet us.

As a result it took us nearly two weeks to reach Charleston. Sister Carolina forthrightly refused to go by sea—"As God is my witness, I'll never board a ship again!"—so we were forced to make our way over land. With the rails and the roads disrupted, the journey was interminable and marked by miserable nights in stinking, overcrowded inns along the way. I couldn't sleep in those places—the cold and the smell were bad enough, but the labyrinthine drawing Katherine Wells had given me kept me fitfully awake. Some nights I crept out of bed with a candle to puzzle over it again and again, harassed by the sense that I had seen something like it before. To add to my anxiety, one night I caught someone watching me from a window—a lean shadow that jerked out of sight as soon as I became conscious of it. I was indescribably relieved when at last we arrived to find Charleston, fortunately, intact.

I immediately carried out Holmes's instructions with precision, placing an advertisement in the Charleston and Atlanta newspapers, as I had been charged to do. I also wrote Holmes a long letter describing my experiences on the water and lamenting the fact that he would not receive it perhaps for weeks. In those days the Atlantic mail always slowed to a trickle in the winter months.

Conversely, within only three days of my advertisement, I received a curious visitor.

"Father Grosjean, sir? My name is . . . Joe Harris of the, of the . . . Atlanta *Constitution.*" He stood there hat in hand, lisping and stammering, his blazing red hair as abundant as his chin was scarce.

"Yes, Mr. Harris. What can I do for you?"

"You, um, you placed this item, sir?" He held out a dirty, wrinkled fragment of newsprint. It was my advertisement.

"Yes, I did. Now, how can I help you?"

"It's I who can, who can help you, sir. You, um, you must know about the . . . the scuffle over yonder . . . in Atlanta?"

"Scuffle? No, I don't know what you mean. Won't you come in and sit down?"

In my heart, I was excited at this first response to my advertisement, but did not want to appear so. Instead I tried to use Holmes's methods to discern as much as I could about this odd stranger as he bowed and bobbed his way into a chair. From his frail albeit pudgy appearance, I deduced a poor diet. The undersleeves of his coat were glossy to the point of transparency—this coupled with the ink stains on his fingers indicated that he spent a good amount of time writing. His extraordinary diffidence, his stammering and shyness, pointed to humble origins. He could barely raise his eyes to mine, and my heart went out a little to Joe Harris.

I offered him a glass, which he gulped gratefully, and then I urged him on to his story.

"Your notice, F . . . Father, your notice has caused some . . . disquiet. In Atlanta. A good many people want to know . . . the same thing."

I glanced again at the paper:

$500 reward for information regarding the murder of the Tarleton brothers of Jonesboro at battle of Gettysburg. Inquire at this newspaper, &c.

"Surely your publication must feature many such inquiries. The late war resulted in so many unresolved cases like this one."

"Yes, sir, you are correct there, sir. But not many . . . cause such a stir. $500, for one thing . . . a lot of money. A lot of money. But another thing. It's the word . . . the word . . ."

"Which word?"

The muscles in Harris's forehead worked hard to get the word out: "M . . . murder, sir."

"Oh, I see. I've created a stir by representing the death of the Tarletons as an instance of murder rather than a battlefield killing?"

Harris nodded. His face bore a look of pained and permanent surprise, as if he were never sure what sounds his mouth might produce. "May I ask, Father, what is . . . what is your interest in this m . . . matter?"

"I am the pastor to a friend of the Tarletons, a member of the Order of Sisters of Mercy here in Charleston. She is convinced that her friends were deliberately murdered and has undertaken to resolve the matter if possible. I am merely acting on her behalf. Now, may I ask *you*, what kind of a stir are you talking about?"

"In Atlanta, the Tarletons had m-many friends, sir. The idea of m-murder . . . it's raised suspicions, sir. Yes. Suspicions falling on one per . . . person."

"On whom?"

"As you might expect, sir, on someone who . . . who isn't likely to be able to de . . . to defend himself, sir."

"Please, Mr. Harris, you needn't keep calling me 'sir.' Who can't defend himself?"

"Oh, I'm s-sorry, sir. I mean, I'm *sorry*. His name is James. Just . . . just James. An old family retainer. He was . . . a dog robber. A dog robber to the Tarleton brothers."

"What on earth is a dog robber, Mr. Harris?"

"A cook . . . a servant . . . in the Army. James was their s-slave on the plantation and went to war with the brothers. To keep the pack horse, cook, clean . . . take care of the weapons."

"Why would suspicion fall on their servant?"

"The Tarletons . . . and James . . . no love lost. They whipped him. For eavesdropping, spreading tales, and the like. Everyone knows he hate . . . hated them."

"I see." It was the old story in this part of the country: the colored man as scapegoat. Of course, I knew immediately it was not true; besides the knowledge I had from Holmes, the intrigue surrounding the Tarletons could not be the result of a mere fit of temper on the part of a mistreated slave.

"So when I read your n-notice, Father, I thought there might be more to the story. I'm only a cornfield journalist, but . . . but I, I cherish a good story."

"Perhaps you'd like to meet the person who is offering the reward," I suggested. "I'm sure she can tell you more about it."

The reporter looked doubtful, but I walked him to the convent where we asked to see Sister Carolina. While we waited, I tried to calm his nerves. I asked him a few innocuous questions about himself, and gradually he relaxed with me. He told me he had been a fatherless boy who had made his way laboring on a farm and selling rabbit skins for twenty cents apiece. Like many journalists, he had begun as a printer's devil and became adept at "listening at keyholes," as he put it.

I smiled at this, and Harris shyly smiled back. I decided I liked him.

"A good reporter . . . is a death hunter," he said. "Nothing, nothing seizes a reader's attention like death, and mysterious death . . . well, there's nothing like mysterious death for a good story."

"And that explains why you have come three hundred miles to see me, instead of telegraphing—which you could have done much more easily?"

"In part," he replied. "In part."

I gave him an inquisitive look.

Harris looked up and away as if talking to an audience in the air. "I hoped the war would have mowed down the old prejudices like weeds." His stammer had subsided almost completely. "But now the same old evils are blossoming again . . . with vengeance."

I was impressed with his fluency and, at the same time, depressed by the scene he painted. "Then you came in part for a story you could print, but also in part to help this man James. I gather he is now in some peril."

"Serious peril. I thought you might have . . . information? That would help?"

My mind seized up. The fragments of information I had—how to explain them when I didn't even know myself what to make of them? What might the luckless servant James have to do with this murky trans-Atlantic mystery, if anything at all? And what was my duty to the poor man? I cursed Holmes for leaving me alone like this.

Fortunately, just then Sister Carolina appeared. "We'll pose that question to her," I said, relieved that I had more time to think.

Introductions were made. Sister Carolina still looked waxy and wobbly from our voyage, and Harris—well, he could have been a fugitive fleeing the law, he was so skittish. One leg bounced rhythmically, his eyes vibrated, he twisted one hand round another.

I explained to Sister why Mr. Harris had come.

"James? The Tarletons' *James*?" A livid light came into her eyes, as if she were surfacing a memory not quite solid but illuminating. "I should have known, I should have known!" Her face tightened with fury.

"What do you mean, Sister?" I asked.

"It's in their nature, that's what I mean. The blacks! The Yankees tried to get us to bend the knee to the most degraded of mankind, to bring them up to our level—and you see the consequence? Buckshot in the back!"

I glanced at Harris, who was now agitated to the point of speechlessness.

"That skinny boy James!" she went on. "He always was insolent, sneaking and prying and listening in on his betters. The Tarletons raised him up by hand to serve their own sons, gave him food and clothes and the gospel and clean straw to sleep on. And how did the ungrateful swine repay their generosity?"

"Apparently nothing is proven. There are allegations . . ." I tried to calm her.

Sister Carolina leapt to her feet—or rather what constituted a leap for her, more of a hop, actually—and charged back toward the nuns' quarters.

"What are you doing?"

"Packing!" she spit over her shoulder. "I'm going to Atlanta to make sure justice is done. I'm going to see that black-hearted murderer hang."

Thus did Sister Carolina love her brother as herself, and I was left alone with Harris.

So I decided to take Harris into my confidence. What else could I do? The poor former slave was about to be tried—or worse—for a crime which to my nearly certain knowledge he did not commit, and he would be getting no help from Sister. It was likely that the only person standing between this unfortunate man and a rope was myself.

Back in my room, Harris stared in amazement at the now creased and greasy pyramidal "sonnet" I had received so many weeks before and gaped at the story I told him. Now quite calm, he let out a torrent of questions at me, which I answered as best I could. Although outwardly the most faint-hearted of men, Harris showed me a glimpse of a truly ardent intellect—he saw the whole picture in no time at all.

"You must tell this story to them in Atlanta. It may be . . ." There was a catch in his voice, this time not attributable to his stammer . . . "It may be you are the only hope James has left."

ATLANTA

Chapter 17

I secured permission from my superiors to accompany Sister Carolina, and Mr. Harris traveled back with us on the railroad that meandered through Augusta and Macon to Atlanta. We sat in our compartment in stiff silence, reading newspapers and watching Sister impaling the tough, dried berries she used to make rosaries and then stringing them together. At length I motioned to Harris to join me for a drink in the corridor.

"She's furious," I said, understating things considerably.

"Wha . . . what is she doing with those beads?"

"She makes rosaries—they're bracelets or necklaces used for prayer. The beads help keep count so one can meditate on the mysteries of the faith more easily. There are fifteen mysteries of the rosary, and each bead represents a mystery."

"Oh, I see. I remember now."

"Are you a Catholic, Mr. Harris?"

"N-no. I mean, yes. . . . I mean, I'd like to be. I think I am. Red hair, you see. . . . Irish."

"Yes," I smiled. I offered him a swallow from my small flask and we opened the corridor window to watch the cold, winter-lit forest flash by.

"It isn't a popular religion in the South. Catholicism," I reflected. "The Klan used to breathe out threatenings and slaughter against Catholics, didn't they? Before my time?"

"Catholics, Jews—mostly blacks. Anyone . . . anyone they didn't like."

"What can you tell me about the Klan, Mr. Harris? Folks round here don't like to speak of it."

Harris was quiet for a moment, working up the energy to speak. Another long draught from my flask relaxed him. "It is important to . . . to know . . . that the war has never really ended. Not here. Deep down, every Southerner imagines that it is forever afternoon on a day in July 1863 at a place called Gett . . . Gettysburg. The whole world stopped there. Now the Klansmen put on their ghostly costumes, ghosts still fighting that battle that cannot end without the end of honor, too. They fight on for their meager honor, their dismal honor . . . with the lash and the torch and the . . . branding iron. And the r . . . rope."

"Have you ever seen them?"

"Not for a long time. When Grant became president, he sent the Yankees to chase them off into the woods, but . . . but they're still here." He gestured toward the dimming forest where only the outermost trees were visible to us as we chugged past. "And now the Yankees are gone. What did Shake—Shakespeare say about the woods moving?"

I smiled at the allusion. "Macbeth. He was doomed by an army bearing tree branches as they descended on his castle."

"Right. The Klan is coming. They used to dress up to hide their faces and scare the colored folks. Some of them . . . pretend to be ghosts and they surround a sharecropper's cabin in the night and take themselves apart. They sits on their horses and make like they can cut off their own heads and put 'em back . . . back on, or fling off a hand holding a torch. You sees that once and you gits out of there and you don't come back."

Harris had slipped into some kind of backwoods banter that flowed with strange fluency.

"You have seen the Klan at work," I said.

"I have," he nodded, staring out the window into the approaching night. "You understand, I had nothing—nothing. I was less than a slave on the plantation, and I lived out there . . . in the . . . in the slave quarters with them. I had a mother who taught me how to read, but she couldn't keep me . . . so I went to work.

"The slaves . . . they were good to me. We worked hard and at night the fires were done up and they told st . . . stories, about the little wars amongst the animals in the woods, and they'd sing their hopeless songs.

"Then Sherman came. All was confusion and distress. They sent me off with the horses and mules . . . I hid out in the swamp, but the Yankees . . . I could hear 'em treading through the mud. They took the stock and I beat it back to the plantation, but it was all quiet, everything stripped. Even the slaves were gone . . . following Sherman like he was the M-Messiah himself.

"After the war I got work in a print . . . a printing shop, but I still liked to pass the time down in the quarters. The slaves weren't slaves anymore. Some had their own land, they were sending the little ones to Yankee schools, and they were so proud being free, and their songs and their stories were mostly hopeful.

"Until one night r . . . riders came. They came right up to our fire and kicked it apart. And one big rider took hold of the peak of his hood and pulled it up and I could swear he had no head!

"That was the end of everything, just everything for my friends. . . they took their young ones out of the white schools and they disappeared and some were found hanging in the trees like moldy fruit . . . and certain parties took back their land claims, saying they were abandoned."

I had to take another drink myself. Night had come, and we could see sparks from the engine and the occasional flicker of fire deep in the woods that surrounded us.

"I understand now why you're anxious about this situation with the Tarletons' servant," I said. "It must feel like demons closing in."

Harris nodded. "The war goes on, Father. Gettysburg . . . it's not over. I don't know if it will ever end . . . but there's mowing to be done."

"Mowing?"

"On the plantation, we mowed down the weeds or they'd take over, and when they dried just a spark could burn us out. It's . . . it's a war you don't stop fighting . . . fighting the weeds of prejudice, Father."

"'Cursed is the earth,'" I replied. "'Thorns and thistles shall it bring forth to thee.'"

"Genesis?"

I laid my hand on Harris's shoulder.

When we arrived in Atlanta, we separated—Harris to his home, Sister to her family's imposing gray-stone mansion, and myself to the rectory near the new Church of the Immaculate Conception. I had wired to the curates, and they put me up nicely.

Morning came slowly to Atlanta, but once awake it was noisy. Sister's wagon called for me and we dodged through the streets of a city that was springing anew from the charred earth of the war. The "heart of Atlanta," once incinerated by the Union army, sprouted dozens of new buildings, among them the newspaper office where we stopped to collect Joe Harris.

Our plan was to travel to the Tarleton plantation where James was hiding and "bring him to justice." We had learned that the boss there was a formidable person who wouldn't give him up, but that any day a mob was liable to storm the place. Sister felt that she had enough influence to extract James from the plantation.

Our wagon was under the command of a lean little sprite of fourteen, perhaps sixteen, named Marta, the daughter of one of Sister's "house workers." Despite her size, everything about her looked strong—arms, hands, face, even the stiff hair that popped out of her head like fistfuls of straw.

Marta chattered without ceasing, her birdsong of a voice twittering incomprehensibly above the wind and noise of the street, mostly about "the folks," I gathered. As a lover of gossip, I tried hard to make out what she was saying and did pick up a few words, but her back-country dialect defeated me. Occasionally, Sister Carolina would bark at her to be quiet—to no avail. Marta kept singing through her soliloquy as effortlessly as she steered the big bay horse through the labyrinth of the city.

Soon we were in the countryside, headed south into red hills undulating like the waves on the sea. The day was fine, cold and bright, the trees had discarded their leaves, and I would have enjoyed the ride except for two things: the very real possibility of a calamity ahead and the unnerving feeling that someone was watching us.

It was not a distinct impression, but it grew stronger as we passed patches of woods between empty cotton fields. I fancied there were shadows moving with us within the thickets, and while nothing solid emerged, I found myself trembling and not just from the cold.

At length we dropped into a hollow where a small stream splayed through the forest and turned the road into a blood colored mire.

"That little r-river's right . . . right out of Exodus," Harris said, and it was just a moment before I realized he had made a joke. The man continually surprised me.

Sister Carolina commanded Marta to stop. The horse needed a drink, and Sister had caught sight of what looked like berries hanging from the pine trees. Marta collected a prickly ball of wood studded with the red-and-black beans that Sister used for making rosaries.

"Don't touch them," Sister said as she reached out for the ball.

I asked her what they were called.

"They's jequirity beans," Marta crowed. "They grows all over creation, chokin' the trees, and they'll kill a cow that eats 'em."

Ignoring Marta, Sister explained, "They're called rosary peas. They harden and hold a lovely gloss, just right for a rosary."

"They are pretty things," I said, picking one out of its pod. "Symmetrical, red as a cherry with a tiny black spot on the base of each one. Not edible, I suppose."

"No," Sister retorted, rather curtly I thought, and seized the bean from my hand.

Harris murmured, "They're something of a . . . a scourge to the planters roundabout. The runners spread deep under the g-ground and come up everywhere, taking over the cotton fields. They poison the stock, too."

I then realized that the rosary peavines webbed the trees all round us, the beans protruding like little red eyes from their spindly pods.

"Marta, go get me some more of those pods—and don't touch the beans!"

Marta shrank back. "I ain't no field hand," she protested. "I a wagon driver!"

But the little wagon driver relented under threats rather uncharacteristic of a religious woman, and harvested all she could reach for Sister to pack into her ever-present rosary case. Sister examined each pod carefully. "You've handled some of these beans!"

"I sorry, I try not."

Marta climbed back up to the spring seat and we were ready to push on when I thought I heard the crackle of a broken stick in the woods.

"What was that noise?" I said, a little more loudly than I intended. Everyone fell quiet, including Marta. We listened for a moment, hearing no sound but the wind in the tall pitch pines, so Marta urged the horse across the bloody Nile and up the hill toward our destination.

Chapter 18

Before the war the Tarleton place had been a great plantation, but the house now looked like a vast shack roosting precariously on its hill just waiting for the wind to carry it off for good. When we approached, black workers blocked our way with shovels and pitchforks—one carrying a rifle almost as a big as a cannon—until Sister Carolina identified herself and the guards fell back to let us pass. Stretching away from the house was the largest paddock I had ever seen, and a dozen or so lovely young horses romping round in it.

A skeletal lady in riding clothes sat on a rail intently observing the horses, while two stable men at her side observed our approach just as intently.

"Miz Bea!" Sister called, and the skeleton noticed us for the first time. She leapt from the railing.

"Careen! It's absolutely not *you!*" This inconceivably thin lady could actually walk, and quite energetically too. Tottering toward us, she had a face as white as a dry bone and hair red like the clay beneath our feet. She greeted Sister with kisses and Joe Harris, whom she had already met, with a curt but respectful bow.

"Miz Bea" was the mother of the late Tarleton brothers. Despite her thinness, she was an abundant soul and invited us all for the midday meal—cornbread and pork belly served from a pot of steaming greens by a frail cook named Tildy. The dining room was returning to nature. Moss grew from the moldings and vines curled round the chandeliers, taking root in the sooty dust of the ceiling.

The lady would hear nothing of our business until we had eaten, and then having laden the hearth with fresh pine, she motioned us into a circle round the fire.

"So your plan is to take James with you to Fulton County and let the sheriff look after him. Mr. Harris, I know you have his interests at heart, but to trust him to the sheriff like that . . ."

"He . . . he would be safe there, I be-believe," Harris stammered quietly, "M-Ma'am. Up in Atlanta they have a r-r-rock-walled jail to hold him until the t . . . trial."

"So you think there'd be a trial, do you?" Miz Bea snorted.

"The *Constitution* would s-see to it."

"Your newspaper is mighty influential, but I don't know if your printer's ink is a strong enough potion to repel the Klan, even from behind rock walls."

"Begging your p-pardon, Ma'am, but newsprint is . . . often stronger th-than rock walls."

"Eloquently put, young man." She was clearly delighted with him. "I suppose I ought to trust a man with red hair like yours," she chuckled, tossing her own bloodshot tresses. "Well, Careen, what do you think?"

"Justice must be done, and done proper." Sister's white chin shivered. "That's all I have to say."

The old lady contemplated this. "Sending James cross country in bold daylight with a nun, a priest, and a shy little scribbler. I suppose it might work. It's not what they would expect, them roarers and redshirts just looking to get drunk and hang a darky.

"And you started all this," she turned her shrewd eye on me. "All due to your notice in the *Constitution*. You know, Father, they came up here last Tuesday week with their torches and their foolishness wearing flour sacks over their heads. They said they would hang James up with the rotten apples, and shouldn't I be glad my sons are getting their due requital at last.

"I held up my big old Enfield musket and told 'em my sons were illiterate louts who misspent their lives chasing women and shooting at dogs and Yankees, and they were just fine where they were—six feet under—and they didn't need no requiting.

"And furthermore, my foreman James never hurt those boys even though they mistreated him every day of his life. And now he's got a wife and children and nobody's goin' to mistreat him again. So you all can turn 'round and get off my land. And they did."

I couldn't help but stare at her in admiration, although I quickly apologized. "I'm sorry to have caused you this trouble."

"Why did you go about stirrin' up this pot in the first place?" she asked.

I didn't think it was right to cast blame on Sister, so I didn't know how to answer.

"Not your fault, I know." She turned to Sister. "Careen, you couldn't leave it. You couldn't just let it go, could you? My boys died in a battle more'n fifteen years now—there's nothing more to say or do about it. It's done."

This awkward exchange was interrupted by the arrival of two strangers. "Misters Beaufort, ma'am," Tildy announced, and our hostess arose to make introductions.

"This is General Abraham Beaufort and his brother, Colonel Tom."

Apparently they were expected. Both men were square and solid, both smoking identical cigars, the only difference between them the cut of their beards. In addition to his aggressive mustache, the general's beard circled his face like a hairy halo, while Tom appeared about to be consumed by his. Only two eyes and a blistered nose stood out from the tangle.

"General Beaufort owns the largest horse farm in Kentucky, but he likes to come south in the winter to buy and sell," our hostess explained. Now I understood the clank and rattle of their elaborate spurs. "I owe him a great deal, as he helped me replenish my stock after the Yankees took all of my horses."

"You owe me nothin', Miz Bea," said the general, his voice amiable but viscous with the chimney residue of thousands of cigars. "And it appears you have greatly improved your stock since the last time we met."

As soon as he spoke, I had the impression that I had met the general before, but could not isolate him in my memory.

Chairs were brought and she motioned the new arrivals into our circle. "I'm so sorry, we just took our noses out of the manger, but you are welcome to what's left of dinner."

While he ate, the general and our hostess bantered a bit on the subject of horses. Brother Tom sat erect eating quietly and politely, and I thought there must be some culture in him despite his haggard, beaten look. At length, Tildy brought us coffee (which made me grimace) and a dessert she called "Republican pudding," just a dish of sweet rice custard.

"Are you gentlemen Republicans?" Tom asked Harris and me, abruptly breaking into the conversation. Tom's culture evidently didn't extend to refraining from the taboo subject of politics in polite society.

Surprised, I tried to sound amusing. "I am an Englishman and a monarchist. I frankly don't know about my friend Mr. Harris." The latter squeaked out the word "D-Democrat."

"I declare, Colonel Tom, whatever does it matter?" Miz Bea said, pouring out the coffee that was bubbling on the hearth. "In my view it's time to put our political differences aside. Politics brings war . . . and war brought us nothin' but trouble. It's all in the dead past now."

"The past isn't dead—it's alive. And it's not even past." Tom was being mystical.

"Good coffee! And this is a fine pudding, ma'am," the general observed, ignoring his brother's indiscretion.

"It's just humble rice and sugar."

"During the war we would have given all our back pay and then some for a little rice and sugar, wouldn't we, Tom?" the general poked his brother. "And some decent coffee. Remember drinking coffee made out of dried acorns and bacon grease?"

"And the bacon was wormy," growled Tom.

"Of course it turned out our back pay brought us nothing at all," the general added. As with so many Southerners, the cloud of bitterness at the loss of the war still hung over these men, a gray, drizzling cloud that persisted and would not move on.

"You're an Englishman, but your name is French," Tom remarked to me. "Like our'n—Beaufort. We were Huguenots, chased out of France by the Catholic Church." And so he brought into our little circle the other great taboo subject: religion.

Embarrassed by this, the general laughed and said, "My brother is a student of history. We were brought up by scholarly parents who provided well for our education. Unfortunately, my studies began and ended with horses, while my brother learned the Latin and the 'decline and fall' and all of that."

Tom went on unfazed. He fixed me with his eyes and said, "It was Riche-loo who expelled us from France. He was a Jezzawit. You a Jezzawit?"

"I am a Jesuit." Although no more than ordinarily brave, I have never—nor would I ever—diminish my vocation. The man's opinion meant nothing to me in any case. "And it may interest you to know that the Jesuits were themselves expelled from France for more than fifty years. It seems the French like to be exclusive," I went on airily, and everyone chuckled except Tom Beaufort.

I decided to divert the conversation. "So, General, you've been touring the South collecting horseflesh?"

"Every winter since the war, and long before," he replied. "Charlottesville, Middleburg, Edgefield County over in Carolina, and here. Miz Bea used to have the biggest and best horse farm in the South, so we're trying to build it up again. We spend a few weeks in each place. Sometimes we buy, sometimes we sell."

"Do you ever stop at Charleston?" I asked. I was trying to pin down where and when I might have encountered him before.

"Yes. There's a fine equestrian club at the college."

Miz Bea broke in. "And my own horses are getting lonely while we sit here conversin' like a ladies' sewing circle. Let's go tend to business, gentlemen. Careen, y'all want to come with us?"

But Sister preferred to stay behind to work on her rosaries, while the rest of us adjourned to the paddock to marvel at the stock. After an hour or so, Miz Bea pulled

Harris and me aside and whispered that she would meet us "at the smokehouse" a little later. So we wandered away and found the place.

In the shade of two huge pines, the smokehouse was a windowless brick building, the only entrance a door made of wooden slats locked together by ironmongery so rusted it looked like dirt. Harris knocked at it quietly.

"Who?" came the throaty question from inside.

"It's . . . It's Joe Harris, James. I've brought a f-friend." The door opened and we were admitted into a treasure house of aromas—salty, smoky hams and wedges of meat hanging like amber jewelry from the rafters. The light from the door fell on a frightened, black man of forty or so huddled against the wall and wielding a pitchfork.

"James, this is Father Simon"—Harris had given up trying to enunciate my last name—"he's come to h-help us get you to s-safety."

"I ain't goin' to no jail," said James.

"It's the safest . . . place for you. The Fulton sheriff will p-protect you."

"No sheriff ever protect no black man." I thought James had a good point.

"Y-you're in jail *here*, James," Harris replied. "But this jail ain't safe like the one in A'lanta. You only got a . . . a old woman and her darkies betwixt you and the K-Klan. The Fulton sheriff doesn't like Sheriff Wallop from down here. He'll be more'n happy to t-take you in, just to t-tweak ol' Wallop's nose." Harris too had a good point. I began to understand his canny way of dealing with Georgian realities.

We all jumped at a noise from outside, but it was just a thin black boy of about fourteen carrying a panier of hot, fresh cornbread. James kissed the boy and gobbled the bread.

"This is my son James Albert." He looked longingly at his son and then shook his head. "If I go to jail I never get out, except for hangin'."

Harris gave a bleak sigh. "Looky here, James. You're stuck betwixt two wolves that h-hate each other. You gotta throw in with one of them and h-hope he's happy just watching the other one howl. You got . . . no choice."

I thought I'd add a sliver of hope, although even I was skeptical. "James, I don't know Atlanta, but I trust you'd get more justice in town than out here in the country amongst these Klan scoundrels. After all, there may not even be a prosecution. They have only some baseless rumor to try you on—no evidence at all."

James looked wistfully at me. "No, suh, Mister Priest. You sure don't know A'lanta. In this world the black man got no rights. Evidence . . . trial . . . none of that don't matter at all. They'd lynch me of a Sunday afternoon comin' out of church just to entertain the ladies."

James's young son trembled at this, and I saw bitterness awakening in his eyes. "Daddy, why do white folks treat colored folks so mean?"

At that moment I had never wished for anything so much as that Sherlock Holmes were there.

Chapter 19

After Miz Bea had seen the Beauforts off, she came rustling down to the smokehouse. "James? James?" Her whisper was so loud I would have preferred her ordinary voice.

"I reckon you *should* go to Atlanta with these gentlemen, James. I can't protect you here. You just think you got endless pasturage here, but once them roarers get drunk enough, my snapping at 'em won't keep 'em away. Not the next time. And you know what'll happen then."

James looked miserable.

"What is a 'roarer,' ma'am?" I asked, unconsciously echoing her whisper.

"A roarer is a horse with a sick lung. Also a drunken, no 'count grayback with leather for brains and revenge in his soul—a big old boy that hides under a flour sack in the dark, bless his heart."

"Do you know these scoundrels?"

"There's a tall ugly one with one arm from over in Edgefield, named Wash Thurman. He drags a bunch of juveniles from his so-called 'rifle club' around with him. Then there's a state senator they call General Mart that keeps men like Thurman busy terrorizing the black folks."

Joe Harris interrupted. "We need to . . . get going. Before it's dark."

"Yes, you do," our hostess agreed, all business and giving orders. "Albert, you fetch down a ham for your daddy. James, you run over and tell your family you're going and be back here in a half hour. Joe, Reverend, let's get that wagon packed up and light a fire under Careen and that silly little hack of yours."

James shot off on a run without hesitating, which surprised me. As we walked back to the house, I asked Miz Bea, "Why was James so willing to come with us when you told him to? Our arguments seemed to carry no weight with him."

"Arguments? With a Negro? You can't argue them into anything. They take no thought of the morrow. They just sleep and feed and do as they're told, as they always have."

Evidently, our hostess saw no appreciable distinction between her horses and her ex-slaves, except that she could still buy and sell the horses. I reflected that it would be a long time—if ever—before things changed in the South.

Within the hour, we were taking our leave of the big hill farm. Marta drove with Sister next to her on the spring seat, Joe Harris and myself riding in the wagon bed, and James concealed in a supine position under a pile of quilts Miz Bea had given us.

Once again, Marta talked us to death. Now that the wind had ceased, she warbled like a crazed bird in the still afternoon air. "I knows where to hide James. I knows all about A'lanta, bettern anybody, I knows every street and street corner, I can take you anywheres you wants to go in A'lanta. We'll find a good place for James, he's the foreman, he deserve better, he the king of the Hill Farm, that's what they calls him, James, King of the Hill Farm."

"Shush!" Sister Carolina snarled at her. "You'll bring the devil and all of hell down on us! Can't you be quiet?" Marta went into a sulk.

I found the ensuing silence disturbing. The cotton fields had been picked over, frost had parched what was left, and a wintry slumber was descending over the rumpled blanket of the hills. We were evidently alone on the road, but I couldn't shake the feeling that someone else was out there with us.

All at once I was frightened by a thunderous sound rising from a thicket down the road, and then I saw spreading across the sky a cloud like a disintegrating rainbow. It was a flock of the most unusual birds, sparkling in the late sun like the points of color I had seen in Mary Cassatt's painting.

"Buttons!" Marta cried, throwing her arms wide. "Buttons!" James poked his head up from his quilts and smiled cautiously at the heavens.

"Buntings," Sister Carolina corrected Marta. "Painted buntings moving south for the winter." I had never seen such birds. They did look painted—even splashed—with streaks of red, blue, and gold as they flowed like a river of flowers through the air.

"It's a sign. A good sign," Marta dared a shout and then fell silent again.

But to Joe Harris it was a sign that something had startled the birds out of the woods ahead of us. He grasped my forearm and held it tight, pushing James down again and covering him with his other hand. "I'd hoped . . . I'd hoped . . ." he repeated over and over.

"What did you hope?" I whispered.

"That they w . . . wouldn't come after us. The Klan."

"I thought the Klan operated only at night?"

"They operate when they p-please," murmured Harris.

Soon we arrived at the ravine where the stream of red mud crossed the road, and again the horse stopped to lick at the water. When the Klansmen came upon us, their approach was so silent I wasn't even startled.

We were surrounded.

Three men, clearly the leaders, sat astride their horses in identical long white robes trimmed with a scarlet cross that shimmered in the afternoon sun. Each wore a horned hood with holes for the eyes and mouth, edged with red like circles of blood, and each carried a sleek carbine in one hand. One of the horsemen had only one arm. A dozen or so others were afoot, draped with dirty robes of all kinds—calico, burlap, old bedsheets—and their heads covered in flour sacks perforated with long holes that made their eyes look as though they were melting.

And we were absolutely in their power. I cursed myself for a fool—I realized I had blundered blindly into this predicament. Holmes would never have allowed it to happen.

The one-armed horseman cantered up to me. "You was warned, you Irish pot-licker."

"I have no idea what you mean," I replied. "And I'm not Irish, I'm an Englishman."

"You was warned to let things lie. And we give only *one* warning."

"Again, you have the advantage. I know nothing about any warning, nor do I know what you are talking about."

"I'm talking about *this*," the ruffian said, pushing the quilt away from James's terrified face with the end of his carbine. "As you well know."

I decided not to give these men the satisfaction of showing the very real fear that I felt. "We are escorting James to the city, where he can receive a fair hearing."

"Where he can get justice. Proper justice." Sister Carolina cut in. "I want to see him hang just as you all do." I thought the tone of her plea rather passive, as if the means to achieving her goal mattered far less than the end.

"He's gonna get justice right here, ma'am," he snarled. "And we'll do it proper, you can be sure."

"How is that possible?" I interjected. "Where is the law? What is the charge? Where are the judge and jury, prosecution and defense, and the presentation of evidence?"

At this, a second horseman lumbered toward us. When he spoke, he sounded unexpectedly literate: "We believe that the administration of justice is best left to popular opinion. *Vox populi, vox dei.*"

I appealed to him. "And you pretend to be the voice of the people? Isn't that wildly presumptuous on your part?"

"You presume to absolve or condemn in the name of God, don't you, Father? Isn't that just a little presumptuous as well?"

Joe Harris had at last mustered his voice. "I . . . I represent the Atlanta C-*Constitution*. If you lynch this man, we-we'll publish the at-atrocity from coast to coast."

"From c-c-c-coast to c-c-c-coast," One-Arm mocked Harris. "You'll stay quiet enough, you stammerin' little scalawag. You got a wife and daughters to think about. And your noosepaper ain't so stupid as that. Did you hear that boys, I said 'noosepaper!'"

There was a good deal of haw-hawing.

It was a nightmare. I struggled with my fear and tried to focus my mind on what Holmes would do. He would be alert for opportunities to escape or at least to persuade. He would be attentive to every detail of their dress, manner, and speech. If I get out of this alive, I thought, at least I want to be able to identify these ruffians in some future court of law.

The third horseman was getting impatient. "Let's get on with this. Make these men fast to those bitts over there."

A half dozen louts descended on Harris and me, forced us to the ground, and tied us to a pair of dead tree trunks. I have always had a horror of being constrained, and I clamped my teeth shut to control myself. I tried to concentrate my mind on details about the three leaders.

Of course, One-Arm I felt I could easily recognize again: his tongue bespoke homemade liquor and the backwoods. The literate man controlled his horse with a certain flair and wore elaborate spurs on his boots. The third man used nautical language—"make fast" instead of tie, "bitt" instead of tree trunk. He must be a sailor or an officer of a ship.

They tied Sister and Marta more lightly, leaving them on the wagon, while they literally threw James to the ground and roped him up head to foot.

Again I cried, "This is an outrage! That man is innocent." I must have been in a self-sacrificing mood. "I know who killed the Tarletons, and he is not here."

"*You* know? *You know?*" One-Arm snarled at me. "Them that knows too much sleeps under the ash-hopper. Gag them two." Cotton rags were rammed into our mouths.

The literate one dismounted and stood towering over me. He spoke calmly. "That black soulless beast is going to pay the price for that crime, just like the scapegoat paid for the sins of the old Jews in the Bible. He is the one for Azazel. And then it will all be expiated. You're a priest, you should understand expiation."

I understood the reference to the scapegoat that was sacrificed to pay for the sins of Israel, and that this man was cruelly distorting the Bible. I wanted to inform this calm villain that *he* was Azazel, the devil himself, but the gag prevented me.

Instead I memorized details of his hands and feet. The most striking detail was his spurs—though they were muddy and scratched, I suspected they were made of gold, or at least gold-plated. The rowels were intricately made; instead of six or eight rough barbs, dozens of finely etched points radiated from each.

I had seen them before—only hours before. This man was one of the Beaufort brothers, probably Tom, who had asked me if I were a "Jezzawit."

"You have opened Pandora's box, Reverend," he said quietly, "but by our sacrificial rites, we will close it again. For good." He walked away.

Taking draughts from a bottle, building a bonfire, kicking twigs into it, the ghouls—as the Klansmen called themselves—seemed in no hurry to carry out their awful sacrament. The sun went down early and the humid cold went right to my bones as darkness gripped the pine grove. I could smell the pitch in the burning wood and wondered if I would live to see morning.

Well, a Jesuit is made for martyrdom, I thought, and there are worse ways to end a life than in trying to save one.

Chapter 20

"If this ain't the thunderinest dreary place," one of the lesser ghouls complained. It was true. In the creek bottom among these naked pines, the winter night grew intense. Lying in the dirt, poor, frozen James had ceased struggling against his bonds. The leaders, crouched round the bonfire with their men, were waiting for something, I didn't know what.

"I wished I was a button!" came a shriek from the wagon. It was Marta. She had spent several fruitless hours denouncing our captors, but we hadn't heard her noisy trill for a while.

"I wished I was a button! I could fly away from here." She sounded a bit strange, her voice strangled.

"Quiet her down," One-Arm barked from his perch near the fire.

"We'll quiet her down," one of the ghouls said. "We'll just take her over into them bushes and teach her how to stay quiet."

Under my gag I roared my protest. Rather than sit by and watch them take advantage of that poor girl, I was ready to die that instant. If I couldn't speak, I would roar, and I refused to stop roaring even as they slapped me repeatedly.

"She's right skinny," one ghoul looked skeptically down in the wagon. Another one grabbed her and picked her up.

"She's fevered," he said. Then I heard the sounds of vomiting and choking, and the man dropped her.

One-Arm pulled my gag out and lifted me by my belt to my feet. "Englishman! Come over here and take a look. What's got into this gal?"

Marta lay there restless in the wagon bed, delirious, her face inflamed and almost dried up with fever. An opportunity glimmered in my head.

"It's variola," I pronounced.

"Smallpox," breathed Tom Beaufort.

"We've been with her all day," I said mournfully. "That means we've all been exposed. Before this night is over, we'll all be lying here gasping out our last."

This alarmed the men who were now crowding round the wagon. I didn't reveal that I at least had been vaccinated, and in any case had no idea what was wrong with Marta.

"What can we do?" a guard asked.

"We burn the ship and row away from her fast," said the nautical horseman, who was already creeping away on his bowed legs.

"Now *you* have opened Pandora's box," I said with a side glance at Tom Beaufort. "There's no closing it now. The thing to do is to get to a doctor straightaway—if you want to save yourselves."

"Hold on," said One-Arm, who had lighted a torch and lifted it over the girl. "This ain't the smallpox. I seen the smallpox before, and this ain't it." He examined her more closely. "She's most likely got the other kind of pox. You boys are welcome to her if you want to get it, too," he snorted with laughter, and the men dispersed. My feint had failed.

One-Arm marched me back to my frozen log and tied me down again. Harris was chilled to the point of convulsions. One-Arm prodded me with his foot. "You're sly, Mr. English Man. Sly like a fox. But you ain't the only sly one in the woods."

"You're a bigot and a bully," I replied. "And you're about to become a murderer."

"*About* to? *About* to? Mister, you have no idea how many of them tar-faced barracoons I've left in the mud."

I simply stared at him. With his steepled hood, he bore an unsettling resemblance to the *penitentes* of Rome.

"You think I'm prejudice, don't you," he said. "You think I'm prejudice against the coloreds. Let me tell you, I've done more for the coloreds than any man. I've filled a whole nation with mulatto babies, and they'll grow up and marry each other, and purty soon they'll be cart-loads of quadroons. Eventually I reckon the tar will breed out of 'em, and they'll all thank me."

"You are indeed proof of Mr. Darwin's theory. In more than one way."

He ignored that. "But I ain't particular. White women does just as well for me. All created equal." He waltzed to the wagon and held up Sister Carolina's nodding chin with the end of his carbine.

"Get down," he commanded.

Sister Carolina clambered off the wagon seat, her hands tied behind her, her face as immobile as ice. One-Arm held his torch up to examine her features.

"Walk."

She looked at him, confused.

"Just walk."

She took a few slow steps forward.

"She looks well. She walks good. Let's see how she kisses."

"Swine!" It was Harris, who had managed to spit out his gag. He was in a frenzy of trembling now, and not just with cold. "F-Filth! Leave her . . . be!"

Harris's shouts alarmed the other two leaders, who turned from the bonfire. "What's going on?"

I spoke up plainly. "Your associate here intends to violate this holy sister."

One-Arm took his hands off her as Tom Beaufort and the seaman glared at him. They accompanied her back to the wagon and lifted her into her seat. Then the seaman took an oversized silver watch from his saddlebag.

"Almost eight bells. Near midnight," he said to the others. "It's time."

"May I know your intentions?" I asked, putting on my most defiant tone (which wasn't very convincing even to my ears).

Tom Beaufort answered. "Our intentions, sir, are to do justice to this tar man. Then we will release that pathetic scribbler to return to his family. His concern for them will ensure his silence. Oh, he may write about us just to quieten his conscience, but in such cloaked words that no one will ever discern his meaning."

"And the women?"

"The nun will say nothing. She wants to see a hanging tonight. As for that muddy stick in the wagon, she'll likely be dead by morning."

"What about this English Man?" One-Arm asked, scowling at me.

"That . . . will require some thought."

"Yes, Colonel Tom Beaufort," I said, facing his masked eyes. "I expect it will."

"He knows your name, Cyclops!" One-Arm shouted. "How does he know your name?"

"At this point it matters very little. He's a Jezza-wit. He knows what a martyr is." Beaufort turned from me.

"Beaufort! If you're going to release Harris and the women, let them go now," I called after him. "The girl needs a doctor. There's no reason to keep them here and subject them to any more of this outrage."

This was ignored. The three leaders climbed onto a fallen log and called their men to form a circle round us. In the dull blaze of the bonfire, they looked like a horrible circus of ghosts. Quietly, they began to chant."

"Yah Oh Ee Ay Oh, Yah Oh Ee Ay Oh, Yah Oh Ee Ay Oh . . . ." they repeated, louder each time until it was a raucous shout.

Then Beaufort called for silence and chanted alone.

> "Shadowed Brotherhood! Murdered heroes!
> Fling off the bloody dirt that covers you to the four winds.
> Prepare Charon for his task! Row back across Styx! Mark well your foes!
> The keyword is Revenge! Revenge! Revenge!"

At this signal, James was raised to his feet and a noose was put round his neck. Each ruffian came forward to beat the poor man, slapping him, spitting on him, and jabbing him with the butts of their guns, as if to lay on him the whole burden of their own shattering defeat in the great war.

Harris and I turned away from this horrid spectacle. And then I looked at Sister—she gazed on the scene almost without interest, impassive, remote, the face of Lady Justice, as she supposed.

I was sickened. I let out a howl of rage, "Stop this! Stop at once!"

But it went on until the last brave ghoul in the circle had a go at the defenseless James.

Beaufort called for calm, then paused.

> "By my order as the Great Cyclops, bring forward the tar and the turpentine,
> Boil and bubble like a hell broth,
> Rain brimstone on him."

Some of the ghosts brought a small cauldron that had been heating on the fire. They poured the contents over James, who awoke and shrieked with pain.

> "We mighty goblins in the Kuklux of Hell-a-balloo assembled,
> Offended ghosts,
> Condemn this creature to the gibbet for the blood of the Lost Cause!
> FLECTERE SI NEQUEO SUPEROS,
> ACHERONTA MOVEBO!"

With this flourish of Latin trumpery, Beaufort gave the signal to hang poor James. I closed my eyes in impotent anger, murmuring the prayer for the dying: *Profiscere anima christiana de hoc mundo in nomine Dei Patris . . .*

But all went silent.

When I opened my eyes again, the whole company of ghouls stood as if frozen to the ground. Then I heard a loud voice behind me.

"STOP!"

I had never laid eyes on such an apparition. Amongst the dark pines, on a great red horse sat a giant figure enwrapped in the robes of the Klan, his hood towering into the branches of the trees. His shoulders were immense and his hands monstrous white bones.

But most horribly, both horse and man glowed like the devil's own fire.

"IN THE NAME OF THE GREAT GRAND WIZARD!" his voice was a peal of brass. "I CLAIM THE PRISONER FOR MYSELF!"

The flaming red horse charged a few steps forward, and the ghouls fell back.

"RELEASE HIM TO ME AND BE GONE!"

Two ghouls started hastily to untie James, but One-Arm roared back. "Whoever you be, this ain't your Den. I'm the Night Hawk here, and yonder's the Grand Cyclops, and we ain't never heard of you before."

"AND I AM THE HYDRA OF THE GRAND WIZARD. RELEASE HIM!" Then the apparition's head slowly rose from his neck until the hood blazed among the trees like a tongue of unearthly fire. The ghouls began to whimper.

"Stand your ground!" One-Arm shouted to his men.

The monster then raised his sleeve and brought it down like a swordstroke: his spidery hand flew through the air, catching One-Arm full in the throat and knocking him to the ground.

At this, the ghouls scattered screaming through the trees. The two remaining leaders jumped onto their horses and were gone, leaving us alone in the firelight with the mounted monster and One-Arm, groaning on his back in the dirt.

The burning apparition on the red horse drew near to One-Arm, who was grasping at his throat, and looked down at him.

"Who . . . who are you really?" One-Arm pleaded.

The answer came in a clenched whisper: "I . . . AM . . . *AZAZEL!*"

With a frightened gurgle, One-Arm got to his feet and ran off into the darkness shouting for his horse, which had long since fled.

"Right," said the horseman, pulling off his flaming regalia. "Now hurry. We must get to town straightaway."

It was Holmes.

Chapter 21

That night is a blister in my memory—a freezing, burning, black night.

Holmes took the reins and the wagon plunged into the winter wilderness at great speed. The bay and the red horse, now tethered to the wagon, raced each other nearly out of control. Mercifully, they seemed to feel the road ahead, although I had no doubt that Holmes was sure of the way.

As we dashed up and down hills, I felt as though I were again being flung about on the black waves of the sea. Harris and I lay low in the wagon bed giving what little comfort we could to Marta and James and watching for pursuers. We saw nothing.

While Marta groaned loudly, I heard no sound at all from James. I feared for his life, but as I held tight to the poor man to keep him from bouncing off the bed, I could tell from his powerful muscles that there was great stamina in him. I prayed for him—what else could I do?

At last the glow of gaslight from Atlanta came into view, and I felt I could breathe again. Harris directed Holmes to the city jail, a castle-like building made of rock, where we pounded at the gate and delivered James to the infirmary. Harris's explanations appeared to satisfy the keepers. James was safe for now.

By the time we deposited Sister at her family home, Marta felt better. Her groaning grew even louder, which we decided was a good sign, and she was able to walk on her own to the back of the house. Harris went home; then I entreated Holmes to come to the rectory with me, but he wouldn't hear of it—we were both to retire to a clapboard hotel in the warren of the railroad district.

"Those blackguards will go to the rectory first if they decide to look for you," he said. "My hotel, being more obscure, will provide a measure of safety." The place was decidedly seedy, but there was a bed and an armchair that looked like a mass of threads with no frame to hold it together.

I had built up a good deal of resentment at Holmes for thrusting me alone into these dangerous circumstances, but my joy and relief at seeing him again overcame it all; and when we were at last in private, I involuntarily embraced him.

He stiffened and smoothly pushed me aside.

"It's just that I'm so glad to see you, Holmes . . . and grateful." The thought of our near escape made me weak in the stomach.

"As well you should be. Your judgment has been utterly appalling, Tuck. Knowing as you do the nature of the Klan, and the fact that you are in their sights, I'm astonished that you would put yourself and others in such an indefensible position."

"I know. I've cursed myself over and over. But . . . how is it you are here? And how the devil did you manage that spectacle tonight? I confess I was as frightened as those ruffians were."

Holmes shrugged. "Sulphur and zinc powder, mixed with a little copper dust," he pointed at a washbowl filled with a glittering substance that looked like sand. "An old chemist's trick. Sprinkled on my *penitente's* robes, it becomes luminous in firelight. Together with my black walking stick to raise my hood into the trees, some beef bones from the butcher to serve as my projectile hands, and I become a howling phantom to the eye of the superstitious."

"How you astound me, Holmes."

"Child's play. *Omne ignotum pro magnifico*, as our Latin tutor would say."

"'To the ignorant, everything unknown appears miraculous.' But I thought you were in London—I've been writing to you there! When did you cross over?"

"How you underestimate me, Tuck. As before, you haven't been out of my sight for a moment since we parted at the Liverpool docks."

"You were aboard the Nebraska?"

"Of course. I'm gratified, though not surprised, that you weren't able to see through that brilliant Norwegian violinist, Sigerson." A transitory smile crossed his lips.

"That was you? But you said . . ."

"I know. I said I was going back to London, but then I became aware of a startling development—Moriarty himself, or rather Adam Worth, had booked passage aboard the Nebraska, and suddenly there was no reason to stay in England. Having found him, I determined to unravel what he was up to."

"So it was you who you passed me the cipher warning me that Adam Worth was aboard. I came to suspect that Adam Verver was Worth. The wealthy American with the beautiful wife? Holmes, is it he?"

"A logical suspicion," Holmes nodded. "Verver is pure economic man, who sees the acquisition of a beautiful wife as essentially no different from the acquisition of, say, an exquisite Persian carpet. In this he is similar to our Moriarty, but men of his mentality acquire power in order to shape the law in their favor rather than to violate it."

"If Verver is not Adam Worth, then who is it? Why didn't you take me into your confidence on the ship?"

"I couldn't risk being seen with you and recognized. Your ignorance was much more useful to me in any case. Knowing your social nature, I counted on you to mingle with the passengers and write to me your findings; when the purser collected your missives, he brought them straight to me. I had an arrangement with him. As it was, I believe Worth suspected Sigerson all along. He nearly killed me on the deck the night of the storm . . . ."

"I thought I saw Sigerson—you—wrestling with . . . .Raymond!" At once all was clear. "Henry J. Raymond is Adam Worth!"

"Precisely."

"But I thought Henry J. Raymond was the editor of the New York Times."

Holmes laughed. "The editor of the Times was one Henry B. Raymond, a very influential figure indeed—when he was living. He died years ago. Our master criminal delights in slanting the truth ever so little, just enough to establish himself in the eyes of his dupes but not enough to invite scrutiny. I'm sure he never actually admitted to being the editor of the Times."

"No, as I think of it now, he didn't."

"He likes to leave a small door of escape—sometimes as small as a single initial or a transposed letter. No, he is no journalist. When directly queried, Henry J. Raymond represents himself to be a financier, and so he is. He finances most of the criminal activity in Britain and on the Continent and earns a healthy return from it. Like any wise investor, he has his hand in diverse enterprises—bank robbery, prostitution, the theft of jewelry and art, the occasional assassination. . . ."

"And the theater!" I broke in. "He seemed to be recruiting theatrical types. . . ."

"Yes, the two young performers. The demimonde of the theater provides our Moriarty with endless illegitimate profits as well as entertainment."

"Mrs. Wells did say he was a sort of 'impresario.' And he recruited that counterfeit clergyman Shlessinger with his magic lantern, who in my mind was another candidate for Adam Worth."

Holmes was amused. "Ah, your instinct there was not far wrong. That rascal with the mangled ear is well known to me. His real name is Peters—in the confidence trade he is called 'Holy' Peters. A crude type, he lacks the mental acuity of an Adam Worth, but together with his vicious wife he preys successfully upon lonely ladies who suffer from a surfeit of religion and money. Worth will no doubt find him valuable. I was in no position to foil Peters on the ship, but no doubt we will cross paths again. "

"I gathered as much. But I thought Adam Worth's operation was in London. What brings him to this side of the Atlantic?"

"That is what I intend to find out, and why I followed you instead of him. We left him at Philadelphia, but the game will be played out here in Atlanta, I'm convinced of it."

"I cannot imagine what that game consists of."

"Imagination does not enter into it. Facts, Tuck, facts. We now have two cryptograms that involve both you and Adam Worth. The original cryptogram by itself would be enough to justify a full investigation, but this second puzzle—the one delivered to you by Mrs. Wells—raises the stakes infinitely."

"Have you made anything of it, Holmes? I have cudgeled my brains over it every waking hour, yet I confess to being completely baffled."

Holmes pulled the document out of a carpetbag and smoothed it out. "Here is your document, which you gave to the purser on the Nebraska and which he in turn delivered to me. It has been carefully drafted on a type and size of stationery I have not seen in Europe—it is possibly American, as it is made of wood pulp. Someone has traced over it—presumably yourself—to make a copy; however, I believe the document itself is also a copy of an original. The diagram consists of a 36-point wheel imposed upon a spiral, in turn imposed upon a step pyramid, to which is appended a table of figures."

He was silent for a moment.

"Do you see anything in it?"

Reaching again into the carpetbag, he removed the small leather box he had received from the Pope in Rome and opened it.

"Examine it carefully, Tuck." There on its bed of velvet was the jewel of the Order of the Golden Spur. I kneaded my tired eyes and tried to focus on it. A cross of ivory. Rays of gold. A carving of a cavalier's spur. I saw nothing I hadn't seen before.

"The rowel, Tuck. Count the barbs on the rowel."

I looked perplexed at him. The tiny golden circle was far too small to see clearly. Annoyed, Holmes handed me his smudged magnifying glass. "Look!"

Laboriously, trying to stay awake, I counted. There were thirty-six points on the rowel. A coincidence?

"Not a coincidence," Holmes said, as if reading my mind. "You'll remember that Adam Worth—otherwise known as Henry J. Raymond—wore the Order of the Golden Spur round his neck, as did his associate, known to you as Count Schindler. Clearly, the symbol has great significance for Worth and his gang."

And then it struck me in my torpor like a blast from a gun. The jangling boots of the brothers Beaufort. The erudite Klansman and his beautifully tooled spurs. The intricate golden rowel . . .

"You see it, don't you?" Holmes's smile could not have been wider. "The two curious characters you encountered today wear the golden spurs openly, and one of them—the younger of the two—followed you into the arena of death this very night."

"Their name is Beaufort—Abraham and Thomas Beaufort. They profess to be horse dealers from Kentucky."

"So I gather. Unfortunately I was not privy to your conversation at the plantation house."

I recounted my exchange with Tom Beaufort and his strange mixture of erudition and prejudice.

"He cried out in Latin tonight. Did you understand what he said?" Holmes asked.

"*Flectere nequeo* something or other. I think I have heard it before, but I could not place it."

"Perhaps you can trace its meaning. In the morning," Holmes said, noting my obvious fatigue. "The golden spur is one key to the cipher delivered to you by Mrs. Wells. The other key is the underlying pyramid. We must have both keys if we are to make sense of this." He scowled as he examined the paper once again in the light of a fading candle.

As if the shades of the room were going down, darkness enfolded me, and in my exhaustion I realized that I was only beginning to glimpse the true extent of this arena of death into which I had stumbled.

"This game is deeply dangerous, Holmes," I said wearily.

"For me, it is life, Tuck. Give me the most abstruse cryptogram. Give me the most grotesque puzzle, add to it the danger of losing all, and I am in my own proper atmosphere."

"I am not in mine!" I spoke more abruptly than I intended. "I followed your instructions to the letter. I posted an advertisement in the newspapers just as you asked, in the very words you gave me. You assured me that the Tarleton murders would then be solved and the entire affair *safely* concluded."

Holmes sniffed at this. "*I* did not instruct you to ride into the wolves' lair and attempt to smuggle away their prey from under their noses. That was your choice."

"I had no choice. I could not stand by while a mob executed an innocent man for a crime he did not commit."

"Of course not," he responded quietly. "Still, I should have approached the matter differently. It is of no consequence now. And I do apologize for showing such relish over this case. Most of the affairs I deal with are important but not particularly interesting; indeed, I have found that importance often saps the charm from an investigation. But here in Atlanta we are presented with a matter that is of both the highest interest and, if I am not mistaken, the utmost importance."

"In what respect?"

"It concerns nothing less than the future of the American Union."

Chapter 22

Although I was mightily intrigued, consideration of the future of the Union exhausted me. I couldn't begin to focus on so large a subject and fell asleep in Holmes's thready armchair.

Well into the next morning, I woke up choking. The room was so flooded with smoke that I thought it was on fire, but it was only Holmes buried in a mountain of blankets fuming away at his pipe and gazing at Mrs. Wells's cryptogram. Someone was hammering on the door.

"It's . . . it's Joe Harris!"

I leapt up and ushered the fellow in. "What is it?"

His red face burning from the cold and excitement, Harris could barely speak.

"Well?" Holmes shouted at him.

"Let him calm himself for a moment." I snatched up some cold tea and gave it to him; he swallowed, grimaced, and rapidly penciled his message on a piece of paper.

"'Klan on way to jail to take James. Help please!'" I read.

Holmes threw off his blankets and pulled on his boots. "No time to lose, Tuck."

Thankfully, Harris had brought a carriage, and the big rock jail was only minutes away. At our arrival, I noticed with dread three road-worn horses tied to the gatepost. While Harris and I made for the gate, Holmes hung back.

"Holmes! Through here!" I called.

"Go ahead. I'll be with you straightaway." He was standing on the pavement, looking over the neighborhood and the mournful old jail.

I followed Harris through the gates and into a bluish rock corridor, up several flights of stairs and into the jail keeper's office. Large and littered, the office reminded me of the donjon tower of an old English castle. Piles of rusty paper, empty, corroded bottles, and all sorts of ominous ironmongery encumbered every surface. A spittoon leaked into the floorboards. The place smelled of wood rot and chamber pots. In the midst of this grandeur a ponderous gent of about sixty sat munching on a doughnut and dribbling crumbs into a beard that looked like a giant, meat-stained ball of cotton. Behind him sat two men as big as bulls and at his feet a red-nosed dog that I could swear was breathing fire.

The bearded jail keeper was interviewing three men who were coated with road dust, one of whom, I noticed with alarm, was missing an arm.

The jail keeper's jolly laugh greeted Harris and me. "Ah! We *must* be near Christmas! Here are the three wise men already, and now the shepherd joins them!" He pointed at my collar. "Well, I hope you've all come bearing gifts."

Harris tried to introduce me. "Reverend Grosjean, this . . . this is Mr. Frost, the super . . . super . . ."

"Superintendent of the Atlanta Jail!" the bearded one interrupted. "Mr. Harris of the Atlanta *Constitution*, with his verbal idiosyncrasies, is well known to me. But I have not made *your* acquaintance before, reverend suh. Doughnut?"

He held up a huge tray of greasy pastry. "Mother of one of our inmates sends up a load of these buttermilk doughnuts, and in return we make sure her son gets to keep the rest of his teeth, poor boy. Now how can I help you?"

Appalled, I demurred. "I am here in regard to one of your prisoners, Mr. James King, who was brought to your infirmary last night after being savagely beaten . . ."

"Yes, yes. Well, suh, this is a remarkable coincidence indeed, for these gentlemen are here on the same errand."

"Are you going to give him to us, Frost?" The one-armed man spoke and I instantly recognized his vulpine voice as belonging to the ruffian who had kidnapped us the night before. In daylight, he was a skinny, evil-looking fellow with a sparse red beard. Dandling rifles, two other toughs stood with him; neither of them was Thomas Beaufort. Though truly tempted, I decided it was the better part of valor not to confront them there and then.

"Now, Wash, I know this is the season of givin'," but there's givin' and then there's gettin.' Let's hear out this reverend gentleman fuhst."

I looked round for Holmes, but as usual he had disappeared again. So I ignored One-Arm and spoke directly to Frost.

"James King has been accused of murder in the case of the Tarleton brothers, as you are no doubt aware. In accord with our civic duty, Mr. Harris and I convinced him to turn himself in to the representatives of the law here in Atlanta. We were on our way to the county sheriff's when we were waylaid by a gang of hooded ruffians who mercilessly beat James and tried to hang him."

Beneath his pile of beard, Frost was grinning—I could tell.

I went on. "Fortunately, the mob was frightened away and we brought him here. Now we wish to ensure that James receives his rights under the law and remains safely in your custody until the sheriff is notified."

"The sheriff has been notified, Reverend suh," Frost said, then chuckled and turned to One-Arm. "Not quite the story you told me, Wash. *Frightened away*, he says."

"It's all lawful," the man called Wash protested. "We're deputies of Sheriff Wallop and he wants his priz'ner back. Are you going to give him up or not?"

I blustered in. "These are men are deputies? Where are their credentials, their papers, their badges?"

Frost ignored me for the moment. "Sheriff Wallop, you say? You know right well that Wallop and the Fulton County sheriff's department don't quite see eye to eye on most things. I'm thinking there could be quite a process here, quite a legal process involved. And that process could be right costly for Sheriff Wallop . . . and his deputies."

One of Wash's men noisily cocked his rifle. The dog showed his fangs, and the two bull-like creatures behind Frost stood up on heavy legs and glowered at the rifleman.

"It's all right," Frost said to his men, then turned back to me. "I must apologize. I have neglected to introduce to you my assistants, Reverend suh. This is Julius and this is Hannibal. I raised 'em from calves. Don't snort much, but they can do a powerful head butt."

The rifleman lowered his weapon and looked away.

"As I was sayin'," Wash, that process of, um, extramaditin' costs a good deal of money. So you just go back and tell Wallop that and see what his treasury can tolerate with regard to this point o' law."

"I can bring a good many more deputies to this place in the wink of an eye, Frost, and you know what I mean."

Frost hesitated. "Yes, Wash, I do. But I'm afeard that the Fulton County Sheriff's department has already made its disposition in regard to James King. Even though he's beat blue, he's a valuable commodity, and when he's standin' again, he'll be shipped off to Dade to work in the mines. We don't consider it morally defensible for a man to sit in a cell all day and get his cornbread and beans on the county without givin' back in the form of honest labor."

I was stunned. "That sounds like a sentence! James hasn't even had a trial yet, much less a conviction."

"Oooooh," Frost intoned. "I understand there *has* been a trial, and a mighty fair one at that. Ain't that so, Wash?"

"There has. But no execution!"

"Execution don't pay the bottler, as my old daddy used to say. And we use up a lot of bottles 'round here, right, Julius? Hannibal?" The two giants rumbled their assent. Frost cocked his head to one side. "Why do you want him so bad, anyways, Wash? How this colored boy any diff'ent from any other colored boy?"

"He killed the Tarleton boys."

"That has yet to be proven in an *actual* trial!" I protested. "Not a mockery of a trial at midnight in the woods. I know for myself that it is a baseless charge."

One-armed Wash looked at me with hatred. To this point he had avoided my eyes; now I stared him down as best I could.

"Gotta be more to it than that," Frost jeered through his pillow of a beard, ignoring me. Evidently, the shrewd old man could smell unexpected profits lurking in the woods. "Tarletons been dead fifteen years. Why all this commotion now?"

"Makes no diff'ence," One-Arm was getting heated, and the rifles came up. "You won't give him up, we take him. Now!"

At that instant, Holmes entered the room. Coatless, bent over like an old man, he was in his shirt sleeves and wearing the green baize visor of a clerk. He spoke with a whistling Georgia accent. "Mr. Harris! Y'all are wanted at the office."

Harris gave Holmes an astounded glance, but immediately understood the game. "Mr. Grady himself asked for you."

"If Mr. Henry W. Grady of the Atlanta *Constitution* summoned me, I would go," said Frost with a chuckle.

As if catching sight of the guns for the first time, Holmes began to tremble. "What . . . what's going on here?" he quavered. "Why the armaments?"

I answered him, glaring with as much meaning as I could into his eyes. "These three men are about to kidnap an inmate at gunpoint. A colored man named James King."

"A colored man, looks like he wuz beaten up?" Holmes croaked. "He just went out the front gate on his way down Butler Street."

"He's escaped?" Frost fought to get to his feet.

Everyone sprang for the door at once. The three Klansmen screeched curses as they clattered down the stairs with Frost, his dog, and his two giants close behind. We heard the crashing of cell doors as they verified that James was gone, and then angry yelps and shrieking horses in the courtyard below.

Holmes sneered, straightening up and pulling off the visor.

"What has happened?" I whispered too loudly. "What have you done? Where is James? Shouldn't we pursue them?"

"A childish game," Holmes answered with contempt. "I deduced what was going on here, so I lagged behind, found my way to the infirmary, and informed the guard that I was a plainclothes officer from the city police here to take James to his arraignment. The fool believed me. I helped James outside to our wagon, covered him with my coat and hat, and gave him my key and instructions to drive to my hotel. He's well away from here by now, driving west toward the depot while our fatuous friends are riding hell-bent toward the south."

"And the visor you wear?"

"Borrowed from a clerk at the bank next door. We must hurry—I'm afraid James was just able to stand when I put him in the wagon. I want to talk to him before he dies."

"Do you think he is as badly off as that?" I asked.

"I don't know. I only wish you were a medical man so you could be of some use. Whether he lives or dies, we must talk to him as soon as possible."

We three leapt on a horse-car that appeared to be propelled by an old mule, but soon realized we could walk the length of Decatur Street much faster than the counterfeit horse could pull the car. Harris and I struggled to keep up with Holmes, whose weightless stride made me feel as though I had anvils locked to my legs.

Fortunately, Holmes's hotel was run by a clerk who was so blind he could not have distinguished a half-dead black man wearing Holmes's coat and hat from Holmes himself. When we arrived, James had managed to pull himself up the stairs to the bedsit, where he collapsed snoring.

"Let him sleep," I insisted, as Holmes prepared to wake him.

"Very well. You," he pointed at Harris, "Go find him some nourishment. Tea. Hot."

Without a word, Harris obeyed, and Holmes and I were left alone with the shivering man on the bed. Holmes did not take his eyes off him.

"Why are you so anxious to speak with him?" I asked.

"Isn't it obvious? Why are all these villains so concentrated on eliminating this one hapless Negro? Why cast him as the scapegoat? Why go to the trouble of bringing in night riders from another state to kill him?"

I shook my head.

"Because he is the only witness to the Tarleton murders."

Chapter 23

When Harris returned with tea and bread, we consumed it like animals and I got some of the hot liquid into James. The poor man's head was blistered from pine tar, much of which still adhered to his skin. His beaten face bloated the color of iridescent flint, he could hardly speak—he merely groaned a few quiet words of thanks and then slipped back into a swoon.

After breakfast Harris returned to his office. Feeling the need to bathe and change out of my filthy cassock, I decided to go back to the rectory and then ascertain how Sister and her servant were getting along. I told Holmes of my intention.

"When you see Sister, ask her why she betrayed us."

"What do you mean?"

"Only she could have communicated to the Klansmen the whereabouts of James. We have her to thank for our encounter of this morning."

"You think she . . . ?"

"I'm sure of it. Of course, I already know what her answer will be. She is determined to see James hang for the murder of her friends."

Holmes was no doubt right. I promised to return later and spent the forenoon as planned. At Sister's house I was told she was sleeping and could not be disturbed, while I found the servant Marta completely recovered and frolicking about in the mews at the side of the big gray-stone mansion. She went on and on about the dozen or so well-kept horses who were her best friends.

Then without notice she turned to me.

"Oh, Pastor," she said, "last night I had the most horriblest dream about big red spots on my eyes and the Klan comin' to get me and then a giant burnin' ghost of a Klansman flyin' through the dark. . . ."

"You know it was not a dream, Marta."

She stopped me and went quiet. "I knows, but my mamma so skeered I can't tell her it weren't no dream, and I was so sick 'n all. . . ."

"I understand."

She changed the subject at once. "They's beauties, ain't they?" nattering again about the horses. "You want one to use? I can ask missus if you can borrow one."

Tired of walking the streets of Atlanta, I took up the suggestion and received permission from the family, who were loyal Catholics. I chose a lovely chestnut mare. Bathed and refreshed, I felt a vibration of contentment cantering through the streets in the clear cold and was reminded of gallops in the lake country when I was a schoolboy.

At the telegraph office, I followed Holmes's instruction and sent off a wire to my former Latin tutor, a model of erudition who was now a curate at Oxford: "Please advise origin of Latin phrase 'flectere nequeo'. Very urgently required." I knew how to translate the words—the only ones I could recall from Beauchamp's incantation of the previous night—but without the right context they were meaningless: *I cannot divert or deflect.* Divert or deflect what? I put it out of my mind until I could get a response from Oxford.

I bought a pot of mild soup and returned with it to Holmes's bedsit to see how James was coming along. Holmes was exactly where I had left him, sitting hunched over James and watching him sleep. He seemed to be better now—his breathing was more even and his bruises more dull in color. Gently I woke him for a swallow of soup.

Thankfully, James ate until he was satisfied and appeared somewhat invigorated. Then with terror in his eyes, he saw Holmes and sat up in the bed.

"It's all right," I soothed him. "This is a friend, Sherlock Holmes. You might recall he helped you out of the jail this morning."

James nodded and relaxed a bit. "Thank you," he mumbled, "I b'lieved I would never leave that jail."

"It was for your protection at first, but then it became necessary to bring you out." I rehearsed for him the events of the night and morning, which were all a fog to him.

"Why?" he asked hoarsely. "Why they come for me? I ain't never done nothin' to the Talton boys. I worked for 'em. They uz no good, but I never laid a hand on 'em nor never answered back."

"That is precisely what we want to know," Holmes said with precision, his hands in the attitude of prayer. "Why would they come for you? What can you tell us? What happened to the Tarletons at Gettysburg?"

"Holmes," I admonished. "He's still very weak. Perhaps later. . . ."

But James had sunk back into the bed, his voice almost calm as he told the story. "It was a big battle. A big battle. I dragged the luggage for days over them Maryland hills and then we wuz in Pennsylvania. The boys astride them horses in front of me, never looked back at me, never gave a fig for me."

He coughed. I gave him a drink of water and he continued.

"Night before the battle I got up some sheet-iron crackers and some acorn coffee and they cussed at me cuz it was so bad, but there weren't nothin' else to eat. And I was ireful myself, and hungry, too; but I said nothin'. I didn' know the nex' day they'd all be dead, did I? All three of 'em? Just like that. Last I ever saw of 'em. They wuz gone before mornin'."

He paused again to cough and get his breath back.

"They wuz always annoyed with me, but that night extra annoyed, I guess cuz they afraid of what was comin'. And then there was that aggravatin' little bounty jumper, a-wantin' some food."

Holmes twitched and sat up. "Bounty jumper? Who?"

Just then Harris knocked on the door and joined us. His wife had baked us a pie, which I eyed with greed and Holmes with contempt.

"Sit down and be quiet!" he commanded Harris, who looked bewildered at him. "James, you were speaking of a bounty jumper. What is that?"

But James had dropped off again. The effort to speak was tiring him out.

"A b . . . bounty . . ." Harris tried to answer the question. "A bounty j. . . jun . . .jum . . . ."

Holmes turned to him. "Speak up, man. What's the matter with you?"

"He has difficulty," I said. "He stammers when he is disturbed."

"Perhaps he is just stupid," Holmes growled.

I thoroughly lost my temper and leapt to my feet. "Holmes, you cross a line. Harris is an intelligent man, a decent man who has put himself in danger for the sake of another. You, on the other hand, put yourself in danger for the sake of your obsessions—you care nothing for your fellow man. You care nothing for justice, as long as you have a diverting puzzle to solve." I mocked his voice: "'It is the mystery that matters.' Nothing else."

Holmes was quiet. Slowly he narrowed his gaze on Harris, who looked embarrassed by my outburst. "Well, then," Holmes finally said in the calmest of tones, "*mea culpa*, Padre. *Mea culpa*. Mr. Harris, kindly forgive me and please go on with your explanations."

Harris gradually found his voice. "During the war . . . both sides paid a b-bounty for recruits. Thirty doll . . . thirty dollars, I believe. Anyone who joined the army could get . . . get the money. A bounty jum . . . jumper would collect his money and then . . . desert and do it all over again. Hundreds of dollars some people collected this way." Racing his breath to get this far, Harris sighed.

But Holmes was already talking to himself. "Petty treason. What some men will sell their souls for." He extracted a flask from his carpetbag and held it to James's lips: abruptly, our patient sat up breathing fire.

"What the tarnation?!" He choked and wheezed and was wide awake. "What *is* that stuff?"

"Just a stiffener," Holmes smiled. "A bit of London gin. Never had it before?"

"Miz Bea don't hold with much liquor, so what we do get is mighty watered down."

"Well," Holmes reminded him, "you were telling us about a bounty jumper." James took up where he left off as if he had never gone to sleep. Harris began taking notes.

"Taltons wouldn't give this bounty jumper no food, so he cussed at 'em pretty sore."

"What was he like?"

"Little man—shabby, shabby. Tunic all yellow, boots all played out. He tells 'em he's gonna kill 'em, so Master Brent aims his pepperbox at the little creature and he skedaddles like a rabbit down a hole."

Holmes was intrigued. "Did you see this man again?"

"Nope. Went to sleep and never seen him nor Taltons alive never again."

"Do you think the bounty jumper killed the Tarletons?"

"Well, suh, I don't know. He might-a laid for 'em. But later I hears they died in the battle, like everybody say. I don't know nothin' diff'ent. Oh, it was a time, I tell you. The fightin' went on and on and they was dead everywhere. When my masters didn' come back and didn' come back, I swear I didn' know what to do. By and by I calculate to go home, and that's what I did. Soldiers took all the supplies, and I was most famished when I gets home."

James had finished his narrative, and Holmes sat back to contemplate it.

"Yes, suh, I sure was famished." I realized James's eye was on the pie—a very good sign!—so I vaulted up to get him a piece. It was sumptuous and buttery, rich with pecans, and James gobbled it down heartily. I had more than my share, as Holmes refused to touch it.

"And what have you done since the war, James?" Holmes asked, taking only a sip of tea.

"We wuz about destitute after ol' Sherman march through. Not a chicken or a chicken egg lef' behind. If it warn't Billy Yank it wuz Johnny Reb a-stealin' everything in sight. The day they took them horses, I thought Miz Bea would just lie down and die. But she never did, never. . . .

"Me and Miz Bea kep' things together, I guess—there warn't nobody else. I wuz a house worker before, but there's no call for that now—I learn how to grow hay and cotton and I got my own house and fambly, and by and by we wuz raisin' horses again. But it ain' like before." He shook his head.

"But now you're free," I said.

"Free. Yes, suh. I spoze so." He started worrying a tar blister in his hair, so I dipped a cloth in cool water from the washbowl and helped him clean it.

"You have suffered a great many troubles," Holmes said with a sudden catch of breath and gave him another swallow of gin.

James smiled painfully as I rubbed at the bloody wax welded to his temples. "My ol' uncle used to say troubles are seasoning," he reflected. "A persimmon's no good till it's frost-bit."

"A final question, James, and then I shall leave you in peace. Did the Tarletons have any dealings with Colonel or General Beaufort during the war?"

"No suh, far as I know. I didn' see Beaufort brothers for a long time after, when they come 'round to look at the horses." James was alert now and suddenly suspicious. "And now, Mister, mebbe you could answer me a question. Who the devil are you anyways?"

Holmes laughed gently. "My name is Sherlock Holmes. I am a consulting detective."

"A policeman!"

"No, no. I am merely trying to solve the problem of who shot the Tarleton brothers in the back—and why. I am rather persuaded it wasn't you, but it would obviously be to your benefit if I could determine who actually did the deed."

"It warn't me!" James sat up straight, and I nearly pulled his ear off trying to remove the tar.

"As I said, I am rather persuaded it wasn't you, but certainty is rarely a luxury I can permit myself at this stage of an investigation."

"If you so persuaded I didn' do it, then I asks it again—why is everybody comin' down on me for it?"

"I can think of two possibilities." Holmes spoke in his laboratory voice. "First: the true culprit suspects you saw or heard something that might lead to him; therefore, it would be in his interest to shut down any further inquiry by accusing and silencing you. The second possibility is more abstruse: he has a deep psychological need for a scapegoat, someone to blame and to expiate his guilt for him. It would likely be a Southerner with a profound sense of personal honor, a man who is deeply devoted to the pitiful mythology of the 'Lost Cause' and the depravity imputed to the Negro race."

I remonstrated with Holmes, "You might speak in a way that James would understand."

"Now who is evincing a lack of respect?" Holmes turned halfway to me. "I speak to all men in the same way, as all men are mathematically and logically equal to me."

"I never thought to hear you admit that anyone was your equal," I muttered.

"A third . . . a third possibility," Harris said, looking up from his writing, "is the little b-bounty jumper. Maybe he was . . . just mad enough to shoot 'em up."

"Of course that is a possible explanation for the original crime, but how could it enter into the accusations against James?" He stopped abruptly and swung round to face Harris. "Unless . . . ."

"Unless what?" I asked.

"I can't say as yet. It is a capital error . . ."

". . . to theorize before the facts," I interrupted him. "Yes, I know."

"Precisely." Holmes was up and putting on his greatcoat and bowler. "And in the service of the facts, I must go to the telegraph office without delay, and from there to consult the railroad timetables."

"He do come and go," James said, as Harris and I laughed. Harris excused himself to go back to work, while I continued to strip the raw tar off of poor James. Eventually, however, we both fell asleep until evening, when I was awakened by Holmes's return.

He came in, lit a low lamp, and raised his finger to his lips. "Let the poor fellow rest," he said, gesturing at James. "'Sleep that knits up the raveled sleeve of care.'"

"*Macbeth*, Holmes?" I whispered.

"I have done a bit of reading since my benighted school days. Yes, *Macbeth*. The greatest mystery of all, Tuck—the perverseness of the human heart. We saw it working last night at the witching hour in the pine grove." He sat down heavily in the precarious old chair.

"It was an unruly night, with 'lamentings heard in the air and strange screams of death,'" I added. "Holmes, I have been thinking over your observations about the character of the murderer. The need for a scapegoat driven by guilt and shame and defeat, a profoundly offended sense of honor—there are many such men of the South. But from what we have seen, such a description exactly fits one man in particular: Tom Beaufort."

Holmes quietly agreed. "The hood and robes could not conceal him. His malice against James, his evident determination to make the poor man a scapegoat does add up to a strong presumption of guilt. At present I cannot see a motivation for killing the Tarletons, but then we simply don't know enough. That is why I have sent a volley of wires off to various places, including the American War Department. We must understand the story of the brothers Beaufort."

Chapter 24

When I returned to Holmes's hotel the next morning, I was stunned to find him stretched out alone on the bed in his voluminous dressing gown. "Where is James?"

"Gone."

"Gone where?"

"I do not know, nor do I want to know."

"He left of his own will? Was he well enough? What did he say?"

"He thanked me for saving him from 'the vultures,' as he put it, and told me he must be on his way. I understood his point of view—it would be only a matter of time before he is traced here. This city is not so large that our comings and goings are not marked."

"When did he leave?"

"In the night. I expressed some concern about his safety, but he answered me rather obliquely. He said, 'The black snake knows the way to the hidden nest.' Charming how his people cloak their meanings—must be the result of centuries of fearing the slave master. I gather he has found a secure place of concealment."

"I pray so. And I have news. I have been to the telegraph office this morning, where I collected an answer to my wire from our old Latin tutor."

"Excellent." Holmes gestured to a pot of fresh tea and invited me to sit down and read the wire.

"To Reverend S. P. Grosjean, S. J., Church of the Immaculate Conception, Atlanta, etc. Dear Tuck (oh, I wish you hadn't hung that sobriquet on me, Holmes), Delighted to hear from you. No doubt reference cited is to Aeneid Book VII: FLECTERE SI NEQUEO SUPEROS ACHERONTA MOVEBO. Spoken by Juno in protest of Trojan invasion of Italy, which Jupiter had destined should happen. Translation: 'If I cannot turn aside the decree of Heaven, I will move Acheron.' Praying this finds you well, Fr. Gerard Manley Hopkins, M.A., S.J. St. Aloysius, Oxford, etc."

Holmes took the telegram from me. "You Jesuits are men of many initials. I remember Hopkins from Stonyhurst. Dreamy, poetic, not my sort of chap." He tapped the document to his chin, mumbling to himself. "Acheron . . . Acheron. . . ."

I explained. "In antique mythology, Acheron is the river surrounding hell. After receiving this wire, I went to the Young Men's Library and copied some of the text from the Aeneid. In this passage, the goddess Juno complains that if she can't move heaven, she will move Acheron to block the accord between Aeneas and the king of Latium. . . ."

"Yes, yes, I'm sure," Holmes cut in. "The River Acheron appears in your poison-pen poem, does it not?"

I stopped short. There were so many arcane references in that document, I hadn't remembered that one.

Holmes drew the rumpled paper from his bag. "Here it is."

Even Thy Goddess in the depths of Acheron shall fall!

He repeated the phrase several times between sips of tea. "What did you make of this?"

"I considered it a Protestant calumny. Many of them accuse Catholics of worshipping the Virgin Mother as if she were a goddess, and I assume they anticipate toppling her and ourselves into hell together."

"Yes, very likely," Holmes said. "I really should study more religion. At any rate, the river Acheron stands for hell. It goes on to say . . .

Revenge! Thou shalt drink the shame of it Sweet!
Shadowed Brotherhood! If we Heaven's will cannot avert, Hell
Let us move. . . .

"It seems to be an appeal to the 'shadowed brotherhood' to rise up and take revenge."

"The shadowed brotherhood? Dead rebel soldiers?" I guessed.

"More likely a reference to the Klan. The most telling sentence is the next one: 'If we heaven's will cannot avert, hell let us move,' which is clearly a paraphrase of the verse from the Aeneid. Perhaps they have taken it as a motto—a conquered army battling against destiny, invoking the powers of hell to help them throw off their conquerors."

"The Lost Cause resurrected," I shook my head. "I can still hear that voice shrieking those words in the night—*If we can't move heaven, we shall move hell!* Holmes, I begin to see why you believe this case is about more than a fifteen-year-old murder."

"I have believed that from the moment I saw this paper in your hand. Still, I am baffled by the lack of connection between that fifteen-year-old murder and this movement to renew the great rebellion—a movement of which we can see only shadows."

"Thomas Beaufort connects them. You said yesterday that his scapegoating of James pointed to his own guilt, and now we find Virgil's very words both in his mouth and in the hand of whoever wrote this letter."

"Yes, there is a possible connection, unless the verse from the Aeneid is a general motto within the Klan; if so, Klansmen might use it in many contexts. Recall also that the motivating force for the murders seems to be revenge for 'Bloody' Ban's massacre at the Waxhaws. How would the Beauforts enter into that picture, if at all?"

We sat in silence for a moment while my mind tried to twist itself round these complications. The small pot of tea was empty, and I could have murdered another cup; but just then I was shocked to my feet by a rap on the door. It was James.

"Please, suh, let me in. They after me again."

Holmes was a blur as he took the stairs in a couple of leaps. I pulled James inside the room.

"What happened? Why did you come back?"

Sweating and out of breath, James sagged to the floor. I struggled to get him back on the bed—he was still weak from his ordeal of two nights before, and now bore further marks of a wild race through miry streets.

Holmes returned to give me a hand. "I saw no one in the street. That is of course no guarantee that they are not out there. We hoped you had found safety, James."

"Oh, I been plumb stupid. I knows how to hide in the back country so nobody kin find me, but I stops at a colored tavern on the way out of town—just for a stiffener, you know."

Holmes glanced at his flask on the dressing table and groaned.

"Well, the bartender, he ain't never heard of no London gin," James went on, "all he has is corn liquor, so I has me some of that, just a touch cuz it don't stiffen. But when I walks out to git on my way, who do I see 'cross the street? A one-arm man. And he looks at me and I looks at him and I knowed it was the same one-arm devil tried to hang me.

"He shouts at me to stop, but I takes off like li'l brother rabbit, over fences and through trees and even a nasty briar patch, and I been hidin' in a mudhole under the railroad tracks since sun-up."

"You must have succeeded in evading them or they would be upon us now," Holmes said. "But we must lose no time to be quit of this place. Tuck, take him into the back garden and see that he cleans himself."

Holmes stood utterly still for a moment, his arm raised as if turned to stone. I thought perhaps he had heard something.

"James, this misfortune may turn our way yet," he said. "I have an idea. Can you read and write?"

"Yes, suh. I learned at the Freedmen's school before they shut it."

"Excellent. I must send a wire or two and I will return," and out the door he went.

"He *sure* do come and go," James said.

Scarcely a half hour later, James was clean (after the application of several pails of cold water from a well behind the hotel) and barely dressed in a dry shirt and trousers borrowed from Holmes—a much leaner man. Just then Holmes came back.

"Great heavens, Tuck. This man needs clothing. To the rectory!"

Holmes packed his carpetbag in an instant and the three of us were on horseback headed for the church. Covered by Holmes's greatcoat and hat, James looked almost respectable—except for his bare, freezing feet. At the rectory, we found some proper clothes for him among the discards collected for the poor, and Holmes donated his coat and hat. Although no gentleman, James now looked at least respectable.

"Now James," said Holmes, seated at a table and writing at high speed, "I propose to put you beyond the reach of these pointy-capped scoundrels for a time, and meanwhile you could do us all a great service—that is, if you're willing."

"For a time? How long is 'for a time'? I'm already missin' my fam'ly."

"Three weeks!" Holmes exclaimed. "Mind, the success of that effort now rests partially with you. If you can succeed with my plan, you shall be completely exonerated and free to return to your family, possibly within the month."

James look at us skeptically. He was no fool. "What I got to do?

"I want you to take ship for Jamaica and stay there until I call you back. Here are two letters. The first is your introduction to a certain gentleman. In the second, I have written instructions for you which you must follow exactly if you are to have any hope of returning."

James regarded me as if to ask if Holmes had lost his mind.

"James," I said, "I know it sounds like a mad request. But if I were you, I would do as Mr. Holmes asks—and do it *exactly* as he asks. Believe me, I speak from experience."

"Jamaica? I ain' hardly been out of Georgia but once in my life."

Holmes began rushing him out the door. "We will accompany you as far as the station. The rest is up to you. Give him some money, Tuck."

I was relieved when the red-brick Union Station came into view, its maw like a whale's mouth breathing out steam—all the better for us, who were doing our best to be inconspicuous. We bought passage for James to Savannah, where he could board a ship for the West Indies, and saw him safely off on the train.

"And now I must bid you farewell also, Tuck," Holmes said.

I was startled, to say the least. "What? Where are you going?"

"Lexington, Kentucky."

"Of course," I said with inescapable sarcasm. "Where else?"

Shivering in the misty depot without his coat and hat, Holmes shrugged and started walking away. I struggled after him.

"Lexington?" I whispered. "Why?"

"I am an English gent touring the Kentucky horse country with an eye to acquiring some horseflesh. Why else would anyone go there?"

"All right, but would you at least enlighten me about James? Why have you sent him to Jamaica? What is he to do there?"

"I have asked him to find employment at the Tarleton property in Jamaica and to find out as much as he can about the Tarletons, their history there, and what happened to the son of Perdita and Bloody Ban."

"And how is James to accomplish all of this? He has no education, no money, no references—and how is he to insinuate himself into a position with the Tarleton plantation?"

"I gather you have little faith in James," Holmes responded as we raced across the depot. "I believe he is perfectly equal to the task. And I am giving him a little help.

"At Oxford, I knew a student named Reginald Musgrave—he is the tenant of Hurlstone Hall and a scion of one of the oldest Tory families in England. He and I were much alike, not generally popular among the undergraduates and too diffident to make friends with any but each other. Through him, I met his uncle Sir Antony Musgrave, the governor of the British West Indies. Without going into particulars, Sir Antony has occasionally required my services and is rather obliged to me. James is armed with a letter from me to Sir Antony. I imagine the governor of the colony will have little difficulty arranging a few things for our friend.

"And now if you will excuse me, I see the train for Nashville is boarding, and I must be on it if I am to make my connections."

"But Holmes, what am I to do in your absence?"

"Do? My dear friend, what does a Jesuit do? I assume you have duties."

He walked rapidly toward the train, turned, and called out, "You shall hear from me."

And he disappeared down the platform into a veil of steam.

Chapter 25

The grinding machinery of the train blasting out fire and smoke brought hell to mind, and my Virgil had abandoned me in the midst of this inferno. Once again, I was forced to go on without Holmes, dropped just like Sprüngli and Jimmy the plumber and his miserable young Deputies of the London streets and everyone else he encountered whose utility was temporary. People were tools to him—to be picked up, used, and packed away when no longer needed. "My dear friend" indeed!

Cut loose in this fashion, I decided to return to Charleston and my duties, as Holmes had suggested. There was nothing for me to do in Atlanta, and I had been too long away in any case. Sister Carolina was very short with me when I called on her, saying she would prefer to stay with her family until after the Christmas holidays. I returned the chestnut mare to Marta, who startled me by giving me a hug and thanking me for saving her from the "gools" that night in the forest. I protested that it was not I who had saved her, but she did not hear me over her insistent sing song.

I also called on Joe Harris to say goodbye. I apologized for Holmes's brusque behavior toward him, but Harris's eyes brightened.

"N-not at all! I found him . . . delightful. His disguises, his brilliant s-schemes . . . I'd never imagined such a character existed!"

Neither had I, I confessed.

"The miracle he p-pulled off in rescuing us from the Klan! . . . and then pretending to be . . . to be a messenger-boy from the *Constitution* and saving James again! R-R-Right under the very nose of the j-jailer. . . ."

"Yes, he is a remarkable fellow."

"So ingenious and . . . unselfish . . . ."

I agreed in a tepid sort of way. "Will you be writing James's story for your newspaper? The people of this city should know about the scoundrels that roam their streets and even run the jails."

Abashed, Harris said no. We were seated at his desk in the newspaper office: he took a sheet of paper, wrote quickly while a finger rested on his lips, and then quietly passed me the message:

"My superiors don't care to publish things that put the South in bad odor. They speak of a 'New South' where the old injustices are long past. In their eyes the Klan is no more, and the colored people are all perfectly satisfied and happy and everyone gets along just fine."

"But these are lies," I whispered.

Harris winced, and we stared helplessly at each other.

"Well," I surrendered, standing. "I'll be on my way. But first I wanted very much to thank you for your acquaintance and help. These few days have been memorable to say the least. I'm sorry Mr. Holmes left you without a word, but it is characteristic of him."

"He d-did leave a word. I have a . . . a job to do for him."

"Oh?"

"Yes. He wants me to . . . to . . . ." Frustrated, he picked up a fresh telegram and showed it to me.

"To J. Harris, Atlanta Constitution. I am leaving town for a few days. Please know I am grateful for your help while in Atlanta. Be kind enough to arrange for Reverend Grosjean to join the Ring as soon as possible. With all good wishes, S. H."

"What podsnappery!" I almost shouted.

"Sorry?"

"Excuse me, dear fellow. It's an English expression meaning, um, 'what effrontery!' He said nothing to me about this. And dash it! I don't even know what it means. 'Join the Ring'?"

Amused, Harris began handwriting again in his quick, ornate style. It was much faster for him to write than to speak. I read:

"The Atlanta Ring is a group of civic promoters headed by my editor, Henry W. Grady. They are mostly businessmen and politicians—the mayor, a senator, railroad men—boosting the New South. No idea why Mr. H. wants you among them, but I have faith in him and will try my best."

"You must have faith bang up the elephant," I was spluttering by now. "Confound his mysteries. Why should the mayor of Atlanta have anything to do with a green Catholic schoolmaster from Charleston!?"

"I am . . . already making the c-case." Harris pulled a document from a machine on his desk that looked like a piano attached to a breadbox. The paper was covered with mechanical writing, the beginnings of a letter.

"Dear Mr. Grady,

It has occurred to me that an invitation might be extended to certain religious and academic leaders to join the Atlanta association for advancement of the New South. I think prominent Catholic, Protestant, and Jewish voices joined to yours could very well add influence to your efforts . . . ."

I looked up at Harris. "But I am not prominent. Grady will want a bishop, not a junior Jesuit."

"I will . . . persuade him."

"You know your business," I sighed. "But I can't imagine what purpose it would serve for me to join such a group."

"Nor I," he replied, and I saw a tiny tinge of mockery in that surprised-looking smile of his.

"Holmes has considerable faith in you," I told him.

"And . . . in you."

Faith in me? I hadn't thought of that—perhaps he expected more of me than was realistic. Was it possible that Holmes, who saw so clearly through what was mysterious to others, could not quite grasp that people like myself were not nearly as clear-sighted as he?

As I put on my coat, I pointed to the piano breadbox and asked, "What is that contraption?"

"It's called a . . . a t-type-writer. . . . a Remington Number Two."

"Remington? I thought they were manufacturers of weapons."

"Indeed they are," said Harris, clear and strong, shaking both of my hands.

He gave me a sheaf of pamphlets and speeches—information about the Atlanta Ring—and we took our leave of each other. I was soon on the train to Charleston and immersed in the transcript of a speech by Mr. Henry W. Grady, editor of the Atlanta *Constitution.*

I could hardly believe my eyes:

The relations of the southern people with the negro are close and cordial. . . . Faith has been kept with him, in spite of calumnious assertions to the contrary. . . . Faith will be kept with him in the future. Nowhere on earth is there kindlier feeling, closer sympathy, or less friction between any classes of society than between the whites and blacks of the South today.

If this were true, then the evidence of my own eyes and ears over the years I had spent in this country was an utter hallucination. Nearly every word of the article was brazen rubbish. If anywhere on earth could be found a more merciless, cold-blooded system of oppression, I could not imagine what it would be. I had seen the freedmen's schools closed and their farms stolen from them; I had heard of colored people intimidated and whipped from the polls. I knew for myself that a whole people had been reduced through plain piracy and mob terror back into slavery—or worse. "Close and cordial relations?" Pitiless, remote, and contemptuous, more like.

In the previous ten years, after the brief spark of "emancipation" was crushed, the blacks had been deprived of the education, land, franchise, and even livelihood they were promised. With the Sisters, I had gone about Charleston to minister to the miserable in Cabbage Row and the destitute on Kittiwah Island. I had encountered starvation at Hilton Head and men in rags worked quite literally to death at the harbor of Port Royal. I had seen these people cheated, cuffed, cursed, and chained together as "leased" convicts—mere slaves by another name.

And, of course, I had just witnessed in a dark wood at midnight the manifestation of what passed for "justice" in this brutal place. If it had not been for Holmes. . . .

At Charleston, my life settled into a curious stillness. Christmas came in peace and went the same way. My charges, two-score or so poor children, were showered with gifts by the more charitable families of the parish. At night the Sisters and I scooped into a wagon a load of surplus dolls, wooden horses, cup-and-balls, jacks and marbles, boxes of dominoes, and took them to the State Orphan Asylum—a tumbledown refuge for abandoned colored children. (I little knew then that the governor of South Carolina was about to close even this poor excuse for a shelter as an "economy measure.")

The day after Christmas I received in the post a most unusual document—the copy of a letter on a piece of what I later understood to be "carbonated paper." It was type-written by Joe Harris.

Dear Mr. Grady,

It has occurred to me that an invitation might be extended to certain religious and academic leaders to join the Atlanta association for the advancement of the New South. I think prominent Catholic, Protestant, and Jewish voices joined to yours could very well add influence to your efforts. Speaking for the Catholic population, I am sure that the bishops of Savannah and Charleston would be most gratified at the invitation. However, as they are exceedingly busy men, they would undoubtedly wish to nominate emissaries who could be permanently attached to the association. A superb candidate would be the Rev. S. P. Grosjean of the diocese of Charleston, a man of intelligence and civic zeal whom I have the privilege of knowing personally. I should be most pleased to discuss this matter further with you at your earliest convenience.

I am yours sincerely, Joel Chandler Harris

Out of the envelope fell a piece of note paper with a handwritten message: "He took the bait. J.C.H."

I laughed out loud. For all his stuttering and shyness, Harris was nevertheless a crafty fellow with a written word.

Now I was a member of the Atlanta Ring. For what reason, I could not begin to guess.

The next day I received a second astonishing missive, possibly connected with the first: A colossal engraved invitation to something called the "St. Cecilia Society Cotillion" on New Year's Eve. I was about to discard it in a rubbish bin when my superior, Father Claudian, walked by and noticed it.

"My dear Father Simon, what are you doing?" he said, scanning the document. "This is a great honor! The St. Cecilia Society is the most exclusive of societies. I have lived in Charleston all my life and never even seen one of these invitations before." Father Claudian had been an eminent lawyer in the city but, like St. Paul, was converted from the error of his ways and became a priest. "The people who are invited to the Cotillion never speak of it, and those who speak of it are never invited. You *have* been invited: you *must* go."

"But it's surely a mistake. Why invite a priest to a ball?"

"The Cotillion is much more than a ball!" Father Claudian exclaimed, his attorney's voice (which he used to great effect in sermons) and his Irish color rising. "The very cream of the cream of Charleston society will be there. Once you are included, all of the most prominent ears in the state will be open to us . . . to you, I meant to say. Think of what it could mean for St. Peter's—for the Church! You *cannot*, you *must not* decline."

CHARLESTON

Chapter 26

The Cotillion of the St. Cecilia Society was held in a lovely Greek revival building called the Hibernian Hall (the name was a mystery to me, as there wasn't an Irishman in sight). Although the night was murky and bitter, the Hall blazed like a gas inferno. Outside, the street was wedged full of motionless carriages, their black drivers hunched over in the biting cold, their dark faces invisible in the shadows.

On approaching, one could hear the chattering of a hundred Southern belles all at the same time, a sound like no other I can describe. On the islands I once heard the scooping yelps of a horde of seabirds caught in an Atlantic squall—it was somewhat similar.

I hesitated before going in. A doorman erect in formal dress examined my invitation and bowed me into the hall, where I was announced by another equally vertical fellow, while yet another occupied himself with my hat and coat.

I entered. Bound up tight in diamond bodices and brandishing their silken bustles, the ladies of Charleston were hailing each other in a sort of panic, as if each feared that she would not be noticed and remarked upon. The men looked excruciating in their cutaway coats and collars, for with fires raging in the fireplaces the interior was as hot as the exterior was cold.

I noticed the presence of other clergy—indeed, the Bishop of Charleston was there, looking like a rumpled old bear, his heavy silver cross propped up on his paunch and his eyeglasses slipping from his sweating nose. He met me with enthusiasm; he seemed positively delighted to see me, as if I were his oldest friend. In fact, he had taken so little notice of me before I wasn't sure he would know me again. In lieu of asking "who the devil are you and how did you get in here?" it was, "Ah! Father Grosjean. What a pleasure!" And then he was off toward the punch bowl.

I stood wondering what to do and why I was there in the first place when two men in sophisticated suiting converged on me. They too greeted me as if I were an old friend, and I realized that I had met them before—at the victory party at the city hall only months before.

"Ah, yes, Mr. Tillman, wasn't it?" I asked the younger of the two, who looked like a bulldog slowly strangling in his white collar.

"It is, and this, if you'll recall, is my good friend General Martin Witherspoon Gary. He is the state senator from Edgefield County." With his white Napoleon III mustaches and tiny pointed beard, the general was almost a caricature of a Southern gentleman. Both men carried themselves with the imperious air of the back-country planter.

"Shall we have a drink together?" Tillman suggested, and we partook of the Society punch—a bizarre, sweetish concoction of brandy and pineapple juice. I immediately thought of my threat letter: *You shall drink the shame of it sweet.*

"It's very good," I lied, to which Tillman replied, "Not enough sugar."

General Gary proposed a toast in a high voice accustomed to command: "Let us drink to the noble and ancient Roman Catholic Church, of which our friend Father Grosjean is such an able representative."

"I thank you," I said, sipping again as little as possible. It recalled to mind the vile sweet tea from my school days.

"I have always honored the Roman Catholic Church," Gary intoned as if giving a public speech. "I was with President Jefferson Davis the day he retreated from the hell-hound Yankees. I led his honor guard after the surrender. His good lady is a devout Catholic, and he himself aspires to become one. I know this, for I saw him with my own eyes kissing his St. Benedict medal." He bowed his head with a choking sigh and took another swallow of the sugary stuff.

"I am pleased to hear it," was my banal reply.

"Did you know that the blessed Pope himself honored Jefferson Davis with his autographed picture? And even sent him a crown of thorns woven by his own hands?" Gary went on. "He addressed him as 'the illustrious and honorable president of the Confederate States of America.' That was a noble act, suh. A noble act." He choked again, then licked at his cup and mustaches, and we all took another ceremonious sip. The punch was actually making me thirsty.

"I, um, I was not aware of that," I said. "The late Pope of blessed memory was a thoughtful man."

The General said, "His successor seems different, but perhaps even more sagacious. You are aware of course, Father Grosjean, of the Pope's encyclical of this week." This was a statement, not a question.

"I fear I haven't read it." In truth, I didn't know there had been an encyclical that week, and General Gary inferred it from my face.

"Your reverend bishop showed it to us. Shall I read a few passages for you?" He extricated a newspaper sheet from inside his coat and held it at arm's length.

I was in the incongruous position of listening to this old planter declaiming the words of the pope at full voice just as the orchestra struck up a rather jovial waltz.

"Date of December 28th, 1878. *Quod Apostolicky mooneris!*" he announced, then in an aside said, "According to the bishop, that means 'from our apostolic office.' The rest of it is in English." Then he took it up in an even louder voice:

"A deadly plague is creepin' into the very fibers of human society and leadin' it on to the verge of destruction. . . .

"We speak of that sect of men who, under various and almost barbarous names, are called socialists, communists, or nihilists, spreadin' all over the world.

"They leave nothin' untouched or whole which by both human and divine laws has been wisely decreed for the health and beauty of life. They refuse obedience to the higher powers, to whom, according to the admonition of the Apostle, every soul ought to be subject, and who derive the right of governin' from God; and *they proclaim the absolute equality of all men in rights and duties!*

"These men of the lowest class, weary of their wretched home or workshop, are eager to attack the homes and fortunes of the rich. . . .

"*The inequality of rights and of power proceeds from the very Author of nature.* . . . He appointed that there should be various orders in civil society, differin' in dignity, rights, and power!"

He lowered the paper and gave me a triumphant frown.

"There it is, suh. From his mouth to your ears. There ain't an equality of men in rights. The inequality of rights proceeds from the very Author of nature!"

Unsure of Gary's purpose in catechizing me in this way, I simply said, "His Holiness is most eloquent, is he not?"

"Confound it!" the General exclaimed. "I'm pitchin' but you ain't catchin'. Here your own Church teaches that the black man is inferior to the white man and needs to get back in his place!"

Asking to see the paper, I pretended to study it—and to be more ingenuous than I was. "With respect, I am not entirely sure that message is intended here.

As the context is economics, it appears to me that the Holy Father is speaking of inequalities of economic rather than racial circumstances. . . ."

Gary lapsed into his gurgling cough, so Tillman spoke up. "We disagree, Reverend sir. The Church clearly damns those who proclaim the equality of men in dignity, rights, and power. We Christians must come together in damning those who seek to substitute the rule of the African for that of the Caucasian in South Carolina!"

Looking into Tillman's face, I realized that these gentlemen were trying to persuade me to their point of view—to what end, I didn't know.

"But should that mean putting the African, as you say, 'back in his place'?" I asked. "Dr. Newman has taught that enslaving other people is a horrible sin. Pope Gregory XVI taught that no Christian should reduce another to bondage, and specifically condemned black servitude. In fact, he said that anyone involved in that inhuman traffic was 'unworthy of the Christian name.'" I added, "That was in, I believe, 1839. *In Supremo Apostolatus*."

The two men regarded me with iron in their eyes. But then, the General relaxed and choked out a laugh. "It is more than presumptuous of us lowly and ill-educated men of the soil to pretend to, as we say, teach the stallion how to trot. You are, naturally, better informed on the credos of your own church than we are. We must, of course, defer to your greater understanding." He offered me another drink of the shameful punch, which I accepted.

"Ah, here are the young ladies," he said, between a sip and a fit of coughing.

The debutante parade began. Dozens of white-gowned girls looked as though they would combust spontaneously as they filed into the fiery ballroom one after another on the hands of their fathers. They took their places for the cotillion, which turned out to be a sort of quadrille as I had seen danced in England.

Hoping this spectacle would distract my two interlocutors, I tried to slip away from them, but they stuck with me. General Gary looked me up and down and asked, "I hope your inquiry on behalf of your religious friend has borne fruit?"

Stunned a little by the question, I pretended to have forgotten about it. "Inquiry?"

"Into the death of those boys at Gettysburg? Your friend from the convent was, if I remember, somewhat agitated about it?"

"Yes, um, no," I stammered. "It . . . it remains a mystery, I'm afraid."

"Too bad. When you asked about it at the victory reception, I was impressed by your solicitude on behalf of your friend. I'm sorry we could not be of help."

Then it struck me. How could I have been so thick-headed? I saw the reception again in my mind, the small ring of men round me—yes, there was Gary, the odious Tillman, governors and mayors who seemed utterly bored, and—a man in Confederate uniform whose name I thought was Buford. I had misheard—it was Beaufort! General Abraham Beaufort! The man I thought I had seen before when I met him again at the Tarleton place. Surely Beaufort authored that menacing poem . . . .

I decided to bowl the ball back at Gary. "General Beaufort did send me an interesting letter on the subject, but I found it unhelpful."

"That's a pity. It's usually wise to pay heed to General Beaufort." He paused to cough into his handkerchief. "May I show you an interesting feature of this hall, Father?"

He and Tillman led me to the portrait of a Confederate officer hanging on the wall. The subject was nearly submerged in beard.

"This is Major General Jeb Stuart," Gary explained, "one of the most gallant soldiers I ever knew. He took a Yankee bullet in the spine in the last year of the war, but as he died, he made a most precious bequest to the wife of Robert E. Lee—his beautiful handmade golden spurs."

"Indeed." I hoped they didn't notice my sudden gulp of air. "Golden spurs, you say?"

"Yes. Jeb Stuart was called 'the Knight of the Golden Spurs.' We loved him. We loved the cause for which he gave his life. Father Grosjean, we are not stupid men. I myself am a graduate of Harvard University. Jeb Stuart was at the top of his class at the Military Academy, as was Jefferson Davis. Mr. Tillman here excelled at the University of South Carolina. I find you to be at least our equal in intelligence. I foresee a luminous future for you here in Charleston . . . but only if our cause becomes your cause."

"I confess I don't entirely follow your meaning," I lied, "but as a servant of our Lord, I must of course put His cause above all others. I'm sure you will understand."

"Naturally, we believe our cause *is* the Lord's cause," Tillman interjected.

"Men generally do," I tried to be ambiguous. "As to your cause, the Apostle wrote that the Lord 'hath made of one blood all mankind.' I believe that verse of the Bible would apply to a humble black sharecropper as well as a lordly gentleman planter."

"But your own Church . . ." Tillman began to say when Gary interrupted him. In a final sort of tone he said, "Let us not quibble. A man is entitled to his beliefs."

The quadrille had ended and the assembly were applauding the debutantes, making that strange, rain-like sound of people clapping gloved hands.

Frightened and tired of hiding it, I wanted to bring this interview to an end and get back to the sanctuary of my church. "Gentlemen," I said, "my day has been very full, and I had hoped only to show my gratitude to the hosts for inviting me here tonight and then return to my duties. Perhaps you could point the way to them . . . ?"

"Mr. Tillman and I invited you."

Nervously, I swallowed the last of my punch, which had warmed to a slightly bitter taste, and bowed. "Then I am most honored by your kindness and will take my leave."

"You will consider our interchange of this evenin'." It was not a question.

Sighing, I said, "General Gary, it seems to me that the destinies of war and the hand of God have already foreclosed your cause. And at this late date, reason militates against it. "

Gary gave me a menacing smile. "Are you familiar with that old philosopher Pascal and his maxim 'The heart has reasons that reason knows not of'?"

"Yes, it is a well-known saying."

He took me by the arm and walked me toward another painting hanging on the wall.

"This picture was a gift to the city by Tillman and myself and a group of our fellow philanthropists. Striking, isn't it?" A mass of writhing peasants were depicted about to cut the throat of a Medieval knight.

"It portrays the Battle of the Golden Spurs," he said. "You know the story, of course."

"I have vaguely heard of it. It was an incident in the war between the French and the Flemish, was it not?"

"The French had utterly defeated the Flemish, occupied their lands, stolen their property, and denied them their rights. Then in 1302 a group of patriotic Flemings arose and murdered the scalawag French governor in the city of Bruges. Outraged, the French king descended on them with a great army of ten thousand soldiers and knights brave in golden spurs.

"They were met by the Fleming militia, which was made up of poor farmers and indignant townsmen armed with the tools of their trades. The Flemings were utterly outmatched; but filled with the righteous fury of their cause and love of their land, they destroyed that French army. It was said that one French knight was worth ten militia, but that day the ratio was reversed! In triumph, the Flemish collected from the bodies of the French knights more than five hundred pairs of golden spurs and offered them up to the church in thanks to God."

"An extraordinary story."

"Isn't it?" Gary was angry now. "Do you think the Flemings would have listened to appeals for *reason*? Do you think *reason* governed them?" Then, as if his throat shut tight, he coughed fiercely and fought for air. Tillman patted his back in useless panic. But just as abruptly, Gary recovered, put his hand on my shoulder, and repeated in my ear, "The heart has its reasons."

A group of tightly gowned ladies who looked as if they had been poured into tall, thin goblets approached us.

"Sallie," Gary said, greeting one of them. "May I present Father Grosjean. This is Mrs. Tillman, Father, and her charming friends."

The lady nodded at me and turned back to Gary. "Are you ill, General?"

"Not at all, not at all. Tillman, isn't it about time you squired your lady to the ball?"

Tillman gave me a final look—his serpent's mouth formed into a perfectly angular frown—and took "Sallie's" arm. She wore a splendid cameo round her neck. Coaxed, reluctant, Gary took another lady's arm, and they and the band waltzed into the beautiful blue Danube while I made my departure.

As I walked anxiously up Meeting Street and then Calhoun Street, I watched for the luminous façade of St. Peter's and would not feel secure again until I was inside its walls. For some reason, I kept muttering those last words of Gary's—"The heart has its reasons . . . The heart has its reasons."

Then it came to me like a lightning strike to the brain. I shouted the name as I entered the church, and it echoed high in the nave lit only by the red altar lamp.

"*Pascal! Pascal! Pascal!*"

Chapter 27

I couldn't wait to get my hands back on that bizarre document that Katherine Wells gave me aboard ship. Without even taking off my coat and hat, I stumbled into my room, pulled the carefully folded paper out of safekeeping, and sat down with it under my desk lamp.

"Pascal's Triangle!" I triumphantly announced to the four walls of my cell. "It's Pascal's Triangle!" It was one of few things I remembered from my otherwise unmemorable mathematics tutor at Stonyhurst. I recalled playing with it for hours.

Embedded within the rowel of the spur was the step pyramid Pascal used to illustrate the workings of the binomial theorem. I took another sheet of paper and inked out the triangle from memory.

Then I started filling it in with numbers. It was easy to do. Put the numeral 1 in the top box, then continue so that each number is the sum of the numbers directly above it. I could do the figures in my head until I got to the eighth and last row, so it went quickly.

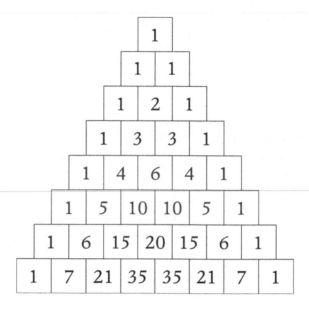

Cheerful and satisfied with myself, I sat back to admire my work. Yes, it was the old Pascal Triangle which we had learned in third year at Stonyhurst as a guide to the coefficients of the binomial theorem. I remembered that it was an intriguing curiosity, but could not for the life of me recollect what it was good for.

Undoubtedly, it was a key to the coded message in the Wells document.

And then my triumph began to fade. I tried first this way then that to match the numbers in the Triangle to the numbers in the message, but I could arrive at no connection at all. I tried a hundred different ways and each time produced nothing but strings of numbers. I tried pairing them with letters of the alphabet: it was no use.

In the end my lamp waned, and so did I. That night I dreamed of dancing ghosts in firelight, ghosts standing like statues in a forest, and two hard-faced men in evening clothes who were trying to warn me of something all through the night. The next thing I knew, someone was tapping at my door and it was morning.

"Father Simon! Come quickly." I opened to Father Claudian, whose eyes as they regarded me were congealed either with cold or disapproval—I could not discern. Perhaps both. "The bishop is here to see you."

"The bishop to see me?" I couldn't credit it. I had slept all night in my clothes and was unsuitably rumpled, but I could do nothing about that. Into the presence I went.

"Father Simon," the bishop greeted me with a damp handshake. He was large, and like many large men sweat a good deal in the humidity of Charleston even in the cold months. At his neck his long hair formed a big coil that was always moist.

"My lord," I said, then catching myself, "Your reverence"—the American usage.

"I have come to see you particularly," he said, glancing at Father Claudian, who took the suggestion and left us alone in his austere study. The bishop invited me to sit.

"A blessed New Year to you, my son," he said.

I offered up the customary blandishments. "Your reverence, I hope my presence at the Cotillion last night was not unseemly. While I did receive an invitation, I had determined not to go—but Father Claudian insisted. It was probably not the place for a clergyman. . . ." I said before I realized it. "I mean . . . for a plain priest like myself."

"Not at all, not at all," he waved his hand. He spoke with the accent of the Georgia hills, a feature of his which had always amused me until this moment. "I understand you have recently returned from Rome, and you had the blessed fortune of meeting His Holiness in person!"

"Yes, your reverence. I was present for a . . . um, presentation. To a friend from England. An old schoolmate."

"A remarkable blessing. I myself had the privilege of his acquaintance when he was Cardinal Pecci and I was a diplomat at the Vatican. A warm and generous soul."

"That he is." I did not demur, nor did I forget the Pope's shrewd face and the baleful wording of his latest encyclical.

As if reading my thoughts, the bishop produced a copy of that very document and laid it on the table between us. "Here is the papal encyclical of December 28. Isn't it miraculous that we in Charleston can read it only a few days after it is given in Rome? The wonders of the telegraph!" He paused. "My son, I enjoin you to study this very carefully."

"Of course I shall, your reverence. Are there passages in particular you would wish to call to my attention?"

He pointed to the same passages General Gary had read to me the night before. I scanned them again and asked, "Why these?"

"My son, you're a foreigner. Your history, your views, are not the same as ours. Here we observe the God-given order of nature where it would result in chaos and confusion if that order were disturbed."

"You refer to the observation that God is the author of inequality."

"I do. Unlike you, I grew up in this country. My family held slaves, and I held slaves. They are free now, but that is only a legal contrivance. It does not change the clear order of things—the Negro is naturally subordinate to the white man. He is very prone to excesses, and plunges madly into the lowest depths of licentiousness. Without the restraint of his white masters, we would be faced with the most deadly antagonism and inhuman warfare in this country."

I felt my spine stiffening against this little lecture. "I'm not sure I understand, your reverence. It is very early on New Year's Day. I know your reverence has duties. Why have you so discommoded yourself to bring these matters to my attention—matters with which I am well acquainted, though I am an alien in your midst?"

"Because, my son, I see no future for the Negro in the South unless he is brought back under the entire charge of civilized men—and I believe you Jesuits are the men for the task. The Society of Jesus has done such miracles before. When we gain our full rights once again . . . ."

Here he stopped. I believe he sensed he had gone too far. For the second time in twelve hours I felt that I was being recruited . . . for what, I did not know. I dearly wished Holmes were there with his analytical powers to make something intelligible of this hidden game.

The bishop reached for my hand. "My dear Father Simon, I must take my leave. Today is the Feast of the Circumcision—there are services to attend to, for both you and myself." Then he laughed nervously. "And after that, as every year, the Irish want me to come round and bless the beer barrels."

I smiled. "That should prove diverting for you, your reverence. I am indebted to you for your kind attentions, and I assure you I am your humble servant in everything."

"I am gratified to hear that, Father. Very gratified." He rose ponderously from his chair and I saw him out of the rectory to his carriage.

When I returned, Father Claudian was waiting behind the door.

"What did he want?"

"I am not sure. He required me to read the new papal encyclical."

"All of it?"

"No. Only the section dealing with inequality of rights."

"Ah. An excellent idea. He is concerned about you. The town is full of talk about how you helped a Negro escape from the Atlanta jail."

"What? How . . .?"

"Unseemly behavior for a priest, don't you think?"

I was indignant. "To begin with, I didn't do anything of the sort. The man escaped without any help from me. I admit that I went there to procure his release because he was jailed unjustly. . . ."

"He is *black*!" Father Claudian hissed at me, then became calm again. "You haven't been here two years, so I suppose allowances must be made. But by doing what you have done, you have put our work—even our very presence here—in jeopardy. We have tried, God knows how we have tried, to minister to the Negroes. Before the war one of our former bishops even started a church for them, but he was forced to shut it. Now because of you anything we try to do may be looked upon with suspicion."

"But the bishop just spoke of a new ministry to them . . . about bringing them back under the 'entire charge' of the white man. He wants me to help. . . ."

"So you should. His vision is right and just, Father Simon. In any case, you owe him obedience. He is your bishop."

"Faith is greater than obedience. Shall I obey a superior who requires me to treat others as my inferiors? Under the charge of white men, indeed!"

Father Claudian exhaled in resignation. "You Jesuits wear me out with your fine reasoning. You're worse than the lawyers I used to joust with. The colored population must be brought to heel or they will run riot over us! Can't you see that?"

"Didn't your own Thomas Jefferson declare that all men are created equal?"

"And the pope declares that they are not! Jefferson was an atheist. I fear you are in danger of your soul, Father Simon. As your immediate superior, I propose that you. . . ."

"I respect you, Father Claudian, but you are not my superior. I belong to the Society of Jesus. My provincial superior is in Baltimore, and it is to him I owe obedience, not to you."

His lips became as tight and white as his hair.

"Now if you will excuse me, Father, I have duties to see to." I stalked back to my cell and washed up. Fortunately, we were occupied with divine service for the rest of the day, so I managed to avoid Father Claudian's icy gaze while longing for the evening when I could shut myself in and return to my study of Pascal's Triangle.

At last the day ended and I could retire. As I approached my cell, I detected a strong odor of cheap ship's tobacco—an unmistakable sign. Holmes had returned!

He had flung his loose limbs onto my only chair and lay staring upward, blowing bluish swirls of smoke at the ceiling. Removing the white alb from my shoulders, I half lay down on my bed. "You're very welcome," I said, trying not to appear too happy to see him. "When did you return?"

"An hour or so ago. I took lodgings at the foot of Meeting Street, and then I came to your service—in the very last chair. You and your co-celebrant are very vexed with one another."

"How on earth . . .? Oh, never mind."

"It takes little skill to see that two men are scrupulously avoiding each other."

"We had an argument over the rights of man—whether all men are created equal," I muttered.

"Of course they are. One man equals another man. It is simple mathematics, is it not?"

"If only it were so. Holmes, I have something remarkable to show you—but I have two questions. First, why did you want me—*me!*—to become a member of the Atlanta Ring, whatever it is?"

"I trust Harris explained what the Atlanta Ring is. It's very simple, Tuck. I want a pair of ears listening in on the meetings of the great conspiracy."

"What great conspiracy? You keep hinting at such a thing but never come down to earth and explain yourself."

Inhaling deeply from his pipe, Holmes leaned back even further on my chair until I thought the legs would snap. "Some men are afflicted with a mania, Tuck. I have a mania for mystery—and shag tobacco. Others are manic for alcohol or sex. Your Southern aristocrats lost everything in the war except their mania for power and wealth. At one time the entire marketplace of the Western world was in their hands, for cotton was truly king. The vast textile mills of England and America undergirded the wealth of both countries, and the slave empire bestrode the ocean.

"Then they overreached and it all came crashing down. But the mania remains, now multiplied manifold by their hatred of the Yankees who defeated them—the Yankees with their iron and steel mills and their railroads and their steamships. Their greedy eyes are upon it all. Do not doubt me—the Atlanta Ring has no small purpose in mind, and if they succeed, many will be crushed under it."

"And what would be my role in such a group?" I asked.

"To listen. To observe. And to report to me."

"Apparently I have been accepted by them. Here is the letter Harris wrote them on my behalf." I handed it to Holmes.

"Ah! A carbonated copy of a type-written document. Extraordinary device, the typewriter. It will be of inestimable value in the detection of crime. Think of it, Tuck! The criminal in the crude maze of his mind will think he can communicate incognito with this device, for nothing in his hand is revealed. But he does not yet realize that each machine has its own character, its own signature, as individual to it as a man's handwriting is to him. Yes! It will be a boon to my work, this new age of the typewriter!"

"A machine has its own signature?"

"Most certainly. Look, here is a slight crevice in the letter 'a,' and a piece of the letter 'n' has broken off." He read the document, his head slightly nodding. "Your friend Harris is just splendid. He has done exactly right. I believe he may prove useful to us yet." He sat up abruptly. "Now for your second question."

"Ah. Why your journey to Kentucky? What did you discover there?"

"Precious little," he sighed out smoke and then gave me a teasing half smile, "except for one thoroughly golden nugget of information!"

Chapter 28

We paused while I made tea and extracted some aging biscuits from a Christmas basket given me by the parishioners. It was all the dinner Holmes needed, and all I was going to get.

"I made the tour of a few horse farms in the vicinity of our friends the Beauforts of Kentucky," he began. "It is capital country for raising horses, which love to graze on the blue grass peculiar to the land, and there are races nearly every day even in winter. Tuck, do you realize that horses race counter-clockwise in this country? I was told it is a sign of protest against the British, who always race clockwise."

"Fine, but what about the Beauforts? The golden nugget?"

"And the Kentuckians hold their own Derby! Fancy the cheek. As for the Beauforts, not much information to be had. They are held in esteem by their neighbors, although Thomas is considered unsocial and unapproachable. He is a single man, has had some trouble in the neighborhood defending his 'honor' against laughable slights, threatening people with dueling pistols, that sort of thing. But the older brother, the general, is well respected.

"Then I happened on an old country tavern at a place called Bardstown. It was a deep well of information, and I dropped a pail in for all I could get. Over at least a gallon of a local distillate called Bourbon (most excellent, by the way), I was able to pry out the history of the Beauforts. They are an enormous family that settled on the blue grass of Kentucky long ago. Some of them fought for the South, some for the North, but the true hero of the family is the grand patriarch two generations back, one Abraham Beaufort, or Buford, a Revolutionary War patriot who . . ."

"Fought at Waxhaws! Another missing link found!"

"Precisely. He it was who tried to surrender to Colonel Tarleton and saw his men sabered to death instead."

"As I suspected! The murderer of the Tarletons would be someone who bore a long grudge against Bloody Ban!"

"Our friend Thomas Beaufort is only a distant relation to the Beaufort of the Waxhaws, but we know he has a mania for honor. The fact that his ancestor was humiliated so famously would gnaw at him, particularly since the rogue Tarleton lived on and prospered. Thomas easily fits the character of the writer of your poisonous poem—and avenger of his family's dishonor."

"The chain grows a little longer each day." I had to tell Holmes about the Cotillion. "I too have added a link—I am sure that it was General Beaufort I spoke to about the Tarleton murders at the victory celebration in the fall. He must have either written the poem himself or inspired his brother to it."

"Very likely."

"And there's more." I rehearsed for him my encounters at the Cotillion ball, the paintings, the story of the battle of the golden spurs, my odd interchange with the bishop—and the dreadful feeling that I was being recruited for a mission to re-enslave the former slaves.

"Capital!" Holmes leaned over and slapped my shoulder. "No doubt the scoundrels felt the need to flatter you, to curry your favor: thus the invitation to the Cotillion. And your bishop—whatever his motives, he must be in sympathy with them."

"I believe I might have offended them—and the bishop. I more or less resisted their appeals . . . perhaps more rather than less."

Alarmed, Holmes sprang up from his chair. "Tuck! You must become their most fervent recruit. They have opened the door into the very heart of the conspiracy and invited you in!"

Of course I agreed, although I had my doubts that there really was a "conspiracy." Then I explained what was most intriguing about that night: my discovery of Pascal's Triangle embedded in the coded message from Mrs. Wells.

Holmes seized my scribbles about the Triangle and studied them closely, then smoothed out the Katherine Wells document on the desk. He stared at it for some time.

"So what have you made of this discovery of yours, Tuck?"

"I make nothing of it. I have flagellated my brains since last night in hopes of finding some application of the Triangle to the figure."

"Then let us put our heads together and try again. I may be able to add yet another link to our chain." From his watch fob he pulled a pocket-compass and laid it before me on the desk. "What do you see here?"

"A compass with a brass lid."

"What else?"

"The manufacturer's name, Negretti and Zambria."

"Good heavens, Tuck. Count them! Thirty-six! Thirty-six points obviously representing the 360 degrees of the compass at a ratio of one to ten. "

"Like the golden spurs." I began to understand.

"Exactly like them. You will recall that the golden spur has 36 points. Now if we lay the wheel over Pascal's Triangle, which contains 36 boxes, what does that give us?"

"No idea."

"I believe it gives us a number and a direction. For example, if we label the arrow pointing straight north 'zero degrees,' and the boxed number immediately beneath it is "1," then we have "zero-1.""

"Or 1-zero."

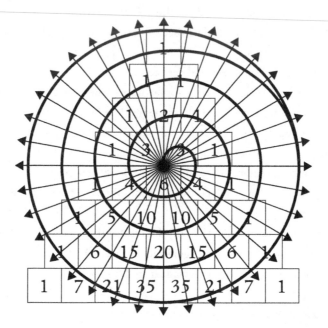

"Yes, of course, it could be so. But in any case, it is the only such combination on the key. Now let's look at the cipher to see if there is a zero-1 combination—or a 1 zero. And . . . here it is. One occurrence. It's the first boxed number in the fourth column."

33-3	4-3	**0-1**	36-1
10-1	1-1	3-1	3-1
26-1	20-21	20-15	3-1
18-20	23-1	4-3	22-5
22-5	20-15	22-5	20-15
18-20	16-10	34-1	25-4
4-3	3-1	4-3	4-3
20-10	18-20	1-1	1-1
18-6	36-1	22-5	20-21
3-1	4-3	4-3	22-7
11-4	1-1	18-6	11-4
20-10	4-3	10-1	18-20
1-1	18-20	4-3	7-1
20-15	18-20	18-20	1-2
25-4	20-10	1-2	14-1

"You might be on to something, Holmes. But what does that tell us?"

Holmes hesitated. "It tells us nothing . . . yet. Perhaps the position of zero-1 in the cipher is significant. Let's see. The cipher contains four columns and 15 rows, which gives us 60 number combinations. Does the number 60 signify anything at all?"

"Nothing to me."

"Of course, the column-and-row arrangement might mean nothing at all. Perhaps it's just a convenient size for the paper."

"It does fill the page. You may be right—and it's unlikely that every message sent by this cipher would always consist of exactly 60 combinations."

"Yes, I see that. Could the boxes represent letters of the alphabet?"

"That occurred to me, Tuck. But there are only 26 letters in the alphabet and we have 60 boxes. However, the remaining boxes might represent the numerals. Let's try that hypothesis."

For the next two hours we tried the hypothesis . . . and tried it and tried it. We arranged the alphabet vertically down the columns, then horizontally across the columns, and even diagonally. We started with the numbers and ended with the numbers. Each attempt resulted in gibberish.

"Perhaps it's just a lot of nonsense," I groaned at last, collapsing on my bed and wishing Holmes gone so I could sleep. It had been a very long, cold, and exhausting day.

"It cannot be. The lady would not have gone to so much trouble and risk to provide you a message that consists of nonsense."

It was true. I pictured her wary, somewhat drained face once again as she passed me the envelope.

"In a substitution cipher, the key depends upon some text, like a passage from the Bible or a poem or a book agreed upon by the conspirators." Holmes was talking to himself, studying the paper even more intently. "But the lady would have provided the text, or some indication of where to find it. There is no such indication, so the entire key must be here—in front of our eyes. It's all right here. What are we missing?"

I got up from the bed, rubbed at my eyes, and looked once more over his shoulder. "What about the snail shell?" I asked.

"Snail shell?"

Holmes leapt up, hugged me to himself, and sang out, "Tuck, you are a miracle, a prodigy! The spiral! The spiral! It's here! I completely overlooked it."

"Well, it is nearly midnight . . . one does overlook things. . . ."

But Holmes abruptly sat down again and continued muttering to himself. "Here is a third figure—imposed upon the compass and the pyramid—the figure of a spiral that begins at the heart of the Triangle and revolves symmetrically outward. What do we know about a spiral?"

"It's found everywhere. In mollusk shells, in the curve of a sheep's horn, in certain flowers. . . . " I was drawn in again and forgetting how tired I was.

Holmes's finger shot straight up like an arrow. "Suppose we arrange the alphabet in a spiral, beginning with 'A' at the apex of the spiral and rotating outward from there." He drew the spiral in the air with his finger.

We fell to work again, filling one of my last sheets of writing paper with a template where each box on the Triangle contained a letter of the alphabet corresponding to the curve of the spiral. As we ended up with ten empty boxes, we proceeded to fill them in with the numerals from one to 10, which seemed reasonable to us.

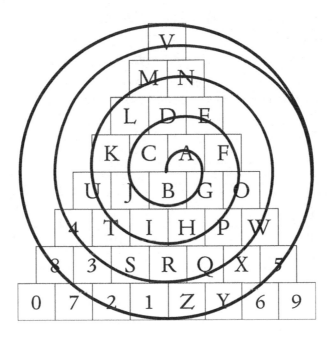

"But Holmes," I said, "are we any further down the road? What is the relationship between the Triangle and the letters in the Spiral?"

"Let us apply our previous hypothesis. Due to the Compass, we now have a degree for each box; due to the Triangle, we now have a number for each box; and due to the Spiral, we now have a letter for each box. If we take the combination zero-1, for example, to stand for one of the letters of the Spiral, we end up with the letter 'V.'

"Now the first combination in the cipher is 33-3. So . . . moving in from 33 degrees, we find the number 3, which stands for the letter 'C.'"

I began putting the letters next to the numbers on the cipher.

"Number 1 at 10 degrees gives us the letter 'O.'

"Number 1 at 26 degrees gives us the letter 'U.'

"Number 20 at 18 degrees gives us the letter 'R.'

"Number 5 at 22 degrees gives us the letter 'T.'"

This was promising. For the first time we had formed an actual English word: COURT. We looked at each other with subdued delight. "We have it!" Holmes whispered and then continued calling out the numbers as I added them to the chart.

"Number 20 at 18 degrees gives us the letter 'R.'

"Number 3 at 4 degrees gives us the letter 'A.'

"Number 10 at 20 degrees gives is the letter 'I.'"

Now we looked at each other disillusioned: "COURTRAI?" I moaned. "It's meaningless to me."

"Perhaps it is only a part of a word. We'll continue. Number 6 at 18 degrees gives us the letter 'B.'"

"COURTRAIB? It's meaningless Holmes. Just more gibberish."

33-3 C	4-3	0-1	36-1
10-1 O	1-1	3-1	3-1
26-1 U	20-21	20-15	3-1
18-20 R	23-1	4-3	22-5
22-5 T	20-15	22-5	20-15
18-20 R	16-10	34-1	25-4
4-3 A	3-1	4-3	4-3
20-10 I	18-20	1-1	1-1
18-6 B	36-1	22-5	20-21
3-1	4-3	4-3	22-7
11-4	1-1	18-6	11-4
20-10	4-3	10-1	18-20
1-1	18-20	4-3	7-1
20-15	18-20	18-20	1-2
25-4	20-10	1-2	14-1

Holmes threw the pen down and wiped his eyes. The gaslight was wearing out, and he looked suddenly exhausted. I'd seen this in him before—the vital energy snuffed from his body like the flame from a lamp.

"Enough!" he said quietly. "This is a fight we cannot win in any case." He picked up his hat and walked out of my room without another word.

Chapter 29

The next day was full and tiring, a teaching day. I had no time to bestow any thought on Holmes but figured I would visit him in the evening if he did not visit me first. It was the coldest day of the year, the air inside the schoolroom almost blue with cold, the stove nearly dead for lack of coal, and the children returning from their Christmas holidays in no mood for catechism. The poor little ones bridled at reciting the four cardinal virtues while they were freezing.

"How does the Christian walk?" I asked as sternly as I could.

One little girl raised her hand and shivered out the answer: "'Walk then as children of the light; for the fruit of the light is in all goodness, and justice and truth, having no fellowship with the unfruitful works of darkness.'"

How could I not love such a child? We moved on to the vision of glory: "What more magnificent can imagination picture than the mansion of heaven, illumined as it is throughout with the blaze of glory which encircles the Godhead!"

Then I let them run circles round my desk. It was the only way I could think of to help them get warm. Heaven knows I wanted to join them. Even my heavy wool cassock wasn't enough to alleviate the chill; but it warmed my heart to see the children's cheeks blaze up with glory and to hear their laughter as they chased each other round a make-believe mansion of heaven.

The noise drew the attention of Father Claudian, who peeped through the door at the uproar and then shouted for silence. The children clustered round me for refuge.

"Let's have an end to this hubbub," Father Claudian commanded. "We are sending you all home early today because a storm is fixing to start. Quickly, children, gather your things. You are dismissed."

They were out the doors in an instant. "A welcome dismissal, Father," I said. "I feared they would turn to ice if I didn't let them run and play a bit." I glanced at the fading fire in the stove.

The old priest gave me a disdainful look. "Coal is expensive," he said.

"Children know only that they are cold."

"Not as cold as they're going to be. If they don't scamper home, they will turn to ice soon enough, all right. It looks to be brewing up a bad storm." It was true: through the window I could see only a seething black cloud, and the afternoon had turned almost to night.

Father laid an envelope on my desk. "This came for you with the post just now."

It was an odd missive: no return address, no stamp, no postmark, and there was something like gravel inside. I ripped it open and out fell what appeared to be five dried white seeds—nothing else. I laughed until I realized that Father Claudian had nearly stopped breathing.

He clutched my shoulder and swore. "What have you brought upon us?"

"I don't follow you. What do you mean?"

"I've heard of such a thing but never seen it." The priest was quaking, and not with the cold.

"No letter. Five pips in an envelope? They look to be from a citron fruit—a lemon or an orange, I'd say. What—does someone want us to start an orangery?"

"It is a warning. It signifies 'join or die.'"

"Join? Join what?"

The priest hushed me. "Join the Klan, you fool. This is an ultimatum!" He took the envelope and opened the flap. There were scrawled the letters "K K K."

"I have no intention of 'joining the Klan.' They threaten me with death if I don't join them? Are they mad?"

"Have they asked something of you? What do they want from you?"

I decided not to burden him with the story—he knew too much already, and I was loth to expose him to danger by embroiling him any further in my troubles.

"Don't worry, Father," I said in as hale a voice as I could muster. "I think I know what this is regarding, and I fear it is just a misunderstanding. I will deal with it."

"It's about that colored man you helped, isn't it? I warned you . . . ."

"Yes, that's it. Now, if you'll excuse me, Father, I have some visits to make which will clear all of this up."

"Not tonight. You'll be making no visits."

"And why not?"

"Look outside." He pointed to the windows.

I looked but saw nothing. Literally, the world had disappeared from view behind a veil of intense sleet that froze the instant it contacted the ground. The pastor was right. I would be making no visits that night.

Nor the next day. When we arose, we found that the door to the rectory had frozen shut, and it was only by pounding at it repeatedly with my shoulder that I was able to budge it.

The morning was still dark, but the landscape mirrored our lamplight like a million tongues of flame. Everything, every surface—trees, walks, shrubbery—was molded into clear ice. My nerves erupted when I heard what I thought was a gunshot, but it was the sound of a plane tree branch cracking explosively overhead. Then I heard the same retort further away, and again and again. The trees were splitting apart under the weight of the ice.

All that day, nothing moved, not man, horse, or dog. Not the milk wagon, the postman, or a single child for school.

I was desperate to talk to Holmes, but when I ventured to put my boot to the ice, I found that even cautious walking was impossible. The ground was as slick as water. I recalled skating on frozen ponds as a child, but in this seaside clime of South Carolina no one conceived of such a thing as ice skates, so there was no means of mobility at all.

Father Claudian and I celebrated a lonely mass together in the darkened church and then huddled ourselves next to the stove in the rectory kitchen for the rest of the day. The pastor squirmed nervously. I could understand why the weather alarmed him—he had grown up in a climate that varied little from the soft and the humid—but it was more than that. Every crack of a branch or echo of falling ice made him jump, and then he would sigh apologetically. I knew he was nervous because of the five orange pips.

At last I looked up from my book. "Have you seen storms like this before, Father?"

"Once or twice. I remember the ice storm of '39, and then just after New Year in '57 when the temperature went to twenty-four below zero."

"You have quite a memory."

"For disasters, yes. I've seen a few."

"If it is any comfort to you, Father, I intend to see the bishop at his earliest convenience and accept his invitation to work with him."

The pastor gave me a pale smile. "That is good. I am glad you can see clear to do your duty."

"Yes, that is what I intend to do."

I spent the rest of the day staring at the Compass, the Spiral, and the Triangle. I had seen Holmes sad, disgusted, and angry, but I had never seen him despondent. Confronted with this maddening cipher, his machine-like mind had come to a stop.

My determination was nothing compared with his, yet I could not sit by and watch as such a remarkable man disintegrated in defeat.

I made a few half attempts, but the cipher seemed more opaque than ever. We had missed something crucial to its solution and I had exhausted every approach I could think of. It was as if my mind had iced over like the world outside the rectory.

The unnerving storm continued for days, spreading layer after layer of ice over streets and houses and tombstones. The cemetery was a desolate field strewn with ice blocks, making the short walk from the rectory to the convent like crossing Siberia. The sisters worried themselves ill over the absent children, imagining little frozen souls scattered through the streets, but they kept busy boiling water for tea and plying the pastor and me with soup. Steam turned their freezing windows rock-hard, but it was warmer in their common room than in the draughty old rectory.

Sister Carolina, who had just returned from Atlanta, took pains to avoid me. Pale and nervous—more than usual---she gave her full attention to the manufacture of her rosaries while the other sisters worked grumbling round her, cooking and laundering and ironing with a vengeance. She was so solitary that one evening after dinner I approached and inquired after her health.

"I am quite well, thank you, Father." It was a seasonably icy response.

"How are your preparations for your final vows progressing?" I asked as gently as I could. My resentment at her betrayal had receded, and I was rather sorry for her sitting alone.

She did not reply, and feeling slighted, I turned to leave her. But then she spoke.

"Once we have detached ourselves forever from the world, it must look as if we have done everything and there is nothing left to contend with." Although she was not really speaking to me, I listened. "But I cannot do that. I cannot feel secure and go to sleep like one who has bolted the door against thieves—for the thief is already in the house."

"I believe Saint Teresa said something like that," I replied. "Surely even behind the veil sin is never completely banished. It is in our nature. We all struggle on."

She appeared not to have heard me. "There is no thief worse than the thief who is *in the house*," she whispered, running her gloved fingers through the pile of red rosary peas in her box.

We sat quietly for a while. I had not been a priest long, but I had begun to catch the tell-tale signs of a penitent who wished to confess. "Would you—like to speak to me in private, Sister?" I asked.

But I had misread the signs. She looked up at me with surprise and then displeasure. "In my case, Father, confession would be a self-indulgence."

Apparently there was no more to be said.

I passed the next day struggling over a letter to the bishop informing him of my 'eagerness' to comply with whatever demand he would make of me. Of course, it was on Holmes's insistence that I become "the fervent recruit." Now it was only a matter of waiting until the weather warmed and the ice "returned from off the earth."

At last one morning there was a sound of melting water and the postman returned like the dove with the olive bough to deposit a week's worth of mail at our feet. The city streets stirred once more with the rush of a pent-up populace. Determined to find Holmes without delay, I sallied out after mass to find the inn on Meeting Street where he was lodging. I had to wade through lumps of ice and wood litter, cautiously avoiding a catastrophe on the slick mess the storm had made of the streets, and at last got to the doors of the inn. There I found that Holmes was a guest but had not been seen since the storm began.

Alarmed, I climbed the stairs to his room along with the innkeeper, who was showing some rather belated concern. After I called out several times with no result, the man opened the door with his master key.

Inside was a deplorable spectacle. The shutters had been jammed shut, the light was dim, and a fog of stale smoke filled the room. On a meager cot lay Holmes, his gaunt, wasted eyes staring up at the ceiling, and I feared the worst.

"Quickly!" I shouted. "A doctor!"

The now fearful innkeeper plunged down the stairs.

Chapter 30

Holmes was barely breathing. I was certain he had eaten nothing in days, but what truly shocked me was the tarnished metal syringe that lay on a chair next to his bed. Someone—perhaps himself—had injected him with morphia or some such noxious substance.

The room stank of sick and sour tobacco. I tried cleaning Holmes and stuffed the wild clutter in the room back into his bags. I found a small bottle of the drug, which I corked and put in my pocket, as well as an unopened bottle of London gin.

At last the doctor arrived, a portly gent who twisted his beard with his fingers and shook like an old drunkard. Indeed he *was* a drunkard and cheerfully confessed it.

"I've been drinking since the storm started. I stopped when the storm stopped and the drink ran out. In a few hours I will be in much the same state as your friend here," he laughed.

I said that I could not understand why people treat themselves so ill.

"Why, the best thing life is intoxication!" the doctor said. "During the war I saw the hectic of death on hundreds of men—men with heads or hearts shredded like persimmon pulp—boys with strong bodies who a second later were nothing but a wine splash across a hillside. The living ones, the ones who would rather die than suffer one more day chopped in pieces . . . I gave them the best time they ever had in their miserable lives. Morphia, spirits, laudanum . . . until it ran out."

"What of my friend?" I asked impatiently. "What can be done?"

"Your besotted friend?" With an idle air the doctor examined Holmes up and down. "The best thing you can do for him is to keep dosing him. He looks the very picture of utter desolation. Why return him to his misery?"

"Because he is desperately needed. Now, what can be *done?*"

The doctor paused and sighed. "If you are so determined, you must destroy the drug. He will have hidden quantities of it in this room. Find it and burn it—or sell it to me. I'll pay . . ."

"I will not. What else?"

"Nothing else. Keep him as comfortable as possible, give him fresh water to drink, and then watch him suffer. It will be excruciating."

"What will?"

"When I was a boy it was known as the 'blue johnnies,' but we learned men of science call it the *delirium tremens*, Reverend suh. He will awake near midday craving the drug. He will be anxious, irritated. Then the sweats and the aches begin. His stomach will cramp and all night he will scream in terror at the vermin crawling over his body—rats, snakes, worms, vile sea snails, oysters and such. He may scratch himself bloody. Through it all he will curse you to hell and back. In three days or so it will pass."

"And then?"

"And then comes the worst thing of all: Sobriety."

I thanked the man of science and paid him with the bottle of London gin.

"I am gratified, Reverend suh, gratified indeed." As he left he whispered, "Give him the last rites, or whatever it is you do to send a soul on to glory. A skinny fellow like that probably will not live through what's coming."

I sent a note back to the rectory pleading with the nuns to take over my catechism classes and stayed beside Holmes day and night. The doctor was right about the course of Holmes's torment—things unfolded exactly as the old sot predicted. I have never, before or since, seen any being suffer as Holmes did. I embraced him to keep him from injuring himself with his wild leaps and tremors. I soaked up the prodigious sweat with a towel. His horrorstruck screams about crawling insects even made me look round in fear.

In his quieter moments I scoured the room and found small bottles of morphine in utterly unlikely places—in a stocking, in his hatband, rolled into a copy of the *Post and Courier*—then I incinerated them in the fire. I thought I had found them all until I picked up the only item of food in the room, a wilting orange on a side table. To my surprise the orange came apart in my hand and out fell another container. Holmes was a devious chap.

Then, on the morning of the third day, he awoke dry and calm. I called for weak tea and toast, which he took without complaint. Relaxed, unruffled, he obeyed me like a child, bathed himself, shaved, even lay down again to rest on my orders. It worried me deeply—I had never experienced a tranquil Sherlock Holmes before. But it was his eyes that troubled me most. They were dead. Lifeless.

After his nap I helped him down the stairs and out to a restaurant for a light lunch. He needed sustenance. He was straightforward with me.

"I am not sorry," he said. "When we could make no sense of the cryptogram, I rebelled at it. Quite abruptly the entire structure of the case collapsed in my mind, and I came to believe I had been weaving a vision out of a baseless fabric. It melted into air—into thin air. Perhaps the ciphers were the work of some crank. Perhaps the Tarleton men had died like any other soldiers. Perhaps I who dismiss the imagination as a pageant without substance had fallen prey to my own imaginary folly.

"And then I received a wire."

I was surprised. I had found no telegram in his room even with all my searching.

"You know we suspected Thomas Beaufort of the golden spurs to be the real murderer of the Tarletons. His malicious scheme to stop your inquiries, his clear connection to the poison poem you received, his accusation of James as a scapegoat for the crime—it all added up."

"Yes, and from my point of view, it still does," I said.

Holmes extracted a telegram from the lining of his coat and held it up between two fingers. "It is from the War Department. 'Dear Sir, In response to your inquiry, the rebel Colonel Thomas Beaufort served with his brother, General Abraham Beaufort, mostly in the western campaign of the war. Together they fought at Vicksburg and ended the war under the command of General Nathan Bedford Forrest'—who, I happen to know, was the leader of the Ku Klux Klan. . . ."

"That might explain the Beauforts' connection with the Klan."

"Indeed. But it doesn't matter now."

"Why not?"

"The wire goes on to explain that during the Battle of Gettysburg on July 3, 1863—the day the Tarletons were killed—the Beaufort brothers were retreating from a Union army at Tullahoma, Tennessee, seven hundred miles away."

"So the Beauforts did not murder the Tarletons?"

"They were not even in the same state at the time," Holmes sighed dismissively.

"But what of the mention of Adam Worth in the cipher?"

"It is an intriguing point. Perhaps even decisive," he murmured, absorbed in the luncheon menu. Very strange. Now I was truly worried about him. He appeared to have lost all interest in the case, so I asked him if that were so.

"It is less a case for investigation than flotsam on the inexorable tide of history," Holmes replied. "There are certain irresistible forces—the power of money, the power of hatred, for example—that are impervious to our attempts to counter them. We must either destroy these forces or agree to live on their terms; and since I can do neither, my small bottles seem to me the only reasonable response to the dilemma." He rolled up his shirt cuff and revealed innumerable puncture marks.

"But Holmes, you must count the cost! You cannot simply withdraw from the scene in a state of blissful arousal while men like Adam Worth remain free to do their worst."

"Adam Worth is merely a parasite on a dying world. Men like James, women like Katherine Wells, will continue to be enslaved in more and more novel ways. Millions will die in wars for the profit of men like Adam Verver as iron and machines are transformed into nightmarish weaponry we cannot even imagine. Hateful bigots will refine and scatter their venom until it consumes the nations. And, like maggots, Adam Worth and his kind will hang and feed on the death of all things."

I had never heard this kind of outpouring from Holmes. The calmness of his voice made it all the more appalling in its effect on me. But then I had a thought.

"I am reminded of an evening long ago in our digs at Stonyhurst."

"Yes?"

"When you demonstrated a highly efficient procedure for killing maggots."

Holmes's face gradually relaxed into a sort of smile. "Ah. I remember. It seems to me that you found that little experiment revolting."

"So I did. But I also remember that you found it fascinating. You believe that your only alternative is to withdraw into stagnant dreams, but that is not so. You are a scientist. Problems, cryptograms, the secrets of men and nature—it is mental exaltation you crave. You said yourself it is the mystery that matters!"

Holmes was gazing at nothing. I was not sure he had heard me, but then he said, "That . . . and shag tobacco."

I laughed. It was a weak, tentative laugh. Our luncheon came and we ate in silence. Afterwards, he lit a pipe and we went for a stroll in the brisk air along Meeting Street. Shabby black men under an overseer were clearing the street of ice and filling in holes in the paving. Holmes said nothing until he spotted a poster on an advertising column.

"Look at this. The great Camille Urso is playing tonight at the Hibernian Hall."

"Who?"

"Urso, one of a handful of female concert violinists in the world, and from what I have heard, truly accomplished. I wonder if we might go."

Pleased that Holmes was showing interest in something—anything—besides injecting himself with poison, I readily agreed to go with him.

That evening we each paid our two dollars and took seats in the Hibernian Hall, nicely lamp lit and surprisingly warm for such a cold evening. The orchestra played some pleasant music and then a soloist entered, a sparkling, roundish French woman who played Mendelssohn's violin concerto. This was Madame Urso.

I was gratified to see Holmes lost in the music. He listened with eyes closed, swaying just perceptibly and tapping his finger in time. "German music is introspective," he had said when we entered, and he was clearly introspecting. As the concerto unfolded, his countenance became more languid, even dreamy, so unlike the keen-edged machine brain I had come to know. I prayed that henceforth music might take the place in his life occupied by the hateful drugs that had nearly killed him.

After the concert we wandered the hall so that I could show Holmes the painting of Jeb Stuart, the knight of the golden spurs, and his heroic beard. Holmes contemplated the face. "A narcissistic type, I would say, given to the dashing gesture. But the beard conceals an irresolute chin. Were I Robert E. Lee, I would have placed little faith in him."

We followed the crowd toward the exits, and I stopped Holmes to show him the "Battle of the Golden Spurs" hanging in a place of honor by the arched doors. "General Gary told me it was a recent gift to the city of Charleston from himself and his friends."

Once again I contemplated the scene of maddened peasants hacking at the knight with blood surging from his body.

"It is not the original," Holmes reflected in a drowsy monotone. "I believe it to be a preliminary study—as you see, the paint strokes are tentative and the lines somewhat unsettled. . . . Great Scott!"

Abruptly he came to life. His pencil came out and he scratched notes on his concert program as he bent like a great bird over the tiny plaque on the picture frame.

"What is it?" I asked. "What do you see?"

"Quickly!" he hissed. "We must be gone. We have no time to lose."

Chapter 31

We locked ourselves into my cell at the rectory. Once the lamp was blazing, Holmes laid out the papers we had struggled over days before in our attempt to decipher the Katherine Wells document.

"Ah! This is it!"

He had found the last page we worked on.

"COURTRAIB," he spelled out. "We got that far and abandoned the effort. Let us continue now."

"But, Holmes, it's gibberish."

"Not at all. Look at this." He handed me his program from the concert and pointed to the notes he had scratched out with his pencil:

"BATAILLE DE COURTRAI, DITE BATAILLE DES EPERONS D'OR"

It took me a moment to absorb the shock. "The Battle of Courtrai, called the Battle of the Golden Spurs," I translated. "Courtrai?"

I looked at the cipher boxes on the table: "C O U-R-T-R-A-I-B. The Battle of Courtrai! Holmes! It's not gibberish after all!"

"No indeed. Courtrai must be a town, the site of this obscure battle in 1302 that became known as the Battle of the Golden Spurs. We found our way through Mrs. Wells's labyrinth without realizing it!" Holmes looked up at me eagerly.

"I cannot remember how we did it."

"But I can. I've rolled it over and over in my mind since then. The Compass gives us a degree for each box, the Triangle gives us a number for each box, and the Spiral a letter for each box. The alphabet is arranged round the Spiral, beginning with 'A' at the center. The message starts with 'COURTRAIB,' which must have something to do with the Battle of Courtrai. Now we must puzzle out the rest of it."

With my wooden ruler I traced out another set of boxes. Then I inserted the letters next to the numbers on the cipher as Holmes read them to me.

"Number 1 at 3 degrees gives us the letter E."

"Number 4 at 11 degrees gives us the letter G."

"Number 10 at 20 degrees gives us the letter I."

"Number 1 at 1 degree gives us the letter N."

"Number 15 at 20 degrees gives us the letter S."

"We have it!" Holmes cried. "COURTRAIBEGINS. The Battle of Courtrai begins? What could it mean? We must not theorize yet. Let us continue."

The next few boxes gave us JAN28.

"So the battle begins January 28. Only days from now. I wonder what the date signifies."

We kept at it. "S-H-E-R-M-A-N-A-R-R-I. . . ."

"That's it! Sherman arrives! Quickly, Tuck, the newspaper."

For the next half hour we ferreted through the stack of *Post and Couriers* I kept for kindling. Holmes scanned at great speed, tossing sheets of newsprint in all directions, and at last gave a gleeful shout. "Here, Tuck, here!" He handed me a paper several days old.

I read, "*On January 28th, General William T. Sherman will return to Atlanta, the scene of destruction and disaster under his command, and will look upon a proud city, prosperous almost beyond compare, throbbing with vigor and strength; and upon a people brave enough to bury their hatreds in the ruins his hands have made, and wise enough to turn their passion away from revenge. . . .*"

I read further to find that Sherman's visit to Atlanta had been in view for some time, and that the governor, the mayor, and many city worthies would welcome and attend on him.

"Perhaps someone intends to carry on the project begun by John Wilkes Booth," Holmes exclaimed. "The painting of the battle might suggest such a thing."

"That was my thought exactly," I picked up. "The battle of Courtrai was fought by a people who had been conquered by a greater power some years before. That battle began with the garroting of the enemy general."

"Similarly, Sherman conquered and occupied the South, and now he is making a polite visit to the city he burned to the ground in the Civil War. It will be Courtrai re-fought! General Sherman's life is undoubtedly in danger!"

Holmes drew on his pipe and leaned again over the papers on my table. "We are probably on the right scent, but it is unwise to let our theories run too far before the facts. We must finish deciphering this most revealing message."

Interpretation of the cipher went quickly now, and soon all was before us.

[The Wells cipher completely worked out by Holmes and Simon.]

33-3 C	4-3 A	0-1 V	36-1 M
10-1 O	1-1 N	3-1 E	3-1 E
26-1 U	20-21 2	20-15 S	3-1 E
18-20 R	23-1 8	4-3 A	22-5 T
22-5 T	20-15 S	22-5 T	20-15 S
18-20 R	16-10 H	34-1 L	25-4 J
4-3 A	3-1 E	4-3 A	4-3 A
20-10 I	18-20 R	1-1 N	1-1 N
18-6 B	36-1 M	22-5 T	20-21 2
3-1 E	4-3 A	4-3 A	22-7 7
11-4 G	1-1 N	18-6 B	11-4 G
20-10 I	4-3 A	10-1 O	18-20 R
1-1 N	18-20 R	4-3 A	7-1 F
20-15 S	18-20 R	18-20 R	1-2 D
25-4 J	20-10 I	1-2 D	14-1 9

"Sherman will arrive in Atlanta on January 28. The day before that, January 27, the 'board' meets. This is followed by a four-letter compound 'GRFD' and the numeral '9.' So . . . what is the 'board' and what is meant by GRFD9?" Holmes tapped his cheek with the letter. "Indeed, what is the full import of this message?"

"Whatever it is, Katherine Wells thought the message important enough that you should see it, Holmes."

"Yes, but to what end?" he mused. "To prevent an outrage, or to mislead? To betray Moriarty, or to serve his purpose? Are we intended to uncover a crime or to walk into a snare?"

"With such an enigmatical woman, perhaps both."

Holmes looked up at me with raised eyes. "Tuck, you astonish me at times. I am prone to view the softer passions of women as incompatible with reasoned action; however, your insight into the convolutions of the female mind might far exceed mine. You have, of course, the confessional as your laboratory: You hear directly what I may only infer."

"It is true that I have listened to women who struggle with objects in conflict. They are capable of hating and loving at the same instant, but I am inclined to sympathize. Human beings who are exploited often suffer from divided hearts."

Holmes considered this and then sniffed, "So Katherine Wells provides us a coded message and a key to the code, but we must discern the true nature of the message. What does your deep experience with the 'exploited' female mind reveal to you on this point?"

"My experience is neither deep nor revelatory," I replied, "but my instinct tells me that Katherine Wells wishes to help you."

"I care nothing for instinct; however, if we accept your premise, we must act. General Sherman must be warned. We must learn what her friend 'Henry J. Raymond' is up to, what is the nature and purpose of this 'board meeting,' and we must discover what 'GRFD9' stands for."

"I believe, Holmes, that you already have your suspicions about the nature and purpose of this 'board meeting.'"

He leaned back and spoke hesitantly. "I am haunted by the *flectere nequeo*—those men in the forest who, if they cannot move the will of heaven, would move hell instead. This cipher has now sharpened my fears. Consider what would be the likely result if, heaven forbid, a figure as eminent as General Sherman were assassinated in Atlanta, the heart of the South."

"I cannot tell."

"Nor can I; however, for the men of Courtrai, it may be only the starting point."

"Holmes, you have hinted before that the future of the American Union may be at stake. Now I begin to see why. Sherman is perhaps the most honored hero of the Union. An attack on Sherman. . . ."

"Could re-ignite the Civil War. Yes. And that may be precisely the aim of the men of Courtrai." Holmes turned grim and fiercely excited at the same time. "We shall see whither that hypothesis will lead us. I'll leave you now. It's very late and we both have a full day tomorrow—you with your work and I with mine."

He made for the door. All at once he looked like a starved greyhound straining against a lead.

"Holmes," I said, "you will not find your drug at the inn. I disposed of it. All of it."

He gave me a cold look. "I have no need of it now. The game is afoot; therefore, I can dispense with artificial stimulants. And what is this?"

Holmes touched the open envelope on my desk and the desiccated orange pips lying next to it.

I explained what I had learned from Father Claudian.

"'Alas, what baneful shade o'erhangs and dries this seed?'" Holmes murmured, then noting my baffled face, he added, "Petrarch. Well, Tuck, there is a distinct element of danger in this game we are playing. I have not heard of this particular warning sign, although it recalls the ancient practice of the Caribbean pirates in delivering an ace of spades to a traitor who has been condemned to death. You'll remember that the card features one pip. Perhaps for lack of playing cards, the K.K.K. substitutes actual pips. . . ."

"Holmes, please. You have alarmed me enough as it is."

"My advice is to lock your door and to take care of yourself, for there can be no doubt that you are threatened by a very real and imminent danger."

"Thank you, Holmes. I shall do as you say."

"I, um, I do wish to . . . I am extremely obliged to you, Tuck. You have been of material assistance to me."

"It is I who am obliged to you, Holmes, for coming to my aid across ocean and continent. You are truly a remarkable man—and a friend."

He opened the door, then turned. "You *will* take care."

"Yes, I shall, but do not over-concern yourself. This is, after all, God's house."

"So it is," he said abruptly, "and do not delude yourself into thinking that you have found *all* of my drugs." He grinned and was gone.

I lay upon my bed in the dark, my attention wandering continually over the new developments of the day. Supposing that our hypothesis were true, then what hellish destiny hung over the people of the South who have already suffered such calamity? I reflected on the many tales I had heard of the brutality of Sherman and his army, of the burning of cities and the ravening mobs of soldiers who stripped bare the countryside, leaving the inhabitants to starve and leading their legions of hopeful slaves into hopelessness.

Then had come Reconstruction and deepening hatred for the Yankee, who in a foredoomed quest for justice turned the world upside down and made the slaves the masters. Angry, defeated, like whipped wolves, former rebels put on masks and tortured by night and bribed by day their way back into power while gradually crushing the former slaves back into the soil once again. Now they spoke of a "new South" where "the relations of the southern people with the Negro are close and cordial. . . . Nowhere on earth is there kindlier feelings than between the whites and blacks of the South today."

They are succeeding, the "men of Courtrai," I thought. They have lulled the American nation to sleep with their cunning words and lured their unthinking enemy back into their midst. And now for the master stroke.

"Who is it?" I called. I was certain I had heard someone outside my room. I had no idea what time it was, but it was well past midnight. Through the bars of my cell window the moon was a thin, curved knife, giving too little light to see by. Perhaps if I lit the lamp. . . .

There it was again. The barest scraping noise, accompanied by faint breathing. Just outside my door.

"Father Claudian?" I called again.

Nothing.

Then I thought of the dried pips on the table and how foolish I had been to take so little notice. But what should I have done? I would never leave my station. Perhaps a few precautions, though, something more than a feeble locked door. . . .

I could still hear the breathing.

Was there anything in the room to defend myself with? A walking stick? A knife? I could think of nothing—except for my stout ruler.

Slowly and soundlessly I rose from my bed, picked up the ruler from my table, and crept behind the door. With my ear to the door I could hear even more surely that someone was breathing on the other side. I reasoned that, although I am not particularly brave, I am a stout fellow and have held my own in more than one boxing ring. So I decided to venture.

"I know someone is there," I said in my clearest, coldest voice. "Whoever it is, I warn you that I am armed. Identify yourself!"

There came a scratchy whisper: "Father Simon!"

The voice seemed familiar. "Who is it?" I decided to unlock the door, and someone peered round the opening in the darkness—a barely visible face.

"Father Simon. It's me, James!"

Chapter 32

Astounded, I let him in, locked the door behind me, and tried to understand his muffled talk. He was almost frozen, his hands and face like ice, so I lit some coals in the grate and covered him with my quilt. Hot tea did not revive him but put him straightway to sleep.

He lay on my bed while I made myself comfortable next to the fire. Fortunately, the little noise we had made went unnoticed by Father Claudian, and we both slept sound and warm until morning. I awoke to find James still snoring quietly, looking utterly exhausted, so I wrote him a note telling him to stay where he was until I returned; then I went to attend to my duties with the school children. It wasn't until midmorning that I was able to return to my room, where James still slept like a dead man. I sent a message to Holmes at his inn that a certain visitor from Jamaica had arrived and would like to see him.

At luncheon, I managed to get away with a bread roll and some soup for James. Resting his head on my pillow, he was just stirring, so I fed him a little of the food and told him to remain in the room and make no noise—that Mr. Holmes and I were eager to hear what had happened to him.

When I had finished my day's work, I hurried to my room. James was at my table writing; he had decided to make a report for us. A little puzzled that I had heard nothing from Holmes during the day, I was answered by a blustering knock on my door and he himself entered, puffing furiously at his pipe. He seemed a totally different man from the somber pessimist of the day before.

"James!" He greeted my guest in eager whispers and sat down with hardly a nod to me. "I must hear your story. What have you to tell us?"

"Well, suh," James stifled a cough and looked at me pleadingly for tea. He was clearly quite ill. After a long draught, he went on. "I made my way to Savannah and got passage to Kingston. It was a wonderful long voyage and I made fren's with some sailors and they takes me up to the gove'nor's house. Your letter just like magic, Mr. Holmes, 'cause I was brought right in to the gove'nor hisself!'"

"Excellent," Holmes sat back satisfied. "Sir Anthony is a gentleman who honors his debts. Pray, what happened next?"

James's hoarseness had increased and he was struggling to talk. "I done wrote it all down for you all." Taking his report in hand, Holmes read it aloud. It was surprisingly fluent.

The govenor send me recomendation to work at George Town on plantation used to be Tallton fambly land -- I was prentice over seer -- I work long side old Jerry the over seer he work for Talltons long time, he say Master Rafe Tallton was a babby when he come with a fambly slave named Tigona, she raise him but she get et by a corkodile -- Master Rafe he a hard master, he sell out when slaves freed in George Town and he win the Fare Hill in a card game and he go to the States and nobody see him ever agin -- I don know what else to do so I come back on the ship -- no money lef so I walk from Savana and it mighty cold--

"Superb! Now the chain is complete." Holmes stood and paced the room. "Rafe Tarleton was the child of Banastre Tarleton and Perdita, Gainsborough's glowing lady. To conceal the child, the father sent him with a family retainer to the West Indies, where he grew up and became master of the plantation. When the British freed the slaves, Rafe must have found his lands unprofitable and risked all on what is now the Tarleton plantation in Georgia. The unfortunate Tarleton brothers who met their end at Gettysburg are therefore indeed the descendants of the unlamented Bloody Ban Tarleton."

"But as you said, Holmes," I interjected, "what difference does it make? Even if the brothers Beaufort felt to pay a debt of honor by killing the Tarletons, they were both hundreds of miles away at the time."

Holmes put his finger to his lips and smiled. "It's all part of a larger picture that is now coming together in my mind. True, the Beauforts were far away geographically, but perhaps not so far away in spirit. Your original poison letter makes that quite clear."

"Are you saying they employed an agent? Adam Worth?"

"I say nothing for the present. Goodness gracious, Tuck, we must do something for this heroic man who has compassed sea and land on our behalf and looks near to death." He seized James's hand and shook it vigorously.

James only smiled. "I'd sho like to see my fambly again."

"And you shall, James, you shall! A few more days, and all will be revealed. You shall be safe then."

I was disturbed by Holmes's assurances, knowing the likely fate of a colored man under the kind of accusations that James faced. "I hope you are not raising our hopes beyond reason, Holmes. You have spoken of powerful forces. . . ."

"So I have, and powerful they are. But they are about to meet a countervailing force they have not reckoned with."

A knock came at the door. I stepped out to find Father Claudian with the post. "You have a visitor?" he asked.

"Just my friend Captain Basil." I stood outside the door until the priest withdrew, then glanced at the post. There was a letter from Mr. Henry W. Grady of the Atlanta *Constitution*!

Holmes took my arm as I went back into my room. "This news from James crowns a most fruitful day, Tuck. I have spent several useful hours in the Charleston Library Society reading up on the Flemish uprising of 1302 against the French. The famous battle of the Golden Spurs at Courtrai pitted the flower of French knighthood, with horses and chargers of the finest, against common weavers and fullers and foot soldiers. Let me read from my notes: 'The beauty and strength of that great French army was turned into a dung-pit, and the glory of the French made dung and worms.' Isn't it immortal, Tuck? And they brought down the greatest French general of his time, Robert of Artois, with nothing but staves and pokers."

"That is the story I heard from Martin Gary," I replied.

"Yes, and it is the story that Martin Gary and friends intend to re-enact! They will assassinate General Sherman, and it will be Courtrai again."

"Unbelievable."

"You may think so, but here is another piece of information I received today." He waved a telegram over his head. "This from Mr. William Pinkerton, of the Pinkerton Detective Agency, Chicago. *Dear Mr. Holmes, per your inquiry, Study for Battle of Golden Spurs by de Keyser stolen Boijmans Museum Rotterdam 1876.*"

"So Martin Gary presented a *stolen* painting to the city of Charleston?" I exclaimed.

"Yes, and I am quite certain it was stolen by Adam Worth. You see, the tapestry comes together tightly now. These threads are linked."

"But how? Why would the great Adam Worth steal a painting for a wretched gang of old Confederates here in Charleston?"

"Adam Worth, our Moriarty, is a fine hand at art theft. He finds it diverting. He himself stole Gainsborough's celebrated portrait of the Duchess of Devonshire from Christie's auction house in London just two years ago, causing an enormous sensation. I am a man of few deliberate aims in life, but one of them is to recover the Duchess one day from Moriarty's slippery hands."

"How do you know he has not already disposed of it?"

"He carries it always with him, I believe in a case especially constructed for the purpose. Her golden tresses and complexion like blooming roses have entranced him utterly, and he will not part with her. That is why I aim to have her from him. I cannot think of a more direct way to wound him . . . unless . . ." Holmes drifted away in thought, as he often did so infuriatingly.

With James dozing and Holmes mesmerized by his pipe and the bricks in the wall of my cell, I picked up the missive from Mr. Henry W. Grady and opened it. The letter inside was a flowery expression of gratitude for my acceptance of their invitation to join an august band of business, civic, and religious leaders working toward a New South of industry, piety, and prosperity for all, and a welcome to me as the representative of "that worthy and highly regarded divine, The Most Reverend Bishop of the Diocese of Charleston." This ornate expression of respect was accompanied by a humble request to attend a committee meeting of the interested parties to be held in Atlanta at 10 o'clock Monday morning January the twenty-seventh at the Kimball House. As a courtesy, a list of the other invitees was attached for my perusal.

I scanned the list and noted with interest, in addition to my own name, the names of "General Martin Gary and Colonel Benjamin Tillman of South Carolina," my hosts at the New Year's Cotillion, along with other worthies whose names I recognized only from reading the political columns of the newspapers—senators, representatives, mayors, and a whole parade of Confederate colonels, captains, and majors. But the most intriguing name on the list was "General Abraham Beaufort of Kentucky."

"Well, Holmes," I announced, holding up the letter, "it appears that I will be entering the door, as you say, into the very heart of the conspiracy. I have been invited to meet with the Atlanta Ring."

Holmes started from his reverie. "When?"

"Monday week, at the Kimball House, the finest hotel in Atlanta."

Holmes grasped my letter, read it, and did what I can only describe as a few steps of an awkward jig. "It is better than I could have hoped for. Look at the date, Tuck! January the twenty-seventh! 'The board meets!'"

"Do you think this is the board meeting referred to in Mrs. Wells's cryptogram?"

"It is the right date. It is the right city."

"But it is a 'committee' that meets, not a 'board.'"

"True." Holmes stopped dancing. "That may signify. Also, we are still at sea over the expression 'GRFD9.' This invitation does not help us with that little problem."

"There is also an attached list of invitees."

"Why didn't you say so?" Seizing the list, Holmes examined it with widening eyes. "Our dear friend General Beaufort will be there."

"As well as the two baleful gentlemen who escorted me to the ball and introduced me to the glorious history of the Battle of the Golden Spurs."

"It is the right date," Holmes repeated, whispering. "It is the right city. And it is at least in part the right set of scoundrels. We must learn as much as we can of every person on this list."

"I shall write to Joe Harris. He will no doubt know who they are."

"Excellent idea. And inform him that the consulting firm of Escott and Tuck will be arriving in Atlanta shortly to take stock of the proceedings."

I smiled eagerly. "Plumbers?"

"Who better to plumb this mystery?"

ATLANTA

Chapter 33

Over the next few days I made preparations to go to Atlanta. Father Claudian, who couldn't be more pleased, promised to take my teaching duties for me. For his part, the Bishop was heartily glad for me and sent me off with a purse of silver coins and a gabble of blessings, along with an expression of his good will to the "committee." He also asked if I would accompany Sister Carolina back to Atlanta for a last visit with her family before her perpetual vows. I agreed to do so, although I was averse to her company and knew that Holmes would consider her a hindrance to our true purposes.

Before dawn one day James and I went to the vegetable market where I knew a seller who would give him work. In the half darkness, turbaned old ladies from the islands were already setting out their baskets of okra and savory herbs. We shared a bowl of hot boiled peanuts for breakfast, and I left him to blend in with the sea-island farmers until we could ensure his safety.

Holmes and I arrived in Atlanta on a Saturday afternoon and were met at Union Station by the amiable Joe Harris. He wore a reddish-orange check suit that exactly matched the color of his hair, which was of a full and rich tint. In the brisk air his florid face gleamed so that he left the impression of a man who had burst into flame.

"S-so pleased to see you again," he cried, taking our bags from us and loading them into his carriage. "Shall we go?"

"Not yet," Holmes said. He walked slowly along the street and back, looking keenly at the buildings opposite the station, his eyes shining. Then abruptly he vaulted into the carriage and we were off.

We deposited Sister Carolina at the gray-stone mansion, where the voluble servant Marta shrieked to see us. More meager than ever, she bestowed blessings on us and particularly on Holmes, whom she called her "saver and bestes' fren'."

Sister Carolina cut her off with a few razor-like commands and walked on, leaving the spidery little creature to bear the luggage inside.

The Kimball House, our destination, glowed like a golden fortress. Although I had been inside some fine London hotels, I had never entered such a luxurious space as the Kimball, with its lobby open to the sky and frescoed walls cascading flowers and palms. Chandeliers burned even in daylight, warming air heavy with vapor from a rococo fountain playing in the midst of it all.

We obtained the smallest, remotest room in the hotel—a sixth-floor garret that was at least new and clean—and passed the rest of the afternoon going over the list of invitees to the committee meeting that was to take place Monday morning. Harris knew every name, except for those from out of town. They were indeed the *crème* of Atlanta business leaders, including Harris's own employers at the *Constitution*.

Sherlock Holmes frowned. "There is nothing about this meeting that seems covert or questionable at all. If it is the 'board meeting' referred to in Mrs. Wells's cipher, why create such an elaborately cryptic notice of it? And what possible connection could it have to the visit of General Sherman, who is due the next day?"

When the meeting convened on Monday morning, I couldn't help but feel the same way. I gathered with a crowd of mumbling businessmen, most of them bearded, corpulent, and connected with the railroads, in a gas-lit "board room." I greeted the only ones I had met before: General Gary, Colonel Tillman, and General Abraham Beaufort, whose bush-encircled face looked drained and depleted. After a few stilted introductions, we all took our places in leather chairs so lavish I was afraid I would be off to sleep—that is, until two gentlemen entered who had not been named in the invitee list.

One of them was Adam Verver, the industrialist I had met on the *Nebraska*, looking as gray and urbane as I remembered him—the other was the man I knew as Henry J. Raymond, known to Holmes as "Moriarty," the master criminal of two continents, the "Napoleon of crime." Both of them bowed slightly to me as they entered.

This black-suited congregation reminded me of a funeral, ever more so as the meeting progressed. One mournful optimist after another gave speeches about the everlasting glory of the South that would someday arise from the ashes of death and dominate world commerce once again: A former Governor Brown, a current Mayor Calhoun, a Senator Gordon whose hair had migrated to his peninsular chin, and the current governor, who looked as if he were being consumed by his massive collar. By this time I was genuinely in danger of falling into a state of prolonged unconsciousness.

At last Mr. Henry Grady arose, the editor of the *Constitution* and convener of the meeting, and gracefully delivered himself of some of the bold rubbish I had read in his pamphlet—blandishments about the "kindly feelings and close sympathy between the whites and blacks of the South today." He greatly praised the fatherly sharecropping program that deprived blacks of any hope of owning property, as well as the humane "convict leasing" system that enabled unruly blacks to do "honest work" while paying their debt to society.

Grady topped off his speech with an appeal to his "brother Americans from the North" to put away former bad feelings and invest in the brilliant prospects of a South rising like a phoenix from the cinders of war.

This was followed by an aimless discussion of railroad routes and freight rates, which mercifully came to an end when "Henry J. Raymond" seized the floor with a sharp clearing of his throat.

"Gentlemen, in the end there is only one interest here: money." At the evocation of this magical word, everyone in the room leaned in to listen. "And as much of it as possible in *our* hands. Some of us in the North are creating fortunes the like of which the world has never seen, and our only interest in the South is to do the same here. If you would care to hear more, my friend Mr. Verver here can enlighten you."

Verver's hypnotic voice filled the room with a sort of dry enchantment. "It's called a *trust,* gentlemen. Mr. John D. Rockefeller, the oilman from Cleveland, now has full control of the oil market through this mechanism. Until now, a trust was simply a legal arrangement to supervise the affairs of an incompetent person—but now, a trust can be used to buy up entire companies and thus control any market.

"In short, gentlemen, as a trust you can own the entire railroad network of the Southern states—you can undersell competition, dictate prices, and ensure yourselves as much income as you want."

At this, the room burst with noise. Men began shouting over each other, some in favor of the scheme, others violently opposed. In the middle of it all, Raymond and Verver sat quietly smiling.

"Why, it's an outright attack on the customers!" The loudest voice belonged to a little Northern investor named Plant, whose yellow mustache curved like a banana over his lip. "The freer and more general the competition, the more advantage to the public!"

He was answered by the high-pitched and eloquent profanity of Martin Gary. "You damned little Yankee devil!"

This persuasive argument led nearly to a brawl; but as most of the attendees were of the torpid type, they eventually lined up like boxcars behind the engine of Verver's reasoning.

"Frankly, gentlemen, the trust keeps money power in the hands of those who know how to use it," Verver intoned.

"It's like keeping political power in the hands of the white man and out of the hands of the ignorant Negroes," Gary screeched. "It's 'zackly the same thing!" There was a general nodding of heads at this.

"It does seem a useful way to ensure our independence," said another. "And to build up our capital."

The mayor started laughing, "No Sherman can come along and knock down *this* capital." The meeting dissolved in giggles, and Grady invited one and all to bring their ladies to a reception that evening in the ball room.

I made my way out shaking a few hands along the way, including the hand of the sad-faced Abraham Beaufort, who had said nothing during the proceedings. I asked after his brother.

"Tom? Oh, he is not part of this . . . assembly. I think he's, uh, still sleeping upstairs."

"Henry J. Raymond" stood in the doorway as I tried to leave. He gave me a sly look. "How very pleased I am to encounter you again, Padre. It conjures up lively memories of our Atlantic crossing."

"Indeed it does. Your, um, ideas appear to have been well received this morning."

"Mr. Verver is the one with the head for business," he replied. "I merely follow in the wake of his capital flow, which is prodigious. I do hope you will be joining us at the reception this evening. I know Mrs. Wells would be delighted to see you once more."

"She is here with you?"

"Yes, taking a respite from caring for her dear husband, who is still indisposed, poor fellow. We thought Georgia would be warmer at this time of year."

"It has been uncommonly cold, I am sorry to say."

"No matter. It is proving to be a most profitable journey." He nodded, smiled, and left me.

Back in our garret, Holmes was pacing like a captive tiger. "Well?" he growled at me. "What happened?"

I described the meeting in as much detail as I could, while his scowls grew deeper and his pipe erupted clouds of smoke.

"It is all useless, Tuck! Useless! Sherman will arrive tomorrow, and we are no closer to penetrating the scheme. You say Moriarty—Raymond—was there?"

"Yes, but only to introduce Verver and his plan for a trust."

"The little beast has far more than that in view. I anticipated he would show his hand here at some point, but I cannot find my way through the maze he has created. If this was indeed the board meeting referred to in the Wells document, it was decidedly unhelpful."

"Well, they did talk of an enterprise that would in theory make them all fabulously wealthy."

"I do not believe that signifies much. In the end, it is not even money that motivates our Moriarty—at center, it's a kind of inventive perverseness. Crime is a gamut of notes, Tuck. Some crimes are simple, like some melodies. Others are repetitious, like a canon or fugue. A few are strikingly original.

"But the rarest crimes are as intricately constructed as a great symphony or a concerto. One must be able to read the entire score, not just one or two lines. Our Moriarty is an artist of crime who takes pleasure in the creation of the work; now he is awaiting an interpreter to come along—I myself—and I am failing at the task."

"If only we knew why Mrs. Wells wanted you to have the cryptogram in the first place."

Holmes brightened. "Tuck, you've hit on it. You say she will be at the reception this evening? Then I shall simply ask her why."

"You're joking. You might possibly be putting her in the most dreadful danger."

"I shall be subtle about it. But if she is in danger, she herself must take the responsibility. After all, she has chosen to consort with the most treacherous man alive."

"But is it by choice or compulsion?"

"That we shall discover. I wonder where I might hire formal suiting for the evening."

"You intend to go to the reception? But you are not invited."

"Oh, come, Tuck. The men are bringing their wives. You obviously cannot bring a wife, so you will bring me."

Chapter 34

And that is how Sherlock Holmes and I found ourselves a few hours later in the ballroom of the Kimball House among some of the most prominent men of the New South—and a good many holdovers from the Old South. A band played sentimental dances while dozens of wives, mostly well past the heyday of their beauty, were steered about the floor by their solemn husbands.

We were announced as Reverend Grosjean and Captain Basil.

The audacious Holmes displayed his Order of the Golden Spur on his cutaway coat and looked as grand as any English gentleman ever did in his hired clothes. More than one woman gazed at him from behind her fan as he deftly made his way round the silken trains that swept the floor. I followed in his wake, trying to look saintly under my Roman hat. Holmes had particularly wished that I behave like a priest this evening, a request that left me somewhat bewildered.

I was stunned once again at the sight of Mrs. Charlotte Verver on her husband's arm. Like a porcelain goddess, she dispensed no looks on anyone but kept her eyes immovably fixed on nothing. I greeted them, and Verver gave me a dignified bow; his wife glided past me without a glimmer of recognition.

Holmes had adopted the heavy-lidded aloofness of the English, which made him even more attractive to the wives, several of whom insisted on introductions. "Captain Basil" relaxed into military small talk with their husbands, while I tried to resist a third glass of champagne from the drinks table. I surveyed the room, but Raymond and Mrs. Wells had not appeared.

Then someone touched my shoulder, and I turned to greet Joe Harris! He looked exceedingly uncomfortable in evening dress that fit him not at all and relieved to find a friend who was as out of place as he. Grady had required his presence so that he could write about the affair for the next morning's edition. I handed him a glass to stabilize his nerves, but it had the opposite effect as the wine trembled and trickled in his hand.

The announcement came, "Mr. Henry J. Raymond and Mrs. Katherine Wells."

I made my way toward them as Holmes had instructed, while he spoke to the band leader.

"Mrs. Wells! I can't express what a pleasure it is to see you again," I said, meaning every word.

Radiant in a white silk gown without lace or flounce, she advanced to meet me and gave me her hand. "Padre! What a delightful surprise." In her fair hair she wore a circlet of diamonds and round her neck a magnificent cameo on a black ribbon. "Henry, see, it's Father Simon from the ship."

"Yes, we met again this morning," Raymond's good-humored smile gleamed through his black whiskers. "How is the Lord's work coming, Padre?"

"Considering how God works for me in all things, it could not come any better."

"God works for you, does he? Up north we suspect he works for Rockefeller."

Laughing at this, I said to Mrs. Wells, "An acquaintance of yours is here: My cousin, Captain Basil, who I'm sure would be charmed to see you again."

I thought I saw a flash of red in her cheek. "Certainly," she replied, and I motioned to Holmes to join us.

Holmes took her gloved hand and held it. "Ah, Mrs. Wells, the daintiest thing under a coronet on this planet, so say we." He nodded curtly as I introduced Raymond to him. "I see we are members of the same distinguished club, sir," he said, indicating the badges of the Order of the Golden Spur, which they both wore.

"I have done some small services for the Church," Raymond smiled, "although I am Catholic only on festival days."

"I too have done the Holy See a small favor. Mrs. Wells, may I compliment you on your choice of cameo," Holmes said. "It is a remarkable piece and of great antiquity. Ariadne with Bacchus, I believe."

"So it is," Raymond replied.

"Captain Basil is a collector, Henry, a particular *devoté* of antique cameos. We met on the train from Paris," Katherine explained.

"There is a specimen very like it in the Vatican catalogues," Holmes mused. "Are you a collector, Mr. Raymond?"

"Indeed I am."

"I don't suppose you would part with this one piece."

"Not on any terms you could name, Captain Basil."

"Ah, well, forgive me. It was unseemly of me to ask," Holmes sighed. "I was so taken by it . . . the story of Ariadne captivates me so. It is a romance heroic, but no less enigmatical for that. You will recall that Ariadne was intended for the Minotaur, the beast at the heart of the labyrinth; but she supposedly became enthralled by Theseus and gave him a key to finding his way through the famous maze."

"In what sense is the story enigmatical?" asked Katherine Wells.

Holmes gazed into her eyes. "Because no one has ever been quite sure of Ariadne. Was she for the beast or the hero?"

"For the hero, without question," she responded.

"You will recall also that once the beast was conquered, the hero abandoned Ariadne straightaway, leaving her to the mercies of Bacchus the wine god—thus, this glossy piece of incised black-and-white shell." Holmes nearly touched the cameo in the delicate hollow of her neck.

Abruptly, he met Raymond's narrowing eyes. "Men who say they will give you no terms sometimes soften in the end."

"I do not," Raymond said, his voice colorless. "What brings you to the New World, Captain?"

"As a naval person, I am conducting my own informal study of the history of the late American war. I was drawn to the site of the famous battle of Atlanta, and my cousin has been kind enough to accompany me. Now we hope to meet General Sherman when he arrives tomorrow. Will you be there, Mr. Raymond?"

"I fear I shall be elsewhere," Raymond replied, taking champagne from a waiter. "I must say, Captain, you do have a broad range of interests: jewelry, military history . . . plumbing?"

Holmes laughed. "All of my interests are purely artistic, including plumbing. A fascinating maze of mysteries beyond our ken, don't you see? And the occasional mass of corruption lurking in the walls, ready to be rooted out. But you too have an array of interests, I take it, Mr. Raymond—art, musicales, business monopolies?"

"Like you, Captain, I have only aesthetic interests," Raymond took a sip of champagne. "Primarily lovely ladies like Mrs. Wells."

The band finished a waltz and struck up a tune I had heard many times back in England. "Oh! Listen to that, won't you?" Holmes said. "'Sweet Molly Mogg of the Rose.' Lovely old English tune about a bonny barmaid." He bowed to Mrs. Wells and Raymond and withdrew to the drinks table, where a gaggle of ladies swarmed him.

Baffled, I tried to make excuses for him. "Please," Mrs. Wells said airily, "allowances must be made for brilliant men like Captain Basil. Let him know, won't you, that I would enjoy a dance before the end of the evening."

I assured her that I would, and she and Raymond bowed and moved on. As he passed me, he murmured, "I still owe you a debt, Padre, so I will say this—it's wisest to stay indoors on an unruly night."

I conveyed these messages to Holmes, who stood with Joe Harris surveying the crowd.

"An unruly night?" Holmes smiled. "A reference to *Julius Caesar*? 'The night has been unruly . . . Lamentings heard in the air; strange screams of death, and prophesying with accents terrible of dire combustion and confused events.'"

"And Caesar assassinated the next day," I added grimly.

"You caught the allusion, Tuck? Well, it *is* a land of accents terrible, if you'll pardon me, Joe Harris. I just spent two minutes in an effort to comprehend the speech of some of your indigenous ladies, to no avail. That charming expression they use, 'fiddle-dee-dee.' What on earth could it mean?"

"I th-think it is the equivalent of a dis-dismissive gesture," Harris grinned.

"What do you think, Tuck?" Holmes was watching Mrs. Wells in her snowy gown doing a progress among the fat wives and their equally fat businessmen husbands. "Is our Ariadne on our side, or the side of the bull?"

"She insisted she was on the hero's side."

"Of course, she would. . . ." His voice trailed off. "Your two angels, General Martin Gary and Colonel Tillman, just collected hats and coats and withdrew from the party. No wives. It's early—where could they be off to?"

"To a meeting of 'the board'?" I wondered aloud.

Holmes had the same thought. "Could there be a second board meeting? A meeting of a different kind of 'board'? Look, several other men are making their way to the coat check stand, yet this party is just starting. I must follow them."

"If only we knew what G.R.F.D. 9 meant," I muttered.

Joe Harris asked, "G.R.F.D. 9?"

"Yes, Mrs. Wells's cryptogram ended with those letters and the number 9," I explained. "We thought perhaps it was some kind of signature. . . ."

"I d-don't know what the number signi-signifies," Harris murmured, "but in Atlanta G.R.F.D. refers to the new Georgia Railroad Freight Depot."

Holmes snapped round and asked Harris to repeat himself. "G.R.F.D. They j-just finished building it. Spanking n-new depot, only three city blocks from here."

We both embraced Harris, then realized we were drawing attention. "What time is it, Tuck?" Holmes asked.

My pocket watch indicated eight o'clock.

"I have one hour to find my way to the depot. I'll wager that there is another meeting at nine—a more ominous meeting than the one you attended this morning, Tuck."

"The Georgia Railroad Freight Depot at nine on the 27th. I see now!"

"Yes, we all see now," Holmes said impatiently. "I must fetch my carpetbag and then be on my way."

I protested, "You cannot go alone. *You mustn't.* We know how dangerous these men are, and even if you forbid it, I am going with you."

"And . . . and so am I," said Harris.

"A priest and a journalist should make excellent bodyguards," Holmes scoffed. "One can absolve my killers, the other can write it up for the morning edition. As you insist on coming, I require you to remain silent and out of sight. We must leave now, and separately."

A half hour later, Joe Harris was leading us through the darkened streets of Atlanta toward a long, low brick building hemmed in by rails on all sides. Holmes held out his hand for us to stop in a particularly gloomy corner from which we could observe the depot at a distance. Through the windows we could see wobbling lights, clearly from a number of lamps. Two ghouls in robe and cap stood sentinel in the shadows under the arch of the doorway; and as we watched, three more ghouls arrived and were admitted by the men standing guard.

Holmes whispered to Harris, "I have genuine misgivings about your coming with us. You have a family to think of. No one would miss Tuck or myself, but . . . ."

"I'm c-coming," Harris interrupted him.

"You must stay here with Tuck. I, on the other hand, am prepared for this meeting," he said, pulling his *penitente* robes from his carpetbag and putting them on. "It is obvious you would not get through the door."

Harris grasped Holmes by the shoulder. "There is always . . . always a k-keyword," he hissed.

"I anticipated that as well. Remember, Tuck? In the woods? 'The keyword is *Revenge!*'" Fully robed and phantomlike, Holmes gave us a last instruction. "Gentlemen, if I do not emerge safely, seek out the commandant of the federal outpost at Fort MacPherson and tell him all you know. He must dissuade Sherman from coming to Atlanta."

With that, Holmes strode away. We hardly breathed as he approached the sentinels guarding the doorway; they stopped him, exchanged a few words, and to our amazement let him enter.

Then Harris murmured in my ear, "There is a-a-another way to g-get inside."

"Old man, Holmes wants us to stay here. We must alert the Army if he doesn't return."

"I don't . . . don't believe he will r-return without our help," and he was off.

Chapter 35

Against my better judgment, I decided to follow. We crouched and crept in the shadows along a wall opposite the depot until we came to the rails, where Harris sure-footedly made his way in the darkness toward a great open maw in the side of the building. This was one of the loading docks. We clambered up a platform and slipped into the warehouse. It was utterly black inside, although from the clean, earthy odor of raw cotton, I gathered we were surrounded by bales of the stuff awaiting shipment. My repeater watch beat nine o'clock, and instantly a chant echoed through the shadowy building:

"Yah Oh Ee Ay Oh, Yah Oh Ee Ay Oh, Yah Oh Ee Ay Oh . . . !"

The sound sent a horrid thrill through my bones. I was back in that haunted grove once again, my hands and feet frozen, my heart hammering with fear. Harris and I took a few steps in the direction of the sound, but it was so murky we found ourselves disoriented. He took a match from his pocket and risked lighting it—for a moment we could see our path ahead—then he put it out and we walked straight, feeling our way through the cotton bales until we reached the opposite wall. At this point we detected a glow far above our heads.

"We—we should be able to see into the receiving hall if we c-climb up there," Harris whispered. He lit another match, and we caught sight of a staircase only yards away. The chant grew louder as we climbed, then stopped abruptly. A harsh, high voice sang out as we reached the top of the stairs, and if we held our heads up in the rafters, we could see through cracks in the wallboard into the next room.

It was a dim well crowded with ghouls in all manner of fancy dress—some in immaculate white sheeting from head to foot, others in ragged red hats that looked like stockings pulled over their heads, and still others wearing black uniforms with gray piping and the black cap of an executioner. No faces were visible. I immediately picked out Holmes, who stood erect and still in his silk robes.

On a high shiplap platform sat a handful of ghouls who must constitute "the board." Addressing the crowd was one whom I recognized even beneath his hood as General Martin Gary. He looked like a priest in a chasuble, his tall, lean form trembling, his hands spread as if he were celebrating the mass. His voice was unmistakable.

"Shadowed Brotherhood! Murdered heroes!
Fling off the bloody dirt that covers you to the four winds.
Prepare Charon for his task! Row back across Styx! Mark well your foes!
The keyword is Revenge! Revenge! Revenge!"

The crowd echoed the strident word. "Revenge!" they cried, lifting their lamps toward the speaker.

"We mighty goblins in the Kuklux of Hell-a-balloo assembled,
Offended ghosts,
Condemn General William Tecumseh Sherman for the blood of the Lost Cause!
FLECTERE SI NEQUEO SUPEROS,
ACHERONTA MOVEBO!
If we cannot move heaven, we shall move hell!"

The ghouls cheered, whistled, and gave out a deafening cry I later learned was known as the "rebel yell."

The speaker paused to cough and drink from a flask secreted in the folds of his robe.

"Tomorrow, my friends, tomorrow the Battle of the Golden Spurs begins."

There was another yell.

"Five-hundred years ago, the Dutch had their breeches beaten off. The French beat 'em, took everything they had worked for, and occupied their country. But a handful of Dutchmen bided their time and waited for the French to relax, and then they struck! They cut the throat of the French general!"

Another cheer.

"And what did the King of the French do? He sent ten thousand knights with golden spurs to beat them down again. But this time, the Dutchmen wuz ready! They rose up and thrashed that French army into the mud!"

Passing round bottles of corn liquor, the ghouls cheered again.

"Tomorrow, we will cut off the hero of the Yankees. This will enrage the Yankees, and they will come against us in force. We met 'em on the field once, and we are ready to meet them again; but this time will be different. The Yankees have lost their will to fight. They have pulled out and gone home to their soft women and their soft jobs. Their blood is dried up, but ours is smoking with revenge!

"They think we have forgotten how they slaughtered our brothers, raped our women, and burnt our cities. They think our cause is lost and we are resigned. But we are organized in every state of the old Confederacy, and what a surprise they have in store when they come at us again!

"Now . . ." he paused to cough, "there are traitors amongst us, scalawags who love the Union and Yankee-lovin' top-dog Negroes. We must be rid of them directly Sherman is dead. I tell you there are certain men you must put out of the way—men you must kill. If you get rid of them we can carry things as we want them.

"Go, arm your masses against these scalawags. Shoot them down and cut off their ears, and I warrant you this will teach them a lesson. Take every statehouse in the South and tear it down if you must, to show them *we will rule!*"

With this effort, Gary fell into a coughing fit, which was drowned out by the liquor-soaked singing of the throng.

> *O, I'm a good ol' rebel, that's just what I am,*
> *and for this Yankee nation I do not give a damn,*
> *I'm glad I fought agin' her, I only wish we'd won,*
> *and I ask no pardon for anything I've done,*
> *I hates the glorious union, 'tis drippin' with our blood,*
> *I hates the stripèd banner and fought it all I could. . . .*

This charming song eventually faded, and Gary shrieked for order once again.

"Gentlemen, now I introduce to you a man whose name is known to only a few of us, and that's all right because you don't need to know it. Just know that he is a generous, shrewd, and sympathetic benefactor who has provided us the means to lop off the head of the Yankee Butcher. He has kindly agreed to say a few words."

The figure who stepped forward in evening dress wore an elegant top hat from which a silken black hood covered his face. The badge of the Golden Spur gleamed on his breast. It was Raymond.

"Gentlemen, I honor and applaud your noble struggle and your glorious future. I believe in both. Now let me be brief. Tomorrow, Sherman will arrive at the Union Station, he will descend from the train, but he will not leave the environs of the station. How this will be done is of no concern to you, but you must be ready for the inevitable onslaught of the Union army. It is true they are now mostly dispersed across the West fighting Indians, and it is also true that the President is a fraud and a weakling, but you must not underestimate the North as you did before.

"Now let me present to you the hero who has volunteered to do this bloody, fiery, and terrible work tomorrow—a man who loves the name of honor more than he fears death—a Grand Cyclops worthy of the title . . ."

A stocky figure in a long white robe trimmed with a scarlet cross stood forth among the crowd, which shrank away from him. The holes in his hood were edged with red, and his spurs glinted in the lamplight. I had seen him before—it was certainly Tom Beaufort.

The ghouls hailed him as he raised his arms in triumph.

Gary stepped up next to Raymond and took the floor again. "Now you Dragons with your Hydras, take note of your duties and be ready. Tomorrow we take the golden spurs from the Yankees! You all are dismissed."

But then Raymond raised his hand for silence. "All of you *except* that tall man by the door. Take him. He is a traitor."

Raymond pointed at Holmes, and a set of burly ghouls seized him.

I shrank from the crack in the wall and grasped Harris by the hand. "What can we do?" I whispered. "They've got him! But how . . .?"

The crowd, mumbling with anger at Holmes, withdrew as he was dragged to the platform and his hood ripped from his head. "This man is not one of you," Raymond told Gary calmly. "He goes by the name of Basil, but his real name is Sherlock Holmes. He is a detective from London, a clever fellow who diverts himself by snapping at my heels."

He squatted to look Holmes in the eye. "I knew you would be here, my friend. You and your two associates." Then, astonishingly, he turned his gaze directly up at Harris and me.

"You can come down from your theater box now, Father Simon, Mr. Harris. The play is over. It is time to pay the ticket."

We heard a noise at the bottom of the stair, and turned to see three ghouls there with lamps lit and revolvers trained on us. We descended and soon found ourselves in the well standing next to Holmes. I felt Gary's eyes on me.

"I had thought we made our peace with you, Father Simon," Gary said, his voice high and threatening. "Now you betray us."

"Betrayal is *your* business," Holmes said. "General, I am not the only masquerader in this room. I wonder if you know with whom you are dealing. This man's real name is Adam Worth, a subtle thief, the foulest criminal mastermind on two continents.

His speciality is binding men to him with silken threads, promises of wealth and glory, until those threads become chains. . . ."

"Shut your mouth, Mr. Holmes," said Adam Worth almost amiably. "Take them to the wagon."

We were harried out to the dark street, tied up, and locked with two ghouls into a van marked "Decatur Bakers." When the Klansmen lit a lamp and removed their hoods I recognized one of them as One-Arm, the gaunt, grizzled torturer from the woods. The face of the other was almost charred from the sun and branded with purple marks.

"Where are you taking us?" I demanded to know, as the van lurched forward.

"Nowhere," One-Arm laughed, his pistol resting in his elbow. "At least that is where you will be when we have done with you."

Chapter 36

"You had best let us go now," came the cool voice of Sherlock Holmes. "You are already conspirators in the assassination of a great war hero. If the crime comes off, it would be well for you to remember the fate of the conspirators against Lincoln. If I recall, Union soldiers would not rest until they were apprehended and hanged."

At this the man with the seared face looked uncomfortable, but One-Arm laughed even louder.

"There is a great deal of affection for Sherman among the Union armies," Holmes added. "Do not plan to live long once you are discovered."

"And who d'ye think will do the discoverin'?" One-Arm cackled. "You?"

"Yes. I have every intention of revealing you to the authorities. This man, for example," Holmes gestured with his chin at One-Arm's partner. "He is clearly a seaman. His complexion and bowed legs attest as much, as well as the expert hitch knot used to secure us. On his knuckles are tattooed the words 'Hold Fast,' which a sailor must do when mounted in the rigging, so his must be a sailing ship rather than a steamer. I gather she is known as the 'Lone Star,' from the fresh tattoo on his left deltoid, and that his name is J. Calhoun, from an older tattoo which is easily read on the inside of his right forearm."

The mariner's eyes turned to fire as he snarled at Holmes. "Ye'll die for that."

"Oh, and his teeth show clear evidence of scurvy, a common ailment among seamen," Holmes added, smiling back at the man. "Once free, I shall no doubt find the bark 'Lone Star' tied up at Savannah, the nearest port, and will be able to identify this man to the Assizes, or whatever your American courts are called."

Calhoun held up the butt of his gun to strike Holmes, but One-Arm stopped him with a curse. "The General said to leave 'em alone."

"But he knows all about me," Calhoun hissed, then sank into his corner to glare angrily at Holmes.

It was deep night, and despite our predicament, I had been fighting sleep for hours when at last we jolted to a stop. Pulled from the van, we found ourselves in woods next to a burnt brick ruin that might have been a house at one time. Shards of glass lay all round from broken windows, which now were blocked tight with boards.

"Where are we?" I shouted, but Calhoun cuffed me across the mouth to silence me. One-Arm lit a torch and pushed us roughly forward. Holmes stumbled, fell against the cracked brick, and rolled face down into the dust. Calhoun jerked him to his feet and led us inside the building, where lamps were already burning and a reception committee of ghouls, among them Adam Worth, stood waiting.

The interior of the building had collapsed, revealing a frame of desiccated wood against which the outer walls leaned at shaky angles. Still wearing his top hat and enwrapped in a black greatcoat, Adam Worth approached me.

"Murdering swine," I said to his face.

He regarded me seriously and asked, "Is it murder to rid a nation of a tyrant? Of a Caesar who burned entire cities and left famine in his wake? Or is it rather not an honorable thing to do?"

"So you are playing the noble Roman, are you, Mr. Worth—or whatever your name is? I should remind you of the fate of Marcus Brutus. . . ."

"I respect you, Padre," he interrupted me, "and have reason to be grateful to you; therefore, I have warned you many times to stand clear. I warned you this very night in order to discharge my debt to you. Now that you have disregarded my warnings, your congregation will lose a bold and intelligent pastor—but not a wise one."

I answered nothing, and he turned to Holmes with a calm smile.

"You are no doubt wondering how I knew you would be attending our soirée this evening." From an inner pocket, he extracted and unfolded a leaf of paper, holding it up to our view—it was Mrs. Wells's cryptogram.

"The woman," Holmes said, looking away.

"Yes, but not in the way you think. It was not you she betrayed."

Holmes looked at the paper more closely. "Ah. I see. It has been traced over with a rough pencil."

"Precisely. A copy was made without my knowledge, and it fell inopportunely into your hands. I knew that of all men you alone could conquer our cipher. Thus I anticipated your arrival this evening in this charming costume—a relic of our Roman adventure, if I do not mistake—and it was a small matter to keep an eye on the movements of your friends."

Holmes gave him an indifferent look. "I assume you will deal with her."

"In my own way. I did not want to be forced to kill you, Holmes. We have given each other much sport these last years, and we have often come up even in our attempts to block one another. Now, however, there is a great deal at stake, and you must disappear without a trace, along with these two gentlemen."

"Mr. Harris is the father of young children," Holmes replied. "I am sure he will undertake to remain silent if you let him go."

"I w-will not," Harris protested.

"Do you hear?" Worth chuckled. "The press is not to be silenced. Do not concern yourself, Mr. Harris. I will have a word with Grady and your family will be seen to. What time is it?" he turned to Calhoun, who consulted a big silver watch.

"It's comin' on four in the morning."

"Then we must be on our way. This appalling fellow here," Worth nodded at One-Arm, "will ensure that nothing remains to testify of your existence. You yourself will become an unsolved mystery—ironically, the sort of thing you have lived for, Holmes. It should give you some pleasure to reflect on all the puzzled souls who will sift the evidence forever trying to discover what happened to you—all to no avail.

"Meanwhile, the honor of a great nation is about to be avenged. Lincoln's assassination did not suffice; the death of Sherman will re-ignite the conflict. 'This same day must end the work the Ides of March begun.'"

His face dusty, his arms tightly bound, Holmes smiled boldly into our tormentor's eyes. "To your immense profit, no doubt, as you and your associated villains take control of the entire economy of the South.

"Do not delude yourself, Adam Worth. You have no honor. You are a thief. An inventive one, yes, but in the end no more than a vile little thief. You are also a coward. You will not commit murder yourself—that would bloody your hands too much. Oh . . . except once . . . long ago . . . when for a few dollars you shot three young soldiers in the back."

At this Worth turned to go, his face white with anger. He glared once again at Holmes as he left the room, and then we heard him ride away with his guards.

"What'll we do to make these men disappear, Calhoun?" One-Arm asked his cohort. "How to carry out this order?"

"Just shoot 'em, mate, and be done with it."

Holmes smiled at the nervous sailor. "J. Calhoun. J for John? Joseph? James? Ah, I see by your slight flinch that I have hit on it. James Calhoun of the bark 'Lone Star.' You will have a heavy reckoning to pay, James Calhoun."

"I'll smash your mouth if you say ought else," the sailor roared.

"Quiet, man. We can't just shoot 'em. We got to leave not a hint of bone or flesh or linen. Weight 'em down in the river? Bury 'em alive? How about a bonfire?"

Suddenly Holmes tugged violently at his ropes. "Not fire," he murmured. "Not that."

"I see the English man is a-feared of fire," One-Arm clucked his tongue.

Holmes sank to the ground and pleaded. "Don't burn me. I'll die any way you wish, but not by fire. Please don't burn me!"

Astonished, I glanced at Harris, who was equally amazed. I had seen Holmes enraged, desperate, and deadly ill, but I had never seen him afraid of anything.

"Then fire it shall be," One-Arm announced, and began to build a pyre out of straw and dry twigs against the decayed wood of the wall. "Go get some more kindling, Calhoun, so we can barbecue these gentlemen. It's a fine answer to our quand'ry. A big, hot fire . . . nothing left but ashes we can blow to the winds."

Whimpering, Holmes curled himself into the dust and struggled in a panic against his bonds. The two ghouls shook wet wax from the lamps over the kindling, set it afire, and fled, fastening the only door behind themselves.

The wall opposite us shimmered with flame much faster than I had expected; it would be only moments before the rotting roof blazed down upon us.

"I-I wished I was a button," Harris said in my ear, and I turned to see him smiling at me. What a bizarre sense of humor—and what a streak of bravery. I felt it strangely comforting to die in his company.

I knew I would have no time for a dying prayer, so I closed my eyes and simply whispered, "Jesus, Mary, and Joseph, I give you my heart and my soul. . . ."

But abruptly I felt my ropes relax. Holmes was freeing my hands.

"Quickly, Tuck," he muttered as the wooden skeleton of the house began to crack and sizzle. "Untie Harris."

Dumbstruck, I leapt to work, freed Harris, and we joined Holmes, who was butting his shoulder against the brick wall with all of his strength. The mortar had gone to mold, and as we threw our bodies at it, a seam opened up.

A shower of flaming shingles nearly engulfed us, but the wall gave way just in time and we rolled out on the fresh ground. Scurrying into the shelter of the woods, we crouched down to watch the conflagration we had barely escaped.

When I found my breath, I embraced Holmes, whose eyes mirrored the fire as he crouched at the foot of an oak. "How? How did you get free?"

He grinned, holding up a savage piece of window glass that flashed with reflected sparks. "Do you recall that I 'stumbled' when we were being marched into the house?

I picked this up and used it to cut my bonds. I also noted that the brick overlay of the house was mildewed and cracked—I knew it would take only a few well-placed blows to bring it down."

Harris was quietly chuckling. "Ain't it nice to have such a w-warm fire this c-cold night?"

But Holmes was sober again. Carefully, he removed his *penitente* robe and secreted it under a log. "We must get away from here as soundlessly as possible. Those two villains are not far, and they will sift the ashes to assure themselves of our death."

Chilled through in the January night, we crept among the trees while Holmes watched the ground for traces of the party that had brought us here. The fire was fading, and soon it would be blind darkness. A few times I thought I heard rough laughter from somewhere in the forest; every tiny crackle of a leaf beneath my foot took my breath away.

All at once Holmes stopped and pointed at the ground. He had spied the vague marks of wheels in the dust and the scuffing made by horses' hooves—we would have to follow this trail backwards to escape, for we had no idea at all where we were.

Keeping close to the woods, we filed along behind Holmes who kept his eye fixed on the ground like a dog on the scent. Soon the tracks turned into a rough back road visible by starlight, and we walked a little easier as the fire behind us died away.

"It will be dawn soon," Holmes whispered. "We must make quick progress. From the time elapsed between the Depot and our destination, I estimate we have fifteen miles of ground to cover."

"Fifteen!" I choked. I was already exhausted.

"We cannot rest. Behind us are two bloodthirsty ghouls who soon will discover our escape, and will surely track us down this road. More urgently, General Sherman arrives in Atlanta in about seven hours—if he is to be saved, we *must* hurry."

Bit by bit, the sky lightened as we trudged silently through a never-ending forest, Holmes skittering along like an animal sniffing at the ground and feeling for the van tracks with his fingers. Then Joe Harris stopped and pointed to a long, low silhouette on the horizon.

"I-I know where we are! That's Stone Mountain. We'll be c-coming up on the Georgia Railroad and then Decatur. . . ."

He was right. We walked along the railroad tracks until I thought we would drop, at last arriving in the village of Decatur where Harris hired a rockaway carriage and horse. Speeding on toward Atlanta, I lay back and closed my eyes while Holmes sat erect watching the road behind us. Despite the cold, I had nearly fallen asleep when Holmes barked at Harris.

"Drive into that grove!"

I leaped up as our carriage dashed into a dense stand of pines just off the road and came to a stop.

"Be perfectly still," Holmes whispered.

Down the road a puff of dust was moving toward us, and we heard a rapid echo of horses' hooves. Our own horse nickered; Harris jumped from the carriage to calm the animal. After several minutes, the riders whipped past us—it was One-Arm and Calhoun, looking desperately angry.

When all was quiet again, Holmes muttered, "Imbeciles." And soon we were back on the road, making our furtive way into Atlanta.

Chapter 37

"Holmes, I suspect that your fear of fire was all a sham," I observed as we proceeded down Decatur Street toward the Union Station.

He snorted and gave me a supercilious smile. "I had to get those two villains out of the house if we were to escape. Of course they would not remain if the place were on fire, so I made certain that they chose fire as our manner of death. But what is this?"

Approaching the station, we were caught in a knot of carriage traffic and people swarming the street.

"They have c-come to see Sherman," Harris called over his shoulder. "What shall we do?" We could not move forward or back.

"Abandon ship," Holmes cried. We left the trap and horse caught in the crowd and bumped and shouldered our way toward the station platform.

"Press!" Harris shouted, leading us on. "Press!" At last we jostled through to the front of the mob where the police had hung ropes to hold us back. A band of trumpets tooted, the station was hung with the Union colors, and a small contingent of bluecoats guarded the bearded, bloated dignitaries on the platform awaiting the great man. I recognized the mayor and senator I had met at the Kimball House meeting, as well as Henry W. Grady, who was beaming like the luminary of the sky.

It was a clear, cold day with a pleasant tang of spring. It surprised me to see the people so eager to greet Sherman: after all, his soldiers had devastated this city only a few years before. Yet there was a hopefulness in the faces; perhaps the future might not be as dark as I feared it would be. Even an old soldier in gray and gold braid, a saber hanging from his belt, stood smiling up at the sunshine and whistling along with the band.

A newspaperman with a press ticket in his hat called out, "Mr. Mayor! Will you be offering the freedom of the city to General Sherman?"

At this some wag shouted, "He made too free with it when he was here before!" The crowd bellowed with laughter.

A be-medaled Union officer stepped out of the building and shook the mayor's hand; there were scattered hisses from the crowd.

"Who is he?" I asked a bystander.

"That is General Ruger. He was the military governor of Georgia."

Sherman's train could now be heard rumbling into the station, and another man cried out, "Ring the fire bells! The town will be gone in forty minutes!"

Everyone smiled but Holmes, who was anxiously searching the windows of the buildings opposite the platform: clearly he feared a sharpshooter waited behind one of them. Exhaustion lined his face. I too began systematically examining each window, imagining a chessboard where each square could contain death.

The band blared out a tattoo and the crowd fell silent. "There he is," someone shouted.

I turned to see General Sherman emerging with two lovely girls in his train. He raised his hat quickly, not ungracefully, and spoke to Ruger. Sherman was an erect, modest-looking man; his face had a gentle sort of firmness about it, as if he were accustomed to being politely but rapidly obeyed.

"There!" Holmes snapped, and was off like a hound after prey. He had found the right window. Brushing people aside, he subtly drew the old gray soldier's saber from its sheath before the man could realize it and pelted, sword in hand, toward a warehouse that overlooked the street. Harris had got lost among the press men, so I followed alone.

I caught up to find Holmes hammering at the warehouse door, but it was impenetrable. "There's nothing for it," he said, "help me up." He pulled off a boot, put his foot in my hand, and I lifted him with all my strength toward a first-floor window. Smashing the glass with his boot, he hurled himself through and disappeared inside.

I hesitated, but could not let him go alone. As I have said, I have considerable strength in my shoulders, so I leaped for the window sill and pulled myself up, my toes catching just enough leverage from the bricks in the wall.

The interior was dusty and dark, the only sound the boom of drums from the station. I kicked at a door and found myself in a hall with a stairway, which Holmes had clearly mounted, judging from the sweeping of dust from the banister. I ran up the stairs, pausing at each landing to glance out the window at the platform across the street. Sherman was now advancing through the line of dignitaries, shaking each man's hand.

Reaching the top floor, I heard shouts from a room facing the street.

Inside the room was Holmes, saber outstretched and pointed at Tom Beaufort.

"Get away from it, I say!" cried Holmes. Propped in an open window was a murderous air gun, a twin to the infernal machine I had seen in Rome. Ignoring Holmes, Beaufort peered through a glass and went on adjusting his aim. He wore a gray uniform rusted with time and a blackish sword at his belt.

Holmes reared back and slapped the man with the flat of his saber. "I shall run you through if you do not step away!"

Beaufort twisted round and went at Holmes with his own sword. "Revenge!" he shouted. "Revenge is the keyword!"

"So it is," Holmes replied, assuming the fencing pose I remembered keenly from our days at Stonyhurst. Beaufort could not know that Holmes was the champion.

But Tom Beaufort was a powerful man. They struck at each other with force; the swords banged together again and again. I tried to get round them so I could knock the gun out of the window, but Beaufort snarled and took a swing at me that could have split my head from my body.

Holmes pushed me back with his free hand and charged at the man, who coiled round and clouted Holmes in the head with the hilt of his sword. Holmes reeled backward. Beaufort leapt for the air gun and cranked it a turn. I could see beyond him through the window that Sherman was still a plain target in the midst of his pleasantries. I ran toward the brute; he turned just in time to give me a blow to my head as well.

I was sure my skull was cracked; I felt blood on my hands. Then Holmes jumped between us, coming close to carving Beaufort in two, but the big man staggered back and away. He raised his sword and made to spear Holmes with it.

"Stop!" came a voice like thunder in a hollow chimney.

Tom Beaufort froze against the wall. Holmes stood erect and turned, as did I, to see General Abraham Beaufort in the doorway, hatless, his face slack and flowing with sweat and dirt. In his hand he held a weighty revolver pointed, it appeared, at all of us.

"Stop," he repeated between tightened teeth, this time softly. "I damn near killed two horses gettin' here from Edgefield. You been mixin' with that mob of Kluxers, and now you just about shamed us to hell." He spoke to his brother as if no one else were present. "Thank God I put an end to this." It was a rattling whisper.

Trembling, Tom cried, "*Flectere nequeo . . . !*"

"Shut your mouth. No more of that devil talk."

There was silence.

"H-how did you find me, brother?"

"I just now sweat it out of that drunken one-arm fiend in that tavern over yonder. When you came up missin' in Edgefield, I knew you what you was after. . ."

"Let me shoot Sherman, brother, for the honor of it. You know what he done. You know what he is."

"Honor? It's pride—damnable pride, that's what it is. 'Before destruction the heart of man is haughty.' Pride destroys as sure as the weatherglass promises rain. The pomp and pride of the South was all kindling, and that man out there . . . all he did was supply the spark. Get up now. You're comin' with me."

"I ain't comin'."

"No, he's not" said Holmes. Abruptly the point of his blade touched Tom's throat. He turned to the General, "Your brother is in my hands now."

"As you are in mine, sir," the General turned the revolver on Holmes.

"I intend to put your brother in the hands of the Federal army out there," Holmes gestured at the window, "for the attempted assassination of General Sherman."

"You will not have the opportunity," Abraham Beaufort replied.

"Then your brother will not leave this room alive."

"Nor will you."

"I should take that chance," Holmes said, almost casually. "But there is a way for us both to get what we want."

"Yes?"

"If your brother will give me a full confession of his part in the murder of the Tarleton brothers and the plot to kill Sherman—in writing—I will let him go. I will keep the confession to myself unless I am forced to use it to clear another party."

The General wiped the filthy sweat from his eyes and stared more closely at Holmes. He could see that Holmes was not shamming.

"Agreed. Where are pen and paper?"

"I'll get them," I leaped up, sponging the blood from my hands onto my cassock. I made a frenzied search of the warehouse offices and found an iron pen, ink, and foolscap.

"I will write your confession for you," I told Tom.

"I confess nothing."

"You will," his brother growled in his tobacco-corroded voice. "You will tell. How you grew up readin' about knights and ladies and Greek heroes and feats of honor and passed your days in a fantasy. How we was raised hearin' about the dishonor of the family and how our ancestor was shamed by Bloody Ban Tarleton, and when we come south to do horse trading we found out that there was Tarletons still living. And you couldn't leave it alone. You was goin' to murder the sons, wipe out their name, burn their farm, kill their horses. . . .

"It was all talk till that scum heard you, that yellow-pants little bounty jumper who said he'd do all the Tarleton boys for fifty dollars."

"What was the name of the bounty jumper?" Holmes interrupted eagerly.

Slumped in the corner, Tom Beaufort was staring at the floor. "We called him Worthless," he finally muttered. "He'd do anything for a nickel. Worth was his name. Adam Worth."

"You thought you'd seen the last of him years ago, but then he re-appeared?" Holmes urged him on.

"I never figured he'd shoot 'em in the ba-ack," Tom began to sob. "He called on me . . . , oh, ten year ago, now. He'd turned into a fancy gentleman, gives me his calling card, says, 'You remember me? I remember you.' I cursed him, but he said he done a favor for me and someday I better return it for him."

"Killing Sherman," said Holmes.

"Yes. He gives me this air gun, tells me where to go, and I'm glad to do it. I swore I'd do it. Now he'll kill me and you and all of us . . . I've failed him."

"We shall see about that. Tuck, have you got it all down?"

I had been scribbling all the while. "Yes, now we must have his signature and those of the witnesses."

The General lifted his brother with one hand and held the gun to his head with the other. "Sign."

Tom glared through his tears at the sheet of paper—I had rarely seen a man so miserable. At last he took the pen and slowly scrawled his name, then the three of us signed as witnesses.

"Reverend sir, I am not blameless in this," General Beaufort turned to me. "I have known the truth for fifteen years. When I heard you asking questions about the Tarletons at the fête in Charleston, I became afraid for my brother. I told him about you, and he composed one of his fancy riddles to warn you off. I fear it has caused you much distress of mind; for that, I am heartily sorry."

"I have been much distressed, that is true. Thank you for your apology, sir. What will you do now?"

The General held his brother's arm firmly but without rancor. "I intend to take him home now. I trust you will live by our agreement."

"You may depend upon it," Holmes gave the General a little bow.

The brothers shuffled down the stairs, two shaggy creatures almost identical from the back, their golden spurs clanking against the iron steps.

From the window we watched a sort of pathway opening up in the muted crowd, and the people stood alongside looking on as Sherman and his party passed by.

"Come, Tuck. We haven't a moment to lose!"

Chapter 38

We charged down the stairs and followed the Beauforts out a back entrance that the General had found, but Holmes was oblivious to the two brothers, who were climbing slowly onto a horse. Instead, we fought our way through a narrow alley overgrown with weeds and rubbish back into the main street where the crowd was scattering.

"Harris!" shouted Holmes. From the window he had spotted Harris, who was himself searching for us.

"Wh-what-what...?"

"I'll explain everything, but we must get to your office without delay."

"My office?" Harris looked puzzled.

"Yes, specifically your type-writing machine."

As it happened, our carriage and bored-looking horse still stood at the corner, and we were at Harris's desk within a few minutes. Holmes whipped out Tom Beaufort's confession.

"Do you have a supply of carbonated paper? Please make two carbon copies of this document."

As Harris plucked at the typewriter he grew more and more agitated. "This . . . this is the story of the decade," he murmured, his fingers speeding through the task. I marveled at how quickly it was done: there were now three typed copies of the confession in our hands. Holmes scribbled on the typewritten document and gave both it and the original back to Harris.

"Harris, is there a safe or strongbox in this office? Please lock up the original signed confession immediately. It must remain absolutely secure. I have written instructions to you on your copy."

Harris read Holmes's note and nodded solemnly. "What-what will you do with the other two copies?"

"One of them will go into my scrapbook of murderers. The other—I have a special use for it."

Harris folded the original and sealed it in an envelope. "The-the story of the d-decade," he stammered again.

"You must not print it," said Holmes.

"I would not if I c-could," Harris replied. "Good luck!"

And we were out the door. I did not have to ask where we were going, for I knew—and the dire look on Holmes's face confirmed—that the life of Mrs. Katherine Wells was now in the most profound danger. Holmes lashed the horse to speed, dodging through the streets until we arrived at the Kimball House. He literally leapt from the carriage, and I had to run to follow him into the hotel and to the lift.

The door of the Garden Suite, Adam Worth's room, was open, with trunks piled about in the hallway.

"Leaving Atlanta so soon?" Holmes and I stood in the open door. The brassy yellow walls and draperies the color of blood bespoke a gaudy luxury. Worth stood looking out the window, his face spectral, enigmatic, and Mrs. Wells, in traveling cloak and hat, was seated at the fireplace in a Queen Anne chair with great golden wings. A thin case made of fine wood sat on a table in the middle of the room.

"Business calls, Mr Holmes," said Worth. He looked like any stout, well-to-do merchant in his lavish whiskers and greatcoat. "We are taking the 2:40 to Savannah, and thence to New York."

"By now you are aware that your business here has not prospered," Holmes replied. "I have seen to that."

"Yes, you have seriously incommoded me twice now—once in my Roman affairs and now in my Atlanta arrangements. It has been an intellectual treat to see the way in which you have grappled with me. By the by, how did you manage your escape last night?"

Holmes explained.

"Your power of observation is formidable, Mr. Holmes. Think of it—a piece of glass and a mildewed crack in a wall. Very resourceful."

"The power is in the small things, Mr. Adam Worth. The things others don't see, the light-catching things that go unobserved by duller eyes."

It was incredible. Here they were, each the other's nemesis, conversing like two painters on the art of observation.

Mrs. Wells stood and came toward us. "It was a dull evening last night after you left," she said to Holmes. "I missed my dance with you."

"Your companion led us a merry dance even so," Holmes replied. "It was an ardent experience for us."

"It did become quite hot, though," she fanned herself. "The fires were too high. Americans are always too hot or too cold—never satisfied. I take it, then, that your name is not Captain Basil but Sherlock Holmes?"

"Yes, and your name is not Katherine Wells but Kitty Flynn, a barmaid from Liverpool who has fallen in with a thieving mob of murderers and does not know how to extricate herself."

"What?" I cried, inadvertently. Mrs. Wells colored and looked back at the fire.

"Yes, Tuck, it's a most diverting story. For years, Mr. Worth had a partner in crime called Piano Charley, a music-loving safecracker. A decade ago they opened a little ale-and-bitters shop together in Boston, which just happened to be situated next to the Boylston National Bank. By tunneling underground, they broke into the bank and stole nearly a half a million dollars.

"That heist drew the attention of the Pinkerton Agency, so the lads escaped with their loot to Liverpool, where they began to compete for the favors of a girl they met in a public house. To impress her, Piano Charley pretended to be a Texas oilman named Charles Wells, and Worth played the part of a big New York businessman named Henry J. Raymond. The competition for Kitty's hand ended in a draw, although she did contract a marriage with Charles Wells."

"He is the husband she speaks of?" I asked.

"Yes. Charley is a man with the delicate hands of a pianist, well suited for safecracking, while Adam was clever, and she was devoted to them both. She joined them when, as I've told you, they set up the American Bar in Paris; but Charley is a hopeless drunkard, and when the partners inevitably fell out, Charley returned to North America and promptly ended up in jail for bank robbery. He has been there ever since. This much I have learned from corresponding with the Pinkertons.

"Meanwhile, Kitty moved with Mr. Worth to London, where he plotted crimes in every corner of the globe from number 198 Piccadilly—among them the assassination of General William T. Sherman, a coup that would garner him a very large fee indeed—so large that he felt the need to supervise things in person. Hence his presence here.

"Now at some point, Kitty became aware of the true nature of her two husbands. . . ."

"Really!" Katherine Wells objected, but with a coquettish smile.

Holmes went on, "And of the rogues that surround him, such as the faux Count Schindler we encountered aboard the ship, actually one Max Shinburn, a notorious master burglar. Kitty has been contemplating for some time the wisdom of remaining in the thrall of such villains. In me, she found what she hoped was her means of escape; thus, she transferred to me, through you, Tuck, a copy of the cryptic announcement of the impending plot against Sherman. Although I say it myself, her hopes were not misplaced."

Worth's sham smile had faded. He drew a small pistol from his greatcoat. "You have provided me such sport, Mr. Holmes, I say unaffectedly that it would be a grief to me to be forced to an extreme measure. I had a bit of fun with you in Rome by shooting out the window of your little *pensione*. . . ."

"Yes, poor Stepnyak. He failed you. No doubt he will accidentally step in front of a train one of these dark nights, if he has not already. As will that miserable, poetic wretch Tom Beaufort. . . ."

"It is only a question of time," Worth replied in his soft, precise voice. "But I have had my fun with you. We will be leaving here in a few moments, and you two will be coming along. A tavern near the station is frequented by a band of fanatics who ride about the countryside in fancy dress tormenting the blacks. I've had some dealings with them, and they will be happy to make provision for your disappearance."

"Henry . . ." Katherine Wells advanced a step. "You go too far."

"Oh, Tuck," Holmes said, his voice almost casual. "I forgot to tell you how Mr. Worth began his career. In his youth, he was a Union soldier who calculated how to make a profit from the war. Both the North and the South paid a bounty to anyone who enlisted. The little wretch could desert, get his fifty-dollar bounty, serve for a few weeks, and then desert again. Who knows how many times he jumped bounty from the blue to the gray and back again?

"Once, while on the gray side, he took another fifty dollars for shooting three innocent men in the back. Perhaps he would like to repeat that feat of honor now." Holmes abruptly turned his back on Worth.

Worth stood still, icy with anger. "To the tavern, gentlemen."

"You had better read this first." Holmes held over his head a carbon copy of Tom Beaufort's confession. "It is a chronicle of your 'honorable' role in the Battle of Gettysburg, as well as your part in an assassination attempt on General Sherman."

Worth scanned the paper quickly. "This is rubbish! Anyone could have written it—no signature, no witnesses. . . ."

Holmes laughed. "I assure you, it is merely a mechanical copy of a signed and witnessed original that is locked in a very secure place. Revealed to certain people—to the Pinkertons, for example—it would provide more than enough evidence to help you to lodgings with your friend Piano Charley, or perhaps even to the end of a rope."

"I assume that you have arranged such a revelation," murmured Worth.

"I have indeed. If we are not heard from within the next few hours, this document will be put in the hands of those who can make best use of it."

"Why has it not already been done?"

"Because I wish to make a bargain with you. You may leave here without hindrance if you will undertake to give Kitty Flynn her freedom, and furthermore never to molest her again."

Worth sniffed and gave the woman a long, hard look. "Is that all?" She glared back at him with sudden contempt in her eyes.

"No, that is not all. Additionally, there will be no 'trust,' there will be no 'Battle of Courtrai,' and there will be no new civil war."

Worth considered this for a moment, smiled, and said, "To the best of my ability, I shall comply with your requests."

"If you break your word, I will know it."

"No doubt. I am aware that your sources of information equal my own," said Worth, coolly. "Anything else?"

"One more thing," Holmes pointed to the case on the table. "The Duchess."

"Ah, there. Now you cross a line. You may do your worst, Mr. Holmes, but the Duchess remains with me."

"Very well," Holmes sighed. "But you will return her someday?"

"She will not be buried with me. I will give her back, I swear, before I die."

"Then in lieu of the Duchess, and as earnest of your promise, I do require the return of the Vatican cameos. I cannot come away empty-handed; you must agree it would not be fair."

"It is a reasonable trade." Worth extracted a long walnut box from the case and gave it to Holmes. "You may return it to the Holy See with my compliments."

Holmes inspected the contents of the box, showed it to me, and bowed to Worth. Then he extended a hand to Mrs. Wells. "Are you remaining with us, Kitty?"

"With pleasure," she replied, removing her coat and hat and tossing a wintry glance at Worth. The baggage porters arrived and we took our leave of Adam Worth, who looked bemused at us as he followed his precious case out the door.

"St. George has saved the princess from the dragon," I whispered to Holmes.

"It seems so," he replied with satisfaction.

Looking back at Mrs. Wells, I added, "Now you have only the princess to fear."

Chapter 39

Shattered with fatigue, I dropped to sleep on the bed in our room and was aware of nothing until Holmes woke me hours later. The window light was fading.

"Up, Tuck. We have one more task to perform." He had shaved and dressed for the evening, while I felt like a filthy vagrant. Holmes allowed me a few ablutions.

"What now?" I asked sleepily as I washed my face.

"There is a public reception for General Sherman in the lobby and a splendid infantry band in the grand parlor. Mrs. Wells must be escorted."

The great atrium was mobbed with people of all sorts—ladies in everything from the latest Paris fashion to worn pre-war crinolines and gigantic bustles; men in tight old uniforms, their swords slapping and tripping people; rich and poor; black and white; young girls supporting their mothers in dusky silk—war widows grim-faced but respectful—all queued up to meet the congenial old Butcher of Atlanta. Katherine Wells entered the crowd like a shaft of light, and Holmes and I basked in her reflection.

There was a fracas behind us: it developed that an old black man was trying to join the queue. "I want to see Mars' Sherman!" A clot of rough young bloods was blocking his way, laughing at him. "It'll cost you a quarter dollar," they said.

He plunged his hand into his pocket. "Here's de money! I'se bound to see him now."

"That's a quarter for *each* of us," said one of the youths, a dandy with a spotted face and greasy hair.

Holmes spoke to the dandy. "Entry to this reception is free to the public. Please return this man's money to him."

"I think I won't," snarled the impertinent wretch.

"I think you will. Otherwise, I shall inform your friends here that the money you have taken from them, ostensibly to invest in a stock-sharing scheme, you have spent on expensive clothes and gambled away on horse races."

Shock spread over the dandy's face.

"Is this true?" one of the young men asked. "I gave him all my savings in gold!"

Another said, "And so did I. He said Florida land was a sure thing."

No longer laughing, the men closed in on the dandy. "Where is our money? What have you done with it? You scoundrel!" They began to pull at him, but Holmes put his hand on the man.

"The quarter, please?"

The dandy threw the coin on the floor as he was propelled into the street, and Holmes returned it to the old man, who, undaunted, took his place in the queue.

Delighted, Mrs. Wells confronted Holmes. "I insist on knowing how you knew all of those things about that man!"

"It was perfectly obvious," Holmes replied. "His grooming does not match the quality of his new tweeds, so he paid more for them than he is accustomed to. His pocket is full of ripped bookmaker's receipts, indicating heavy losses on the horses. Thus, he must have come into money and rapidly consumed it. Where would such a rotter pick up money? I inferred, from defrauding his friends with some investment scheme."

Mrs. Wells beamed. "It seems so simple!"

"Mr. Homes! Mr. Homes!" The little housemaid Marta came squealing up to us. In a blue-green shawl over a bright orange dress, she resembled an exotic little bird. "My saver!" Behind her glided Sister Carolina in stolid black, upright, eyes cast down. A path opened for her through the crowd.

"Marta!" she snapped. "Be quiet."

"Welcome, Sister, Marta," I exclaimed. "Won't you please join us? I presume you are here to greet the General."

"Yes, I would like to lay my eyes on the Yankee destroyer and see for myself the kind of man who could burn a city filled with women and children."

I disregarded this and whispered in her ear, "We have important news for you. Holmes has solved the murder of the Tarletons." She looked at me, expressionless. "We'll explain it all later, after the reception."

We were now rapidly approaching the General's party. First we shook hands with stoical army officers in blue and blinding brass, then a series of ladies. The General himself, snowy beard clipped close, hat under his arm, greeted us cordially and introduced to us his daughters, Lizzie and Ellie. I have rarely met such embodiments of grace as the two misses Sherman—their pale, mild eyes should have misted over with *ennui* by now, but instead gleamed with affection for every new guest. Each wore a delicate crucifix on her breast.

I presented Sister to them. They curtsied, and Sister nodded soberly. "My servant has a remembrance, a rosary for each of you, made with my own hands. May you delight in the blessing in store for you."

Eagerly, Marta drew two rosaries strung with fresh berries from Sister's bag, stepped up on tiptoe, and began to lace one of them round the soft, white neck of Lizzie Sherman.

A hand reached out and caught both rosaries away from Marta. It was Holmes. With a courtly smile, he addressed the daughters, "I shall hold these for you until the reception is over," then backed away bowing. The sisters nodded and turned to greet the next guests in the queue.

Sister Carolina whipped round, her face paralyzed with fury. "What are you doing, Mr. Holmes?"

"Come, Marta. Come quickly," Holmes whispered as he draped the rosaries round his walking stick. Hands bleeding from the berry juice, Marta chirped questions at him but went with him into a side parlor where a few visitors were lounging with drinks at the far end of a bar.

Sister Carolina stalked after them, and Mrs. Wells and I followed.

"You dare? What do you mean by this . . . this outrage?" Sister's voice was a hiss. "Why did you interrupt my presentation to the General's daughters?"

Holmes asked for a moistened bar towel and dabbed Marta's hands with it. "To prevent an outrage of your own, Sister Carolina." His eyes fixed hers. "Why did you want to poison those young ladies?"

"Poison?" exclaimed Mrs. Wells.

"Yes, Kitty," Holmes replied. "The juice of the rosary pea, known to science as *abrus precatorius*, is one of the most potent of poisons. I have made such vegetable toxins a special interest of mine. One drop can produce violent illness—intense fever, hives, restricted breathing, and in many cases, death. Marta has struggled with its effects at least once, when she was waylaid by those ruffians in the forest, and possibly many times before."

"I . . . I didn't know . . ." Sister stammered.

"Please," Holmes glared back at her. "You know full well the dangers of the rosary pea. You dare not handle it yourself without gloves, which is the reason for your copious collection of them. The dried pea presents little danger, but when it is fresh—when the liquid poison runs from it like water—you cannot afford the slightest exposure of your skin. Therefore, you send Marta to harvest fresh prayer beads for your dainty trinkets rather than doing it yourself."

Startled by this news, Marta began to cry under Holmes's arm. "I been sick so many times," she moaned. "So many times, so many times. I never touch jequirity beans again."

"So I repeat, Sister Carolina. Why did you wish to poison the General's daughters?"

Sister squared herself up to look Holmes in the face. "For the sake of justice! *Justice!* Why should that fiend, that fire-breathing animal Sherman, enjoy the company of his daughters when I have lost all . . . *all!* Yankee vermin! *Cursed Yankee vermin!*" She was sobbing, panting for breath. "They took everything from me! Every hope, every prospect for happiness. My beautiful beau, my beautiful Tarleton. . . ."

"Oh, fiddle-dee-dee," said Holmes.

I gasped. Mrs. Wells stifled a surprised laugh.

"Why such mournful yelps for 'justice' from those who have held millions of their fellows in bondage for centuries?" Holmes barked at Sister, dangling the deadly rosaries on his cane. "Year after hopeless year, armies of men like James broke their backs in the cotton fields so ladies like you could sit all day under your parasols in your silks and flounces and sip your Sazeracs. Slave women like Marta stood sweating in the heat, fainting from exhaustion, fanning you while you took your precious afternoon naps.

"Then the war came, and your beaux went out to fight for their evil prerogative to enslave others. It ended badly for them, as God knows it should, and you found out for yourself what it meant to break your back in the fields. I do not diminish your suffering, but instead of chastening you it has made you bitter. Along with so many of your countrymen, it has filled you with malice.

"My advice to you is to go straightway into the cloister and contemplate your own history of hellish cruelty. And before you do so, read this!"

Holmes handed Sister a copy of Beaufort's confession. Curiosity overcame her anger; her whitish skin became inflamed as she read it.

"I presume, Sister, you will now cease persecuting James, who, as I have maintained all along, is innocent of the Tarleton murders. May you find in your new life of prayer a balm for your bitterness."

Wordlessly, she backed away from Holmes and fled, with a more sober Marta hopping along behind her; however, leaving the room, Marta turned and tossed a spritely grin at Holmes.

Surprised, he grinned back.

Mrs. Wells and I looked at each other utterly flummoxed, then despite ourselves we laughed out loud.

Holmes's grin instantly dissolved into a scowl. Wiping the toxic sap from his walking stick, he let the lethal beads drop into a waste basket. As he did so, I murmured to myself, "St. George no longer need fear the dragon—*nor* the princess."

"What did you say, Tuck?" Holmes asked.

"Just remembering something my nephew once told me."

"All right now," said Holmes, "I am beginning to feel listless with hunger."

"We'll have dinner," said Mrs. Wells, collecting her skirts, "but dancing first. You deprived me once before, Mr. Holmes, but you shall not deprive me tonight."

"Well, then," Holmes exclaimed, "strike up, pipers!"

The reception had ended, the band blared out the grand march, and we followed the General's party into a radiant ballroom. Waiters spiraled round carrying trays of shimmering champagne. With one of his superb daughters in hand, Sherman himself led the first quadrille. I watched as Mrs. Wells gracefully swept Holmes into the maze of swirling figures, and was pleased to see that he could dance very creditably. The night had turned all light, and although a priest, a Jesuit, and a chaplain to the Order of Our Lady of Mercy, I could not help but dance a little jig myself.

Chapter 40

My door and my head crashed open at the same time.

"Sorry to knock you up so early, Tuck," Holmes said, striding into my room and throwing himself down on my bed.

"Don't think of it," I was struggling to open my eyes. The previous night's champagne was exerting some kind of hydraulic pressure on my eyelids.

"But I must return to England," he announced.

"Now? Today?"

"Without delay. This side of the Atlantic has become too hot for Mr. 'Moriarty,' so he will be on the first steamer for London, where his web of crime remains intact. Remember, he is the manager, director, and controller of half that is evil and nearly all that goes undetected in that great city. His agents remain numerous and splendidly organized. If it requires the rest of my life and the devotion of all of my energies, he must be exposed, broken, and brought down. So I have come to say goodbye."

"At least, stop for breakfast. I shall join you."

"Very well. I would not mind a cup of insipid American coffee, if I could indulge a pipe of excellent American tobacco before I go."

In the hotel restaurant I consumed an English breakfast superior to any I had experienced in England—except for the coffee, which as Holmes said was quite without character—while he sipped, smoked, and talked quietly.

"This morning I have seen Mrs. Wells off on the train to New York. With the money and jewels she had of Adam Worth, she should be able to establish herself independently."

"She just left?"

Holmes nodded. I felt a twinge of disappointment that she had not taken her leave of me. "She asked me to express her gratitude to you, and her best wishes."

"Thank you," I said, although a sad little ache caught at my heart. "Do you think Moriarty will keep his word? To leave her in peace?"

"He has no choice but to keep his word, Tuck. Kitty will stay in the States, while he and I will be in England under one another's watchful eyes. Beyond that, I don't believe he's truly inclined to harm her . . . or myself, for that matter." He took a last sip of coffee, scowling. "I give him too much sport."

"Perhaps the reverse is also true," I said between bites of bacon.

"Mr. H-Holmes! Father S-Simon!" It was the familiar, faltering voice of Joe Harris, who stood over our table grinning. "I t-tried . . . to get an interview with Sh-Sherman last night," he chuckled, "and this is the result." He showed us his notebook: *At the reception, a modest reporter from the Constitution attempted to interview the general but was repulsed with stately dignity.*

"Your modesty, Harris, is awe inspiring," said Holmes. "Please, won't you sit down? We too attended the reception—for us, it was even less eventful than for you." He shook his head once at me: there was no need to say anything to Harris about Sister or her rosaries, and I silently concurred.

Harris leaned eagerly toward us. "So . . . what did you d-do with the Beaufort document? I received your note that I should not r-release it to the Pinkertons after all."

In a quiet voice, Holmes described our dealings with 'Moriarty' while Harris listened with mounting satisfaction.

"There will b-be no railroad trust, then. No cabal of money men. . . ," Harris smiled.

"And no renewed civil war," I added. "Incidentally, Holmes, why would Adam Worth promote a money trust in the South and at the same time plot a new outbreak of war?"

"Worth always has more than one aim in mind. If one scheme fails, another may succeed," Holmes explained, veiling himself in pipe smoke. "Although in this case, an even larger scheme encompassed both aims—a monopoly can be immensely profitable, but nothing is more profitable than war. Put them together . . . ."

"And you have profit on a g-grand scale," Harris concluded.

"It all seems out of line for a professional burglar," I said.

Holmes barked out a laugh. "Adam Worth wants to transcend ordinary crime! He now aims to be a baron of industry, in a world where the law bends itself obediently round the money power. Thus the involvement of a magnate like Verver, who is not overly encumbered with scruples."

"'The law grinds the poor, and rich men rule the law,'" Harris murmured without stammering.

"Goldsmith?" I was again surprised at Harris's erudition. "*The Vicar of Wakefield?*"

"We do r-read books in America now and then," Harris chuckled, then turned back to Holmes. "So . . . you let him go? You let Adam Worth go f-free?"

"It was unavoidable. 'We have scotched the snake, not killed it.' It'll close and be itself soon enough."

"Shakespeare. . . . *Macbeth*, I b-believe," Harris smirked at Holmes.

"There *is* hope for America after all," Holmes said wryly, feigning to punch Harris in the shoulder. "As for your money power, it will continue to rule, however—and your New South, despite its industrial renaissance, will continue to oppress the former slave."

Harris looked down at his hands. "Sadly, I see no . . . no end to that. Henry Grady's belief in the New S-South is genuine, but he remains blind to that greatest of wrongs. Still," he smiled up at Holmes, "you have saved the life and liberty of at least one poor sh-sharecropper named James. That is by itself . . . heroic."

"Not so," Holmes replied. "James saved himself. With his courage, his cleverness in carrying out his mission to Jamaica, his unbelievable powers of endurance, he is his own salvation. I am a mere brain; James is a full-souled hero. Now, you are a fine brain yourself, Joe Harris. What heroics are in your power? What will you do to slow the mills that are grinding the poor?"

Harris thought about this. "I intend to t-tell stories. I shall speak for the poor people I lived with, the people I loved." Then he brightened. "I'll tell tales about a clever rabbit who b-begs the fox not to throw him in the briar patch . . . even though that is exactly what the rabbit wants him to do."

"That reminds *me* of a story," I broke in, "about a man who begs not to be thrown into the fire."

"So it does. I can t-tell any story I wish . . . so long as the people in the story are all animals. That way I c-can undermine the fortress of hatred like a sapper, and—who knows?—maybe h-help topple it." Harris stood and shook our hands. "Goodbye, Mr. Holmes, Father Simon. I have w-work to do."

I bade him farewell affectionately, and then it was time for Holmes's train. I accompanied him to the platform, where in the humid cold he was creating his own fog bank with his voluminous pipe.

"You have been materially useful to me, Tuck," he said, extending his hand. "I have been solitary too long. When I return to London, I shall take more spacious rooms and advertise for a congenial partner to help with expenses—and perhaps with other things as well."

He then turned his back and mounted the train, leaving me feeling rather empty and rubbing my eyes, which watered all at once. I never saw Sherlock Holmes again.

Over the years, like everyone else I followed his adventures with Dr. Watson from afar as he became world famous. I was bemused when Holmes gave his biographer a thoroughly misleading description of Moriarty—undoubtedly to protect Watson from too much dangerous knowledge—and gratified to read of Moriarty's ultimate fall. As for Mrs. Katherine Wells, Holmes, rather to my disappointment, manifested no further interest in her.

Our friend James returned home on my assurances that he would not be molested again, and to my best knowledge he enjoyed a long life in the heart of his family. I now hear with satisfaction that his grandson Michael has entered the ministry.

One day I happened across an item in the newspapers regarding the fate of one Thomas Beaufort in Kentucky. A lawsuit had gone against the Beaufort family, and Thomas calmly walked up to the judge in the case and shot him dead. In the consequent murder trial, Thomas Beaufort was pronounced insane and committed to the state asylum for the remainder of his life.

My own career wavered for a while—I could not rekindle my enthusiasm for teaching the catechism—and I eventually found myself aging away in a Catholic college in Boston as a professor of theology. So I lived and prayed and took it upon myself to solve the mystery of existence, spying on God, as it were; and in applying my friend's methods to God's workings, I have passed my life attempting to discern His cryptic designs . . . with little success, I must admit.

But then I am not Sherlock Holmes, and in the end I can only be grateful that for one winter of my youth I was privileged to witness his uncanny powers at work; and more than that, to befriend him, to detest him, and finally to love him—the best and the wisest man I have ever known.

THE END

CAMEOS

"Cameo: an appearance of a known person in a work, typically unnamed or appearing as themselves."

For your interest, here is further information on some of the characters, real and fictional, who make cameo appearances in *The Tarleton Murders*.

James Calhoun: A character in A. Conan Doyle's "The Five Orange Pips" (1891). A leader in the Ku Klux Klan and captain of the bark "Lone Star," he hounds the recipient of the five pips to death for stealing the confidential records of the Klan. Calhoun and his gang are lost at sea before Holmes can engineer their arrest.

Mary Cassatt (1844-1926): Groundbreaking American artist, associated with the impressionist movement in Paris during the later 19th century. Harshly criticized for her work, she nevertheless persisted. An 1879 impressionist exhibit in Paris marked a turning point for her, and she began to be recognized as an important painter.

G.K. Chesterton, aka "Gibby" (1874-1936): British philosopher, dramatist, critic, and author of detective fiction (the "Father Brown" series) about a sleuthing Catholic priest, son of Marie-Louise Grosjean and Edward Chesterton. A child prodigy, Chesterton was considered by George Bernard Shaw "a man of colossal genius."

Martin Witherspoon Gary (1831-1881): Fire-breathing Confederate general and politician who practiced violent intimidation on freed slaves in the South during Reconstruction. He organized the "Red Shirt" gangs in South Carolina to suppress the black vote, leading to the 1876 victory of the "redeemers," the anti-Reconstruction party that instituted nearly a century of racial segregation in that state.

Henry W. Grady (1850-1889): Atlanta journalist and civic leader, part owner of the *Atlanta Constitution* and booster of the "New South." An articulate spokesman for the Atlanta Ring, he traveled the United States giving speeches to encourage investment in Southern industry, arguing that the South had re-integrated into the Union, that the racial segregation system was benevolent, and that freed slaves were happy with their new status.

Marie-Louise Grosjean Chesterton (1844-1933): Mother of G.K. Chesterton ("Gibby") and one of 23 Grosjean siblings. Perhaps there was a Simon among them. . . .

Joel Chandler Harris (1848-1908): Journalist for the Atlanta *Constitution* and folklorist from Georgia, beloved author of the "Uncle Remus" tales, fables about Brer Rabbit, Fox, and Bear and other animal characters who stood for the types of people Harris knew in the South. Harris grew up in poverty among slaves and was sympathetic to them all of his life. Afflicted with a speech impediment, he was intensely shy but highly articulate in his writing. Some scholars view his tales as carefully veiled attacks on the racial inequities he observed all around him during his life.

Mycroft Holmes: A character in a number of stories by A. Conan Doyle, among them "The Greek Interpreter" and "The Final Problem." He is the brother of Sherlock Holmes and a mysterious, dominating presence in the British government. Said by Sherlock to be more intelligent than himself, Mycroft is a heavy, lethargic man who stays in his office or his club and occasionally calls on Sherlock for help when there is a sensitive political issue to be resolved.

Gerard Manley Hopkins (1844-1889): English classicist and Jesuit, among the most eminent English poets of the Victorian period. Studied philosophy and lectured at Stonyhurst College from 1870 to 1874.

John Jasper: A character in *The Mystery of Edwin Drood* (1870), a famous unfinished novel by Charles Dickens. Jasper, a choirmaster and genteel opium addict, is jealous of Edwin Drood, the fiancé of a young woman Jasper apparently loves. Jasper just might be the murderer of Edwin Drood, although Dickens died before revealing "who done it." Perhaps Sherlock Holmes might someday solve the mystery of Edwin Drood.

Leo XIII, Pope from 1878-1903: Relatively liberal leader of the Catholic Church known as the "Rosary Pope" due to his veneration for the rosary. He did much to reconcile the Church to modern science and the changing political landscape of the 19th century. Although in 1878 he issued *Quod Apostolici Muneris*, an encyclical disputing the idea of human equality, he later issued *Rerum Novarum*, which defended the rights of laboring people against unrestrained capitalism.

Patrick Neeson Lynch (1817-1882): Roman Catholic bishop of Charleston from 1857. He represented the Confederate government to the Vatican, attempting to get official recognition from Pope Pius IX, who, however, condemned slavery and would not recognize the Confederacy.

James McCartney (?): Plumber and painter in Liverpool during the 1860s and 1870s. Great-grandfather of Paul McCartney of the Beatles.

Mrs. Ezra Miller and Randolph Miller: Characters in the novella *Daisy Miller* (1878) by Henry James. The conventional Mrs. Miller, her daughter Daisy, and son Randolph are expatriates living in Italy when Daisy falls in love with an "unacceptable" Italian and dies of fever. Mrs. Miller returns downcast to the United States. Randolph is an unpleasant, jingoistic youth who dislikes Europe and Europeans.

Sir Antony Musgrave (1828-1888): Governor of Jamaica, 1877-1883, who did much to advance education and economic development on the island. Was he related to Reginald, Holmes's friend and client in Doyle's story "The Musgrave Ritual" (1893)?

Perdita: A character in Shakespeare's "The Winter's Tale," the daughter of a jealous king and a spurned queen. The king orders his servant Antigonus to leave the baby on the seashore to die of exposure. The servant takes pity on the child and goes to retrieve her, but is attacked and killed by a bear. The child is found and brought up by a shepherd. "Perdita" is "the lost one" in Latin.

Henry Peters, aka "Shlessinger," aka "Holy Peters": A character in A. Conan Doyle's story "The Disappearance of Lady Frances Carfax" (1911). An Australian charlatan masquerading as a clergyman. Along with his wife, Peters dupes wealthy women into giving him their valuables ostensibly to benefit a non-existent mission in Brazil.

Henry B. Plant (1819-1899): American businessman who bought up the Southern coastal railroads and initiated the Florida land rush.

Princess Puffer: A character in The Mystery of Edwin Drood (1870) by Charles Dickens. She is the proprietor of a London opium den and highly knowledgeable about the criminal element in the city.

Mary Robinson, aka "Perdita" (1757-1800): Famous English actress of her time, notorious for affairs with the Prince of Wales and Col. Banastre Tarleton. In 1783 she miscarried Tarleton's child, according to confidential reports. She was a famous beauty painted by Gainsborough, and in her later years an accomplished poet of Romantic verse. Nicknamed "Perdita" because she played a character by that name in Shakespeare's "The Winter's Tale."

George Bernard Shaw (1856-1950): Renowned Anglo-Irish playwright, the leading dramatist of his time. In the late 1870s he was an employee of the new Edison Telephone Company in London. When the Bell group bought the company, Shaw left to write plays and essays full time.

William T. Sherman (1820-1891): Union General in the Civil War who led the famous "March to the Sea," a scorched-earth campaign in late 1864 intended to demoralize and break the back of the Confederate States. Sherman's army burned Atlanta in mid-November, thus disrupting the hub of Confederate railroad traffic. Long after the war, in January 1879, Sherman visited the renovated city with his daughters Elizabeth and Eleanor, who had been brought up Catholic by their mother. His reception in Atlanta was cordial. Sherman's brother, U.S. Senator John Sherman, was the father of the Sherman Anti-Trust Act, which eventually broke up John D. Rockefeller's Standard Oil Trust.

Max Shinburn, aka "Count Schindler" (1840-1917): An ambitious German criminal who joined Adam Worth's gang in Europe, went by the name of "Baron" or "Count Shindle" or "Schindler."

Sergey Stepnyak (1851-1895), Russian revolutionary, mercenary, and assassin, known primarily for killing the head of the Russian secret police in the summer of 1878. He became an expert on guerrilla warfare and assassination while fighting in the Balkans. In 1895 he was killed in London when he stepped (or was pushed) in front of a moving train.

Banastre Tarleton (1754-1833): A British soldier who fought the colonials in the American Revolution. He was most famous for leading the Waxhaws Massacre (1780) in which 113 American soldiers were killed, by some accounts after raising a flag of surrender. Tarleton's alleged brutality gave new impetus to the American cause. Tarleton returned to England, and as a member of Parliament championed the slave trade, which was his family business. He carried on an affair with the actress Mary Robinson ("Perdita") for 15 years, after which he married a nobleman's daughter.

Benjamin Tillman (1847-1918): South Carolina governor and U.S. Senator, white supremacist who is said to have murdered African-American voters in the violent election of 1876. He was a principal author of South Carolina's constitution of 1895, which prohibited blacks from voting for more than 50 years.

Camille Urso (1840-1902): French concert violinist who settled with her family in Nashville, Tennessee, from 1855. Renowned for her emotional range as a musician, she carried on a successful concert career through the United States and Europe for more than 40 years.

Adam and Charlotte Verver: Characters in *The Golden Bowl* (1904) by Henry James. After an impassioned affair with her Italian son-in-law, Charlotte returns to America with her much older husband, an industrialist and art collector, to face a bleak and loveless future.

Charles Wells, aka "Piano Charley" or Charles Bullard (? – 1891): An American criminal and glamorous rake, said to be a superb safecracker and pianist, partnered with Adam Worth in robberies and gambling operations. He was the husband of Katherine "Kitty" Flynn. On an 1878 trip to Canada, he went to jail for five years for robbery. In 1883, he was captured while robbing a bank in Belgium and sentenced to 17 years. He served seven years and died in prison.

Katherine Wells, aka Kitty Flynn (1852?-1894): Born Katherine Louise Flynn, Kitty was a Liverpool barmaid when she was courted by Charlie Bullard and Adam Worth. They took her with them to Paris and London. Nominally, she was married to Charlie Bullard, but she might have had two children by Adam Worth. She broke free of the pair and established herself in New York, where she married Wall-Street banker Juan Terry. *Kitty*, a 1945 film about her life, starred Paulette Goddard. Her grandson Juan Terry Trippe founded Pan-American Airlines.

Adam Worth (1844-1902): Identified by many Holmes commentaries as the model for Moriarty, Worth was born in Central Europe of a Jewish family. After immigrating to the United States, he became a petty thief, bounty jumper in the Civil War, and a member of the storied Mandelbaum gang in New York. The huge haul from the Boylston Bank robbery enabled him to set up as a gentleman and major criminal organizer in Paris and London, where he went by the name of Henry J. Raymond. Although he became wealthy, even buying a luxury yacht called "The Shamrock," organizing crime remotely was not enough for him; he liked hands-on crime. For example, he personally stole 700,000 francs in Egyptian and Spanish bonds from the Paris-Calais Express, a half-million dollars in diamonds from South Africa, and the famed Gainsborough portrait of the Duchess of Devonshire—which traveled with him in a special case for years, until he voluntarily turned it over to the Pinkerton Agency in 1901. Worth was eventually caught during a robbery in Belgium and sentenced to seven years in prison. He died in London and is buried in Highgate Cemetery.

Clym Yeobright: A character in *The Return of the Native* by Thomas Hardy (1878) who ruins his wife's happiness by his bitter dissatisfaction with life and insistent "yearning" for a more meaningful existence.

ABOUT THE AUTHOR

Breck England juggles writing mysteries with composing classical music, French cooking, ghostwriting for authors such as Stephen R. Covey, and (formerly) singing in the Mormon Tabernacle Choir. He writes widely, mostly books and articles for business people, and occasionally contributes to social media on subjects ranging from education to politics to religion to French pastry. He holds a Ph.D. in English from the University of Utah. Breck lives with his wife Valerie in the Rocky Mountains of Utah among nearly innumerable grandchildren.

CPSIA information can be obtained
at www.ICGtesting.com
Printed in the USA
BVOW08s1252100917
494433BV00002B/2/P

9 781633 536494